DESERT MAGIC

Desert Magic

Witches of Wiccanburg

Book One

Dharma Kelleher

For my wife, Eileen,
who fills me with joy every day,
and is my best friend and greatest cheerleader.

And for Nancy Smith,
who believed in me in high school.

By the pricking of my thumbs,
Something wicked this way comes.
From *Macbeth* by William Shakespeare

Chapter 1

"Morgana?" A voice cut through the fog of my spiraling thoughts.

Do not *start crying*, I warned myself. *If you do, you'll never stop. You'll only embarrass yourself. Everyone will stare at you and know what a loser you are. Just get your shit together, girl.*

Sure, my life was falling apart. But a public meltdown at the Driftwood Café, my favorite Santa Monica hangout, would only make things worse.

I closed my eyes, took a deep breath, and slowly let it out—the way my mothers had taught me.

It usually helped—when my ADHD brain wasn't stuck in emotional overdrive.

Love, peace, and happiness in. Hate, anger, and bitterness out.

Positivity in. Negativity out.

You got this. You're fine. Everything's fine.

Nope. Didn't help. The memory of my girlfriend, Saffron Blaise, tangled in the sheets of our bed with some bleach-blond bimbo was forever seared into my brain, her passionate moans ripping me apart from the inside.

The Edison-style light bulb above me flickered erratically. A strange electric charge rippled through the air, raising the tiny hairs on my arms. That meant something—something important—but my brain refused to hold on to the thought. It slipped away like everything else when I was overwhelmed.

"Earth to Morgana Quinn! Your vanilla latte is ready."

I wiped my face, rose from my chair, and approached the counter.

Mila, who owned the café, handed me a ceramic mug printed with the coffee shop's logo in retro bubble letters. A little espressy for my depressy.

"Hey, girl! Haven't seen you in forever." Mila was cute with a purple bob and major lez vibes. Always flirting with me. Or maybe she was just being nice. Hard to tell with lesbians sometimes.

The cup's warmth helped ground me. "Yeah, well, I've been—"

"Actually, that's not technically true, is it?" she interrupted, giving me a knowing look. "I saw you on TV a few weeks ago."

"On TV?"

"At the Emmys? On the arm of one Saffron Blaise, star of *LA Murder Squad*? I'm such a stan for her. Can't believe you two are dating. I'm totally jelly!"

And that's when the chaos erupted in earnest.

Lights throughout the shop flared and buzzed before shorting out in a series of sharp pops. Customers' phones began ringing, dinging, and beeping all at once in a raucous chorus of ringtones. The electric charge in the air sent a tingling sensation through my body. Then came the mothball-like smell of creosote after a rainstorm.

Déjà vu bubbled up in my mind. I'd experienced this before. Long ago. But what was it?

A memory from my adolescence hit me.

Magic. Someone's using magic. But not spell magic like my mothers use. No, this smells... different. Mama Joyce had called it Faerie magic.

I scanned the room and caught a sus-looking dude watching me. Like me, he had black hair and olive-brown skin. But unlike me, he was wearing prosthetic elf ears and dressed in a forest-green cloak. *Like, seriously, dude? Halloween's still a few weeks away. A little early to play dress-up, don't ya think?*

Is he the one using magic? Could he be a Faerie? wondered my inner child, who still believed in such things. My brain latched on to the idea and ran with it like a terrier with a sock. *Hyperfocus, much?*

That's ridiculous, my rational brain countered. *He's not a Faerie. Faeries don't exist. He's an actor on break from a movie shoot. Or a cosplayer attending LA Comic Con, taking a break at the beach.*

But why was he *glaring* at me? He was the one dressed like an extra from *The Lord of the Rings*. Surely, he didn't think *I* was responsible for the flickering lights or the phones going berserk.

It must be him, my inner child assured me.

Impossible! Faeries. Do. Not. Exist. There must be another explanation.

Mila stared, aghast, at the blown bulbs. "That was weird, huh? Must've been a power surge."

Thunder rumbled, drawing my attention to the street outside. Dark, brooding clouds drifted in from the ocean, swallowing the early-afternoon sun. Pedestrians scrambled for cover while heavy raindrops battered the sidewalk.

Weird, indeed. The forecast had called for clear skies until late tonight. But on par for how my day was going.

I struggled to compose myself. "Faeries," I replied, trying to act nonchalant.

"Excuse me?" Mila said.

"That's what my maternal units always said when strange things happened."

"Faeries, huh? Could be." Mila entertained the thought with a grin. "Well, I'll get the ladder and replace the bulbs. Enjoy your coffee."

"Gracias." I quietly returned to my table.

Mom and Mama Joyce, in addition to being my mothers, were the head priestesses of a coven back home in Arizona—something that had earned me no end of grief from classmates while growing up.

I don't believe in Faeries. I don't believe in Faeries.

Unlike my mothers, I preferred to live in the real world. I was twenty-six, not twelve. I had adulting things to worry about. Like finding a new job as a screenwriter, since the studio I worked for had canned me that morning. Never mind that I won them an Emmy a month ago. That's gratitude for ya.

I also had to figure out where the hell I was going to live, now that I'd caught Saffron cheating on me with her little side piece.

My phone rang the moment I sat down. I dug it out of my purse, hoping it was a job offer. Marc Luna, one of my friends in the writers' room, said he had a lead on a new gig and would mention my name.

My heart sank when Saffron's name appeared on the caller ID. Bitch had some nerve.

A briny gust of wind blew the café's front door open and whipped through the shop with all the fury of an Arizona monsoon. Napkins and cups went flying. A glass canister of biscotti fell from the counter and smashed on the floor.

I took a shaky breath, sent Saffron's call to voicemail, and shoved the phone back into my purse.

Again, I tried the relaxation techniques that Mom and Mama Joyce had taught me. Maybe if I closed my eyes for a few moments, I would open them to find the morning's dumpster fire had been an awful anxiety dream. That I still had a career I loved and a girlfriend who hadn't cheated on me.

Positivity in. Negativity out. Peace and love in. Fear and shame out.

I opened my eyes. Nope, not a dream. Though the rush of wind had quieted, I was still sitting in the café. Still unemployed. Saffron was still a cheating skank. And Legolas over there was still staring daggers at me.

Seriously, what is his damage?

Mila had replaced the bulbs over the counter and now perched on a ladder above my table.

"Congrats on the Emmy win, by the way. That's huge," Mila said.

I shrugged. "Not sure I deserved it, honestly."

"Nonsense. Too bad Saffron didn't win Best Actress."

"Yeah, too bad," I echoed. I'd felt sorry for Saffron at the time. Now, not so much.

Mila climbed down and leaned against the ladder. "Everything all right, girl? You don't seem your usual cheery self."

Translation: I looked like a wreck.

"Another beautiful day in Santa Monica." Thunder rumbled again outside, as if to prove what a horrible liar I was. No one believed me when I lied anyway.

She cocked her head, clearly not buying it. "Morgana, what's really going on?"

"Been a rough morning." I didn't feel like burdening her with my problems. She had enough to deal with, what with the lights, the spilled cups, and the smashed biscotti canister.

"How about a chocolate croissant? On the house." Her generosity caught me off guard. I still couldn't tell if she was flirting or just being nice. Probably feeling sorry for me.

"I'd like that. Gracias, Mila." Maybe a pity pastry could fill the swirling pit of despair in my heart. Doubtful, but worth a shot.

My phone rang again. No doubt Saffron trying to justify her betrayal. Nope, not gonna answer it.

But what if it's a job offer? Shit.

I pulled out the phone and let out a sigh. Not a job offer. Or Saffron, thank Goddess.

I answered, trying to sound casual. "Hi, Mom. What's up?"

CHAPTER 2

"How's my favorite daughter?" Mom asked, her voice brimming with excitement. "You're not busy, are you?"

"I'm your only daughter, Mom. And no, I'm not too busy to talk."

"Oh, good. Mama Joyce and I just heard the good news and wanted to tell you how proud we are of you."

"Good news?"

I racked my brain for anything remotely positive from the last few days, but my memory was a jumble of emotional static. They'd already congratulated me on the Emmy. So, what was this good news?

"That *LA Murder Squad*'s been renewed for a fourth season. You must be so excited."

I swallowed hard. "So excited," I echoed, hating how my voice trembled. Any second now, she'd hear the truth in it —that I'd failed. The last thing I needed was for her to think I was a disappointment.

"Are you getting a pay raise?"

I blinked back the tears that threatened to spill over. "Too soon to say."

"Morgana?"

"Yeah, Mom?"

"Is everything okay?"

"Why wouldn't it be?"

I wasn't ready to say it out loud. Saying it made it real. It meant my career as a screenwriter was over. My relationship with Saffron? Over. My dream of getting the hell out of that shithole Arizona town and making something of myself? Dead.

"So, work's good?"

"Like you said, renewed for a fourth season. Woo-hoo!" I tried to inject some enthusiasm, but my voice fell flat. Even I couldn't believe my pathetic lies.

"Uh-huh." She didn't sound convinced.

Well, she was one of my mothers and a self-described empath. She always knew when something was up, even when I was trying my damnedest to hide it. "And things are good between you and Saffron?"

That did it. The dam broke. I sobbed into the phone. My shoulders shook as the weight of my failures crashed down upon me. Unemployed. Cheated on. Homeless. Hopeless.

My ADHD brain wasn't just spiraling—it was in total free fall. I couldn't stop crying, couldn't stop feeling everything all at once. And I hated it. Why was I such a failure?

Once again, the lights flickered throughout the coffee shop. The scent of creosote returned, stronger than before. Goose bumps raced up my arms as static electricity crackled in the air.

Stupid Faeries! Why can't they leave me alone, today of all days?

I cried for what felt like an eternity.

When I finally caught my breath, I whispered, "Sorry."

Mom's response was broken up as the connection cut in

and out. "No nee... to apol... swee... you tell... wha... wrong?"

Now the damned Faeries were futzing with the connection. Naturally.

My words tumbled out in a cascade of tears and humiliation. "Paragon Pictures bought Ruby Productions. They fired me... and the rest of the writers' room."

"Oh, sweetie... so sor... when... this happ...?"

I took a cleansing breath, trying to let go of all the bitterness as I exhaled. "It happened this morning."

"Well, that was a rotten thing for them to do." The phone connection improved. "But that's Hollywood, sweetie. Most shows don't get renewed for a second season, much less a fourth. You'll get another job soon."

"I can't."

"Why not?"

"I..." The words felt like boulders in my throat. "I got nowhere to live."

"Oh, sweetie. Did you and Saffron have another fight?"

I swallowed hard. "Not exactly."

"Well, then what exactly?"

"I caught her. An hour ago. She was..." Deep breath. "She was in bed with someone."

"Another woman?"

"Yes."

"And it's her condo, isn't it?"

"Uh-huh." Each admission felt like a punch to the gut.

"Want me to hex her?" She was joking to cheer me up. Or was she? "I've got a return-to-sender spell to make her feel the pain she caused you. A nasty one that uses chipotle powder, broken glass, and cactus spines. She'll show up on set so blotchy and swollen no amount of makeup will cover it up. Or maybe an itchy-asshole spell."

"No. Don't."

Snot was dribbling onto the table. *Goddess, could I be any more pathetic?*

I wiped my nose with a paper napkin and caught the other customers staring. Two had their phones out, recording me.

Just how I wanted to become a YouTube sensation. *Emmy Winner Melts Down at Santa Monica Coffee Shop. Like and subscribe.*

Mila set down the chocolate croissant in front of me and briefly put a reassuring hand on my back. Probably thinking, *Glad I never hooked up with that loser.*

"I don't know what to do, Mom," I mumbled. "I've got no savings and nowhere to live."

"You can always move back to Wickenburg. Give yourself time to find a new job, maybe do a little freelance editing like you did in college. Mama Joyce and I would love having you home again, especially for Samhain."

Wickenburg, Arizona. Last place in the universe I wanted to be. The small town I couldn't wait to escape from. Ultraconservative. Bigoted. Suffocating. I grew up feeling like an outsider because of my mothers' relationship and witchy ways, compounded by my own repressed sexuality.

The thought of skulking back with my tail between my legs to a town full of MAGA supporters made me ill.

"But this was my dream," I protested.

"And it still can be. Sometimes, the Universe throws us curveballs. You just gotta roll with the punches."

"Nice mixed metaphor, Mom."

"When I learned I was pregnant with you, I thought my life was over, convinced my dream of making something of myself was history."

"Good to know I ruined your life too. Super motivational. You should write for Hallmark."

I was being rude and disrespectful, but I couldn't stop myself. My emotions were completely dysregulated. The words flew out, bypassing the filter I wished I had.

"Honey, that's not what I meant. Sure, I was scared about becoming a single mother. But you turned out to be the greatest blessing of my life. Mine and Mama Joyce's both. In fact, you're the reason we got together. Every morning, I thank the Goddess for you."

"I don't know why. I'm just a loser who can't keep a job. Or a girlfriend." Self-pity, party of one—your table is ready.

"Sweetie, you are the furthest thing from a loser. Jobs come and go in Hollywood. You know that. But you're talented, smart, and you just won an Emmy. How many writers can claim that? Any studio would be proud to have you."

"Paragon obviously wasn't."

"Then those brain-dead producers at Paragon are the losers. Not you. You still taking your meds?"

"Yes, Mom," I replied with an eye roll. "Every morning. First thing."

"Good. Then maybe you just need to take a step back and reassess. You can stay in your old room while you figure out your next move. And if you need spending money, I can always use a hand at the bookshop. I can't pay you what you made as a screenwriter, but you'll have free room and board. Not a bad deal, is it?"

"Having to move back to a town full of fascists? Seems like a bad deal to me."

"Not everyone here in Wickenburg is a fascist, honey. There are a lot of good, caring people here too."

"Not that I remember. And I can't imagine things have improved much since I left."

"I won't deny these are troubled times. But how you show up in the world affects how people respond to you.

Look for the good, and good will find you. Like attracts like. So what do you say? Move back home for a bit until you can find a new screenwriting gig?"

I wanted to say no. I wanted to have to click over to another call because Netflix or HBO were offering me a seven-figure deal as head writer of a new series. But the odds of that fantasy scenario happening were worse than me winning the lottery.

Resignation settled over me like a heavy blanket. "Yeah, okay. I'll move back home."

"Chin up, sweetie. The Goddess has great things planned for you."

"Thanks, Mom."

I hung up and stared at the chocolate croissant. Moving back to Wickenburg and living in my old bedroom—not the future I'd envisioned for myself.

I took a deep breath, and my phone chimed. *Now what?*

Saffron had left a voicemail. Probably telling me to move my crap out of her condo.

Fine. I would. But not while she was around. I didn't want to talk to her. And I sure didn't want to see her surgically enhanced face.

I wanted to wriggle my nose, snap my fingers, and have everything moved back to Arizona in an instant.

Unfortunately, even my mothers, with all their witchy magic, couldn't accomplish that. No amount of wishing was going to pack up my shit. And the thought of organizing, boxing, and loading everything into my car sent me into an executive-dysfunction panic spiral. Ugh!

Chapter 3

LA Murder Squad's showrunner was hosting a party that night up in the hills to celebrate the show's fourth-season renewal. All cast and crew invited. Everyone except us writers, who got the axe that morning.

Saffron had sent me a couple of texts, asking if I was going with her, because she didn't want to go alone. I didn't bother responding. Her cheating ass had answered that question. Let her do the math.

Instead, I waited across the street in my Kia Soul, feeling like a stalker, until she drove off to the party in her top-of-the-line Lexus. I then spent the next few hours packing all of my belongings into a couple of suitcases, left-over cardboard boxes, and a bunch of garbage bags.

The sad truth was that I didn't own a lot of stuff. But the upside was I managed to fit what I did have into the back of my car.

It was midnight by the time I was done. I was tempted to drive through the night back to Wickenburg. But the packing and the day's trauma had wiped me out. No amount of coffee would have kept me awake for a six-hour drive. So I grabbed a motel room in West Covina to get some much-needed sleep.

I woke the next morning, feeling bleak and empty. A cold and broken hallelujah.

Saff had left me a long, rambling voicemail. She sounded drunk. "Morgana, where the hell are you? I went to the party all by myself. Do you know how embarrassing that was? And then I come home to find your stuff gone? Are you screwing around on me? It's that bitch set designer, isn't it? Stupid cow was always—"

Click. Delete. I was not interested in her paranoid accusations when she knew good and well why I was gone.

Breakfast consisted of convenience-store coffee, a stale French cruller, two granola bars, a package of beef jerky, and a bag of Gardetto's. Wasn't like the Circle K offered a breakfast buffet. I could've grabbed an Egg McMuffin at Mickey D's but was eager to get on the road.

As the miles slowly piled up behind me, I reflected on the life I was leaving. I'd had fun and loved the work. But I never fit in with the Hollywood crowd. I wasn't tall enough. Not skinny enough. Not pretty enough. Not white enough. Not social enough. Not shallow enough. Not fake enough.

Whenever Saffron dragged me to those dreadful parties, I inevitably found myself alone in the corner, petting a cat. Or staring at my phone while she schmoozed and flirted, making connections and discussing upcoming roles.

Still, the drive back to Wickenburg felt like being banished to one of those places where people were never heard from again. Like Guantanamo or Area 51, or Adak, Alaska.

Sure, Arizona had a certain "glad I don't live there" kind of beauty. Vast stretches of scrub desert intersected by jagged mountain ranges. And the sunsets were often breathtaking.

On the flip side were the triple-digit temperatures six months out of the year. Every plant had spines. And every animal was trying to sting you, bite you, or otherwise kill you—scorpions, tarantulas, Africanized bees, rattlesnakes, Gila monsters, pumas, bobcats, and javelinas. Not to mention, the deadliest, most vicious creatures of all—humans.

It was almost noon when I turned off Highway 60 and began the all-too-familiar climb up Hummingbird Hill Lane. Near the summit, my childhood home came into view—a three-bedroom wood-frame house next to a small, weathered barn, which my maternal units used for storage and occasional rituals when the weather was bad.

I parked in front of the house and checked my phone. Mom had sent me a text: *Welcome home, sweetheart. You know how to get in. Once you're settled, come by the shop.*

The subtext of her message was clear. Getting into the house required magic. Great!

As I stepped out of the car, I was assaulted by the dusty aroma of the Sonoran Desert and the lingering summer heat. Sure, it was mid-October, but the face-melting temps lingered later each year.

A subtle magical energy pervaded the area, like standing too close to a power line. Mom and Mama Joyce claimed the house was built on a mystical vortex like the ones up in Sedona. As witches, I guessed they'd know about such things.

A throaty croak followed by a couple of clicks caught my attention. Perched in a cottonwood tree sat a raven with a single white feather in her otherwise onyx tail.

She stared at me, as if to say, "Look what the cat dragged in."

"Hello, Lenore," I said.

"Hi," she said back. "Boop, boop. Merry meet. Nevermore. Mwah, mwah."

It was more a parroting response than an actual greeting. Ravens were great mimics, though Mom swore she understood what the bird was saying, even if it sounded like nonsense.

She'd been Mom's familiar since I was a child. I wondered if all ravens lived this long or if being a familiar extended her natural life.

Lenore cocked her head and let out a series of croaks.

I ignored the bird and approached the front porch. A wave of nostalgia and guilt washed over me. In the past six years, I'd only visited a few times. I was a bad daughter.

The sun-bleached walls begged for fresh paint, their fading color a testament to decades in the Arizona sun. Wind chimes swayed in the warm breeze, playing a lazy, melodic tune.

On the heavy oaken front door was carved a stylized tree surrounded by sigils. The design always reminded me of an illustration from a Tolkien novel. Like those elvish doors of Middle-earth, it hummed with magical energy.

A twist of the doorknob confirmed my fears. Locked.

I checked under the "Blessed Be" doormat, hoping to find a spare key. Nothing but a dead bark scorpion and desert grit. *Crap!* No hide-a-key rock in the front yard either. Too mundane for my witchy moms.

Still, I wasn't ready to admit defeat. Nor would I embarrass myself by calling Mom and telling her I couldn't do it. There had to be a window or door that had been left unlocked. Mom could be as scatterbrained as I was about such things.

I circled the house, my hand trailing along the rough, sunbaked walls. A path on the east side led to a hilltop clearing where my moms' coven, the Siblings of the Desert Moon, held rituals to celebrate the full moons and Sabbats.

Originally called the Sisterhood of the Desert Moon, the coven's officers had switched to a more gender-inclusive name to allow male and nonbinary members.

I'd participated in the rituals as a child, invoking the elements and lighting candles. That stopped when Mom had the brilliant idea of doing a Beltane ritual skyclad. I'd seen things a twelve-year-old girl shouldn't ever witness—grown-ups standing around a bonfire, stark naked.

Major eww! Not enough mind bleach in the world to erase that memory.

Near the screened-in back porch, I caught a whiff of weed. Mom occasionally indulged in the evenings to help her unwind. Not my jam, but I never judged. Granted, she'd been doing it long before it was legal in Arizona.

A low hum caught my attention when I walked past my old bedroom window at the back of the house. A pair of hummingbirds flitted around my head. I looked up at them and gasped.

For an instant, they looked like pixies rather than birds. Human faces, dragonfly wings, the works.

I rubbed my eyes and looked again. They were back to being normal hummingbirds.

What the hell's going on with me?

I sighed with disappointment when I reached the front porch again. Every entry was locked, except for a small high-set pet door in the kitchen that allowed Lenore to come and go as she pleased. I was too big to fit through.

I resigned myself to the inevitable. I either had to use magic, or I wasn't getting in on my own.

Mama Joyce always explained that magic was a combo of intention and focus, drawing on universal energies. Wands, candles, crystals, herbs, and incantations could help direct that energy, but bottom line—it came down to intention and focus.

As an ADHDer, focus was *not* my strong suit.

Technically, any words would work for an incantation if they were meaningful to the user. And our home being built on a vortex supposedly made this easier. Supposedly.

I approached the front door, attempting to focus on the lock.

"Lorem ipsum dolor sit amet," I intoned solemnly.

I know. Not really an incantation. Just fake Latin filler text that appeared in my screenwriting app whenever I started a new project.

Nothing magical about it, unless I wanted to summon a demonic editor from the Ninth Circle of Literary Hell. Or the ghost of Ms. Mankiewicz, my tenth-grade English teacher, who would, no doubt, lecture me on comma splices and my overuse of em dashes.

Intention was what mattered. And my intention was to unlock the door.

I repeated the phrase over and over, all while thinking, *Unlock, unlock, unlock!*

I'll admit, I was more than a little surprised when the doorknob unlocked with a soft click.

"Ha! Easy-peasy lemon squeezy." The thrill of accomplishment energized me.

But when I turned the knob, a sharp zap of electricity shot into my hand.

"Shit, shit, shit!" I shook my stinging fingers.

The wards. I'd forgotten about the Goddess-blessed wards. Mama Joyce had first set them years ago after a few of my schoolmates showed up on Samhain night, looking to have some fun at the witches' house. Broke into the barn and wrecked my mothers' library.

The next year, when they came round again, they got more than they bargained for.

Taking a deep breath, I tried to calm my mind, reaching back into my memory for the spell to disarm Mama Joyce's protective magic. It had something to do with that book she loved so much—*Women Who Run with the Wolves* by Clarissa Pinkola Estés.

But what were the words she used to release the wards? Not the author's name or any of the stories in the book. No, it was the title of one of Estés's poems. But which one? Mama Joyce used to recite so many of them.

Goddess, why can't I remember things?

Closing my eyes, I focused inward, extending my consciousness like the roots of a tree, deep into the very foundation of the house. As my energy connected with the lingering traces of my own history and my mothers' love, I felt a flicker of recognition—the house remembered me.

Okay, that's a little scary.

The words I needed rose from the depths of memory.

"Abre la puerta," I whispered, my voice barely audible. *Open the door.*

The wards shuddered and yielded, their protective magic surrendering to me at last. With no small amount of trepidation, I once again turned the doorknob.

No shock.

With a sigh of relief, I opened the door and stepped into the house where I'd grown up.

CHAPTER 4

THE LIVING ROOM hadn't changed much. Dust motes danced in the golden sunlight shining through the windows, while Swarovski crystals suspended on strings painted rainbows across the room.

A well-worn faux leather couch rested beneath a collection of throw pillows in celestial prints and earth-tone African patterns. A red-and-black checked flannel blanket hung over the back for keeping warm on winter evenings.

The walls were a mosaic of memories and magic—framed family photos, African tribal masks, a variety of pentacles, and woven tapestries dyed in desert hues.

A bookcase dominated the far wall, lined with books on every magical subject, along with deity and Faerie statues, crystals, and spell jars.

A signed copy of Brian Froud's book *Fairies* lay next to a small bowl of cowrie shells and half-melted candles on an antique mesquite coffee table. The table's edge bore a scar from where I'd dropped a small cast-iron cauldron years ago.

The interwoven scents of patchouli, lavender, and vanilla incense still filled the air. Grounding. Calming.

No matter how desperate I was to leave Wickenburg or how long I'd been gone—this house still felt like home. It wasn't filled with elegant designer furnishings like Saffron's condo. There was no identifiable decorative style. Nothing matched. There was no ocean view.

But there was a comfortable energy about this place that the condo had always lacked. It was like a worn pair of jeans that fit perfectly in all the right places.

Growing up with two amazing, yet distinctly different mothers, I always felt loved. Here I was encouraged to try new things, to cherish nature, and to embrace everything that made us human and unique. This home had been a refuge from the harassment I faced in school.

I had been twelve—and halfway through the coven's year-and-a-day program—when word spread like wildfire through my seventh-grade class that I had two moms of different races who practiced witchcraft. I might as well have painted a target on my forehead. Prejudice metastasized into cruelty.

My main tormentors were the Meanlindas, a vicious clique of girls whose names—I kid you not—were Melinda, Belinda, Delinda, Rosalinda, and just plain Linda. All of them were cheerleader-pretty and came from rich, evangelical families. Melinda Fox ruled the pack, hell-bent on making my life a daily nightmare.

They shoved me, tripped me, and elbowed me "by accident" in the crowded halls between classes. They churned out vile rumors about me and my moms. They pasted my face onto porno stills and sent them to each other's phones. On multiple occasions, they broke into my gym locker and trashed my street clothes, though I could never prove it was them.

The relentless abuse was enough to make me not want to do magic anymore, much less go to school. I quit the year-and-a-day program, and my grades began to suffer.

Mom and Mama Joyce begged the school to intervene —but nothing changed. The teachers and the principal brushed it off, saying some "teasing" was expected when I "shoved my family's perversions down everyone's throats."

Never mind that I *never* talked about my moms in school, much less their sexuality or their spiritual path. Not once. Not ever.

With the school doing jack to help me, Mom and Mama Joyce decided it was time for a magical intervention. They crafted a protective charm inside a small, hand-carved wooden box for me to carry in my purse.

Inside was a tiny mirror, a shard of black obsidian, a small cowrie shell, and a tightly rolled paper scroll. I never peeked at the scroll, but knowing Mama Joyce, it was likely a plea to the Morrigan—the Irish Goddess of war—and Ayelala, the Yoruba goddess of justice.

Before giving it to me, Mama Joyce sat me down and hit me with *the look*. "This is for protection *only*, Morgana. We don't use magic to harm people. We don't manipulate them. That's not who we are. Understand?"

"I don't care about magic," I muttered, sulking. "It's stupid."

"Nevertheless, I want you to carry this with you at all times and listen to what I'm saying."

"Yeah, yeah." I rolled my eyes. "Do no harm but take no shit. Got it."

"Good. Now this is a return-to-sender protection charm. As long as no one messes with you—or your stuff—no harm will come to anyone."

"And if they do? What?"

She paused then dropped her voice to pure steel. "Let's

just say the Morrigan and Ayelala don't play. And neither do I when it comes to anyone who hurts my baby girl."

The next day after gym class, I braced myself as we filed back into the locker room. My heart sank when I found my street clothes had been glitter-bombed again. So much for magical protection.

Then a blood-chilling shriek of terror echoed through the locker room. I sprinted toward the showers.

Melinda Fox sat sobbing, on the wet tile floor, the water from the shower raining down on her naked body. Her cheerleader-perfect hair was falling out in clumps into her hands. Tangled, horrifying clumps. Her scalp was bright red, splotchy, and blistered like she'd washed it in acid.

For a heartbeat, I stood there, frozen. Part from horror, part from shock, but mostly from satisfaction.

Holy shit. The protection charm worked.

The other Meanlindas gathered around her, screaming, crying, and gagging.

"Somebody get a nurse!" Rosalinda demanded.

I backed away slowly, suppressing the smile that tugged at my cheeks.

The name-calling and taunts continued. Not much to be done about that, according to Mama Joyce. But my stuff was never messed with again. No one tripped me or "accidentally" knocked my books out of my hands. They were afraid of me for once.

The creak of my old bedroom door yanked me back to the present, revealing a time capsule of my teenage years. LED Faerie lights still glowed blue above posters of Orla Gartland, Girl in Red, and P!nk on the walls. A faded quilt that Mama Joyce's grandmother had made lay across my bed. Glow-in-the-dark stars dotted the ceiling.

An envelope rested on the pillow, my name penned across the front in Mom's loopy handwriting. The greeting card inside featured a cheesy cartoon witch, zipping through a starry sky on a broom. I recognized it from Mom's bookshop.

The printed message read, "Nothing says lovin' like something from the coven." Beneath it, Mom had written, "Welcome home, Morgana. Blessed be, sweetie. Love, Mom and Mama Joyce."

My dream of becoming a screenwriter might have fizzled—along with my relationship with Saffron. But I still had two moms who loved me, flaws and all, and always had my back when life went sideways. And that, I had to admit, wasn't nothing.

I hauled in the suitcases, boxes, and garbage bags from my car. While unpacking my embarrassingly meager belongings, I found a framed photo of me and Erin O'Brien —my former best friend—taken during a tubing trip down the Salt River and set it down on my old desk.

Her pale skin was sunburned, but her smile was still as radiant as always.

Through all the bullying, Erin stuck by me—one of the few who did. She, too, was gay but made no effort to hide it. Unlike me. Harassment from the Meanlindas—or the jock squad they orbited—never fazed her. She hurled it right back at them and laughed like it was a joke at their expense.

I envied her brazenness. Her fire.

She was the queer rebel I lacked the courage to be. And I had no excuse, considering I had two loving, supportive mothers. Sometimes, I wondered if they secretly wished Erin were their daughter instead of me.

Staring at that photo of us on the Salt River, I couldn't help wondering how her life had turned out. She used to dream of becoming a professional chef. I'd always encouraged her to audition for one of those cooking competition shows she binge-watched religiously.

Wherever she was, I hoped she was living her dream and having more success than I was.

From one of my suitcases, I lifted out the Emmy statuette, wrapped in a seldom-used cashmere sweater. It was heavier than I'd expected. The gleaming figure looked out of place on the old wooden desk where I'd written my first stories—cringeworthy fanfic pairing Jane Rizzoli and Maura Isles as lovers.

The memory of accepting the award onstage amidst the roar of applause and the blinding lights seemed like a distant dream. I'd never much cared about awards. It was the work I loved. And that was the one thing I didn't have right now.

By the time I'd emptied the last of the boxes and found a place for everything, I was drenched in sweat and exhausted, both physically and emotionally. I refilled my water bottle, stepped outside to reset the wards, and drove into town to see Mom at Wiccanburg Books.

CHAPTER 5

Mom's bookshop—and yes, she called it a bookshop rather than a bookstore because she thought it sounded more elegant—was wedged between a cowboy art gallery and an overpriced ice cream parlor in quaint downtown Wickenburg.

The sign above the door read, Wiccanburg Books: A Metaphysical Experience. A handwritten sign taped inside the glass door announced the store offered tarot and psychic readings.

Mom was sweeping the sidewalk in front of the shop. As always, she looked like she'd wandered out of a Stevie Nicks music video—flowing skirt, peasant blouse, silver goddess earrings, and bangles that jingled with every sweep of her broom. No surprise that my middle name was Rhiannon.

She was tall with pale freckled skin, long sandy-blond hair, and eyes that were either blue or green, depending on what she wore.

Aside from my nose, I looked nothing like her. I was petite with olive-brown skin, hazel eyes, and long black hair, due to my paternal heritage, no doubt. Despite being in my mid-twenties, I still looked like a teenager.

I assumed my biological father was Latino, but Mom never talked about him. And when I asked Mama Joyce, she always said, "Talk to Mom."

Mom was so focused on sweeping the sidewalk, she didn't look up when I approached. A faint energy rippled through the air, and I caught the pungent scent of black salt and burning sage. *Magic.* Mom was using magic to banish something.

"Hi, Mom. Whatcha doing?"

"What—?" She startled then beamed when she saw me, rushing over for a hug. "Oh, sweetheart, you're home! How was the drive?"

"Six delightful hours of long and boring. TL;DR—it sucked."

A lump formed in my throat. As much as I hated moving back to Wickenburg, I'd missed her and Mama Joyce more than I wanted to admit.

"I know you're disappointed about getting laid off, especially after you worked your butt off for that show. But something better's on the way. I can feel it." She tucked a strand of my hair behind my ear. "As for that skank who broke your heart, you sure you don't want me to hex her? Because I could. Like, maybe she loses her eyebrows for a month."

"No," I said despondently.

"Eh, you're right. She'd just draw them back on. Although I could hex just one, so she'd have to shave off the other one to make them look even. Or I could make all her teeth fall out one at a time. Ooh! Or I could—"

"Mom, no. Aren't you always saying magic's not to be used to hurt people? *Harm none* and all that jazz?"

"That's more Mama Joyce's rule than mine," she admitted. "I've always leaned toward the 'play stupid games, win stupid prizes' school of thought. And Miss Saffron Blaise won herself the deluxe prize pack. Don't ya think?"

Her words triggered the memory of Saffron in bed with that other woman. Anger and hurt threatened to summon tears.

"No, don't do anything. I'd rather just forget her."

"Of course. Give yourself time to process and heal. I've got the perfect spell to help you do just that. It uses a—"

"No offense, Mom, but I'd rather grieve the old-fashioned way—Ben & Jerry's, Netflix, and crying in the shower. No candles. No spells. No incantations."

"Lavender-scented bath oils?" She really was trying to help.

"Let me think about it. So, what are you doing out here?"

"Oh, just keeping the sidewalk clean."

"With black salt?"

"Good for banishing negative energy. You know that."

What I knew was that she wasn't telling me the whole truth. But I let it slide.

She patted my cheek. "Go on inside. Mama Joyce is manning the counter. I'll be along in a moment."

I pushed open the door and caught a whiff of incense—dragon's blood, if memory served. *Ugh, so not a fan.*

Shelves and display cases overflowed not only with books but crystals, tarot decks, statues, candles, spell ingredients, and every other metaphysical trinket under the sun. The soft strains of a Celtic harp melody drifted from the sound system.

Customers browsed the aisles. One was getting help from a slender white woman I vaguely remembered—Bernice something-or-other. Along the far wall, an employee named Garry McGowan—a guy a few years older than me with electric-blue hair and a face full of piercings —was shelving books.

A tall Black woman with long thin braids and dressed in cobalt-blue scrubs stood behind the counter, ringing up a customer. That color always looked so good on her.

"Morning, Mama," I said after the customer walked off, bag in hand.

"Goddess bless me! Come here, peanut!" She rushed around the counter and pulled me into an embrace so tight I felt my spine crack like a glow stick.

Joyce Coleman had been Mom's midwife nurse when she was pregnant with me. They began dating a few months after I was born. At first, she was Auntie Joyce. By the time I was a toddler, I called her Mama Joyce, or some-times just Mama.

She pulled back, holding my shoulders. "Good to have you home, baby girl. I'm sorry about the job and, well, *her*."

"Guess I'm just not Hollywood material."

"Nonsense! Screenwriting jobs are always temporary. You know that. This is just a little detour, not the end of your career. I ever tell you what happened at the first prac-tice where I worked as a labor and delivery nurse?"

"No."

"They fired me. After only two days. Two days!"

"Why?"

"The arrogant little shit of an administrator found out I was a witch. He was worried I'd hex the patients or steal their babies. As if. I had half a mind to hex *him*."

"That sucks."

"But that's my point. Getting canned pushed me to become certified as a nurse-midwife. No regrets."

"I don't think more classes will help me, Mama."

"Perhaps not. But don't think your career's dead just because you got fired and moved back home. You're a talented writer with two years' experience on a critically acclaimed show and an Emmy to boot. Don't let that imposter syndrome get the better of you."

I appreciated her confidence in me, even if I didn't share it. "So, what are you doing here at the shop? Shouldn't you be helping an expecting mother give birth?"

"Call shift today. Probably be pretty quiet, but one never knows. Thought I'd help out here and have lunch with Mom. She ordered gourmet sandwiches from the Wicked Grille. I can call and add one to the order for you, if you'd like."

"No thanks. I'm not all that hungry. I grabbed something on the way in."

"Lemme guess—fast food?"

"Spicy chicken taquitos and a milkshake from the QT in Quartzsite."

"Processed foods." She rolled her eyes. "Full of salt, sugar, and saturated fats. The evil trinity."

"More like the holy trinity of yum!"

"Your body deserves better."

"It's road-trip food, Mama. None of that counts when you're on the road." I gave her my most innocent look, but she wasn't buying it.

"I suppose."

"I see Bernice and Garry are still here."

"Yep. Bernice's son will be graduating from U of A next spring. Meanwhile, her daughter recently started at ASU. A bit of school rivalry between the two of them."

"Should make for interesting visits during the holidays."

"No doubt. And Garry has taken up bookbinding. He's created some exquisite hand-bound journals. We have some on the other side of the tarot cards display. You should check them out."

"Speaking of tarot, you have someone giving readings now?"

"We do. I think you know them—Angel Lopez?"

"Oh yeah. I remember Angel. He was the only other gay kid in school besides Erin and me."

"Angel came out as nonbinary a few years ago. Their pronouns are they/them now," Mama Joyce corrected gently. "Come on. Let's go say hi."

Mama Joyce led me to a corner of the shop sectioned off by folding screens painted with Goddess figures, sugar skulls, and crescent moons against a black background. A wooden sign read, "Tarot readings $50. Uncover your truth. Discover your future."

Personally, I lumped tarot readings in with astrology, Ouija boards, and other woo-woo nonsense. But hey, if someone wanted to throw away their money like that, who was I to argue?

Mama Joyce knocked on the screen's frame. "Angel? You busy?"

"Always got time for you, Mama J," replied a familiar voice.

I followed Mama around the partition to where Angel sat behind a table, studying cards laid out in an elaborate spread. They gathered the cards into a neat pile as we entered.

The light overhead was off, allowing the space to be lit by a single pillar candle that threw flickering shadows over the sharp lines of Angel's face. They wore a leather corset over a black lace top and makeup with a strong goth vibe. Their pronouns may have changed, but their queer goth vibe remained the same.

"Angel, you remember my daughter, Morgana? She's back in town for a while."

"How's it going?" I asked casually.

Angel studied me for a moment while shuffling the cards loosely in their hands then held them out to me. "Cut the deck into three piles."

"Sorry, I don't have fifty bucks," I said, a little too defensively. Even if I did have a spare fifty, I wouldn't spend it on this.

Angel smiled seductively. "On the house, chica. Sit."

Chapter 6

I shot Mama Joyce a look that said, *Really?* She nodded.

I sat obediently. *As if this small-minded town isn't bad enough. Now I'm humoring a goth who fancies themself a psychic. This just isn't my week.*

The card backs were black, embossed with sugar skulls circled by thorny roses. Not exactly the standard Smith-Rider-Waite deck but fitting Angel's brujo aesthetic.

I cut the deck into three and set the piles in a row on the table.

"Now choose a pile."

I felt like an audience volunteer from a Vegas magician show. What next? Pick a card, and they'll guess what it is? "One on the left."

Angel gathered the cards, with the pile I'd chosen on top, then dealt three cards in a column. The art on the face sides was dark and morbid—a bleeding heart pierced by daggers, a decaying corpse impaled with swords, and a crumbling stone tower engulfed in flames.

"Ay, mamacita! Someone's been through hell recently," Angel said, examining the cards.

"Excuse me?"

"Betrayal, heartbreak, and some other major loss... a job or a home, perhaps?"

I shot Mama Joyce a quick glare. "You're telling people my business?"

She held up a hand as if swearing an oath. "Haven't said a word."

"Nobody told me, chica," Angel replied. "It's all in the cards."

"Right."

A faint tingle wriggled up my spine, and the temperature seemed to drop ten degrees. I caught a whiff of ginger and cinnamon.

Magic! declared my inner child.

Don't be ridiculous, my rational mind countered. *Tarot reading is nothing more than random cards and mentalism. Angel was always good at reading people.*

But what if it is *magic? Could this be what divination smells like? Why have I never noticed it before?*

They laid down another three cards. The first depicted Santa Muerte, Mexico's folk saint of healing and protection. Her skeletal hands poured water from a pitcher beneath a golden star. Only it was inverted. Never a good sign.

The next card featured a bone-white hand, reaching out of a stormy cloud and holding a wand. The third showed a half-rotted jester, grinning as he danced across a graveyard.

More doom and gloom? Do I even want to know?

Angel nodded appraisingly. "Well, that's interesting."

"What?"

"You're feeling hopeless. You've lost faith in yourself. Understandable, considering what you've been through recently. But here—Ace of Wands? New inspiration. And this cabrón?" They tapped the jester. "He's Death's fool. He walks through endings like it's a party."

"Meaning?"

"Exciting opportunities are on the horizon, possibly new creative projects."

Generic horoscope drivel, I assured myself. *Vague enough to fit anyone, any situation.*

But the crackle of magic in the air told me Angel might be on to something.

Angel dealt three more cards. "Death. Two of Swords. The Hanged Man. Oh yeah, this tracks."

I stared at the Death card. "I'm going to die? What happened to these so-called exciting opportunities on my horizon?"

"We're all gonna die, sweet cheeks. But the Death card doesn't necessarily mean physical death. It represents change. Shedding your skin. Letting go of old stories, old guilt, the old you. Time to embrace new perspectives. Could be there's something you're avoiding—a choice or a truth. Face it and level up. Or ignore it and stay stuck in limbo. Your decision."

"And what have I been avoiding, exactly?" I folded my arms across my chest.

They shrugged. "No idea. But I think you know."

"No offense, but it sounds like a steaming pile of mystical crap."

Mama Joyce shot me a scolding look. Yeah, yeah, I was being rude.

"Sorry. Thanks for the reading, Angel. Good seeing you again."

I stalked away and nearly bumped into Mom, who was breezing into the shop, broom in hand. "Sorry. What were you sweeping off the sidewalk?" Something told me it wasn't just desert dust.

"Oh, nothing."

"Nothing, my ass." Garry approached, breaking down

an empty cardboard box. "Some jerk spray-painted 'Witches Burn in Hell' on the sidewalk. Again."

Bitterness coiled in my chest like a rattlesnake. Some things never changed in this town.

"Mom, that's not nothing," I exclaimed. "That's a threat."

"That's what I told her," Mama Joyce added.

"Did you at least call the cops?"

"It's just harmless graffiti. Nothing to get worked up over. The police have bigger things to worry about than some kid with a spray can and a rebellious streak."

"What if it's not just harmless graffiti?"

"The shop is warded. No harm can come to us in here. Besides, I took care of it. A little black salt, my enchanted broom—swish, swish, problem gone!" Mom mimed sweeping with the broom. "Like it never happened."

The bell above the door jingled, followed by a voice from my past. "Lunch delivery!"

I turned, and my pulse quickened. *No! Can't be!*

Erin O'Brien strode in, a large wicker basket hooked over one arm. Her coppery hair gleamed against the crisp white of her chef's coat. The name Wicked Grille was stitched neatly over the pocket.

Memories of secret kisses and slick, fumbling fingers in the dark came rushing back. Heat blossomed in my core, coupled with a pang of guilt.

Her eyes landed on me, and she beamed. "Oh my Goddess! Morgana! When did you get into town?"

"Couple hours ago," I said, trying to play it cool. "It's good to see you."

How does she not hate me after what I did to her in school?

She set the basket on the counter and pulled me into a quick hug before I could mentally prepare. Her arms around me felt strong, warm, and familiar. She smelled of grilled meat, garlic, and spices.

It hurt how much I missed her. Missed us. *Get it together, Morgana.*

"Good to see you too. I heard about your Emmy. Major kudos!"

The compliment only amplified my sense of failure. "Thanks."

"I hope everyone's hungry." Erin pulled a cylinder wrapped in white butcher paper from the basket. "Garden Goddess sub with shiitake, cucumber, and avocado for Selene."

"Yum!" Mom beamed and took the sandwich.

"Grilled chicken and tomato for Joyce, smoked salmon club for Garry, ham and gouda for Bernice..."

"Thanks," Bernice said, already unwrapping hers.

"And last but never least—an LGBT for Angel."

"Thank Santa Muerte. I'm starving." Angel took the sandwich from her.

"LGBT?" I raised a brow. "As in lesbian, gay, bi, and trans?"

"Lettuce, guac, bacon, and tomato." She winked at me. "What can I say? I love to tease the straights. Which I see you're not anymore. You and Saffron Blaise looked amazing together on the red carpet."

"Thanks. You look great too."

"I've got to rush back to the restaurant, but let's catch up soon. Maybe grab drinks sometime?"

"Absolutely." Her mention of Saffron stung but was mitigated by the prospect of us getting together. Who knew where it might lead?

"Bon appétit, everyone!" She turned to leave, calling back over her shoulder, "Catch you later, Morgana."

"Most definitely." A smile tugged at my lips. Maybe coming home wasn't a total disaster after all.

Chapter 7

The afternoon flew by. For the first time in weeks, I wasn't circling the drain emotionally. Sure, my life was still a blazing dumpster fire—no job, no girlfriend, no more beachside condo, no friends. And I couldn't forget the death threat spray-painted outside Mom's bookshop.

But seeing Erin shifted something. Even if I didn't believe in miracles or fate, I *did* believe in second chances.

Maybe I could make up for being a shitty girlfriend and causing our breakup back in high school. We'd both matured. I wasn't hiding in the closet anymore. Hell, the whole world had seen me walk the red carpet at the Emmys, arm in arm with Saffron Blaise.

Maybe, just maybe, we could give romance another shot. Who cared if I was on the rebound?

That evening, Mom, Mama Joyce, and I ate dinner by candlelight—Mom's idea to celebrate my return home. A Fleetwood Mac album played quietly on the living room stereo.

How long had it been since the three of us had shared a meal here? Almost a year. I'd forgotten how much I enjoyed this—sharing a simple meal with the women who loved and raised me. And the thought of getting back together with Erin had left me absolutely giddy.

"What's got you grinning, baby girl?" Mama Joyce asked between bites of eggplant parm. "You look like the Cheshire cat."

"Nothing."

"Oh really? Earlier, you looked like an orphaned kitten," she continued. "Now you're practically glowing. Not that I'm complaining, but what happened? Why the sudden change in demeanor?"

Before I could answer, Mom jumped in. "I think Erin O'Brien happened."

My face flushed. Dammit, was I that easy to read?

"It was nice seeing her again," I said, trying to sound casual. "She wants to get together and catch up. I'm curious what she's been up to."

The two of them exchanged a knowing glance. *What was up with that?*

"After graduation, Erin joined the CIA," Mom said, deadpan.

I choked on a piece of eggplant. "She what? Erin's a spy?"

"Mom's messing with you." Mama Joyce made a face at her. "Erin did *not* join the Central Intelligence Agency. She attended the Culinary Institute of America in New York."

"Sounds prestigious. So why's she back here working in a sandwich shop?"

"For starters, the Wicked Grille isn't a sandwich shop, it's a gourmet restaurant," she explained. "They earned a Michelin star last year. First restaurant in town to do that."

"But why here in Wickenburg of all places? Why not New York or Chicago or even Phoenix?"

"Remember Suzanne Wilcox? She owned the Hassayampa Tavern."

"And was a beloved member of the coven," Mom added.

"I remember. Erin worked in the tavern's kitchen after school."

"Suzanne died a few years ago. Fatal car crash. Tragic loss," Mama Joyce continued. "She left the tavern to Erin in her will."

"Erin's the owner?" I asked. She really *was* doing well for herself.

"She changed the name and upscaled the menu. The place is packed six nights a week."

"Good thing she gives us the coven discount," Mom said. "Or we couldn't afford to eat there often."

"Wait—Erin's also a member of the coven?" I wasn't completely surprised. She'd wanted to join when we were in school, but her staunch Irish Catholic parents refused to allow it.

"She joined after moving back to town."

Mama Joyce nodded. "Talented little kitchen witch too. She supplies the cakes and ales for our full moon rituals."

"Oh my Goddess!" Mom gasped. "Those sweet-potato-and-sage cakes she made for the harvest moon ritual were out of this world."

"Maybe it's time I joined the coven." Anything to spend more time with Erin.

Mom's face lit up. "You mean it? You're staying?"

"For a little while, anyway. If that's all right?"

"Of course, it's all right," Mama Joyce assured me. "I'm just surprised. I thought you weren't interested in walking the path of the Goddess."

"I liked it as a kid. Before kids at school started bullying me."

A memory surfaced, uninvited, from the wreckage of my teenage years.

After Erin and I broke up, I'd been lonely. Vulnerable. Desperate for friends. So I did what any emotionally unstable teenage daughter of witches might do—I crafted a charm to make people like me.

I crept into the old barn next to the house. No longer a shelter for animals, the former barn was now Mom and Mama Joyce's library and place for spell work. An altar stood in the center. Their coven conducted rituals around it when the weather didn't permit using the outdoor circle up the hill.

One wall was crammed with books on every magical subject imaginable, alongside stacks of journals and grimoires. Another set of shelves overflowed with herbs, crystals, candles, and spell components. Statues of deities from various pantheons—Greco-Roman, Celtic, Yoruba, Norse, and more—stood in reverent rows, watching over it all. My moms tended to be rather eclectic.

I had thumbed through Mom's main grimoire and *Cunningham's Encyclopedia of Magical Herbs*, cobbling together a spell to transform me from a high-school pariah into one of the cool kids.

I chose a rose quartz crystal, a few gold ring cowrie shells, and a handful of herbs associated with friendship. I added a spoonful of sugar crystals to sweeten people's perception of me then placed everything in a small earthenware bowl surrounded by red and pink candles. On either side, I placed statues of Aphrodite and Oshun.

With the candles lit, I recited an incantation.

"Aphrodite, empower me,

Oshun, bless my charm to be.

Change their minds to welcome me,

And grant me popularity."

Not exactly Chaucer or even Dr. Seuss. But I was a desperate, lonely teenager.

As I chanted, I pictured my new life— laughing and hanging with the Meanlindas, going on shopping sprees, attending wild parties. Maybe becoming class president. Hell, maybe even homecoming queen. *A girl can dream, right?*

When the spell was done, I stuffed the crystal, cowrie shells, and herbs into a cloth pouch and tucked the newly made charm into my purse.

It worked like magic—literally. The next day at school, I got invited to two different parties. People saved me a seat at lunch. Melinda Fox, of all people, complimented my hair. No more sneers or insults. Just validation and respect. I felt normal for once. And I liked it.

A month later, I was sitting at the kitchen table, writing a story on my laptop.

Mama Joyce came in. "Honey, I need to scan your driver's license for an insurance policy. Where is it?"

I should have brought it to her myself, but I was deep into a scene and didn't want to interrupt my creative flow.

"My purse is on the desk in my bedroom," I replied without looking up.

When she returned a moment later, she cleared her throat. "Morgana?"

I glanced up to find her expression cold and hard.

Yikes! Was I in trouble?

"Something wrong?"

She held up the charm. "What's this?"

Aw, crap! I was so busted.

"Nothing." I was such a horrible liar.

"Not nothing. This is a charm. Who made it?"

"I did." I sat a little taller, proud of how well it had worked.

She looked incredulous. "Really? You're doing magic now?"

I shrugged.

"What's the charm for?"

"Just to have." *Why did I even bother lying?*

"Morgana…"

"Fine. I wanted people at school to like me. To be popular for once. Is that so wrong?"

"Morgana Rhiannon Quinn! Magic is not a toy. We do not use it to manipulate people."

"You made me that protection charm!" I defended. "It caused Melinda Fox's hair to fall out. She's still got scars on her scalp. How's this any worse?"

"Protection charms are for self-defense. Harmless until someone hurts you." She shook the sachet like it was a dead rat. "But this? This is mind control. It violates the coven's most sacred rule of consent."

She tossed the charm onto the floor and stomped on it. The quartz crystal and cowrie shells crunched under her heel. I felt the charm's magic evaporate along with my future social life.

"You're so mean!" I cried. Like, ugly cried. Years of trauma unleashed in an explosion of rage and tears and snot. *Yeah, it was gross!*

The lights in the kitchen flickered then flared. My laptop flashed the Blue Screen of Death and went dark. *Shit! Shit! Shit!*

Then came the wind, roaring through the house like a summer haboob, knocking dishes off shelves, and toppling houseplants. A salt lamp exploded. I caught a bitter whiff of ozone mixed with creosote and desert dust.

"What's going on?" I screamed, terrified. Had her destroying my charm unleashed this chaos?

Even Mama Joyce, who was normally unflappable, looked freaked out.

Not good. Not good at all.

"It's Faerie magic," she said. "They're attracted to your negative emotions. They'll stop once you calm down."

That only made me panic harder. Faeries were real? And they were attacking me? Why? Had I inadvertently involved them in the spell to make the charm?

"Just breathe, baby." She sat beside me and held my hand. "Nice and slow. Positivity in, negativity out."

Gradually, I released my fury and fear. As I did, the chaos around me abated.

"Why... why would Faeries do this?" I asked once I'd stopped shaking. "What'd I ever do to them?"

"I don't know. But it'll be all right. I'll make an amulet to protect you from the Faerie magic. Okay?"

That night, I heard her and Mom arguing in hushed voices behind their bedroom door. I couldn't make out the words, but I heard the tension and the fear. Was this about me? About the Faerie attack? Or something else they didn't want me to worry about?

The next morning, Mama Joyce handed me a pendant. Three metal discs—brass, steel, and copper—stacked and strung on a silk cord.

"What's this?" I asked her.

"An amulet. It will protect you from the Faerie magic. They'll leave you alone as long as you're wearing it."

The tone of her voice suggested there was something she wasn't saying. Something that bothered her. Maybe something she and Mom had been discussing last night.

"What about you and Mom?"

"It's you they're drawn to. You're young. Emotional. Open."

"Is something wrong?" I asked, hoping she'd share whatever it was she was holding back.

"Wrong? No, of course not, honey." She kissed the top of my head. "Nothing's wrong."

I'd worn the amulet ever since and never had a problem with the Faeries. No flickering lights, weird smells, or unexplained gusts of wind. Until recently.

I put a hand on my chest and realized the amulet was missing.

Mama Joyce must have noticed me reaching for it. "Morgana, where's your Faerie protection amulet?" Her voice was tight, eyes narrow with concern.

When's the last time I wore it? Oh, yeah. That *night.*

"It's... I don't know. I took it off a month ago, when Saffron and I attended the Emmys. She said it looked tacky and refused to let me wear it."

"It's not a fashion statement, Morgana. It's for your protection."

"I know. I could've sworn I put it back on after we got home. It must be in my dresser." But I didn't remember seeing it when I was unpacking everything.

"You need to put it back on. Right now."

"Joyce, it's okay," Mom reassured her. "Maybe it's time she knew."

"Knew what?" I looked at Mom then at Mama.

Mama looked hesitant. I could see the wheels turning. "After we've finished dinner."

"Seriously, what the hell's going on? You two are acting weird."

I waited for a more complete explanation, but it never came.

"Fine. Be weird." I took a long sip of wine. "I'm glad Erin's doing well, at least. Maybe she and I can pick up where we left off."

Mom winced. "Uh, about that."

"What?"

"Erin's dating someone," she said. "She and Kari Sullivan have been together about a year or so."

It shouldn't have been a big deal. Of course she'd be dating someone. She was gorgeous and funny and sweet and smart. Who wouldn't want to be with her?

But I felt like I was lost deep in a cave and my flashlight had just died. All my failures came rushing back, enveloping me in a smothering darkness.

A gust of air whipped through the room, extinguishing the candles and knocking over my wineglass. The stereo in the living room began blasting Fleetwood Mac's "Rhiannon" at full volume. I caught a strong whiff of ozone, creosote, and rotting plant matter. *Faeries!*

A question niggled at the back of my mind. *Am I causing this?*

No, can't be, I assured myself. *I don't do magic anymore. It's the damn Faeries again.*

Mom rushed out of the room to turn off the stereo.

Mama Joyce shouted above the din, "Morgana, calm down!"

"When has yelling at someone to calm down ever worked?" I screamed back.

She reached for my hand, and her touch grounded me. "Just breathe, baby girl. Slow deep breaths. In and out. That's it."

I matched my breathing with hers, and the tempest in the kitchen subsided. The music stopped mid-chorus.

Mom returned to the dining room. "Are you all right, sweetie?"

"I'm okay." I pushed my plate away, having lost my appetite.

"What say you and me go out on the back porch, smoke a little, and talk?"

By "smoke a little," I knew she meant weed, not tobacco.

"But I promised to clean up the kitchen after dinner." I surveyed the mess caused by this latest attack. "Damned Faeries."

"I'll handle the cleanup," Mama Joyce said. "You and Mom need to talk."

"Fine." Maybe I'd finally learn why the two of them had been acting so weird. "Weed's not my jam. But you smoke and talk. I'll listen." And try not to get a contact high.

I followed her out onto the porch. She fished out a preroll, lit it, and took a drag.

"Sure you don't want a hit?" she offered in a strained voice.

"I'm good, Mom. Thanks. Just tell me what the hell's going on."

CHAPTER 8

"IT'S ABOUT YOUR FATHER," Mom said.

Wow. After all these years. "You never talked about him. I figured he was just a one-night stand and you didn't know who he was."

"Yeah, well, I hoped I'd never have to bring up the subject. But after what happened at dinner, I suppose now is the time."

"What's my father got to do with it? I thought Faeries were causing things to go crazy."

"It's a little more complicated."

"It always is." *This should be good.*

"Your father and I met at a Beltane festival up in Sedona."

I wasn't exactly shocked. I'd done the math years ago. I was born on Groundhog Day, which meant I was conceived in May. On Beltane, as it turned out—a Pagan fertility celebration for the start of summer.

"As fate would have it, I was selected as that year's May Queen. Your father was chosen to play the Green Man." The embodiments of the Goddess and the God.

"And they made you sleep with him? Like, as part of the ritual? That seems a bit medieval."

"No, it wasn't part of the ritual. We just kinda... hooked up." She offered an embarrassed smile.

"But you're... gay."

"Pansexual, actually, with lesbian leanings. But he was hot." Again, she blushed. "Just looking at him got me wet."

"Eww, Mom! Seriously? I do *not* want to hear that." I pressed my hands against my ears.

"Surprise, kiddo. Your mom's a sexual being, just like you. It *was* a fertility festival, after all. Besides, he and I were a little..."

"Stoned?"

"I was going to say, 'caught up in the spirit of the festival.' But yes, if we're being blunt—pun intended—I was a little high."

"Who was he? What was he like? And what's he got to do with what happened earlier tonight?"

"His name was Ray. Dark olive skin, black hair, golden eyes."

"Like me?"

"Yes."

"So, Latino?" I was curious where in Latin America he or his family was from originally. And if he still lived in the States or had been deported by Trump's ICE stormtroopers.

"He wasn't Latino."

I blinked. Not expecting that answer.

"Native American?"

"Not that either."

Okay... "Italian? Greek? Arab?" I was fast running out of possibilities.

"He was Fae, sweetie."

My brain did a full record scratch. "Wait, wait, wait! Back up. Did you say my father was Fae?"

"Yeah." She stared at the floor.

I laughed before I could stop myself. "Fae? Ray the Fae? As in a Faerie? Wings and pixie dust and all that? Like Tinker Bell from *Peter Pan*?"

"Not a pixie. No wings. And Ray was sort of a nickname. Short for Rhaedoryal. He's Desert Fae."

"Desert Fae? That's a thing?" I stared at her. She couldn't be serious.

She took another drag on the joint. "Just what he said."

"How stoned were you?"

"I'll admit, I was pretty baked when Ray and I slept together. But I was clearheaded the next morning. That was when he told me." Her face flushed.

"And how do you know he was really Fae and not a delusional cosplaying elf-wannabe?"

It wouldn't be the first time Mom had attributed something mundane as having magical origins. When I was seven, she was convinced gremlins were messing with our internet. Turned out the coax cable hadn't been properly screwed into the modem. And my freshman year at Wickenburg High, she was convinced my history teacher was an ogre. Like, a literal ogre. He wasn't.

"Believe it or not, I was skeptical too. At first," she said.

"Were you now? And how'd he convince you he was the real deal?" Not that it would take much.

"For starters, he had olive skin."

"A lot of people have olive skin, Mom."

"Not olive tan. His skin was dark olive green."

"Oh, come on. He was playing the part of the Green Man. Probably covered in body paint."

"Not body paint. He was olive green all over. Even his..." She gestured toward her groin.

I winced. "Green junk? I get the picture. Anything else?"

"His ears were pointed. Not silicone extensions like they sell at the Ren Faire. They were real. He let me feel them."

Without thinking, I touched my own ears—not quite pointed but not quite round. Somewhere in between. One more thing the kids at school had made fun of.

"He could've had plastic surgery," I suggested, though I wasn't convinced.

"He also showed me his magic."

"What magic?"

"For starters, he summoned wind. Inside our tent."

"Could've been a breeze sneaking through the flap."

"It wasn't. It was him. I watched him control it like a performance artist. And when I stepped outside, wildflowers had blossomed all around our tent. Just ours. No one else's."

"Mom, it sounds like you had a magical, albeit chemically enhanced, Beltane festival. But seriously? You think my father was an actual Faerie?"

"I know you think I'm a flake," she said. "But when I hired Mama Joyce as my midwife, she confirmed it."

"How?"

"She noticed... anomalies."

"What anomalies? Cravings for cakes and ale? A sudden urge to binge-watch *The Lord of the Rings*?"

"Morgana, I'm serious. While I was pregnant with you, my magic kicked into overdrive—especially any spells involving air or water. I could summon wind and rain with a thought. Best monsoon season we had for years or since. And you know how I don't exactly have a green thumb?"

"Yeah." She'd buy a houseplant and set it in the kitchen window. Within a month, it'd be a dried-up husk. Mostly because she'd forget to water it.

"While I was pregnant, every plant in the house was thriving. I wasn't even watering them. Outside, wildflowers bloomed—months after they'd withered and died. Every cactus, shrub, and ocotillo flowered again. And it lasted *for months.*"

"Okay. That is a little weird."

"Mama Joyce and I conducted a ritual to be sure—one that detects Faeries. We confirmed a Fae presence in my womb. You."

I swallowed hard, remembering the guy dressed as an elf in the café. And the hummingbirds when I arrived home that for an instant looked like Faeries. The world tilted slightly. I knew I was biracial. But Fae? What did that make me? Bi-species? Bi-special?

"You're telling me I'm a freakin' Faerie?"

"It's why you always looked younger than other girls your age. And why iron and steel irritate your skin."

It was true. When I went to a bar, not only did I get carded, but I'd be accused of using a fake ID half the time. Not my fault I was petite with good skin.

And the thing about iron and steel was true too. My moms had to buy nickel-plated flatware because stainless steel gave me rashes. Vaccines left welts for days. Even touching steel grocery carts, door handles, or steel zippers on my jeans could trigger a reaction.

Suddenly, the weird quirks in my life started to make sense. "And why I can't lie worth shit."

"Not the worst trait to inherit," Mom said, laughing.

I laughed too. I had to. It was either that or fall apart.

Everything I thought I knew about myself just... cracked. I wasn't fully human. I was something else. A half-breed. A freak.

"How did you *not* know before you slept with him?" I asked. "Aren't witches supposed to—I don't know—sense stuff like that?"

The porch lights flickered then flared too bright. Wind

surged through the porch, crackling with electricity. The sharp tang of ozone burned in my nose. Shit! It was happening again.

"Morgana, calm down. Here, take a hit." She offered the joint.

I shook my head and waved it away as hair whipped in my face. Damned Faeries again!

No, wait. It was me. *I* was the Faerie. This was *my* magic! Fear rippled through me.

"Why is this happening?" I shouted over the rising wind, blowing through the screens.

"Morgana, listen to me. You've got to ground yourself." She set the joint in an abalone shell she used as an ashtray and took my hand. "Close your eyes and imagine calming energy rising up through your feet. Like a plant soaking up water through its roots. Breathe in for six seconds, hold for three, and release for eight. And again. Focus on the sensation of your chest rising and falling."

I followed her advice, trying to focus as best I could with a thousand thoughts buzzing through my brain and the overwhelming emotions that came with them. Breathing in, holding, and out. Imagining grounding energy filling my body and all the frenetic energy leaving. Over and over.

The air stilled. The lights dimmed back to normal. The chaos ebbed like a tide going out.

"That—that was me?" I could hardly believe it.

She nodded. "It was. I'm sorry for... well, for all of this. Mostly for not telling you until now."

I took another deep breath, further stilling my tumultuous emotions, quieting my magic. "It's okay, Mom."

When I finally had calmed enough, I asked, "What happened to him? My father. Did you see him again? Did he go back to Faerieland?"

"I never saw him again. I don't know where he is. And while I'm embarrassed about how it all happened, he left me a special gift. And for that, I'm grateful." Her eyes were glassy from the weed, but also with tears.

"What? A freak for a daughter?"

"A freak? Goddess, no. A magical daughter. Beautiful. Brilliant. A blessing I never expected but who I treasure every day."

"So why keep it a secret from me all these years?"

"I wanted to tell you. I really did. But it never seemed the right time. And I... I was ashamed."

"Of me?"

"No, course not. Of myself." She stared out at the dark night. "Because I was tricked. Because I slept with someone I barely knew."

"You have nothing to be ashamed of. When the kids at school bullied me, you and Mama Joyce loved and supported me. You used magic to protect me. And you welcomed me back after everything fell apart in LA. I'm lucky to have you. I love you. You and Mama Joyce both."

"We love you, too, kiddo," Mom said.

"Absolutely," Mama Joyce called from the doorway. "We've got your back, peanut. Always."

A question bubbled up in my mind. "If Faeries are real, what about other supernatural creatures? Do vampires exist?"

Mama Joyce shook her head. "Vampires? Not that I've heard of."

"Although stories about vampire-like beings appear in cultures all over the world, going as far back as ancient Mesopotamia," Mom added. "So maybe they do exist?"

A chilling thought. "What about werewolves or unicorns?"

Mama Joyce looked skeptical but didn't say anything.

Mom shrugged. "Folklore is filled with tales of all kinds of supernatural creatures."

"Tall tales," Mama Joyce scoffed.

"Perhaps, but there's almost always a seed of truth. Stories of gigantic beasts were considered myths—then we discovered the fossils of dinosaurs and prehistoric mammals. Sea serpents and krakens were believed to be the delusions of drunken sailors, but now we know that giant squids and oarfish exist."

"Fair point." Mama Joyce appeared to consider this.

I always enjoyed watching the two of them spar like this —Mom open to the fantastical, Mama Joyce ever the skeptic.

"In the mythology of Arizona Indigenous cultures," Mom continued, "there are creatures who were part human, part animal, like Coyote the trickster. And Lenore swears there's an ancient wise woman living deep in the Superstition Mountains who can shift into a gigantic raven. There are also legends about chupacabras, hoodoos, the Mogollon monster, el cucuy, el duende, and others. As Shakespeare wrote, 'There are more things in heaven and earth, Horatio, than are dreamt of in your philosophy.'"

"You needn't worry about any of that, peanut." Mama Joyce assured me. "Just focus on being you."

"I'm not sure how to do that. How do I use this Faerie magic? Ideally without making lights flicker or triggering a dust storm?"

"That's a good question," Mama Joyce said. "I don't know how Faerie magic works."

"But we can figure it out," Mom said. "Together. As a family."

"Is that why you named me Morgana? After Morgana le Fae, the evil sorceress from the Arthurian legends?"

Mom nodded. "I was reading *The Mists of Avalon* when I

learned I was pregnant. That book changed how I saw Morgana le Fae. She wasn't evil. She was a bold feminist in a world shifting from matriarchal Paganism to patriarchal Christianity. But if you'd rather be called something else..."

What else would I call myself? I couldn't think of anything.

"No, I think Morgana suits me." I smiled. "You chose well."

Thoughts flurried through my mind for the remainder of the evening.

Half-Fae. Doesn't feel real.

Where was my father—this Rhaedoryal dude? Faerieland? Some other dimension? Could I visit? And who were the Desert Fae, anyway? What made them different from other Faeries?

I realized I was also experiencing a deep loss with this revelation. Since as far back as I could remember, I had assumed my father was Latino. I mean, hello! I had brown skin and black hair. And I was born and raised in Arizona.

Latinx culture, and Mexican culture in particular, felt as much a part of who I was as the desert around me. I loved the foods, the music, everything about the many unique and beautiful cultures from south of the border.

I had joyfully learned Spanish even before I formally took it in school, because it felt like a way to connect to the father I never knew. While I might have been ashamed of my sexuality or my moms' spirituality growing up, I had always, *always* proudly been Latina.

Except I wasn't. And that brought feelings of loss and shame. All this time, I'd been unknowingly appropriating Latinx culture when that wasn't my heritage at all. The one thing I had treasured about myself turned out to be a lie.

By the time I climbed into bed, I was wrung out emotionally.

The amulet Mama Joyce had made was still missing, but maybe I didn't need it anymore. As painful as it was to admit, I wasn't Latina. But I was Fae. I was still Brown, just a different kind of Brown.

And with all the fervor I'd once embraced being Latina, I would embrace being Fae—if I could figure out how.

CHAPTER 9

THE NEXT MORNING, I helped Mom out at Wiccanburg Books, since one of her employees was on vacation for the week. She drove us in the Hippie Hearse, an actual used hearse she'd bought from a funeral home.

She'd hand-painted flowers, birds, and cacti against a sky-blue background. It looked like something the Grateful Dead might have driven.

My mothers used it for campouts and Pagan festivals. The interior smelled of sandalwood and patchouli, though I'd swear I could still detect a hint of formaldehyde.

We parked in a public lot a block away and started walking. As we approached the bookshop, I spotted someone sprawled on the sidewalk near the front door. Seemed like an unlikely spot for an unhoused person to crash. Maybe a drunk sleeping off a bender? And what was that around them? Candles?

I sprinted ahead of Mom, horror gripping me as I recognized the person's short red hair and starch-white chef's coat, now stained a deep scarlet.

Erin O'Brien.

Goddess, no!

She lay motionless inside a large pentacle drawn on the sidewalk in chalk. Crude sigils and smaller pentacles had been scrawled inside the large one. At each point of the star, a black candle burned low, wax pooling in thick puddles. Blood seeped from wounds in her chest and belly. An athame, also smeared with blood, lay beside her. Her pale skin looked waxy in the morning light.

"No, no, no!" I dropped to my knees, my chest tightening under the weight of panic. "Erin! Can you hear me?" I pressed two trembling fingers to her neck but couldn't find a pulse.

"I'm calling 911," Mom said, her phone already to her ear.

"Please don't be dead." I pressed my hands against the wounds, trying to stop the bleeding. Maybe there was still time to save her.

A strong wind whipped down the street, desert dust stinging my eyes. Creosote and ozone filled my nostrils. *Damned Faeries!*

No, wait! I'm the Faerie! This is my magic! Could I use it to save her? Did Faeries have healing magic?

Probably not. But I could not risk losing her. Not again. Not now. Not without making up for how I hurt her years ago. I had to save her somehow.

"Please, Goddess. Please save my friend. Maiden, Mother, Crone, please, please, please help me. Show me what to do. Please help me heal her."

Even as my entire body shook with fear and grief, I struggled to ground myself. Calm, peaceful, magical. Breathe in for six, hold for three, out for eight.

I imagined drawing in energy from all around me—from the air, from the earth, from the water in my tears, from the fire in my heart—and pouring it all into her.

I was probably doing it wrong, but I had to try.

"Please, Danu, Goddess of the Faeries, help me save her."

The air crackled with electricity. Tiny hairs on my arms rose. I gasped as a surge of energy coursed down my arms, through my hands, and into Erin.

I'm imagining it, I thought at first. *Wishful thinking.*

But the energy was real. I could feel it. Alive. Electrical. Mystical. Magical.

Beneath the metallic tang of blood and the bitter stench of creosote, I caught the scent of fresh herbs and wildflowers. Life energy. I continued channeling it into Erin.

Her body shifted. A cough rattled out of her, and she spat up blood.

"Hang in there," I whispered. "Help's coming."

Her eyes fluttered open and met mine. She tried to say something, but it came out as a gurgle of blood.

"Don't talk. Just stay with me. Let me heal you."

"Ma'am, move aside," a male voice said.

"No, I have to save her."

"We've got it."

An EMT knelt next to me, another at Erin's other side. "We'll take it from here."

I didn't want to stop. I didn't want to let go of her. I wanted to keep sending healing magic into Erin. But the EMTs were better equipped to save her than I was.

The world tilted when I tried to stand. My legs buckled, but someone caught me.

"Easy. I've got you," said a woman's voice. Not Mom's.

A woman in a dark suit and plum-colored top steadied me. She had long black hair, a narrow tan face, and deep-set eyes. A detective's shield gleamed from her belt.

Uniformed officers now swarmed around us, setting up barricades, corralling curious onlookers, and unrolling yellow crime scene tape. Cruisers blocked off Tegner Street, lights flashing.

"Are you hurt? Do you require medical attention?" the detective asked.

I felt shaky and drained. "N-No, I'm okay. Just... just need to sit."

"Of course. Come with me." She guided me to a nearby bench. "I'm Detective Hatathlie with the Wickenburg Police. What's your name?" she asked in a gentle but firm voice.

"Morgana. Morgana Quinn." I reached to shake her hand then saw mine was covered in blood. My shirt too. I pulled back and curled my fingers. "Sorry."

"It's okay. Why don't you tell me what happened?"

I TOLD her how Mom and I found Erin bleeding out on the sidewalk.

"I... I tried to... to save her. To stop the bleeding." I couldn't exactly tell her I was using magic to heal Erin. Or that I was Fae.

"Did you light the candles and draw the symbols on the sidewalk?"

"What? No! We found her like that." I glanced toward the bookshop. They were loading Erin into the ambulance.

"Do you know the victim?"

"Yes, she's Erin O'Brien. We were friends in high school." No way was I getting into our messy history.

"You're not friends now?"

"We lost touch when I moved to California to attend UCLA."

She raised an eyebrow. "You're in college? How old are you?"

I sighed. My Fae heritage must be the reason why people assumed I was years younger than I was. In twenty years, I'd probably be glad to look so young. But right now, it was an annoyance.

"Graduated four years ago. I'm twenty-six."

"Really? I would have guessed about seventeen."

I showed her my California driver's license.

"What do you do for a living in Santa Monica?"

Why is she asking these unimportant questions? I wondered.

Then I remembered what I'd learned in my research on police procedures. She was establishing rapport, getting a baseline for my honesty, and watching for tells.

"I'm a screenwriter for a TV show." Or was.

"Oh, really? Which one?"

"*LA Murder Squad.*"

"Popular show. You know a lot about solving murders?"

My face burned. Was she mocking me?

"I'm just a writer. I did research for the show. Went on a few ride-alongs. Interviewed LAPD detectives about procedures and such." *Goddess, could I sound more pathetic?*

"So, what brings you back to town, Morgana?"

"Visiting my moms." After getting fired. And cheated on.

"That was your mom with you?"

"Yes, she owns the bookshop. I was helping her out this morning."

"Wiccanburg Books?"

"Yes."

"Wiccan as in witches?" Her tone sharpened. "You specialize in the occult?"

"The bookshop specializes in a wide range of spiritual and metaphysical topics." Mom's usual line when someone asked.

"But you sell candles, knives, spell books, and other supplies for performing rituals? Like what was done to Ms. O'Brien?"

"No!"

"You don't sell ritual supplies?"

"Yes, we do. Or rather, my mom does. But Erin wasn't murdered as part of a ritual. At least, not a Wiccan ritual."

"Then what's with the candles and the pentagram drawn on the sidewalk? Looks a lot like a witchy or Satanic ritual sacrifice to me."

Bitterness burned the back of my throat. I might not be a practicing witch, but I'd be damned if this know-it-all cop was going to disparage my moms and their beliefs.

"Witches don't perform ritual sacrifices. That's a harmful stereotype perpetuated by movies and ignorant Christians."

The wind kicked up. I forced myself to stay calm. Last thing I needed was for my Fae magic to cause something weird to happen.

"So, you and your mom are witches?"

"She is. I'm not."

"What are you?"

I wasn't going to admit I was a Faerie. That was for sure. I could barely admit it to myself.

"Agnostic."

"And Erin?"

"I haven't spoken with her in years. She stopped by the shop yesterday while I was there. We're planning on getting together later to catch up—assuming there is a later."

"Is your mom a member of a coven?"

"What's that got to do with anything?"

"I'll take that as a yes. Is Erin a member of this coven?"

"Why do you care? Despite what some might think in

this town, people still have the freedom of religion and freedom of association. Or has Trump revoked that too?"

"Why'd Erin come into the store yesterday?"

"She delivered a lunch order. She owns a restaurant down the street." I couldn't think of the name all of a sudden.

"The Wicked Grille? That's the name stitched on her jacket."

"That's the one."

"Sounds pretty witchy to me."

"It's a restaurant. A popular one, I'm told."

"When were you and Erin getting together?"

"We hadn't set a date."

"I see. So, you two are dating?"

I recognized this technique from my research. Trip a suspect up by twisting their words. Trigger an emotional reaction. Get them to contradict themselves. Catch them in a lie. Use it to press for more revealing, incriminating admissions.

"What? No! Like I said, I—"

"Just got back into town. Right." Detective Hatathlie nodded. "Did you or your mom have any conflicts with Erin?"

"No, they were friends."

"But you weren't friends with Erin."

"We were, but I was in California. I didn't come home a lot."

"Why not? You having problems with your mom?"

"No. Work kept me busy."

"So, I won't find your fingerprints on the knife found beside her?"

"Absolutely not." My fingers felt sticky with Erin's blood. "Can I wash my hands now?"

I was exhausted, and the endless questions weren't

helping. I needed to find Mom and check on Erin at the hospital.

"We'll need your shirt, a sample of the blood on your hands, and your fingerprints." She waved over a crime scene tech.

I pulled my hands close to my chest. What if they found evidence of my Fae magic? Would it show up somehow? "Why? I told you, I was just trying to stop the bleeding."

"I believe you. But we still must document all potential evidence. And taking your prints will eliminate you from any others we may find. You should know this from all your... research."

I sighed and held still while Hatathlie then pulled out her phone and took photos of me, my hands, and shirt.

The tech swabbed my hands then handed me some wet wipes to clean the blood off my fingers and used an electronic device to collect my fingerprints.

"Are we good?" I asked, starting to feel shaky.

"We need your shirt."

"What am I supposed to wear?"

Hatathlie called over her shoulder, "Turner, grab me a shirt from the van."

One of the other crime scene techs arrived shortly with a navy blue tee and offered it to me.

"You expect me to take off my shirt in front of everyone?" Granted, I was wearing a bra underneath. And the gown I'd worn to the Emmys had been very revealing. But I wasn't exactly used to doing a striptease in public. Especially in this town where half the people knew me.

"We'll all turn our backs and shield you from view," Hatathlie said.

When they faced away from away from me, I slipped off my shirt, set it aside, and pulled on the replacement. The Wickenburg PD emblem was printed in gold on the front.

Great! Now I was a walking advertisement for the cops.

"All right," I said with a sigh. "You can turn around."

I handed one of the techs my bloody shirt, who promptly put it into a paper evidence bag.

"Thank you for your cooperation," Hatathlie said. "We may have further questions for you. How long do you plan to stay in town?"

"A couple weeks." I had no idea, since I had zero prospects on the job front. But it seemed like a reasonable answer.

When she finally let me go, an officer escorted me past the yellow crime scene tape. The shop was off-limits while the cops investigated.

CHAPTER 10

I SPOTTED Mom in the growing crowd of gawkers—a mix of locals, tourists, and leather-clad bikers. She whisked me away to the restroom in a coffee shop down the street.

"Are you okay?" she asked, while I scrubbed furiously at the blood on my hands.

"I feel... jet-lagged and shaky."

"Intense magic can have that effect."

I swallowed hard. "You... You know I used magic?"

She nodded. "I felt it. And why wouldn't you? Erin was badly hurt and needed help."

"Not sure how much good it did. I had no idea what I was doing."

"I'm sure it helped."

"Who would've done this to her?" I asked.

"I don't know." The sadness in her voice matched the ache in my chest. "But they went to a lot of trouble to make it look like a twisted version of a ritual—chalk pentacle, candles, an athame."

"But it wasn't, was it? No one in the coven would do something like this, would they?"

Writing for *LA Murder Squad* had rewired my brain to analyze crime scenes and speculate about suspects and their motives.

"Absolutely not. Like I told the cop who questioned me, this was no Pagan ritual. Whoever did this knows nothing about magic. Those sigils inside the pentacle were nothing but gibberish. The candle and athame, just props. Some psychopath's pathetic attempt to pin this on us."

I remembered Mom sweeping the sidewalk the day before. "Could it be the same person who spray-painted the graffiti?"

"Maybe. But why target Erin? She's kind to everyone. People love her."

"She's also openly gay and Pagan in a town that treats people like us as pariahs," I reminded her.

I dried my hands on a paper towel. "I hope whoever did this rots in prison."

"Me too." She draped an arm around my shoulders. "Let's go see how Erin's doing. I called her girlfriend, Kari. She'll meet us at the hospital."

Wickenburg Medical Center was small compared to most hospitals. I'd been a patient there twice. Once when I was six, after Mama Joyce's best efforts couldn't break my fever from a nasty bout of the flu. And again after I broke my arm during my one and only attempt at rollerblading when I was sixteen.

"We're here for Erin O'Brien," Mom told the man at the emergency check-in desk. "They brought her in by ambulance."

"One moment." He picked up the phone.

Fifteen agonizing minutes crawled by before a man in scrubs stepped into the waiting room. He looked exhausted.

"You're here for Erin O'Brien?"

"Yes," Mom said. "She's a friend of ours. We were the ones who called 911."

"I'm Dr. Espejo." His expression turned grim. "I'm afraid Ms. O'Brien didn't make it. Her wounds were too extensive."

"But she was alive when they loaded her into the ambulance," I said, my voice breaking.

He nodded solemnly. "Unfortunately, a major abdominal artery had been punctured. She bled out before the paramedics could stabilize her. She was already gone by the time she arrived here. I'm truly sorry."

Grief surged through me. The lights flickered. Static crackled on the overhead speakers.

Mom touched my arm. "Morgana."

I fought to steady my emotions, blinking back tears. "Can... Can we see her?"

"She's in the morgue, awaiting transport to the medical examiner. We've notified her parents."

"Erin was estranged from her folks," Mom said firmly. "We're her family. We need a chance to say goodbye. Her girlfriend is on her way."

"I'm sorry, but this was a homicide. By law, only medical examiner staff has access to the body until the autopsy's complete. It's out of my hands. Now, if you'll excuse me, I have other patients." Dr. Espejo gave a weary nod and walked away.

I shuffled back to the waiting area, my heart breaking into a million pieces. Mom grabbed snacks from a vending machine while we waited for Erin's girlfriend to arrive.

She offered me a granola bar, but I shook my head.

"Not hungry."

"You need to eat, sweetie. You expended a lot of energy trying to save Erin."

I took it from her but left it unopened. "What's the use? I failed."

"You tried. She was just too far gone by the time we found her."

"We should be allowed to say goodbye."

I understood the need to maintain chain of custody. A rather dehumanizing label to apply to someone's body. But to the cops, her body was now evidence.

"I know." Mom pulled me close, her voice low and tight. "Hopefully, the cops can figure out who did this."

Silence settled around us, heavy as a weighted blanket. And then the past came rushing in—spring semester of my junior year, when everything changed between Erin and me.

A decade of friendship had quietly developed into something deeper. Every time we were together, new feelings blossomed inside me. Her laugh, the sparkle in her eyes, the curves of her body. Everything about her set my senses on fire.

After our tubing trip down the Salt River, I worked up the nerve to ask her out. I was terrified she'd reject me—or worse, that dating her would ruin our friendship. To my delight—and utter shock—she felt the same way about me.

Soon we were finding every excuse to be alone, to touch, to kiss, to explore.

We told no one but my moms. Erin's strict Catholic parents would've lost their minds if they found out. They barely tolerated me as it was—with two witchy moms and all.

The kids at school had been hurling homophobic slurs at us long before we started dating. I wasn't about to give them more ammo by confirming their accusations.

A few weeks in, Erin wanted to hold hands in public. I resisted.

"Why not?" she asked, her voice soft but urgent. "You're not ashamed of me, are you?"

"What? No, it's just... I don't know. What'll people say?"

She laughed in that disarming way she had. "What people?"

"The other kids at school. Especially the Meanlindas and their jock boyfriends."

"Oh, please. Everyone knows. Worst-kept secret ever."

It was true. "What about your folks? Won't they freak?"

"What are they going to do? Disown me? Sarah was always their favorite anyway." She leaned in, eyes fierce. "Might as well stop pretending. Why let these losers steal our happiness?"

"You sound like my moms."

"They're not hiding, are they? I've seen them hold hands in public."

"Yeah, and have you heard what people yell at them when they do? I'm tired of being treated like a freak. I want to blend in and be normal for once."

"Normal's a snoozefest. Just be your fabulous self. Quit hiding and let your freak flag fly!"

She was right. I needed to stop hiding. But I wasn't ready. And to her credit, she didn't push.

The slurs still came—*lezzies, dykes, rug munchers.* And they still stung. But I never had the guts to fight back the way Erin did.

A month later, she popped the question, right in front of our lockers between third and fourth periods.

"What do ya say? Me and you. Junior-senior prom. You can wear a dress. I'll rent a tux."

"Wait, what?"

Panic struck me—full-blown fight-or-flight, chest-tightening, deer-in-the-headlights panic.

"Come on! Let's show those asshats we're not ashamed."

"They won't let us. Not as a couple," I said, trying to sound reasonable rather than terrified.

"So? We'll lie and say you're going with Angel Lopez. I'll say I'm with Dennis Williams. Once we're in, we swap."

"Dennis Williams? I thought he was dating Becky from algebra. They're always hanging out together."

"Becky Matheson?" She laughed. "She's tutoring him. Dennis is a total gym queen."

"Wait, Dennis is gay?"

"Seriously? You didn't know?"

"But he's not..."

"Effeminate? Girl, please. Not every gay boy is as flamboyant as Angel. I ran into them together once at that queer bookstore in Phoenix. They're so cute together."

"But still... you and me? At prom? Together?"

That's when I noticed Melinda Fox hanging on the arm of Dave Talbot, the football team's top receiver. Bobby Monroe, the team's kicker, stood next to them, smirking.

"Well, if it isn't the sapphic duo." Melinda gave us a fake pout. "What's wrong, girls? Can't find any boys desperate enough to ask you out?"

"Ignore her." Erin's eyes locked on mine. "What do you say? Will you go to prom with me? Please?"

Dave let out an ugly laugh. "Did you just ask her to prom?"

Bobby joined in, his tone threatening. "You think the school's gonna let a couple of lesbos dance together? I don't think so."

Erin squeezed my hand. "Say yes, babe."

I wanted to. Goddess, I ached to kiss her passionately in front of the whole world and tell anyone who didn't like it they could go screw themselves.

But no, I was a coward.

"No, I will *not* go to prom with you!" I shouted, far louder than I meant to. "I'm not gay! So stop asking."

The instant the words left my mouth, I hated myself. Melinda, Dave, and Bobby howled with laughter.

Erin froze. Just for a second. Then she turned on her heel and walked away without a word.

I texted her during fourth-period English. Nothing. When I passed her in the hallway before geometry, she looked right through me.

That night, I tried calling to apologize. She'd already blocked my number.

She had dumped me. And I deserved it. I'd crushed the one person who'd always had my back. Not because I didn't love her. I did. But I was just too chickenshit to show it.

We never spoke again. Not until yesterday. And now... now, she was gone.

"I'm scared, Mom. What if we're next?"

"I'll strengthen the wards around the house and the shop. That should keep us safe while the police search for the killer."

I wasn't convinced. Someone was targeting Mom's shop and the coven. Someone with a lot of rage toward us, judging by the multiple stab wounds in Erin's torso. Could a ward stop someone so intensely driven?

Making matters worse, Detective Hatathlie was fixated on witches. I feared she'd frame my moms or a member of their coven, even if that allowed the real killer to go free. After all, what was one dead witch or even a wrongly convicted one to somebody who believed all witches were evil?

Who then would bring Erin's murderer to justice?

"Could we use magic to track down her killer?" I asked Mom.

She gave me a wary look. "Possibly. Why?"

"I don't trust that detective. She seemed convinced it was one of the coven." Or me.

"What are you suggesting?"

"Remember when Mama Joyce made that charm that caused Melinda Fox's hair to fall out? We could hex Erin's killer. Make them suffer so much they'd wish they were in prison."

"No."

"Why not? You wanted to hex Saffron just for cheating on me."

"That was wrong. I never should have suggested hexing your girlfriend."

"Ex-girlfriend. And you're starting to sound like Mama Joyce."

"Yeah, well, maybe she's right. Magic shouldn't be used as a weapon."

"But Erin deserves justice."

"She does. But we are not cops. Or vigilantes. We can ask the Morrigan to help bring Erin's killer to justice. Beyond that, we should focus on honoring her memory and helping each other heal." She looked at me. "And you're still learning how to handle your Fae magic. It could be dangerous to use it against someone."

This wasn't like her. She was always the one who stepped boldly, who'd rather ask forgiveness than permission. Damn the torpedoes and all that jazz.

"What's going on? Why are you suddenly afraid to use magic?"

My words clearly struck a chord, judging from the look in her eyes.

"I'm not. I'm just..." She took a deep breath and let it out. "Maybe I've been a little too brazen lately. Ignoring the dangers. Like the graffiti. And maybe... maybe that got Erin killed."

"No, Mom. It's not your fault. This is on the asshole who did this to her. It's this town. There are some decent people here. You and Mama and the coven. But there are also so many hateful bigots. It's why I couldn't wait to shake the dust off my shoes and move to LA. It's why I rarely visited."

"I know. We missed you, but we understood. You have a lot of trauma associated with this place."

"But I'm back now. And I'm not gonna let those assholes rob me of my joy. You and Mama taught me that. And I guess it finally sank in. I'm sick of hiding. I'm sick of being afraid of what narrow-minded people think. And now that I have magic, real magic, I'm going to do what I can to protect the people I love. At least once I figure out how it works."

She hugged me. "I love you, sweetie."

She group-messaged her employees to let them know what happened then called Mama Joyce to fill her in.

While they talked, I replayed the events in my head, looking for something, anything, I could have done differently to save Erin. But I had no idea what I'd been doing or how my magic worked. It was all guesswork, based on what I'd picked up living with my moms.

"Selene?" A woman about my age rushed over, a terrified look on her face. "Is Erin okay?"

Mom pulled her into a hug. "I'm so sorry, sweetie. She... She didn't make it."

They clung to each other, sobbing. I hovered nearby, feeling like an intruder.

When they finally pulled apart, Mom gestured toward me. "Kari, this is my daughter, Morgana. Morgana, meet Kari Sullivan, Erin's girlfriend."

"Fiancée, actually," Kari said, staring at her trembling hand. A ring sparkled—blue sapphires flanking a marquise-cut diamond. "We were going to announce it at the Samhain ritual."

I recalled seeing a similar ring on Erin's hand, though it hadn't registered at the time that she was engaged. I'd been more focused on trying to save her.

"I'm so sorry for your—" I started to say, but Kari wrapped me into a sudden hug.

I held her until she pulled back, wiping at her tears. "What happened?"

"We found her outside the bookshop," Mom said once we were seated. "She'd been stabbed."

"They made it look like a ritual killing," I added, bitterness thick in my throat. "A pentacle and sigils drawn in chalk on the sidewalk. Black candles. An athame."

"What?" Kari looked horror-struck. "You're not saying a member of the coven did this."

"No, it was staged," Mom said. "The so-called sigils were nonsensical scribbling. Not a coven member." She reached for my hand. "Morgana tried to save her, but Erin was too far gone, I'm afraid."

"I'm sorry," I whispered. "I really tried."

"Thank you," Kari said softly. "Can I see her?"

Before I could answer, an older couple burst through the entrance, their faces etched in grief.

I recognized them instantly. Erin's parents.

Phillip O'Brien had always been a severe-looking man. Time had only deepened the scowl he wore like a mask. He ran a successful investment firm and sat on the town council.

His wife, Gloria, clung to his arm, looking, as always, like a frightened rabbit.

Dr. Espejo emerged to meet them. I couldn't hear their words, but Mrs. O'Brien quickly broke into sobs.

Mr. O'Brien turned and locked eyes with me.

"You!" he barked. "You filthy witches! This is your fault. Dragging my daughter into your perverted cult!"

"Phillip, please!" Mrs. O'Brien whispered, reaching for his arm.

He shooed her away as if she were a fly. "Quiet!"

Mom stood defiant and unapologetic. "Mr. O'Brien, I'm terribly sorry for your unimaginable loss. But neither my family nor my coven had anything to do with Erin's death. Just the opposite. My daughter and I did everything we could to save her."

"You poisoned her mind with your filth. This never would have happened if not for you people."

He spat in Mom's face.

"Bastard!" I lunged at him, fists clenched, but Mom caught my arm.

"No, don't."

"I swear to you," he roared, eyes wild with fury, "you and your Satanic coven will pay. The Bible says, 'Thou shalt not suffer a witch to live.' I'll make you pay for what you've done. Every last godforsaken one of you."

"Phillip," Mrs. O'Brien pleaded, tugging at his sleeve, but he barely registered her.

"Mr. O'Brien," Dr. Espejo cut in. "Let me take you to your daughter."

"Wait," Mom said. "You told us no one could see her until after the autopsy."

"Technically, yes. But the O'Briens are immediate family."

"I'm her family." Kari held up her ring. "I'm her fiancée."

"Fiancée—not spouse?"

"Not yet."

"Then, no. You are not considered family."

"You'll break the rules for the father who despised her but not the woman who loved her?" I asked.

"Legally, no one should see her before the autopsy. But given Mr. O'Brien's standing in the community..."

"Meaning he's a straight, rich white man in a position of power," Mom snapped. "Goddess forbid he be forced to live by the same rules as the rest of us."

I hadn't seen her this fired up since my school refused to stop the bullying.

Dr. Espejo's expression softened, but his voice remained firm. "Ma'am, please. If you don't leave, I'll have to call security."

CHAPTER 11

We were in the hospital parking lot when Mom's phone rang.

"How can I help you, Detective?" she answered and paused. "Do you have a warrant? Fine. I'll be there in ten."

She hung up and turned to me. "Detective Hatathlie's got a warrant to search the shop."

"Why? We tried to *save* Erin."

"Her body was left on our doorstep, Morgana. The detective's just doing her job."

"Sounds more like she's trying to pin it on us."

"Well, she's got a warrant. So, either I let them in, or they bust down the door. That would only make us look more guilty and cost us money to repair."

"Mind if I come with?" Kari's voice sounded brittle. "I'd rather not be alone right now."

"The more the merrier," I said, hoping to be encouraging.

"Thanks."

Bernice, Mama Joyce, and Angel were already waiting with a growing crowd of onlookers when the three of us arrived. Angel explained they'd already been questioned by the police.

Mama Joyce wrapped me in an embrace. "How you doing, peanut?"

"Shaky. Tired." The memory of me finding Erin and sending my energy into her played on repeat in my mind. The smell of the blood and the healing magic filled my nostrils.

"Mom tells me you used your magic to save Erin."

"Tried. Failed."

"Girl, all you can do is try. Can't succeed if you don't. Failure's part of learning."

"But I should've saved her."

"Why? Because you're Fae?" Mama Joyce asked sweetly. "Morgana, it will take time to master your new skills. Especially healing magic."

"She'd already lost too much blood, sweetie," Mom added. "You did what you could. And you should be proud of that."

I shrugged. "It's just... I owed it to her. After how horrible I was when we broke up."

Kari gave me a reassuring smile. "She forgave you long ago. Water under the bridge."

"Good to know," I told her, though it really didn't alleviate my guilt.

"I better find that detective and let the cops into the shop before they smash through the door," Mom said.

Kari and I followed her to the yellow police line tape cordoning off the crime scene.

A uniformed cop held up a hand. "Sorry, ma'am. Area's closed while we're investigating."

"I'm Selene Quinn, owner of Wiccanburg Books. Detective Hatathlie asked me to let y'all inside." Mom held up a set of keys.

The cop made a call on his radio. "Detective, we have the shop's owner."

A garbled response came back in reply. I never understood how cops made heads or tails of it.

A moment later, Detective Hatathlie walked up. "Ladies. Thank you for your cooperation."

"Why do you need to search my mom's shop?" I asked.

"The weapon found next to the victim's body appears to be what you witches call an athame." She mispronounced it like uh-*thaim*, with the stress on the second syllable.

"The word's *a*-thuh-may," I corrected, stressing the first syllable and adding the third.

"Of course. Double-sided blade. Black handle. Am I right?"

Mom nodded. "I didn't get a good look at it, as I was busy calling 911. But that sounds right."

"And you do sell athames, do you not?"

"We do."

Hatathlie held up her phone with a photo of a bloody athame, the one I'd seen beside Erin's body. "Do you know who bought this one?"

Mom studied the photo. "We don't carry this model. Not with the Celtic knotwork in the handle."

"Nevertheless, we'll need to search the shop to be sure."

"Even if the killer *had* bought the athame from the shop, what would it prove?" I pressed. "Just yesterday, someone spray-painted 'Witches Burn in Hell' on the sidewalk. And today, a member of the coven is murdered in the exact same spot. We're not the perpetrators, Detective. We're the ones being targeted."

That seemed to get Hatathlie's interest. "Did you report the graffiti?"

"I thought it was just a prank," Mom replied. "Didn't seem like a big deal, so we just removed it."

"And neither of you thought to mention this to me when I questioned you earlier?"

"We were in shock and worried about Erin," I said.

"Please understand," Hatathlie replied. "I'm not making any assumptions about the perpetrator's identity. Maybe they were a witch. Maybe not. But if the candles or the athame were purchased here, a search of the bookstore may lead to other evidence that results in an arrest."

Mom handed her key to the detective. "Very well."

"Detective Hatathlie?" Kari asked, just as the detective was turning to go.

"I am. And you are?"

"Kari Sullivan. Erin O'Brien's fiancée. You left a voicemail for me."

"Thank you for coming. I'm sorry for your loss." Hatathlie handed the keys to a patrol officer and instructed them to proceed with the search. She then turned back to Kari. "Let's talk, shall we?"

As the two of them stepped away to have a private conversation, Mom and I walked over to where Mama Joyce, Angel, and Bernice were standing.

"Perhaps we should call Douglas Tremball," Mama Joyce suggested.

Mom shook her head. "I don't see why we need to hire a lawyer. We've done nothing wrong. We've got nothing to hide. The killer didn't get the athame from us. Probably not the candles either."

"That doesn't mean anything," Mama Joyce said. "Cops could look for something to pin on us. Hatathlie seems rather suspicious of witches."

"Admittedly, I don't know Detective Hatathlie well," Mom said, "but she seems like good people. And I think she understands we are too."

"I'm not so convinced," I said.

"Let's just see how things play out," she replied. "We want them to find Erin's killer. Trust the detective to do her job."

Typical Mom, always looking for the best in people. Mama Joyce and I were a little more jaded.

We had an early lunch at Dana's Ranch House Café. Dana was a petite woman in her seventies who'd opened the restaurant back in the 1990s. She and her two granddaughters served customers with friendly smiles and twangy Texas accents.

Although I wasn't normally a big eater, I inhaled two cowboy breakfasts—each one with two sunny-side eggs, hash browns, three pieces of bacon, and a couple of sausages. My failed attempt to save Erin had left me famished.

Two long hours later, Hatathlie and the crime scene techs finished their search and allowed us back into the shop. A sense of violation hung about the place. Books, tarot decks, and statues had been tossed onto the floor.

"They took all the candles." I walked past the now-empty shelves where they'd been stocked. Black fingerprint powder was everywhere.

"All the athames are gone, too," Mama Joyce said. "No surprise there."

Angel stepped into their tarot-reading nook. "¡Mierda! They took my Santa Muerte and Sister Witches decks. And there's black shit all over my Smith-Rider-Waite. ¡Pinches putos!"

"It's fingerprint powder."

I followed Mom to the sales counter, where bins of crystals used to sit in neat rows. Now, the crystals were in a chaotic pile on the floor, dumped like garbage.

"Still think the cops are on our side?" I asked her.

Mom leaned against the counter, her arms folded. The

heartbreak was clearly written across her face. "We should straighten things up and open the shop. But honestly, I don't have the heart to do it right now. It's like we've been violated twice in one morning."

"Three times if you include yesterday's graffiti," Bernice added.

Mom studied each of us for a moment then said, "Circle up. Come on, everybody. Bring it in."

The six of us gathered into a circle, arm in arm. Kari stood next to me, sobbing. I wanted to cry, too, but was afraid my magic might create more havoc. Instead, I squeezed her shoulder in solidarity.

"We have suffered an immeasurable loss," Mom said. "Erin was our beloved sister. Her death is a deep wound in our souls. That her murder was staged to mock our beliefs only deepens our grief. It's important we honor whatever we are feeling. Sorrow, grief, anger, fear. There are no wrong emotions. Let yourself feel them."

"If someone killed Erin, what's to stop them coming after the rest of us?" Bernice sounded terrified.

"We have to trust the police to find the killer."

"Yeah, right." Angel snorted. "The same pendejos who wrecked the shop and stole my tarot decks? I don't think so."

"I understand your distrust," Mama Joyce said. "Do what you can to protect yourself. Carry protection charms. Reinforce the wards around your homes and your vehicles. Be aware of your surroundings. And remember that we have each other. Don't be afraid to rely on that."

Mom nodded. "If anyone needs help with charms or wards, let me know."

"Is there going to be a funeral for Erin?" Bernice asked.

"Her parents will be given custody of her body

following the autopsy," Mom said. "They'll do with it as they see fit."

"They hated her," Angel muttered. "We're her real family. Kari, especially."

"It's unfair, I know," Mama Joyce agreed. "But without a marriage license, the law doesn't care. Legally, her parents are still her next of kin."

Tears streamed down Kari's face. My heart broke for her.

"But all her parents get is her remains," Mama Joyce continued. "Erin was more than a body. She was a brilliant woman, a talented witch, and an award-winning chef. We knew her in ways her birth family did not. So tonight, you and the rest of the coven are invited to our place to celebrate Erin's life and to support each other as we process her passing. It will be a safe space to cry, hug, eat, drink, share stories, even laugh."

"Thank you, all of you," Kari said, barely choking out the words. "I'm so blessed to have you all as family."

When the hug circle broke up, Mom put a sign in the shop window that read, "Closed due to death in family."

CHAPTER 12

THE REST of the day blurred into tasks. I helped Mom, Mama Joyce, and Kari prep for the memorial—ordering flowers, printing photos of Erin, and cooking enough food to feed a small army.

Late in the afternoon, I sat in my room, firing off resumés for screenwriting jobs. An email from Saffron pinged into my inbox. I deleted it without reading it. I was so done with her.

Instead, I dove down a research rabbit hole, digging for any mention of the Desert Fae. There was plenty about Faeries in general—their traits, the endless species, legends of the Summer and Winter Courts. But nothing on the Desert Fae. Had my father made them up? Had my mom misheard him? She was stoned, after all.

People began arriving around five. I recognized a few coven members from before I'd gone away to school. They were happy to see me, though moods were understandably somber. Others were complete strangers to me.

At sunset, more than a dozen of us hiked up the path to where the Siblings of the Desert Moon held their rituals. A stone altar stood at the center of a flat sandy circle. Large rocks marked the cardinal directions. Electric lanterns hung from poles all around.

Mom had already prepared the altar with candles and items representing the four elements, as well as statues of Cerridwen and Cernnunos. Photos of Erin had been arranged so that everyone could see at least one. I had added the one of Erin and me on the tubing trip.

My mind swirled with memories. Attending rituals here as a child. The reverence for nature and the sacred. Leaving out cakes and honey for Faeries. Rejecting it all out of shame after being bullied. And of course, the years Erin and I spent as friends followed by the all-too-short romance.

I had let fear and shame steal so much from me. A life following the path of the Goddess. A loving relationship with Erin. Would she have followed me out to Los Angeles if we'd stayed together? Would she still be alive?

Mama Joyce would caution me against such thinking.

"Woulda, coulda, shoulda, darling," she'd say. "No good can come from chasing such thoughts down that rabbit hole of despair. Feel your feelings, accept what is, and then do what you gotta do to make things better."

Easier said than done, Mama. Easier said than done.

"Would you like to call North?" Mom asked as the group formed a circle.

I hesitated. Part of me just wanted to observe. But this was Erin's memorial. After everything that had happened between us, I owed it to her to show up fully.

"Sure," I told her.

She handed me a laminated index card with writing on both sides. "Calling is on one side, releasing the other."

"Thanks. I remember."

Mom drew her wand and walked the circle three times

sunwise, chanting with each pass, "I cast this circle as a space between worlds. Bound by love, guarded by will." She repeated the words with each time around.

A sphere of energy sprang up around us and shimmered in the moonlight. Even the desert seemed to hush in reverence.

When she returned to her place, Mom lifted her wand and declared, "The circle is cast. So mote it be."

"So mote it be," we echoed and turned to face east.

Kari stepped forward, her hand shaking as she held the card. "We welcome..." Sobs choked her voice for a second.

I wanted to comfort her, but now wasn't the time.

She spoke again, this time with strength and determination in her voice. "We welcome the benevolent elementals of air to this circle. Share your energies of intellect, wisdom, and intuition with us during this ritual. Hail and welcome!"

The group echoed, "Hail and welcome."

Kari lit a yellow candle on the altar then rang a silver bell next to it.

We turned to the south. A woman with dark-blond hair, tan skin, and a lean, athletic build held a card like mine. "We welcome the benevolent elementals of fire to this circle. Share your energies of passion and transformation with us during this ritual. Hail and welcome!"

The group again echoed the welcome, while the woman lit a stick of incense and a red candle.

We pivoted to the west. A tall African American woman on that side of the circle said, "We welcome the benevolent elementals of water to this circle. Share your energies of healing and emotion with us during this ritual. Hail and welcome!"

Her alto voice had a gentle sexiness to it.

"Hail and welcome," I said, along with the group.

The tall woman lifted an earthenware cup, poured out a small amount of water on the ground, then lit a blue candle.

The group turned to face north. A rush of grief and nervousness filled me. A strong breeze whipped around the circle like a dust devil, filling my eyes with grit. Despite the wind, the candles flared high.

"Steady, sweet girl." Mama Joyce stroked my hair in a soothing gesture.

I took a deep breath, imagining the grounding power of the earth flowing into me from my feet to the crown of my head, like a tree soaking in water and nutrients through its roots.

I stared down at the index card in my hand, rubbing the tears and desert dust from my eyes. "We welcome the benevolent elementals of earth to this circle. Share your energies of strength and grounding with us during this ritual. Hail and welcome."

"Hail and welcome," the group echoed while I lit the green candle.

We turned back to toward the altar. Angel stepped forward, athame raised. "We call upon Spirit that dwells in all things. Join us in this moment of grief and healing. Guide and assist us in this ritual. Hail and welcome."

They lit a purple candle as the rest of us said, "Hail and welcome."

Mom again raised her wand. "Blessed Cerridwen, goddess of rebirth, transformation, and the deep mysteries, we welcome you to this circle. Share your healing wisdom and assist us in this ritual. Hail and welcome."

After Mom lit the Goddess candle, a male witch stepped forward, voice calm and reverent. "Blessed Cernnunos, horned god of the wild and the underworld, we welcome you to this circle. Lend us your strength and endurance, while assisting us in this ritual. Hail and welcome."

Once the God candle was lit, Mom said, "We are here to honor and remember our beloved sister, Erin Sagefire O'Brien. Her tragic death has stirred a storm of emotion—grief, anger, sorrow, fear. Whatever you are feeling right now is valid. Let it move through you. This is a safe and sacred space. And while we mourn, let us also remember Erin's life and the joy she gave us in her brief time on this earth."

The group nodded, and Mom continued. "I first met Erin when she was Morgana's best friend in school. She was bright, funny, endlessly curious, and kind to her core. She was also fearless and always true to herself, no matter what anyone else thought. I am truly blessed to have known her."

"She was a teenager when she first asked to join the coven," Mama Joyce shared. "I wanted to welcome her, but her parents forbade it. It was with a heavy heart I told her, 'Not yet.'"

Sad nods from the others assembled.

"But I was all the more overjoyed when she joined us a few years later as a young woman. One of the most gifted kitchen witches I know. Her real magic was food that went beyond the culinary to the transformative. I'm devastated that she's gone but am grateful for the time she was a part of our lives."

Others in the group shared stories, many complimenting her cooking talents, some describing how she had encouraged them through difficult times. It was all I could do to keep control of my emotions and not let my Fae magic create chaos inside the sacred circle.

When nearly everyone else had shared, I found my courage to speak. "More than anything, I remember her fearlessness. She was never afraid to live her truth. No matter what. When the kids at school spewed slurs at her, she let it roll right off her back. I always admired her for it. And her laughter was contagious. I can't count the times something she said made me do a spit take."

I allowed myself to smile at the memory.

"I'm glad she found love with someone. And got to live her dream as a chef. She deserved it all and so much more. And I hope, wherever she is, she knows how much we love and miss her."

When the last person had shared, we released the God, the Goddess, Spirit, and the four elements, working widdershins around the circle.

"The circle is now open but never broken," Mom said. "Merry we meet, merry we part, and merry we meet again. Blessed be."

"Blessed be," replied everyone.

After a round of hugs, we gathered the ritual supplies, extinguished lanterns, and walked silently and solemnly down to the house.

Chapter 13

I HELPED Mom and Mama Joyce set out the food and drinks, while the house filled with the murmur of conversation, bursts of laughter, the occasional sniffle, and Erin's favorite music.

Everyone knew each other well. Everyone except me, that is.

I felt like an outsider in my childhood home. I made a half-hearted attempt to be social. But after twenty minutes of small talk, I'd had enough.

I slipped out to the back porch, nursing a bottle of hard cider. The single bulb on the wall cast harsh shadows. The desert beyond was pitch-black and full of the sounds of insects, birds, and who knew what else. I tried to let it distract me from the barrage of memories, thoughts, and emotions assaulting my neurodivergent brain.

My mind gradually switched from grieving-friend mode to detective mode. Okay, more like screenwriter-pretending-to-think-like-a-detective mode. But it helped to focus on something other than the all-too-vivid memories of Erin's final moments or the mess I'd made of my life.

The fictional detectives I wrote about in *LA Murder Squad* were relentless seekers of justice, chasing the truth no matter where it led and nailing the killer in forty-two minutes or less. But solving murders in real life didn't work like that.

Detective Hatathlie had made her feelings about witches clear. The way she interrogated us, the way her team tore through Mom's bookshop like a pack of wolves... She wasn't looking for the truth. She was looking for someone to blame.

Someone like us.

Erin deserved better. She deserved justice—not a half-assed investigation warped by prejudice. But what could I do? I knew the basics of homicide investigation—enough to write a decent script. But I wasn't a cop. I didn't have a badge or access to suspect interviews or forensic evidence. And my magical abilities were a hot mess.

The sliding glass door whooshed open behind me. Angel strutted onto the porch, dropped into the chair beside me, and propped their boots on a wicker glass-top table. The buckles glittered in the dim light.

"There she is—the prodigal daughter. Hiding from the crowd, are we?"

Their goth makeup was cranked up to eleven. And why not? A cherished friend and coven member had been brutally murdered. If that didn't call for full-on goth, what did?

"Never been much for crowds," I confessed.

Angel let out a sigh. "I hear ya, chica. Peopling is so exhausting. One-on-one? Yeah, okay. But groups?" They shuddered theatrically. "No thank you."

Three more figures emerged onto the porch. I fought the urge to bolt.

The tall woman who'd called West during the memorial claimed the other chair next to me with a bottle of San Pellegrino. Kari settled into a lounge chair, nursing a glass of red wine, her expression somber but composed. And the lean, athletic woman who'd called South took up a seat in the shadowy corner.

"We're not intruding, are we?" the tall woman asked. Her dark hair was in a natural style that beautifully framed her face. She looked familiar, but I couldn't place her.

"No," I said, resigned to the situation. "It's fine."

"I'm Roxy, by the way. You're Morgana, right?"

"I am. Nice to meet you." The name didn't ring a bell. I'd probably seen her at a coven event years ago.

"Wish it were under better circumstances. I remember you and Erin were pretty tight back in school."

Again, I struggled to place her. So familiar and yet... not. "Did we know each other?"

"I was a few years ahead of you. And we didn't exactly travel in the same circles."

"Erin told me about you," Kari added, her voice raw and fragile.

That ratcheted up my awkwardness. The porch light flickered, and a breeze whispered through the screen, carrying the sharp scent of creosote.

My Faerie magic! Shit!

I took a deep breath to ground myself. I didn't need these people thinking I was some sort of freak, even if I was. The porch light stopped flickering.

"What... What'd Erin say about me?" I sputtered.

Kari let out a soft, broken laugh. "Only good things. All PG."

I breathed a sigh of relief. "She was a good person. Better than me. At least she had the courage not to hide in the closet in school."

"Don't beat yourself up, honey," Roxy said. "Wickenburg High wasn't exactly queer-friendly. I didn't come out until after graduation."

"You're queer too?"

She nodded. "Transgender. And lesbian. My senior year, the dysphoria got so bad I started using drugs and alcohol to cope. By the time I hit bottom and got clean, I no longer cared what other people thought. Now I'm a substance abuse counselor for queer youth at the Oasis Treatment Center."

"That's amazing." I meant it. Everyone had their life together but me.

We lapsed into silence, and my brain once again slipped into detective mode. "Kari, when was the last time you saw Erin?"

She seemed taken aback by the question. "Yesterday morning. She headed to work at the Wicked Grille. But she never came home. Why?"

"I'm just trying to put together a timeline of events. I don't trust Detective Hatathlie to find her killer. She seems a little too hung up on pinning the blame on me or someone associated with the coven. So maybe I can find evidence that points to the real killer."

"That's right. You're a screenwriter for *LA Murder Squad*," Roxy said. "That's amazing."

"Well, I was. The studio got bought out and fired the entire writers' room. And to make matters worse, I caught my girlfriend cheating on me. So now I'm unemployed, single, and back living with my moms."

"¡Ay, mami!" Angel winced. "Guess my tarot reading yesterday was spot-on."

I wanted to make a snarky retort but held my tongue. They'd been right about my recent failures. Was being Fae the truth that I had to embrace in order to move on?

And then there was the Death card. Had that predicted

Erin's death? Or did it simply mean change? Or was it all lucky guesses and speculation?

"I'm sorry about your job and your girlfriend." Roxy offered a sympathetic smile. "I hope something better is around the corner."

"You really think you can solve Erin's murder?" Those were the first words from the woman staring at me from the corner. Her voice was smooth and commanding. Something about the way her eyes reflected the light seemed... not quite human. Was she Fae? Did she know I was Fae?

"That's Thalia, by the way," Angel said. "Likes to come off as dark and brooding, but underneath she's a pussycat."

Thalia shot them a glare.

"Admittedly, I'm not a cop, just a writer," I said. "But I'm not going to wait around and be railroaded by a detective with a grudge against witches."

"I thought you didn't practice witchcraft," Angel said.

"I'm starting to embrace it, now that I'm back."

Roxy's expression tightened, concern flickering behind her eyes. "Selene said the crime scene looked like some sort of ritual sacrifice."

The memory scent of blood filled my nose. "Erin's attacker drew a pentacle and sigils around her in chalk and lit candles at the five points. But I didn't smell any magic."

Roxy tilted her head. "Magic has a smell?"

Her question surprised me. Was I the only one who could smell magic? Was this a Fae thing?

"Magic has a variety of smells if your senses are keen enough," Thalia murmured. "Earth magic, healing magic, blood magic, even Faerie magic—they all have a distinct scent."

"Faerie magic?" Angel sounded skeptical. "When have you smelled Faerie magic, chica?"

Thalia's unsettling gaze again locked on mine. "A few times."

My jaw clenched. She must know I was Fae.

"Did Erin receive any threats?" I asked Kari.

She shook her head. "No. Not that she ever told me about."

"Did she have any problem employees? Maybe someone she fired recently?"

"No, all her employees love her. Well, *loved* her. She paid them well, always treated them with respect. And they knew she had their backs on the rare occasion a customer complained about a meal or service."

"Maybe this wasn't about Erin specifically," Thalia suggested.

"Meaning?" I asked.

"Her murder was staged to look like a ritual sacrifice," she explained coolly. "In front of your mother's metaphysical bookstore. And I heard people saying someone had spray-painted anti-witch graffiti on the sidewalk just the day before. You do the math."

"You think someone is targeting my mom?"

"Or the coven."

I considered this. She had a point.

"We should crash the funeral," Angel suggested.

"There won't be one," Kari said softly, staring at the floor. "Not at St. Stephen's, at least."

"Why not?" I asked.

"The church wouldn't allow it, since Erin was Wiccan. Her parents are having a graveside service at Wickenburg Cemetery after the autopsy. The service announcement's on the *Wickenburg Sun*'s website."

"We should go," Angel said. "If the killer shows, maybe we can figure out who it is."

"I think you've watched too many *Veronica Mars* reruns,

Angel," Roxy said. "Why would her murderer go to her burial?"

"To gloat," I said. "Or out of guilt."

All eyes turned to me.

"As a writer for *LA Murder Squad*, I researched criminal behavior, investigation procedures, crime stats, the works. Based on the crime scene, the killer has a grudge against witches. And Erin knew them."

Roxy gave me a doubtful look. "How could you possibly know that?"

"Oh, great. Another psychic." Thalia shot Angel a look, who in turn flipped her off.

"I'm not psychic. Erin was still wearing her engagement ring, so probably not a robbery. The multiple stab wounds indicate a crime of passion. She knew her killer. Her being attacked and left in front of my mom's bookshop—in the exact spot where someone spray-painted 'Witches Burn in Hell' the day before—and staging it to look like a ritual sacrifice—it suggests animosity toward witches. Odds are better than even her killer will be at the burial."

"Wow, our very own Veronica Mars," Angel said. "I love it!"

Roxy still looked skeptical. "Even if you somehow identified them, what would we do about it?"

"Give the evidence to Detective Hatathlie," I suggested. "Maybe then, she'd pursue the actual killer and not one of us."

"I say we *hex* the murderous cabrón," Angel muttered. "And not just some itchy-asshole spell, either. Make their life a living hell."

"I'm all for that. I want that bastard to suffer," Kari said, her voice now steel.

My moms strongly opposed using magic as a weapon.

But this wasn't some petty grudge. Erin had been murdered.

"I say we kill the bastard," Thalia said casually. Her brooding manner and the way she held herself told me she could do it. I wondered if she'd been in the military.

"While I don't trust these cops, we are *not* vigilantes," Roxy warned. "We do *not* use magic to hurt people, much less kill them."

Thalia harrumphed. "I don't need magic to end a threat."

Roxy looked aghast. "Do you even hear yourself? You're talking about murder."

"I'm talking about punishing a killer," Thalia replied. "And making sure they don't hurt anyone else. How is that wrong?"

I considered the question. Hexing a murderer to push them to confess was one thing. But killing them? Was I capable of that, whether by magic or other means?

"What do you suggest, Roxy?" I asked, hoping to find some middle ground.

"Wickenburg relies on tourism to survive, especially now that the snowbirds are back," she said, referring to Arizona's part-time residents. "An unsolved murder is bad for business. And while Erin was one of us, she was also the daughter of a wealthy white business owner. Despite their prejudices, I believe the cops will be doing everything they can to bring her murderer to justice. Or alternatively, if we can find evidence that points to the killer, we can present that to the cops."

Thalia snorted. "So naïve. It's gonna be a witch hunt. A literal witch hunt. Either we let ourselves be hunted, or we become the hunters."

"No!" Roxy said firmly. "We are not killers."

"I vote we hex whoever did this to Erin," Kari said. "Put

the heat on them until they can't stand it any longer and confess to the cops."

"I'm down with that," I said, offering her a smile of support. "We figure out who did it and make their lives miserable."

"Fine," Thalia said. "I'm in."

"Me three. Or is it four?" Angel smirked. "Come on, Rox. What do ya say?"

Roxy didn't look pleased. She sighed and said, "I'm in, reluctantly, for hexing them. No killing."

"Five companions. So be it," Angel announced in a cinematic voice. "And we shall call ourselves the Gutterflies."

"The Gutterflies?" Roxy asked with a look of bemusement. "That's horrible."

"Yeah, like goth butterflies," they explained.

I snorted. "Angel, you're the only goth one here."

They sighed dramatically. "Fine. We can be the Sand Witches. After all, we are witches. In the desert. With sand."

The rest of us groaned.

AFTER EVERYONE LEFT, I helped Mom and Mama Joyce straighten up then retreated to my room, hoping to get some rest after a long, traumatic day.

But my mind buzzed with thoughts. Could we really figure out who killed Erin? And if we did, how far was I willing to go to see justice done? What would Mom and Mama Joyce think?

Just as I was finally drifting off, my phone rang. I grabbed it from the nightstand. "Hello?"

"Morgana? What the hell? You had me worried sick."

Saffron. *Shit.* And she sounded drunk.

"You just disappeared. No explanation. All your stuff is

gone. I left over a dozen messages, and you didn't call me back. Not once. What's going on? Where are you?"

"I'm in Arizona."

"Arizona? What the hell you doing there? Come home."

Part of me wanted to do just that. To slip back into her arms and into the life we'd built together. To feel her warm embrace, her lips on mine and... on other places. Then I remembered her in bed with that woman.

"I don't think so. You cheated on me."

"Cheated? What are you talking about?"

A wisp of my hair fluttered across my forehead. My nightlight brightened on the other side of the room. Faerie magic. *My* magic. I breathed slow and steady to ground myself.

"I saw you, Saff. I *heard* you. Saying all those sweet things you used to say to me, only you were saying them to her."

"Oh, honey, Cheryl and I were just running lines for the new season of the show. It wasn't real—"

"Don't. I'm done with your gaslighting. Done with your manipulations. Done with your Jekyll and Hyde routine. Warm and loving one minute, a cold-ass bitch the next. Always playing on my insecurities, twisting everything to get what you want."

"What are you even talking about? I'd never manipulate you. I love you."

"More lies. You weren't running lines. You were screwing her. For real."

The line went silent for a moment. I wondered if she'd hung up. Kinda hoped she had.

"Look, Morgana, I'm sorry, okay? I made a mistake," she admitted. "It started as rehearsal, but things got... a little carried away. It's method acting. What can I say? But I swear, I was thinking about you the whole time."

"Don't even. By the way, what happened to my pendant?"

"What pendant?"

"The one you made me take off before the Emmys. The one you called Appalachian folk art?"

"Ugh, that horrid thing? I threw it out. Trust me, I did you a favor. You're welcome."

"Screw you, Saffron. You had no right."

"Morg, please. Just come home. I'll buy you a new one."

"Mama Joyce made it for me. It had sentimental value." And magical value. "You can't just buy one on Rodeo Drive."

"Then ask her to make another and mail it to you. Just come home. We'll work things out. I heard the studio replaced the writers' room. They were idiots to let you go. But there's a new crime series about biker lesbians in preproduction. I know the showrunner. Netflix has already green-lit it for two seasons. You'd be perfect as one of their writers. Better yet, as head writer. I can make it happen. Me and the showrunner, we go... we go way back."

Part of me wanted to say yes. I wanted more than anything to get back to screenwriting. To resume living my dream.

But not if it meant going back to Saffron's mercurial temper and her never-ending stream of bullshit.

"We're done, Saffron. Don't call again."

I hung up and blocked her number.

CHAPTER 14

FOR THE NEXT FEW DAYS, the local news was ablaze with stories about the "ritual murder in Wickenburg," complete with plenty of photos of Wiccanburg Books. Endless speculation about witch covens and demonic cults preying on the town's youth.

Mom and I had declined all media interviews. Kari had helped her write a press release condemning the murder, denying that it had anything to do with witchcraft, and informing people that the shop's employees have been cooperating with Wickenburg PD to apprehend the killer.

I asked Mom and Mama Joyce if they knew of anyone specific with a grudge against the bookshop or the coven. Had they received any threats aside from the graffiti? They assured me they hadn't.

Through her contacts at Wickenburg PD, Kari learned that Erin's car had been located in the Wickenburg Hospital parking lot. No word on whether the cops found evidence that might lead to the murderer, much less a motive.

Had Erin injured herself while at work and needed

medical care? I knew the hospital wouldn't give out that information. Nor would they give me access to parking-lot security footage, even assuming they had cameras that showed who parked Erin's car.

I called her sous chef, Charlie Ralston, whose number I'd gotten from Kari. The call went straight to voicemail. So I left a message saying I was a friend of Erin's and had some questions.

I tried to think of other ways I could track down the killer. I supposed I could interview employees at her restaurant, but I wasn't sure what they would know that Kari wouldn't. I already knew there were some people in town who weren't fond of her for being a witch or gay. But that didn't exactly narrow things down.

I then dove headfirst down a research rabbit hole on all things Faerie, starting with books from my moms' personal libraries. Some were compendia of Faerie-like creatures from cultures around the world. One speculated whether Faeries were merely folklore, the embodiments of the elements, or full-on sentient beings.

A few books instructed readers how to attract and work with the Fair Folk as well as the potential risks of doing so. According to these authors, Faeries were capricious, cunning, and fond of making bargains that benefitted them but screwed over the other party. Getting the better of humans was considered entertainment to the Fae.

They couldn't outright lie or break their word but were masters of double meanings and hidden loopholes. Probably make great lawyers in the human world.

Offerings to the Fae were appreciated, but crossing them was asking for trouble. They held grudges like nobody's business and could make a person's life a living hell. Maybe I could find a way to use my Faerie magic to punish Erin's murderer.

Some books went into detail about the Summer and Winter Courts, ruled by Queen Titania and Queen Mab respectively. But not a word about the Desert Fae. A search of the internet turned up zilch. Perhaps they—or we—were a subset of the Summer Court. Or maybe my dad had somehow misled Mom. He couldn't have lied, assuming he really was Fae. But sidestepping the truth sounded very on-brand.

Faeries frequently appeared in novels by Jim Butcher, Yasmine Galenorn, and Julie Kagawa, just to name a few. But I figured the depictions reflected more of the authors' imaginations than their personal experiences. Then again, it was hard to know how much of the so-called nonfiction was fact or speculation.

None of the books offered any instruction on how to use Faerie magic if, you know, one happened to be Fae, or at least half Fae. I supposed full-blooded Fae were born knowing how to use their magic. But what were half-breeds like me supposed to do?

Over dinner, I voiced my frustration to the maternal units.

"I suppose the best thing to do is experiment," Mama Joyce suggested.

"Experiment?"

"Use the scientific method. Try different ways to use your magic. See what works and what doesn't."

"But this is magic, not science," I replied.

Mama Joyce shrugged. "No, but short of luring a Faerie to mentor you, it seems the only approach."

"A Fae mentor? Maybe I should try that."

"No," Mom added sharply. "Don't go making bargains with Faeries."

An idea popped into my head. I asked Mama Joyce,

"That amulet you made to suppress my Faerie magic—how'd you know how to make it?"

"I didn't. A friend of ours named Gina Marten did," Mama Joyce said. "She's a metalsmith who infuses magical energy into her creations. When you were having your..."

"Magical meltdowns?" I suggested.

"For lack of a better term, yes. I explained the situation to Gina."

"You told her I was half Faerie?" *Goddess! How many other people knew my secret?*

"Only because you were in a crisis and we desperately needed help. She'd encountered a similar situation before. Apparently, sandwiching the steel disc between copper and brass traps your magic, allowing you to live a normal life."

"Normal." I scoffed. "I'm the furthest thing from normal. I'm a brown half-Fae lesbian."

"Still, the talisman kept things from escalating while you were young."

She was right. On the few occasions that my Faerie magic had accidentally manifested, I'd been terrified. I dreaded to think what life would have been like dealing with that level of chaos every day on top of everything else.

"Maybe your friend Gina can teach me how to use my Faerie magic."

"She moved to Seattle a few years ago," Mama said. "But I can give you her number."

"Thanks. I'm desperate for any guidance."

After dinner, I called Gina Marten. I explained who I was and why I was calling, stumbling over my words. It felt awkward, reaching out to a stranger who'd shaped my life without ever meeting me. Especially since she'd known I was Fae more than a decade longer than I had.

"I'm trying to learn how to use my magic."

"I'm sorry, Morgana," she answered, her voice warm but frail. "I don't know how Faerie magic works."

"But you must. You made the talisman. And it worked."

"I'm glad it helped. I simply used what I knew about metallurgy and alchemy to prevent magic from manifesting. Faerie magic is wild and unpredictable. My advice is to keep wearing the talisman."

"Unfortunately, I lost it recently."

"Oh. Sorry to hear that. I'd make you a new one, but I suffered a stroke a few months back. I'm unable to do metalwork anymore."

"I'm so sorry. I hope you recover."

"Thank you. I am. Slowly. But my smithing days are over, I'm afraid."

"I don't want to suppress my magic any longer. I want to embrace it and learn to use it. Mama Joyce says you knew someone else who was half Fae."

"I did," Gina said after a pause. "But we lost touch a long time ago."

"Were they Desert Fae?"

"Desert Fae? I'm not familiar with the term, but it's possible. She lived in Phoenix."

"What was her name?" Maybe I could find her and talk to her.

"I'm sorry, but I promised never to out her to anyone. Just as I promised Joyce and Selene I'd never tell anyone about you."

"But I'm not just anyone. I'm half Fae like her."

"I realize that. But I don't break my word, especially when dealing with the Fae."

I appreciated her loyalty, though it left me no closer to the answers I was seeking. "Well, thank you for your time. And thank you for making that talisman back then. It helped. I wish you a full recovery."

After hanging up, I gathered with Mom and Mama Joyce in the barn. Flickering candles filled the space with soft light, dancing shadows, and a sense of magical possibility. I felt nervous but hopeful.

Mom placed an unlit pillar candle on the altar between us. "Let's start simple. Try to light the candle."

"Perhaps this isn't the safest space for her to practice her magic," Mama Joyce said warily.

"Why not?" Mom countered. "We work on a lot of spells here."

"Yeah, normal magic. Wooden barn. Open flames. Shelves of flammable books. And from what we've seen of Morgana's magic in the past, well..."

"Nonsense. Magic is magic. It'll be fine."

Mama Joyce arched an eyebrow. "Let us at least start with something less... incendiary."

"Like what?" Mom asked, bristling.

"Plant magic. I can grab the Christmas cactus from the kitchen. See if she can coax it into blossoming."

"Oh, please! That's too easy. She's always had a green thumb. Let's give her a challenge."

"Still, I think it would be a safe place for her to start."

"Hello? Standing right here." I waved, feeling awkward. "Anyone care what I think, seeing as how it's my magic we're talking about?"

They both turned to me, slightly sheepish.

"Sorry, peanut," Mama Joyce said. "Where do *you* want to start?"

I considered my options. Summoning fire seemed all kinds of risky, given our location and my clear lack of control.

"Let's start with the plant," I said.

"Fine," Mom replied with a dejected sigh.

"Smart choice." Mama Joyce ran up to the house and returned moments later with the Christmas cactus.

When I moved back a week ago, it had looked rather pale, limp, and pathetic. Now it had perked up, and the segments were a healthy deep green.

With the cactus on the altar, I held my palms toward it, feeling like an idiot. "Should I close my eyes?"

"Up to you," Mom replied. "Trust your intuition."

I closed them and imagined sending fertile energy into the plant.

Grow. Blossom. Bloom. Grow. Blossom. Bloom. Grow. Blossom. Bloom.

After a minute or so, I reopened my eyes. The Christmas cactus looked the same. Because of course, it did.

"What am I doing wrong?"

"Nothing," Mama Joyce assured me. "We're just experimenting at this stage."

"Maybe I should try summoning wind. I seem to be good at that," I suggested.

The two of them exchanged a glance.

Mama Joyce nodded. "Go ahead. But easy does it. We don't need a full-on dust storm in here. Just a gentle whisper of air."

"Try blowing out the candle." Mom lit the wick with a lighter. "Okay, sweetheart. Show us what you've got. Blow this baby out."

I stared at the flame, feeling all the more self-conscious.

Come on, girl. You got this, I told myself. *Concentrate. Think wind.*

And... nothing. Not even a flicker.

"I can't do it." Frustration knotted in my chest.

"Sure, you can," Mama Joyce assured me. "Just go deeper and focus."

"I *am* focusing. It's not working."

"You always were a disappointment, Morgana," Mom said.

"What?" I was aghast. Her words hit me like a punch in the throat. She'd never spoken to me that way.

"Selene..." Mama Joyce cautioned.

"No, it's true," Mom said flippantly. "You've been an absolute embarrassment. Our own daughter can't be bothered to learn magic. The whole coven pities us. Erin told me she was glad you turned her down for prom. 'Dodged a bullet,' she told me after she and Kari got together."

Rage and grief exploded through every cell in my body. The rush of blood in my ears became a roar of wind, gusting all around us and whipping my hair into knots. My nose filled with the bitter stench of creosote.

The candles in the barn blew out, pitching us into darkness, except for the silver glow of moonlight spilling through the skylights overhead.

"Morgana, honey, take a breath." Mama Joyce rested a steadying arm over my shoulder. "She didn't mean it."

As my hair whipped in my face, I rallied to regain control of my emotions. *She didn't mean it. She didn't mean it.* I wanted to ask her why she'd said it, but my body was trembling too much to get the words out.

Mom laced her fingers with mine. "Sweetheart, I'm so sorry. Mama's right. I didn't mean a word I said. I was seeing if an emotional reaction would help you tap into your magic."

"That was cruel, Selene."

"But it worked. You did it, darling. You summoned wind."

I inhaled deeply, trying to calm the riot of emotions swirling inside me. The wind died down as I grounded myself.

"It was still a horrible thing to say, Mom." I made no attempt to hide my anger.

"You're right. It was a foolish thing to do."

"Not foolish. It was just mean," I countered, refusing to let her off the hook.

"Yes, I suppose it was." She held up her hands in surrender. "Please forgive me, Morgana. I didn't mean to hurt you."

I still felt the shock and sting of her words. They were so out of character for her, which made them hurt all the more. It was like the ground disappearing out from under me.

"I forgive you," I managed to say. "But it may take a while to forget."

"I understand. Maybe you'd like to try relighting the candle on the altar?"

I drew in another breath, steadier this time. "Fine."

"Just easy does it," Mama Joyce added. "Let's not set the barn ablaze."

Easy does it. Right.

I focused on the candle, its silhouette rimmed in moonlight. *Fire*, I thought.

Nothing.

I tried tapping into my emotions but was careful to avoid burning the place down.

"Light, dammit!" I said to the candle.

A flicker of light appeared above us, then another, then dozens, swirling lazily like fireflies. Only we didn't have fireflies here in Wickenburg. The scent of rain and desert sage replaced the bitterness of creosote.

Mom let out a delighted laugh. "Well, that's different."

Mana Joyce stared, slack-jawed. "I read about Faerie lights, but I've never seen them. This is... amazing."

"Faerie lights?" I watched them swirl and blink in and

out of existence. They were pretty and mesmerizing. But the candle remained unlit.

"You've heard of the will-o'-the-wisp?" Mom asked.

"In folk tales. I thought that was just swamp gas or something."

"Nope, it's this. Faerie lights."

I tried to touch one, but it winked out an instant before I made contact. "But what are they? Pixies? Spirits? Just energy?"

Mama Joyce shook her head. "Honestly, I have no idea, peanut."

"It's magic," Mom said. "Pure Faerie magic."

It was stunning, but I still felt a little disappointed. "Why *this*? Why not fire?"

Mama Joyce shrugged. "You said 'light,' not fire. And light is what you got."

She was right, but I was thinking fire. My magic was still a hot mess. I felt no closer to being able to control it.

The lights danced a while longer then slowly faded, blinking out one by one, leaving us in moonlit darkness.

Mom lit the candle with the lighter. "Shall we try summoning water next?" Mom asked.

I considered it. Erin's burial was scheduled for the morning. "Maybe another time. I'm exhausted and would rather not risk turning the inside of the barn into a sopping mess."

"Wise choice," Mama Joyce said, giving my arm a squeeze. "Let's call it a night."

WICKENBURG CEMETERY SPRAWLED across a dry hillside, its sunbaked soil scattered with mesquite, cacti, and weather-worn gravestones dating back more than a century. No rolling acres of manicured grass found in most cemeteries. No walls keeping the living out after hours. Or, for that matter, keeping the dead in.

Not that escaping corpses were ever really an issue, far as I knew. But the revelation of my Fae heritage still left me wondering what other mythical creatures might be real. Werewolves? Zombies? Chupacabras?

Angel, Thalia, Roxy, and Kari were waiting near their vehicles when I pulled into the gravel lot at the bottom of the hill. The morning air was chilly. High, thin clouds veiled the sky in a mournful gray, washing out the morning sun.

Angel was dressed in their usual attention-grabbing goth attire, right down to the black lipstick, a lace parasol, and Doc Marten boots. Roxy and Kari both wore dresses and heels. Thalia had on a leather jacket over a dark tailored shirt and slacks.

I didn't own anything appropriate to wear. I'd attended only one funeral in my life—for Mama Joyce's father—and I'd been eight at the time. I usually wore jeans and a casual top to work. The dresses I owned were all too bright or revealing for a burial service.

In the end, I borrowed a dress from Mom, the one she'd worn to Erin's memorial ritual. I hoped no one would notice the faint aroma of weed that clung to the fabric. Or if they did, maybe they'd have the decency not to say anything.

"Sorry I'm late," I muttered.

"You're good," Roxy said, flashing a gentle smile. "I think the service just started."

"Time for the Sand Witches to make our presence known," Angel declared, giving their parasol a theatrical spin.

I rolled my eyes. "Gaia help us. We're not really calling ourselves that, are we?"

"What? You'd rather we go back to the Gutterflies? Besides, the Scooby Gang was already taken. Twice."

I rolled my eyes, but weirdly, I liked the collective nickname, corny as it was.

We climbed the gravel path toward the gathering of mourners clustered around an open grave. A wind chime hanging from a nearby mesquite tree clanged a discordant melody, stirred by a restless breeze.

I scanned the faces, watching for guilt—or worse, glee —over Erin's death.

Erin's father stood stone-faced, staring at the bronze-hued casket. His wife trembled with barely contained grief, while their other daughter, Sarah, stood between them, eyes hollow with sorrow. Now fully grown, she looked less like Erin's kid sister and more like her twin.

They'd treated Erin terribly for being gay—worse still

for practicing Wicca—but their sorrow felt genuine. I didn't get a sense that they were responsible for her death.

A priest in his thirties, dressed in a black robe, read from a weathered prayer book. "So, let us commend our sister, Erin Siobhan O'Brien, to the Lord, that He may embrace her in peace and raise up her body on the last day..."

I had nothing against Christianity or even Catholicism per se. But it felt wrong to bury Erin with all this talk of God. She had rejected those beliefs in favor of following the path of the Goddess. Erin would probably have a good laugh over the whole thing.

Still, this was how her family needed to say goodbye. For all their failings, they were grieving too.

Detective Hatathlie stood near the back, her expression unreadable. Did she know the O'Briens? Was she here to pay respects—or to search for suspects, like we were?

I recognized former schoolmates, teachers, and towns-people in the small crowd. I'd forgotten most of their names. Some deliberately.

The priest continued, "For our sister, Erin, let us pray to our Lord Jesus Christ, who said, 'I am the resurrection and the life. Whoever believes in me...'"

I consciously blocked out the priest's words, trying to extend my mind and use my Faerie powers to identify Erin's murderer. Not that I'd had much success using my magic the night before in the barn. But Mama Joyce had encour-aged me to try things to see what worked. So that was what I was doing.

But I didn't notice anything but the priest droning on and the quiet sobs from the crowd. Once again, my Faerie magic had failed. No dust storm or monsoon, thankfully. But no clue who'd killed Erin either—assuming they were even here.

When Erin's casket was lowered into the earth, I whispered to Roxy and the others, "Let's go."

I didn't want to spend another minute with these people who had the audacity to grieve over Erin's death after they'd treated her so horribly in life. Who was I kidding, thinking I could somehow identify the killer in the crowd? I wasn't a detective. Just a screenwriter who had churned out episodes of *LA Murder Squad*, where the crime could be solved in forty-two minutes or less. Real life was not so simple.

Roxy, Kari, Angel, Thalia, and I trudged silently back down the hill.

Erin's sister, Sarah, caught up with us halfway to the parking lot. A guy walked beside her—tall, mid-thirties, with shaggy brown hair that brushed his collar. Boyfriend? Relative? No clue.

"Thank you all for coming," Sarah said.

"I'm so sorry for your loss," I replied.

She choked back a sob and hugged me then Kari and the rest of us. "I still can't believe she's gone. The detective said you're the one who found her."

"I tried to save her, but... I guess she was too far gone. I'm sorry."

"I'm sure you did everything you could."

"Sarah's the only member of her family who still talked to her," Kari explained, locking eyes with her. "Your support meant a lot to her after your folks turned their backs."

"Mom and Dad... They did love her—in their own way. They just... The church filled their heads with a lot of hateful nonsense. I'm just glad she found love before she died."

Her words felt like a punch to the chest, reminding me again how I'd abandoned Erin. "Me too," I managed to say.

The guy with Sarah extended an awkward hand to me. "Hi, I'm Charlie Ralston, sous chef at the Wicked Grille. Well, head chef, now that Erin's gone."

"Nice to meet you, Charlie. I'm Morgana Quinn. Sorry to meet under such circumstances."

"It's a hard blow to us all," Charlie said. "And sorry I didn't call you back. I've just been slammed to the wall without her."

"Any idea why her car would have ended up in the hospital parking lot? Had she injured herself that night?"

He shook his head. "No, she was fine when she left."

That eliminated a serious medical injury as the reason why her car was at the hospital.

"What are you going to do with the restaurant?" I asked.

"I'm talking with my lawyer about taking over as owner."

"Sounds like she poured her soul into that place. I think she'd be proud to see it continue on."

He nodded. "Come have dinner at the Grille tonight. Raise a glass to her memory. It's on me."

"Thank you," I said. "I'd like that."

"I'll make a reservation for the five of you. Say around seven o'clock?"

"Works for me," I said. The others agreed.

"How dare you show your faces here!" an angry voice shouted. "This is my daughter's funeral. Have you people no shame?"

Mr. O'Brien stormed toward us, his face mottled with rage. He seized the front of my dress and pulled me toward him, his eyes wild and accusing. "You got some nerve, showing up after seducing my daughter in school and filling her head with all kinds of perversions."

He cocked his fist, and I braced for the blow. But before he could punch me, Thalia tackled him to the ground.

"Keep your hands off her, you pathetic piece of shit," she growled. "Touch one of us again, I'll put you down for good."

"Bitch." He threw Thalia off him and got to his feet, blood trickling from where the side of his head hit the gravel. "Perverts. You're all a bunch of sick perverts."

"I didn't make Erin gay, Mr. O'Brien," I shouted at him. "She was born that way. We both were."

"Bullshit! You're the reason she's dead, you filthy dyke."

"We had nothing to do with her death, sir," Roxy said. "We're only here to pay our respects."

"Dad, please stop it!" Sarah stepped between us and put a hand against his chest as if to fend him off. "This isn't what Erin would have wanted."

But Mr. O'Brien wasn't listening. "You seduced my daughter and then broke her heart. And now I've lost her forever." His voice broke with grief. "I hope you're pleased with yourself."

His words found their mark, amplifying my grief and guilt. He was right on one point. I'd initiated our romance. And in my cowardice, I'd ended it. And now I'd never have a chance to make it right.

"Stay the hell away from my family, or so help me, I'll make you all wish you'd never been born."

I fled, my heart racing and tears blurring my vision. Past the startled faces of the other mourners, desperate to escape the suffocating weight of my guilt and grief.

I didn't stop until I reached my Kia, fumbling with the keys in my shaky hands. I collapsed into the driver's seat, sobs racking my body, my forehead pressed against the steering wheel.

The air crackled around me, charged with grief and something more volatile—my magic slipping its leash. The stench of creosote and ozone filled the vehicle. I half feared

I might short out the electrical system. But I was too angry and miserable to care.

A tapping on the window roused my attention. I wiped away tears and looked up.

Roxy stood outside my door, wind whipping her hair. Wind I probably summoned with my out-of-control emotions and equally out-of-control magic.

I took a deep cleansing breath and blew it out, stilling my magic as best I could.

"Morgana, you all right?" Her voice was muffled by the glass that separated us.

I started the ignition and lowered the window. "I'm... I'll be okay."

"We're getting together for coffee. Care to join us?"

I shook my head. "I'd rather be alone right now. But thanks."

She handed me a business card. "If you need to talk, call me. Anytime. My cell's on the back. I'm a good listener."

"Thanks," I said.

She was cute and had a calming energy about her that made me feel better just being near her.

"You coming tonight to the Wicked Grille?" she asked.

After what just happened, the last thing I wanted was to be around a bunch of strangers in a noisy restaurant. But then, spending time with Roxy and the other Sand Witches and eating food from Erin's restaurant might just fuel the healing process.

"Sure, I'll be there."

She patted my shoulder. "I'll see you then."

I took a shuddering breath and drove home.

Chapter 16

I spent the rest of the afternoon in the barn, trying to figure out how my magic worked. Trying, failing. Trying again. Failing even more.

But after a few hours, I was getting a handle on some basics. I could coax houseplants into blooming, making their petals unfurl like time-lapse footage. I summoned gusts of wind and drifting banks of mist, careful not to unleash rain inside the barn. Faerie lights danced at my fingertips again, though they were harder to see in the daytime.

Fire, on the other hand, was still a no-go. Probably just as well. Burning down the barn was not on my to-do list.

Part of me wanted to test my healing magic after I'd failed to save Erin. But how?

I recalled an episode of *Heroes* where one of the main characters deliberately injured herself to demonstrate her healing abilities.

I wasn't so brave.

The very thought of cutting myself ooked me out. I sure as hell wasn't going to cut off a toe just to see if I could magically reattach it or somehow sprout a new one like a lizard regrowing a tail.

Plus, most of our knife blades were made of steel. Since I was part Fae, iron could blister, burn, or possibly poison me. If something went wrong, I might not be able to heal it.

By sunset, I was drained—my mind exhausted, every nerve frayed. Magic took more out of me than I'd expected. I wanted nothing more than to collapse onto my bed for a nap.

But my stomach growled, and I'd promised Roxy I'd meet her and the others for dinner at the Wicked Grille. A promise was a promise.

After a quick shower, I slipped into an emerald-green designer dress Saffron had given me when we were dating. It had cost as much as my Kia, and I was afraid of spilling something on it and ruining it. But the bodice hugged my curves in all the right places, and the sweetheart neckline revealed enough cleavage to make me feel sexy. And I deserved to feel good about myself for once.

I added a touch of sparkle—a tiny emerald pendant on a gold chain and a Jennifer Meyer tennis bracelet I'd scored from a swag bag at the Emmys.

Kari, Roxy, Angel, and Thalia were waiting by the hostess stand in the Wicked Grille's packed lobby. The place buzzed with energy. Erin had clearly made her mark early in her culinary career. Too bad she wouldn't get the chance to build on her success.

The décor leaned rustic—dark wood beams, stonework, and wrought iron chandeliers—but mercifully stopped short of taxidermy. No glass-eyed elk or grinning bobcats staring down from the walls. Thank Goddess for that. Those things always creeped me out. Nothing kills an appetite like a dead thing watching you eat.

Savory scents swirled through the air—roasted garlic,

charred meat, something sweet and smoky I couldn't quite place. My stomach let out an embarrassing growl.

The hostess led us to a wooden table tucked near the kitchen doors, the hum of chefs and clatter of pans just beyond. It was set for four, but she quickly added a fifth place at the end. I slid into the seat next to Roxy, whose sophisticated perfume held notes of lavender and rain.

We'd barely ordered our drinks when Charlie appeared, dressed in a crisp white chef's coat and matching toque.

"Sorry for the tight squeeze," he said with a weary smile. "We're slammed tonight. But dinner and drinks are on me. Also, I'm introducing some new menu items—duck confit, coq au vin, and boeuf bourguignon. And for dessert, tarte tatin and crème brûlée."

"How classically French," Roxy observed.

"Thank you," he said. "Bon appétit."

I flipped open the menu and nearly dropped it.

It was a good thing Charlie was comping our meals. The entrées ran in the fifty-to-sixty-dollar range. Each one sounded like it belonged on the cover of a foodie magazine. Elk carpaccio drizzled with citrus herb oil and pickled shallots. A sixteen-ounce coffee-rubbed rib eye paired with cheddar mashed potatoes. Bison tenderloin in a blackberry bourbon reduction. No surprise this place had snagged a Michelin star.

For my main course, I chose the hickory-smoked duck breast glazed with prickly pear, served over rice pilaf. A lot fancier than my usual, but I was ravenous after an afternoon of practicing my magic.

After we placed our orders, I glanced across the table at Thalia.

"Thanks for stepping in with Mr. O'Brien."

She met my gaze, cool-eyed. "Can't stand bigots. Especially those who don't keep their hands to themselves."

"You okay?" Roxy asked me. "You looked a little rattled earlier."

"I'm better now. Showing up at the burial was a mistake. I was an idiot to think I could identify the murderer."

"Detective Hatathlie was there too," Angel added. "Probably had the same idea."

"Only now we look more guilty," I muttered. "Especially after that scuffle with Mr. O'Brien."

"I'm still glad we went," Kari said. "Her parents are awful, and that burial service wasn't what she'd have wanted. But being there... It felt right. Especially after her folks showed up at our house the other day."

That was a shocker. "Why were they there?" I asked.

"Probably to spew more hate," Thalia muttered.

"They were looking for a dress to bury Erin in. They didn't say anything particularly mean, but it felt invasive having them there. *I* should have been the one handling the funeral arrangements."

Raucous laughter at a nearby table caught my attention. I recognized familiar faces from school—Melinda Fox, Linda Swilling, Dave Talbot, and Jimmy Collins. Just great. The bullies who'd made high school a nightmare. Older now but just as smug. Why the hell were they here at Erin's restaurant?

I forced myself to tune them out and focus on the conversation at our table, where Kari shared a story about Erin.

"She almost didn't hire Charlie as her sous chef," she explained.

"Why not?" I asked.

"He trained at Le Cordon Bleu in Paris. Thought Erin's concept of upscale ranch cuisine was beneath him."

"So why'd she hire him?"

"She didn't get many applicants wanting to work so far from the Valley. Of the few who applied, he was the most qualified. And I guess he wasn't getting a lot of offers himself. He'd had some clashes with some of the other chefs he worked with. But he and Erin worked things out, much to the restaurant's success."

Roxy chuckled. "Remember the cranberry-and-orange scones she made for the Imbolc ritual? So good."

"I remember the swarm of pixies they attracted," Angel said. "Ay, mami! What a pain they were."

"Those weren't pixies. They were hummingbirds," Roxy corrected. "Probably drawn to the desert honeysuckle on the altar."

Angel shook their head. "They may have looked like hummingbirds, but trust me, chica, they were pixies using a glamour."

I remembered the hummingbirds outside the house shortly after I arrived back in Wickenburg. I thought I'd been crazy when I thought they were Faeries. But maybe I wasn't. Maybe I'd seen through their glamour for an instant.

"Angel's right, for once. They were pixies," Thalia said. "I could smell their magic. It's why the candles refused to light during the ritual. Damned Faeries. Nothing but troublemakers."

Ouch! My face heated with a rush of humiliation and bitterness. I was starting to like my new friends. But now, the thought of coming out to them as half Fae terrified me. Would they reject me the way Erin's parents rejected her?

Something about Thalia tugged at my curiosity—her ability to smell magic, the way her eyes caught the light. Could she be Fae too? Was her Faephobic talk a cover for her identity? Or was I just projecting?

"What did their magic smell like?" I asked, trying to play it cool.

"Like an approaching monsoon mixed with desert sage."

The same smell I noticed when I intentionally used my magic. Did Thalia know I was half Fae? Did the others?

"You grow up around here?" I asked, curious to learn her story.

"Wittmann." It was a tiny town just south of Wickenburg but smaller.

"How'd you end up in Wickenburg?"

"Joined the army after high school. Now I teach desert survival training. Wickenburg's as good a place as any to do that."

I turned to Kari. "What about you?"

"I write for *Phoenix Living* and the *Wickenburg Sun* and freelance for the *Arizona Republic* and some national queer media. I grew up in Scottsdale."

"You left Scottsdale for Wickenburg? Why?"

She shrugged. "Erin and I met at Phoenix Pride. We hit it off, and I moved to Wickenburg a month later."

"You gonna stay in Wickenburg?" *Now that Erin's gone*, I thought but didn't say.

She seemed to consider my question. "I have the house, and the coven's become like my family. My dad died of a brain aneurysm when I was in college. My mom... We don't talk much since I came out. She's not as bad as Erin's parents but not exactly an ally either. Not like your moms. Or Angel's family."

"I'm lucky, I know," I admitted. "Though I kinda wish I'd known my dad too."

"Ever meet him?" Kari asked.

"My moms never talked about him." Until now.

"Must be hard," Roxy said.

"Just feels like there's a piece of me missing."

"I hear you. But whether you meet him one day or not, you're still a complete person. He might have contributed some DNA, but that's all. You get to decide who you are."

She smiled at me, and I nearly melted. Her warmth and kindness were infectious. I couldn't help feeling good around her. She made me feel seen. Cared for. Why couldn't Saffron have been like that?

Maybe it was the wine or the company, but I didn't feel quite so alone anymore. The grief for Erin and the shame over my failures were still there. But coming home, however temporary, wasn't the worst thing to happen.

"Well, if it isn't the queer little witches."

I looked up. Dave Talbot stared down at us, his arm slung around Melinda Fox. Linda Swilling stood next to them. *Crap!*

CHAPTER 17

A DIAMOND the size of a Volkswagen glittered on Melinda's ring finger. She and Dave must be married. Figures. The two had been high school sweethearts, king and queen of the prom, and the progeny of the richest families in town.

"Oh, look! It's Morgana Quinn," Melinda said with a smirk.

Linda sneered. "Who let you back in town, lesbo?"

I glared at them. "News flash, bitches. I don't need your permission."

"Slinking back for your dead girlfriend's funeral?" Linda said with a fake pout. "I swear, we get rid of one rug muncher, and another one shows up. They're like cockroaches."

"Erin was my best friend," I retorted, struggling to control my emotions. "How dare you talk about her that way."

Melinda scoffed. "Some friend you were. Humiliating her in front of everyone when she asked you to prom? Pretending to be straight? But then—big surprise—you turned out to be a big old dyke anyway. Just like your big old dyke moms."

"Bitch got what was coming to her, if you ask me," Dave said. "One less perv in this town."

"If you hated her so much, why are you here, eating in her restaurant?"

"Celebrating, of course," he replied. "Ding-dong, the wicked witch is dead."

He laughed at his own joke. I wanted to punch his smug face in so hard it'd turn his head inside out.

Jimmie Collins walked up from the restrooms, wiping his hands on his slacks. "Holy shit! Bobby Monroe?" Jimmie barked out a laugh. "In a dress and makeup? Dude!"

"What the hell? You a freaking tranny now?" Dave asked.

I glanced at Roxy, and suddenly, everything clicked. *That* was why she looked so familiar. I hadn't made the connection because she'd had a shaved head in school.

Roxy flinched, cheeks darkening. Her eyes hardened with resolve. "The name's Roxanne now. Why don't you people mind your own business and leave us alone?"

I almost felt bad for her being outed and humiliated like that.

But then I remembered—back in school, Roxy had been one of *them*. My tormentors. Now she knew what it felt like. Maybe that was karma.

"Does tearing people down make you feel superior?" Angel asked. "Because without your daddies' money, you're just a couple of mediocre white boys, struggling with your internalized homophobia."

Jimmie's face turned purple. "Shut the hell up, faggot. We ain't queer like you."

"Oh really? I recall you sucking my dick in the parking lot

after y'all lost a game to Dysart High." They moaned theatrically. "'Oh, Angel, I'm so gay for you. I love your cock in my mouth.' Face it, sweetheart. You're as queer as the rest of us."

"You lying faggot!" Jimmie screamed.

Guess Angel's remark struck home.

"You best watch your backs, you freaks," Dave hissed. "Or what happened to Erin might happen to you next."

Anger flared hot in my veins. The air crackled with electricity, and the scent of creosote filled my nose.

"You threatening us?" I rose to my feet, hands balling into fists.

Thalia stood as well. "Not a smart move."

Jimmie held up his hands in mock surrender. "Whoa there, lesbos. Cops are saying y'all are the ones who killed her. Part of one of your satanic rituals."

"It's a lie," Thalia hissed at him. "Erin was one of ours. We'd never hurt her. I'm thinking it was one of you."

Dave sneered. "You know, Jimmie, maybe it's time to start burning witches again. Says to do so in the Bible. It's our Christian duty."

"Try it. See what happens," Thalia replied. "I will rip you people apart with my bare hands."

The lights above us flared and flickered. I should have reined in my magic, but I wasn't in the mood.

I turned to Melinda. "How's the hair, girl? Be a shame if it all fell out again."

She glared at me, her pretty face darkening with shame. "Don't you *dare*, you filthy Mexican whore."

The light bulbs above her exploded in a cascade of hot glass.

"Best leave us alone. Or a little hair loss will be the least of your worries. That goes for all of you."

"Morgana." A hand landed on my shoulder.

I wheeled around at the touch. Roxy stood next to me, her face pinched with worry. Probably afraid I'd turn the restaurant into a scene from the finale of *Carrie*.

"Let's just leave," she pleaded.

"Don't touch me. You used to be one of them."

I turned back to Jimmie and the others. "If I learn any of y'all killed Erin, I'll make you suffer in ways you can't imagine."

I stormed out, Faerie magic rolling off me in hot waves of energy. Car alarms shrieked, headlights flashed like strobes, and a damp wind swirled through the lot, thick with the scent of ozone and creosote. The air felt like a monsoon about to break.

"Morgana... wait." Roxy approached cautiously, hands up, her eyes bright with fear, softened by guilt.

"Save it."

"Please, Morgana. Hear me out."

I paused, one hand on my car door. "What?"

"I was wrong to bully you in school. I sincerely apologize."

"You bullied Erin, Angel, and me, even though you were as queer as we were."

"I know. I was wrong to do so. Please forgive me."

Thalia, Kari, and Angel caught up to us.

Angel asked, "You okay, chica?"

I turned on them. "You knew who Roxy was?"

They nodded. "Sí, but let's be honest. You were a bit of a puta yourself back then. The way you dumped Erin in front of everyone. And then started hanging out with the Meanlindas? As if you were one of them?"

Touché. Leave it to Angel to twist the knife.

"I'm sorry for everything I did to you, Morgana," Roxy said. "There was no excuse. I wish more than anything I could take it all back. But I know I can't. All I *can* do is make amends."

"And my moms, they know?"

"Yes. As did Erin," Kari said. "And they all forgave her."

"Well, I don't forgive you, Roxy Monroe. You made my life hell for years. You can all go kiss my ass."

I climbed into my car and peeled out of the lot, gripping the wheel tight, praying I didn't short out the electrical system or accidentally summon a thunderstorm inside the vehicle.

CHAPTER 18

I DROVE HOME, haunted by old wounds and simmering anger. The bullies from high school hadn't grown up— they'd only gotten meaner with age.

I fantasized about unleashing my Fae magic on them, but all I'd managed so far was shorting out a few light bulbs, summoning some wind, and making plants grow. I'd tried to heal Erin, but it didn't save her. Oh, and Faerie lights. Pretty but useless.

Mama Joyce sat in the living room, reading on her tablet, glasses perched low on her nose when I walked in. "How was dinner?"

I shrugged. "Okay. Where's Mom?"

"At the bookshop, teaching a class. She should be home sometime after nine." She tilted her head. "Everything all right, peanut?"

"Just tired. Been a long day figuring out my magic."

"How's that going?"

"Slow." I rubbed my temples. "I think I'll crash early."

"Sleep well, honey. I'll see you in the morning." She kissed my forehead, and I headed to my room.

I tried to sleep, but my mind kept drifting back to Roxy. Why was it so hard to forgive her for what she did in high school? That was years ago. And she said she was sorry.

But as I thought about it, I knew the answer. I couldn't forgive her because I couldn't forgive myself for what I'd done to Erin. Roxy and I had both been closeted and afraid. And stupid.

When I finally fell asleep, the nightmares came hard. No surprise, given the burning dumpster fire my life had become.

In a horrible dream that seemed to be on repeat, a dark figure stalked me through the halls of Wickenburg High. I ran in terror but kept stumbling over something. I looked down. Bodies. Everywhere. Dozens of them. Torn apart as if by a lion or bear or some other apex predator.

I tried to hide, but it always found me. I threw things—books, chairs, anything I could grab—but nothing slowed it down. I reached for my magic, but all that came out were Faerie lights. And the dark figure kept coming and coming.

Mom and Mama Joyce sat at the kitchen table, sipping coffee, when I walked in the next morning.

"Hey," I mumbled, still half asleep.

"Good morning, sunshine," Mom said. "How was dinner with your friends?"

"The food was good. More than good. It was amazing. And I had a fun time—until a bunch of kids from school showed up."

"Who?" Mama Joyce asked, setting a mug in front of me.

"Melinda Fox, Linda Swilling, Dave Talbot, and Jimmie Collins."

She shook her head as she sat across from me. "Ugh. Those kids. A bunch of entitled little pricks—just like their parents. Did they bother you?"

"Yeah. But something else upset me worse."

"Oh? What's that?"

"I found out who Roxy used to be."

Mom nodded. "Roxy's transgender. You don't have a problem with that, do you?"

"No, of course not. It's just…" I searched for the words. "She used to hang with Dave and Jimmie. Mom, she used to bully me."

She nodded solemnly. "Yeah, she told me."

"She said you forgave her."

"She told us what she did. She owned it, said she was sorry. But we told her—we're not the ones she needs to make amends to. You are. Did she?"

"Only after Dave Talbot outed her."

Mama Joyce stroked my hair. "Being a lesbian in high school is rough, kiddo. We all know that. I can only imagine how much harder it might be for trans kids."

She wasn't wrong, though I hated to admit it.

"People deal with being queer in all kinds of ways," she continued. "Some, like Erin, live loud and proud from the start. Some, like you, stay in the closet until the time feels right—and that's okay. Then there are people like Roxy, who bully others to avoid dealing with their own internal queerphobia. It's a coping mechanism."

"Don't make excuses for her, Mama."

"I'm not. What she did was wrong. She's acknowledged it. But let's not forget—breaking up with Erin the way you did? That wasn't exactly kind."

"But I didn't bully her."

"Didn't you? You humiliated her. Gaslit her. That was cruel."

I sighed. She was right. And I'd been carrying the guilt for years. "I know."

"We all screw up," Mom said. "We all do things we're

not proud of—especially when we're young and stupid." She grinned. "I sure did."

"Yeah."

"But when we know better, we do better. Roxy was wrong—no question. But she was struggling, same as you were. It took nearly dying from an overdose to snap her out of it."

"She almost died?" The thought shook me more than I expected it to.

"She did. But she got clean and now helps others do the same. And she's become quite adept at healing magic. So maybe it's time to forgive her."

"I just... can't. I know she's sorry, but it doesn't erase what she did. Ignoring it doesn't make the trauma magically go away."

"Of course not," Mama Joyce said. "But forgiveness isn't about ignoring what someone did to you, baby girl. Forgiveness is simply choosing to let go of resentments. It's about freeing yourself of that burden, so it doesn't eat you alive."

"I suppose."

"When I was a little girl, my uncle molested me. And every time I thought of him, I relived it. For years. The pain. The trauma. The rage. The shame."

"Oh, how horrible." The thought of anyone hurting Mama Joyce made my stomach twist.

"It took a long time—and a lot of healing work—for me to finally let it all go. To be free. That's what forgiveness is, baby girl. Freedom. From the trauma. From the anger. From the past."

"Did you ever see him again?"

"A few times, at family reunions. But I made sure he never got close to me—or any other girl—again. Eventually,

I told my grandmother what he did. He stopped coming after that."

"I get it. But that doesn't mean I have to be friends with Roxy now, does it?"

Mama Joyce shook her head. "No, it doesn't. My uncle never admitted what he did. But Roxy has. I think she wants to make things right. Maybe even be the friend she couldn't be back then. Question is—will you give her the chance?"

Her words hit deep. I'd wanted the same shot with Erin —but I never got it.

"I'll think about it."

"Of course. You decide who you let in. I just hope her being in the coven doesn't push you away. Mom and I would love for you to be a part of it, for as long as you're here."

"I'll think about that too."

She hugged me and kissed me on the forehead. "I love you, sweet girl."

"Love you, too, Mama."

I spent the day making calls, following up on job leads, and touching base with former colleagues. Totally not thinking about Roxy. Or Erin. Or forgiveness.

Anyone buying this? Yeah, me neither.

By midafternoon, my frustrations over the job search, my grief over Erin, and my feelings about Roxy got the better of me. I needed a break. So I hopped in my Kia Soul and drove a few miles south of town to the Hassayampa River Preserve.

While most of Wickenburg was mountainous desert, the Hassayampa River Preserve was a true oasis. The river itself ran mostly underground along the bedrock except in this one area, where it reached the surface and created a beautiful riparian environment full of wildlife, trees, and trails. It was enough to make you forget you were in the middle of the Sonoran Desert.

Since I was a kid, it had been my refuge from the craziness of life.

I followed the loop trail around Palm Lake, took a seat on the bench, and stared out at the water, watching the red-eared sliders sunbathe and listening to the bullfrogs croak amongst the cattails.

Mom had told me that moving back home could be a new start. But so far, it had been one disaster after another. Maybe I was cursed somehow. Like the Kennedys or the cast of *Poltergeist*.

The rapid hum of wings beating caught my attention. I looked up and expected to see a hummingbird. Or maybe a bumblebee or a dragonfly.

But it wasn't.

It was a Faerie. A pixie! Hovering just a foot away from my head. And she was staring at me. At least, I assumed she was female. I wondered if she was one of the ones I'd seen near the house.

"Um, uh, hello," I said, unsure of the protocol. "I'm Morgana."

The pixie laughed. As if I'd just told the funniest one-liner anyone had ever heard. I felt a little taken aback.

"And you are?" I continued.

"You're Morgana? Hoo-wee, I do not envy you."

"Why not?" What did this thing know about me?

"If I were you, I'd go back to the land of angels," she said, with a hint of warning in her response.

"Los Angeles? Why? What's going on?"

"Wait? You don't know?" She erupted into another fit of laughter. I was beginning to see why people considered Faeries so annoying. This one was certainly getting on my last nerve.

"Look, pixie, what is it I don't know?"

"You humans sure know how to make a mess of things. Messing with powers you don't understand. Life. And death. And life again. Sort of. And more death. Lots more death."

"What are you even talking about? And for the record, I am half Fae."

"Oh, you'll see. And it's going to take more magic than you seem to possess. Morgana the Half Fae. You're gonna need help."

"And I suppose you're the one to help me."

I was a little wary of asking this pipsqueak with wings for help for this whatever-it-was threat that was headed my way. Bargains with Faeries were not to be entered into lightly.

"Me? Oh, no, no, no! I want no part of this. No, thank you! You need the help of the old raven who lives in the mountain. Of course, she's as likely to eat you as she is to help you."

Again, fits of pixie laughter added to my chagrin.

"What raven? What mountain?"

Rather than answer my question, she flitted away over the lake, leaving a trail of sparkles I assumed was pixie dust in her wake. It smelled like strawberries and cream. I was pretty sure my magic didn't smell like that.

I sat there wondering if she might return when a couple of people walked by on the trail.

"Nice day," said a woman in a tangerine tank and white shorts.

The guy she was with held a camera with a long lens. Probably out shooting nature photos.

I was tempted to ask them if they'd seen the pixie. But then, they'd probably think I was crazy. "Yeah, I'm hoping it cools off more soon," I said, just making conversation.

They continued on the loop trail, and the bullfrogs kept droning on.

Should I tell my moms about this? They wouldn't think I was crazy. Probably. But what would I say about this vague, ominous warning? That someone was doing something they shouldn't? And something about life and death and life? It was just a whole lot of nonsense. Probably nothing more than a pixie playing games with my head. As if I needed that.

CHAPTER 19

Kari's name lit up my phone the next morning, a little after nine.

"Hey, how are you doing?" I asked her and then immediately realized what a stupid question it was.

"I'm... It's hard. Without her. Everything feels so... empty. Like a part of me is missing."

"I can relate. Anything I can do to help?"

"There is. We're getting together tonight. I'd like you to come."

"Who's we?"

"The Sand Witches."

"I don't know, Kari. I'm not even a formal member of my moms' coven. Not even sure I'm a witch. I really don't think I'd fit in." Not that I ever fit in anywhere. Not here in Wickenburg. Not in LA. Probably not even in the land of Faerie, if such a place really existed.

"Is your reluctance because of what Roxy did to you in school?"

Heat crept up my neck. "Maybe."

Mama Joyce's words about forgiveness and freedom

echoed in my skull like an Insta Reel on repeat. But our encounter with the Meanlindas and their jock boyfriends had brought the humiliation and shame into the forefront of my mind. The trauma still felt fresh.

Roxy might not have been the ringleader, but she was no innocent bystander either. Not when she knew damn well what we were going through.

"Look, Morgana, I don't blame you for being angry at Roxy. She bullied Erin and Angel too. They managed to forgive her and start fresh. Roxy's not the same person she was then, and I don't just mean her gender and pronouns. She's really kind."

Kari paused for a moment. "Besides, I really want you there."

"Why? What's going on?"

"We're having a séance."

I barked out a laugh before I could stop myself. I knew I shouldn't have. Kari was grieving Erin's death, as we all were. But a séance? Seriously?

"Do people still do that?"

"Angel's hosted a few before. They're actually pretty good at it."

Angel. Of course. Who else would do such a thing? I loved them like a sibling, but they were just so damned theatrical sometimes.

"Good at what? Bumping tables and making lights flicker?" The latter was more my thing, I had to admit.

"Divination. Talking with the dead. With Samhain just two weeks away, the veil between worlds is already at its thinnest. Angel thinks they can reach Erin. Maybe we can find out who killed her."

My inner skeptic did a major eye roll. Then again, I'd recently found out I was half Fae with actual magic powers.

Who was I to throw shade at Angel's ghost-whispering skills?

I took a breath. "Fine. I'll be there. For Erin. And for you."

"Thank you. Angel says we could do it with four, but it's better with five."

"You really think they can contact the dead? It's not some mentalist trick?"

"I believe so. At least, I hope so." Her voice cracked. "I just want one last chance to say goodbye. And I want whoever did this to pay."

"Same. When and where are we meeting?"

"Midnight at Angel's place, just south of downtown. I'll text you the address. And Morgana?"

"Yes?"

"Thanks for trying to save her." Kari's voice was strained yet strong. "I'm glad she was with someone she loved in her final moments."

Loved. That word hit me hard in the feels.

"Why would she love me after everything I did?"

"Her romantic feelings may have faded, but she never stopped caring about you."

"Thank you. I'm glad she eventually found someone who deserved her."

"Thanks."

I shuffled toward the kitchen in search of more coffee when I heard Mom and Mama Joyce whispering behind their closed bedroom door.

"But what if it *was* her, Joyce?" Mom said. Her voice was muffled, but I could still hear the terror in her tone. "You don't know her like I did. She didn't just hold grudges. She went after people."

Who the hell was she talking about? I didn't normally

eavesdrop on my moms, but something told me this was connected to Erin's murder.

"She killed Oliver Jordan."

"The former mayor's brother?" Mama Joyce sounded skeptical. "As I recall, he died of a heart attack due to a congenital septal wall defect."

"That's what his family told the press. But it was her. Belladonna hexed him."

"Did you tell anyone?"

"Are you kidding? They'd have laughed at me."

"But why would she go after Erin?"

My phone pinged in my pocket—a text from Kari with directions to Angel's apartment. *Dammit!*

Their bedroom door opened. Mama Joyce stepped out, her expression carefully neutral. "Morgana? Did you need something?"

"Uh, no. I was just headed to the kitchen. Who's Belladonna?"

"Nobody."

"Nobody? Didn't sound like nobody. Sounded like..."

"Just someone from Mom's past, peanut," she said too quickly. "Nothing you need worry about."

I wanted to press, but her tone warned me to let it go.

I helped out Mom at the bookshop for several hours—stocking shelves, ringing up purchases, answering customers' questions as best as I could, though deferring to Mom or one of the other employees most of the time. A few asked about Erin's murder. Per Mom's instructions, I replied that we didn't know anything. Which was the truth. Mostly.

Around three, I came home and checked my emails. A few of the jobs I'd applied for had sparked requests for copies of my work. I submitted scripts I'd written for *LA Murder Squad* and a screenplay for a horror movie that I'd been paid for but that never made it to production. Now all I could do was wait.

The thought of resuming my Hollywood dream filled me with a flutter of hope. At the same time, I'd just made some friends. Real friends. Not the fake Hollywood "let's do lunch" types. Kari, Angel, Thalia, and, I had to admit, even Roxy, genuinely cared about each other. Part of me wanted in on that.

And of course, I still wanted to discover who had killed Erin and make sure the perpetrator was brought to justice, one way or another.

After dinner, I hung out with Mom on the back porch and talked about old times. Mama Joyce joined us when she returned from a client who thought she was going into labor—but nope, just Braxton-Hicks and first-time parent panic.

I kept quiet about the séance. Not that they'd think it was ridiculous. They were witches, after all. And Mom trusted Angel enough to feature them at the shop as a resident psychic and tarot reader. But if I told them we were seeking justice for Erin, they might not understand. Especially Mama Joyce.

At a quarter to midnight, I grabbed my purse and headed for the door—only to get zapped by the warded doorknob.

"Shit! Shit! Shit!" I shook my stinging fingers.

Mom had started setting the wards every night since Erin died. I racked my brain, trying to remember how to disarm them without getting fried.

I reached out with my mind, feeling the energy of the wards like an electric force field.

"Abre la puerta," a voice said behind me.

I nearly jumped out of my skin.

Mama Joyce grinned down at me, dressed in her scrubs. "Going somewhere?"

"Um, what are you doing up?" *When busted, use deflection.*

"I have a patient who's in labor. For real this time. And you?"

"Meeting up with Kari and the gang."

"Why so late? Not planning any Halloween pranks, are we?"

"No, nothing like that," I said, a smidge too breezily. "Just, you know, hanging out. Because we're witches. And we like to, you know, hang out at midnight. Do witchy things."

"Peanut..." She wasn't buying it. "What's really going on?"

"Oh, all right. Angel's having a get-together at their place. Fine, it's a séance. Okay?"

"A séance?"

"To say goodbye to Erin and help Kari get some closure."

I figured that'd be enough. But Mama Joyce always knew when I was holding back. "And?"

"And... I need some closure too."

She gave me the mom stare—quiet, serious, seeing straight through me. "Just be careful. There's a killer on the loose. They've already taken one of ours. Don't want to lose you too. Wait here."

She vanished down the hall and returned a moment later with a bracelet of black beads. "Black agate. For protection. Just in case."

Wasn't sure what good a bracelet would do against a crazed killer with a knife, but I slipped it on my wrist and hugged her. "Thanks, Mama."

We stepped outside, and Mama Joyce reset the wards. "How long do you think you'll be gone?"

"Maybe an hour. I didn't ask."

"Be safe. I love you."

"Love you too." I hugged her and climbed into my car.

Chapter 20

Angel's apartment complex consisted of four large mission-style buildings. I followed the signs upstairs to unit number 13, which seemed on-brand for Angel. I rang the buzzer.

A moment later, Angel opened the door, wearing their signature heavy eyeliner and black lipstick. Silver pentacles dangled from each ear. They leaned against the doorway and asked, "May I help you?"

"I'm here for the séance. Kari invited me."

"I know. I was beginning to think you weren't coming. On Lesbian Standard Time, are we, hermana?"

"Sorry. Mama Joyce caught me as I was leaving."

"Well, come on in. Don't want to keep the dead waiting. Not that they've got much else to do."

Candles flickered throughout the living room. I noticed the scent of palo santo, which Angel must have used to cleanse the space.

A bookcase held a dozen or so books and three times as many tarot decks, amidst a collection of small statues, alebrijes, crystals, spell jars, and a painted human skull that I suspected was real.

A round table stood in the center of the room, covered in a black tablecloth embroidered with a large silver pentacle. Kari, Thalia, and Roxy sat at three of the points—a yellow, red, and blue candle in front of them, respectively.

"Hey," Kari said with a weary smile. "I'm glad you came."

"Of course." I wanted to say something comforting but couldn't think of anything.

Thalia's expression was unreadable, though her retinas caught the candlelight like a predator's. Again, I wondered if she was Fae or perhaps some other supernatural creature.

Roxy looked as if she wanted to say something but didn't.

"Have a seat." Angel gestured toward an empty chair between Roxy and Thalia. A green candle glowed brightly at its point of the pentacle.

I would've rather sat between Angel and Kari. I might have forgiven Roxy, at least in theory, but I wasn't ready to sit next to her during a ritual or séance or whatever the hell this was.

And Thalia... Something about her scared me.

But I didn't want to be disruptive. So I held my tongue and took the offered seat. Angel sat in front of a purple candle.

The room was oddly quiet. No music or voices carrying through the walls from other apartments. Not a surprise, considering the hour. But there were also no dogs barking outside, no vehicles driving by on the street, no sound of night birds or crickets. It was unsettling, to say the least.

"Now that we're all here, take each other's hands," Angel

instructed. "Close your eyes and clear your mind of all distractions. Let it go blank. The veil between worlds is near its thinnest for the year. But even one stray thought could lead us off course as we reach across to the realm of the dead."

I tried to clear my mind. Instead, a thousand rabid brain squirrels scurried through my head. Erin's terrified face as she fought for life. Saffron in bed with the blond bitch. Mr. O'Brien's cruel words at the burial. The screen-writing jobs I was applying to. Where I might live if I moved back to LA. Roxy bullying me in school. Me breaking Erin's heart in front of everyone. Getting in Jimmie Collins's face at the restaurant. Detective Hatathlie's judgmental questions.

I opened my eyes, ignoring Angel's instructions. The green candle flickered before me. Earth. Grounding. Strength.

I once again closed my eyes and imagined roots extending out from my feet, reaching into the earth. My spirit connected with it, releasing the toxic flurry of thoughts. My mind quieted and connected to the others in the circle.

Angel's voice dropped to a reverent murmur. "We call upon the Dark Goddess, she who walks in shadow and goes by many names. Santa Muerte. Hekate. The Morrigan. Kali. Lilith. Dark Mother, guide us as we reach across the veil to our beloved sister, Erin Sagefire O'Brien."

Angel inhaled sharply. I felt a tug in my chest, as if something or someone pulled hard at my soul. My magic strained toward them, threads of energy stretching, inter-weaving. Would this work with me being Fae? Should I have warned them?

Energy circled clockwise around us, spiraling faster, tighter. The air thickened. What I could only describe as a doorway between worlds opened, like the parting of a theater curtain. And then—I felt them. Hundreds—perhaps thousands—of spirits gazed back at us across the portal. Anxious. Waiting. Yearning. Hungry.

The air in the room suddenly dropped twenty degrees. The smell of graveyard dirt and rot filled my nose. A shiver ran down my spine.

I drew in the deep pulse of earth—cool soil, damp roots, stone and bone beneath the desert—to steady myself and, by extension, our little circle.

"Erin Sagefire O'Brien, we call to you. Can you hear us?" Angel asked.

Nothing happened. None of the countless souls in the portal responded.

"Erin Sagefire O'Brien, we call to you," Angel said more forcefully. "Can you hear us? We are your coven mates. We come in love and peace."

Again, nothing but the anxious yet still energy from the other beings on the other side.

"Erin Sagefi—"

A soul-rending screech pierced the air, a keening that stabbed at my mind like knitting needles, filling me with a primal terror. My stomach lurched. Every childhood nightmare, every buried trauma, rose like bile in my throat.

Danger! a voice in my head screamed at me. *Run! Run now!*

Just Angel being theatrical. It has to be, my rational mind assured me. But the biting chill in the air and my instinct to flee told me otherwise.

I took in a long breath, grounding myself. Roots to earth.

"Why...." The voice was wrong. Like nails on a chalkboard. Echoing as if it came from everywhere.

I squeezed open an eye. My breath billowed in frosty clouds of mist, illuminated by the guttering candlelight.

And for an instant, it looked like Erin's face, spectral and ghastly, before vanishing once again.

Angel sat with eyes clenched tight, lips firmly shut, face pale as bone.

"Why... have you... done thisssss?" the ragged voice hissed. Not Angel or anyone else in the group.

"Erin Sagefire O'Brien, we come in love and peace." Angel's voice shook with terror.

"Nooo... blooooood... pain... anger... revenge..." Every word was a stab of agony in my brain.

I tried desperately to ground, to strengthen, but it was too much. That voice... It was Erin's. And yet... it wasn't.

The spiral of energy spun out of control. The air buzzed with static. Shelves rattled. The candles sparked wildly before going black.

"Blood... pain... anger... revenge... blood... pain... anger... revenge..."

I ripped my hands free from Roxy and Thalia, as if shocked by a supercharged version of Mom's wards. The portal slammed shut like a vault door, reverberating in my chest. Then came silence so absolute it pressed against my eardrums.

My body trembled, and I gasped for breath. The room was pitch-black except for a dull glow leaking through the blinds. The smell of graveyard dirt and rot still filled the air.

Kari crumpled in on herself, hands clamped over her face as ragged sobs tore from her throat.

Roxy knelt beside her, murmuring soft reassurances that barely hid the tremor in her voice. "Shh... it's okay. You're safe. We've got you."

Thalia clicked a lighter and relit the candle in front of her. The flame danced in her eyes, which blazed with fury and uncertainty.

"What the hell just happened?" I demanded of Angel. "This better not be any of your cheap theatrics."

They stared blankly at the table, visibly shaken. "I... I don't know what that was. Nothing like this has ever happened before. Not in eight years of communing with the dead."

"I think... I think I know." Kari wiped her face with the back of her sleeve. "We... We need to go to Erin's grave."

"What? Why?" I asked.

"You don't think..." Angel started.

Kari nodded vigorously. "Yes."

"But how? Who would do something like that?" Roxy looked bewildered.

Kari shrugged. "Checking her grave is the only way to know for sure."

"Know what?" I asked. "What happened?"

"Necromancy," Thalia said. "Someone brought Erin back."

A memory surfaced. Erin dying on the sidewalk. No, not dying. Dead. No pulse. But then I sent my Fae magic into her. To save her. She had started to revive. What if... No! I couldn't have. Could I?

"Necromancy isn't real," I said. But the words felt hollow. Even to me.

"We have no choice." Angel's tone shifted—hard, certain. "We need to check her grave. See if it's been... disturbed."

Chapter 21

Call me a party pooper, but I wasn't keen on cramming into Roxy's SUV with the other Sand Witches for a late-night visit to Wickenburg Cemetery.

My rational brain insisted this was a complete waste of time. Magic might be real, and sure, I was half Fae. But reanimated corpses? Really? I didn't think so.

Death was death. No one came back from that. No one. Even magic had limits.

And yet, there I was, trailing after Angel and the others among the tombstones, using our phones as flashlights.

Granted, after what just happened, I did *not* want to be alone. That spectral voice still echoed in my mind like an earworm. I feared it would be haunting my dreams for a long, long time.

"Anyone remember where she was buried?" I asked.

The funeral had been easy to find—just followed the crowd. But that was in daylight. In the dark, with only the light from our phones to guide us, I had no idea where Erin's grave was.

"Section six, row D," Kari said.

"Over here." Thalia jogged ahead and stopped two-thirds of the way up the hill. The rest of us hurried after her.

A red marble headstone gleamed in the beam of her light, a mound of freshly turned soil at its base. But in the center of the mound, a large dark hole gaped.

Anywhere else, I might have assumed this was the entrance to a coyote den. But this was no animal burrow. Something had dug its way out.

A faint whiff of embalming fluid drifted on the breeze, a scent I recognized from a funeral home tour I took while researching *LA Murder Squad*.

Beneath it lurked something worse—the unmistakable stench of rotting flesh combined with a grimy tang that clung to the back of my throat. An unsettling sense of magic prickled at the base of my skull, like a spider picking its way through the neurons of my brain.

My stomach lurched. Something was deeply wrong.

"No!" Kari wailed. "This can't be happening."

I shook my head, trying to make sense of what I was seeing. "How could she dig her way out? How could she escape the casket?"

I didn't know what terrified me more—that Erin had become a zombie, or that I was the one responsible for raising her from the dead.

And then I remembered my encounter with that damned pixie. What did she say? Something about messing with powers I didn't understand. Powers of life and death. She was talking about me trying to save Erin. What had I unleashed?

"She couldn't," Roxy insisted. "This is someone's sick joke. First, they killed her. Now they're trying to make it look like someone brought her back."

"Who would do this?" Angel asked. "And why?"

"I can think of some people," Thalia said. "Your former schoolmates, for starters. The ones who harassed us at the Wicked Grille."

I considered the possibility. "I don't know. They're assholes. Might have even killed her. But making it look like she rose from the dead? What would be the point?"

"This isn't a prank." Angel pointed at the hole. "See the patterns in the dirt? No shovel marks—those are hand-prints. Erin clawed her way out."

Thalia crouched beside the grave and inhaled deeply. "Angel's right. I can smell the magic. Necromancy."

"And that voice…" Angel winced. "¡Ay, Santa Muerte!"

The memory sent a chill into my mind as well, raising the hairs on the back of my neck. "But who would know how to do this?"

"No one in the coven," Angel said. "Necromancy's strictly forbidden."

"I think I know," Kari said quietly. "Before Erin joined the coven… she studied with someone else. Another witch."

"Who?" I asked.

"I don't recall her name, but she had Erin doing dark magic. Things so horrible she refused to talk about it. Now I'm wondering if this witch found out Erin died—and brought her back?"

"Or murdered Erin in the first place," Thalia growled.

Roxy shook her head. "Might explain why her murder looked like a ritual sacrifice. Maybe it was."

"I overheard my moms talking in their room earlier," I said. "They think a woman named Belladonna might have gone after Erin. Someone Mom knew who used magic to kill people."

A light went on in Kari's eyes. "Belladonna. That was her name. She was the witch Erin studied with. If anyone could do something like this, it would be Belladonna."

"The thing is, I didn't smell any magic at the scene. I'm pretty sure someone staged it to look like a ritual killing."

Angel pointed at the hole in the ground. "Does this look staged to you?"

The combined stench of rotting flesh, embalming fluid, and blood told me it wasn't. "No, this is real." I swallowed hard. "So, is Erin a zombie now?"

Kari's face looked pained. "Technically, a revenant. But yeah."

"Why would her former mentor do this?" Roxy frowned.

"I don't know. Erin was terrified she might come after her. Hoped never to cross paths with her again. She kept protections everywhere—her purse, her car, our home."

A car pulled into the cemetery lot, its headlights sweeping toward us.

"Who the hell's that?" I switched off my phone light. The others did the same.

"Beats the hell outta me," Angel said.

"Trouble," Thalia said with a growl.

The driver emerged, flashlight in hand, and marched up the hill toward us.

"What are you people doing here?" barked an authoritative male voice.

I shined my phone light at him. A cop. *Busted!*

"Visiting a friend," I said, trying to sound casual.

"Cemetery closes at sundown." The officer reached us and looked down at the grave. His eyes narrowed when he noticed the hole. "What the hell are you people doing? Desecrating a grave is a felony."

"It wasn't us, Officer," Roxy explained. "We found it like this."

But the officer was already calling for backup on his radio.

"Vamanos," Angel whispered.

The officer drew his sidearm. "You people aren't going anywhere. Except to the station to answer questions."

Nope, not happening, buddy!

I closed my eyes and tried to summon wind.

And... nothing happened. *Dammit!*

Dust devil, I summon thee, I pleaded—to the Universe, the Goddess, the Fae, or anyone who might be listening.

Again, nothing. *Because, of course, my magic fails when I need it.*

My mind spiraled with worst-case scenarios—us getting arrested, not just for disturbing Erin's grave but for her murder. No way would the cops believe someone used necromancy. Or that it wasn't us.

The memory of Erin's death rose again. Blood all over her pale face. Her skin cold. Then suddenly, she was gasping for breath, for words. Eyes wild with terror and desperation.

Without warning, a gust of wind, sand, and dust blew all around us. It worked!

"Run!" I shouted.

We raced blindly through the blowing dust and pitch-black darkness. Twice I tripped over grave markers, and once I nearly slammed my head into a gravestone.

Gunshots rang out. I prayed to the Goddess and the Fae that we wouldn't be hit.

Roxy's SUV headlights flashed in the dark ahead, the doors unlocking with a beep. More gunfire split the night.

"Get in!" she shouted.

She didn't have to say it twice. We dove in and hit the floor as Roxy threw it into gear and sped off.

CHAPTER 22

WE RODE in silence back to Angel's apartment. Did they know that I'd summoned the dust storm? Did they suspect I was Fae?

When Roxy parked in the apartment complex lot, I noticed a bullet hole in the rear door—right where I'd been sitting. Another had punched through the interior, inches from my leg. It must've just missed me. Maybe the Goddess was looking out for me after all, or maybe the Fae were. Or maybe I was just lucky.

"Thanks for getting us out of there," I said to Roxy, still feeling ambivalent toward her.

She hugged me, and I didn't pull away. It felt... good.

"You're welcome. Get home safe, okay?"

I nodded. "Kari, you going to be okay?"

She looked like she was in shock. Expression vacant. "I'm... I'm okay. Just trying to make sense of everything."

"We'll figure out who did this. Somehow." I wasn't sure I believed it, but it felt like the right thing to say. "And we'll recover Erin's body and lay her to rest."

The five of us gathered into a group hug—even Thalia,

who always seemed standoffish. We were a bunch of freaks. Misfits. Gaia help us—we were the Sand Witches.

THE NEXT MORNING, I woke from another nightmare of me running from an unseen terror. Clearly a stand-in for whatever killed Erin. But the real nightmare, the one that set my pulse racing, was the possibility that I had accidentally turned Erin into some sort of zombie-ghoul-revenant thing.

Goddess! If the others found out I was to blame, who knew what they'd do? I'd probably lose the only friends I had in town.

When I walked into the kitchen, Mom was sitting alone at the table, which was covered with dishes of food— scrambled eggs, French toast, bacon, sausage, fruit salad.

"Is there a coven brunch this morning I didn't know about?" I poured myself a cup of coffee, fixed a plate, and sat next to her.

"What? Oh, this?" She blinked at the food, as if she'd just noticed it all. "Guess I went a little overboard, huh? You know me—I cook when I'm stressed."

"Or high." I'd caught a whiff of weed coming off her.

"Yeah, I was as stoned as Medusa's boyfriend last night."

"What're you stressed about?" She was always a cup-half-full person, even when the world was a dumpster fire —which it definitely was at the moment.

"Everything. Hoping you'll find a new job you'll love as much as the last one. Still coming to terms with Erin's death, of course. And avoiding the sensationalized news coverage, which has brought sales at the shop to a grinding halt." She sighed. "But with a little luck, the Fall Festival should give us a boost. Halloween tends to bring the witch out in people. You planning on going?"

"When is it?"

"Starts tomorrow and goes the weekend."

"I suppose. Not like I have any other plans." Aside from figuring out how to undo reanimating my ex's corpse.

"You mind helping out with the shop's booth?"

"Sure."

"Also, the coven's having our Samhain ritual on Saturday at midnight. We're having a party afterward. Midnight margaritas and everything. You interested in joining us?"

Samhain was the biggest holiday on the Pagan Wheel of the Year. Like Christmas and Mardi Gras rolled into one.

"Yeah. I'm in."

"Wonderful," she said. "How'd the séance go?"

"I... uh... How'd you know about the séance?" I felt like a teenager again, getting busted for sneaking out after curfew.

"Mama told me. She got in an hour ago. She's sleeping now."

I needed to tell her about the previous night's events and find out who Erin had studied with before joining the coven.

"It didn't exactly go as planned," I said.

Before I could continue, a loud knock rattled the door, followed by a rapid-fire chime of the doorbell. Who the hell could that be? An overzealous Amazon delivery driver? A reporter determined to interview Mom or me about Erin's murder? Another Jehovah's Witness trying to convert my moms from their witchy ways?

"I'll get it," I told her, wanting to spare her from talking to the press.

But when I opened the door, I learned it wasn't a reporter. Or a Jehovah's Witness or even an Amazon delivery driver.

Detective Hatathlie stood on the porch, flanked by two linebacker-sized cops.

Crap! This can't be good.

"Can I help you?"

"Morgana Quinn, you need to come with me."

Shit. Did the cop at the cemetery identify us?

Of course he had. The press had splashed my face on stories with headlines that read "Emmy Winner Finds Body at Shocking Crime Scene" and "Crime Writer Involved with Ritual Murder." No doubt a cop would recognize me at this point.

"Why?" I asked. "I haven't done anything."

Mom stepped up beside me. "Detective? What's going on?"

"Morgana needs to come with us to answer some questions," Hatathlie said.

"I already answered your questions after we found Erin's body."

"There've been new developments."

"What developments?"

Was this about us being at the cemetery? Would she accuse me of grave robbing?

"Three more bodies. Found this morning."

I did a double take. "What?"

Mom gasped. "More people have been killed?"

My heart clenched. Had Erin's killer struck again? Or had Erin's zombified corpse... No! Not possible.

"Who?" I asked, trying to stay calm and hoping it wasn't any of the Sand Witches.

"Best if we discuss this at the station."

"Why me? I haven't done anything."

Mom stepped between the cops and me. "Seriously, Detective? You're accusing my daughter of murder?"

"I'm not accusing anyone, ma'am. But I do have questions."

I sighed. "Fine. Let me get dressed first."

"I'll call Douglas Tremball," Mom said. "He's a lawyer. Don't say a word till he gets there."

"Don't bother," I said, against my better judgment. "I can handle this."

The truth was I couldn't afford a lawyer. I barely had any savings. And I didn't want to further burden my mothers with my problems. Besides, I'd learned a lot about the law and police procedure while writing for the show. I hadn't done anything wrong, aside from accidentally reanimating a corpse. That wasn't technically a crime.

"Morgana, this is serious. You need legal representation."

"Mom, it's okay. I'll be back soon."

Ignoring Mom's pleas, I let Detective Hatathlie drive me to the station. They stuck me in a cold room with cinderblock walls, a small frosted-glass window, and a Formica table bolted to the floor.

After what felt like forever, Detective Hatathlie walked in, carrying a thick case folder.

"You want anything? Soda? Coffee? Bottled water?" she asked, like this was a friendly visit.

"What I *want* is to go home. So why am I here?"

"Three more people are dead."

"So you said. Who?"

"We'll get to that. Were you at the Wicked Grille a few nights ago?"

How the hell did she know that?

"Yes. Along with a hundred other people. What's that got to do with anything?"

"Were you dining alone?"

"I was with friends. Why?"

"Who were you with?"

"Angel Lopez, Roxy Monroe, Kari Sullivan, and a woman named Thalia something-or-other."

"You have an altercation with anyone while you were there?"

From her tone, she already knew the answer and was looking to catch me in a lie.

Nice try, Detective. But I'm not falling for your traps.

"Some people from high school walked over to our table and harassed us."

"Names?"

"Melinda Fox, Linda Swilling, Dave Talbot, and Jimmy Collins."

"Did things get physical?"

"No." Making a lightbulb explode didn't count, did it?

A slight breeze brushed a strand of hair across my face with a faint whiff of creosote. *Keep it together, girl.*

"Did you or your friends threaten them?" she pressed.

"No. They threatened us. Dave threatened to burn us for being witches. Are you going to charge them with assault?"

Again, she ignored my question. "Where were you last night between nine and one o'clock?"

"At home." At least for most of it.

"All night?"

"Where would I go in Wickenburg that late? It's not like there's any queer-friendly bars in town."

"Can anyone confirm you were at home?"

"My moms."

"The one who smelled like weed when we picked you up this morning? Not exactly a solid alibi."

"What do you want me to say? I didn't realize I'd need an alibi, or I'd have made sure I had more reliable witnesses." My snark wasn't helping, but I couldn't help myself. "What's going on here? Who was killed?"

Now I was starting to rethink Mom's offer to call a lawyer.

No! I told myself. *I won't saddle my mothers with legal bills when I didn't do anything wrong.*

"What happened at the Wicked Grille after they threatened you?" She was circling back on the timeline. Another classic technique to catch inconsistencies.

"I told them to go to hell and went home."

"The friends you were with—they're members of your coven?"

"It's not my coven. I'm not a member." *Yet.*

"Right. Your mothers' coven. But your friends are members, right?"

"I don't know who's a member and who's not."

"Did anyone in your group threaten to kill James Collins?" A repeated question, fishing for a slipup.

"Not that I recall."

She shot me a disbelieving look. "You sure about that?"

"Thalia said if they kept harassing us, she'd make them regret it."

I wasn't going to go into details about her threatening to rip them apart with her bare hands.

"How about Linda Swilling? Any threats against her?"

"Not that I recall."

"And Charlie Ralston?"

"What about him?"

"Did you or your friends threaten him?"

"What? No! Why would we do that? He invited us and even comped our dinners. Charlie's great. Why would you ask that?" Unless...

Hatathlie slid over photos from the case folder she'd

brought in. The first was of Jimmie, his chest sliced open, exposing his lungs. A second photo showed Linda Swilling's face and neck, torn up the same way, eyes open but sightless. Then another—someone's decapitated body, bloodied and slashed beyond recognition. I guessed this was Charlie.

I'd seen plenty of crime scene photos during my research for *LA Murder Squad*. They hadn't bothered me. I wasn't squeamish. But these photos sent a chill up my spine.

Four murders in the small town where I grew up.

My gorge rose. *Do not puke in the interrogation room! Do not!*

"When?" I managed to gasp out.

"Town coroner puts time of death between nine o'clock and one last night."

"Why would someone kill Charlie?"

"You don't seem surprised Jimmie and Linda are dead."

"I am, but... Jimmie's a prick. Or was. Pissed off a lot of people. Linda wasn't much better. They used to bully me in school. But Charlie? He seemed like a nice guy."

"Did you and your friends kill Jimmie and Linda?"

"What? No! We're not murderers."

"Sure about that? You move back to town. Next day, your ex turns up dead. Followed by your high school bullies and your ex's business partner. Same slashing knife wounds. And you being a screenwriter for *LA Murder Squad*."

"It's a stupid coincidence. We didn't do anything."

"When do you go back to work?"

"What?"

"To your screenwriting job. I assume you're on a break."

"Not sure."

"Because you got fired from the show. Isn't that right?"

Shit, she'd been checking up on me. What else did she know?

"Yes, the studio replaced the whole writers' room with new people."

"Must've pissed you off. Especially after you won them a slew of Emmys."

"I was a little frustrated. But I'll find another job soon." I hoped.

"And Saffron Blaise. You two looked awful cozy strolling the red carpet. What'd she say about you moving back to Arizona?"

"Who says I moved? Can't a girl visit her folks once in a while? She's filming the next season of the show." That part was true.

"You didn't kill her, too, did you?"

"Dammit! I didn't kill anyone." The overhead lights flickered. *Keep it together, girl.*

"I'm five foot two, Detective. Jimmie was, like, a foot taller than me and jacked. Probably outweighed me by fifty pounds or more. How could I possibly kill him? And Linda. And Charlie."

"Do you own any knives?"

"No."

"Or athames?"

"Again, no."

"But your moms do, right? They use them in their practice as witches."

I didn't answer.

She stared at me and waited, using silence to pressure me to say more. But I knew the waiting game and remained quiet.

Finally, she said, "In our previous interview, you didn't mention you and Erin O'Brien had been lovers."

"We weren't lovers. We dated. Briefly. In high school— seven years ago. But we lost touch."

"Until the day before she was murdered."

Emotions surged through me. The fluorescent light overhead flickered again. "She dropped off sandwiches at my mom's bookshop. Like I told you."

"Did she break your heart? Is that why you killed her?"

"I didn't kill her."

The room filled with the pungent aroma of creosote and ozone. The lights flickered like a manic strobe at a club, then winked out with a sharp pop. Dim daylight filtered in through the small window.

Dammit! Get control of yourself.

Hatathlie regarded the darkened lights for a moment, then turned back to me with an expectant look on her face. "Not even after she dumped you?"

Her probing questions were designed to throw me off balance. To trigger an emotional reaction. And so far, it was working.

"She didn't dump me," I said, steadying my voice. "I dumped her."

"Why? Did she cheat on you?"

"No. I was scared to come out. People at school made our lives hell."

"People like Linda Swilling and Jimmie Collins?"

"Among others."

"You think they might have killed Erin?"

"Maybe. I don't know. At the Wicked Grille, Dave Talbot said Erin got what she deserved. Sounded like a confession."

"Except everything about Erin's murder points to a ritual killing. The candles, the pentagram and symbols drawn in chalk. The ritual knife. And all in front of your mom's bookstore. Looks more like the work of witches."

"The crime scene was staged, obviously. My moms' coven only uses magic to help people. Never to harm. They have very strict rules about that."

"Melinda Talbot says you used magic to make her hair fall out in school. Is that true?"

It took me a second—Melinda Talbot. She must've married Dave. Of course.

"You think magic is real? That it can make someone's hair fall out?" I asked Hatathlie.

"I grew up in Chinle. There was a woman on the rez—a witch—who used magic to destroy crops, kill goat herds, and to hurt people she disliked. Is it real? I believe so. And those who use it are evil."

"You're Navajo?"

"Yes."

"Your people also have healers who use magic, don't they?"

"We have hataałii—medicine women and men who use herbs and other tools to heal our people. But they are different from adiłgąshii—witches who use magic to harm others."

"The coven only uses magic to help and protect. We're not evil."

"You just said 'we.' Are you a witch or not?"

"I don't know what I am." That was the truth. "I stayed away from it in high school to avoid being bullied."

"Where were you really last night between nine and one?"

"I didn't kill Jimmie, Linda, or Charlie, if that's what you're thinking."

"Where were you?"

She held my gaze, playing the waiting game. But I wasn't going to be the first one to speak.

Five minutes later, she said, "Maybe you didn't kill them."

"Of course I didn't."

"But an officer reported trespassers at the Wickenburg Cemetery after hours. He recognized you from your photograph from internet reports on Erin's murder."

"So? That doesn't make me a killer."

"And a Chevy Trailblazer belonging to Roxanne Monroe was spotted in the cemetery parking lot."

"So what? We were visiting a friend's grave after hours. We left as soon as the officer showed up and told us to leave. You want to issue us a fine?"

"Who else was there?"

"Why do you care?"

"Erin O'Brien's grave was desecrated. Her casket was torn open, and her body is missing. What the hell were you and your friends doing last night?" Her tone was sharp, eyes blazing.

So Erin's body really was gone. I'd been clinging to the hope this was all some sick joke, that she couldn't be a zombie, even though I smelled dark magic at her grave.

Guilt hammered at my heart. I shouldn't have used magic to save her when I didn't know what I was doing. But what else could I have done?

"Her body was already gone when we arrived."

"Why were you there?"

Because I'd accidentally reanimated her corpse, I thought.

"We were trying to reach out to her spirit. To find out who killed her." Technically true, though that was before our trip to the cemetery.

"By digging up her corpse?"

"No! I told you, it was already gone."

"Who was with you and Roxy?"

"Kari, Angel, and Thalia. But we wouldn't steal her body. We're not into necromancy."

"Who is?"

"How should I know? I just got back into town."

"Right before these murders started happening. Four bodies inside of a week. How did you know Charlie Ralston?"

"I didn't."

"You never met him?"

"Only on the day we were at the restaurant. He comped our dinners. He was a nice guy. We'd have no reason to hurt him."

"Why do I sense you're holding something back?"

"I'm not." *Aside from me being a half-Fae freak who raised my ex from the dead.*

A knock at the door startled me. Detective Hatathlie opened it a crack. After a quick exchange of words, a man in a rumpled suit stepped in.

"Ms. Quinn, I'm Douglas Tremball. Your mother hired me to represent you. Don't say another word."

Chapter 23

After Detective Hatathlie stepped out, I brought Douglas Tremball up to speed.

When I was done, he said, "You should not have talked to her without me there."

"But I didn't kill anyone."

"Doesn't matter. You're a suspect for four murders, as well as grave robbing."

"Based on what evidence? That I just happened to move back home right before this started? How exactly does a woman my size stab a big guy like Jimmie to death? And take out two other people at the same time? You think I'm some sort of ninja?"

"And yet here you are being interrogated by the police. You need my help, Morgana. Let me help."

When Hatathlie returned, he asked, "Is Ms. Quinn under arrest?"

"Not at this time. But we still have—"

"Then this interview is over. Good day, Detective."

He led me out without another word and offered to drive me home. I didn't argue.

On the way, he said, "If they come calling again, you call me. No ifs, ands, or buts."

"I can't afford you," I muttered. "My moms can't either."

"Your mothers would rather pay my fee than see you in prison. Innocent people get convicted every day because they didn't have a good lawyer. You want to be one of them?"

"No."

When I got home, Mama Joyce was sitting in the living room with Mom. I could smell magic in the air. A protection spell, maybe?

The second I closed the front door, they both rushed in for a hug.

"What happened at the police station, peanut?" Mama Joyce asked when we sat down. "They didn't arrest you, did they?"

"No, not yet anyway."

"What happened last night?" Both she and Mom looked worried.

I told them everything—about the séance, the ghastly voice, the grave. By the end, guilt sat heavy in my chest, tight and suffocating.

"It was me. I brought Erin's body back to life," I said, choking back tears. "When I tried to save her."

"Nonsense, honey," Mom said gently. "You have a gift, but I don't think even your Faerie magic includes necromancy. I don't know anyone capable of such dark and powerful magic."

"But Erin was dead when we found her. And I... I revived her somehow."

"How do you know she was dead?" Mama Joyce asked pointedly.

"I couldn't find a pulse. And her skin was cold."

"Jellybean, you were in shock. It's hard to find a pulse

when your own heart's pounding. And it was chilly that morning. Of course her skin would be cool to the touch."

"But she seemed so dead."

"Probably hanging on by a thread when you found her. Your magic might have revived her but didn't turn her into a zombie."

"There are countless people with near-death experiences," Mom added. "Revived, even after their hearts stopped for several minutes. But that isn't necromancy. And neither is your magic."

Mama Joyce nodded. "Breaking through a casket lid? Digging through six feet of earth? That takes a lot more than healing magic. That's dark spell work. Blood magic. Death magic. This is all someone's idea of a sick joke. Probably the same person who killed her in the first place, trying to pin this on our coven."

They clearly knew more about this than I did. But the guilt clung to me, heavy and persistent.

Then I remembered overhearing my moms talking the day before.

"Who's Belladonna?" I asked, my voice low. "I overheard you talking about her in your bedroom."

Mama's expression darkened. "That was a private conversation, baby girl. You shouldn't have been snooping."

"I wasn't snooping. I was walking past your door when you two were yelling."

Mom looked admonished. "Her name is Donna Loveless. But she called herself Belladonna. And honestly, it fit. She could be as toxic—and as deadly—as the plant she named herself after."

"Who is she? How did you know her?"

"We were friends as kids. Unfortunately, a man named Oliver Jordan molested her when she was twelve. He was her church's youth minister."

"Goddess... that's awful."

"When she told her parents, they didn't believe her. They called her a slut and accused her of smearing the name of a good man. Belladonna turned to witchcraft as a way to get revenge. She used magic to murder that youth minister."

Mama Joyce looked skeptical. "Officially, Mr. Jordan died of a heart attack."

"At twenty-eight? I don't think so. It was Belladonna Loveless. She admitted it to me."

"Not that you could blame her," I said.

"No, but her anger took over. Twisted her. She used magic to lash out at anyone she felt had wronged her. After a while, I didn't feel safe around her, afraid she'd turn on me too."

"Saffron could be like that," I said quietly.

"When I ended our friendship, she called me a traitor. Threatened to hex me. I had to shield myself with charms."

"And Erin studied with her?"

"Erin had wanted to join the Siblings of the Desert Moon, but she was only sixteen at the time. She couldn't join without her parents' permission. So she went searching for a different teacher. Unfortunately, she found Belladonna."

"You think Belladonna killed Erin? And the others?"

"She's capable of it, I suppose. But when she hurts someone, she uses magic, not knives."

"Could she have raised Erin from the dead?"

Mom paused before answering. "Possible. She's gifted— but necromancy? That's advanced stuff. Not something she could do when I knew her."

"But you haven't seen her in years," Mama Joyce told her. "Who knows what that woman can do now? Jellybean, are you certain this wasn't some sick prank?"

I shook my head. "I wish it was. But the voice I heard during the séance... It scared the hell out of me. It wasn't like anything I've ever heard or felt before. And then when we got to Erin's grave, I could sense the magic. Dark. Angry. Twisted. It just felt wrong."

Mom went pale. "That's... troubling."

"What can we do?" Visions of a zombie apocalypse flickered through my mind. "Should we track down Belladonna Loveless and stop her somehow?"

"No," Mama Joyce said firmly. "Let the cops handle this."

"But someone's killing people and reanimating their corpses."

Mama Joyce fixed me with a stern look. "Sweet girl, you're brilliant. You've got a creative mind made for solving mysteries—that's why you're such a gifted writer. But this isn't a fictional murder mystery to solve. This is real. Let the professionals handle it."

I sighed. "Fine."

"And keep away from Belladonna Loveless," Mom added. "She's dangerous. Especially against a novice such as yourself."

"But I'm also half Fae. I used my magic to help us escape the cop at the cemetery."

"Exactly. You're already a prime suspect. You need to stay far away from all of this. We can't have you getting arrested—or worse." She took a breath. "We've got the wards up, and I'll make you a protective charm."

"I don't need a charm. I need to stop whoever's doing this."

"A noble goal. But it's not your fight." Mama Joyce squeezed my hand. "As your mother, I'm asking you to let it go."

Mom's brow furrowed. "Huh."

"What?" I asked her.

"Lenore always stops by for our morning tête-à-tête. But she hasn't shown up today."

I felt a jolt of unease. Had the killer hurt Mom's familiar too? "Maybe she's just out enjoying the cool autumn air," I said, hoping to reassure her.

"Maybe." She didn't look convinced. "I can still feel a connection, so she's alive. But she's far enough away that I can't hear her thoughts."

"She'll turn up," I said softly. "Oh, and thank you for sending Mr. Tremball. I'll pay you back somehow."

"Don't even think about it." Mom kissed my forehead. "Your freedom's worth any price."

"We always got your back, girl," Mama Joyce said. "You know that."

CHAPTER 24

WHILE EATING some of the breakfast Mom had made in her manic munchy state, I wondered if Hatathlie had questioned Kari and the others. Or was the detective fixated on me?

I thought about calling Kari but wasn't sure if she was up yet. So I sent her a text, letting her know about the other murders and that I had been questioned.

My mind then drifted to Roxy.

She was beautiful and kind and smart. She had a knack for letting you know she cared, that you mattered. I even found myself attracted to her, though I had no clue about her sexual orientation.

Which made it all the more painful to realize she'd been one of the asshole jocks, harassing Erin, Angel, and me in school. Even after all these years, the memories still hurt.

But then, who was I to judge? I'd denied being queer, too, just to survive. And I'd hurt Erin in the process.

Could I forgive Roxy? Did I really want to keep carrying around that resentment?

Simple answer was no.

Roxy had changed. Not just her gender or appearance —she wasn't the bully she used to be. Erin had forgiven her. Angel too. Maybe it was time I did the same.

And maybe, just maybe, I could start forgiving myself for how I treated Erin.

I turned my attention back to my job search. Still no offers. Just a bunch of scammy messages from job boards, all trying to hustle cheap labor.

No, thanks! Don't want to crank out screenplays for your script mill at fifty bucks a pop. Hard pass! And no, I don't want to drop a hundred bucks to enter your fake-ass screenwriting competition.

After following up on a few job leads, I started brainstorming a new project about a queer professional bounty hunter. I'd written two seasons for a police procedural, but writing a show about a bounty hunter could be a lot of fun. Somewhere between a cop and a vigilante, operating on the fringes of the law.

Was it likely to be picked up by a studio? Maybe. Maybe not. They kept cranking out spin-off series for *Bosch* and *Dexter*. So why not a series about a bounty hunter? About time for a crime series with a queer protagonist.

But as I tossed around character and story ideas, my mind kept drifting back to the recent murders in town and the horrifying thought that Erin had been turned into a zombie. Whether accidentally by me or intentionally by someone like Belladonna Loveless, I didn't know.

How exactly did necromancy work? Was Erin's soul still inside her reanimated body? Was she sentient? Or just a shambling, decaying monster hungry for human brains?

If Belladonna Loveless was responsible, would she go after Mom next?

Shortly after lunch, my phone rang, yanking me out of my thoughts.

"Hey, Kari," I said after her name popped up on the screen. "What's up?"

"I got your text about the other murders. Detective Hatathlie questioned me too. Roxy and Angel as well. I've spoken with my contact at Wickenburg PD. There's a lot of pressure from the town council to make an arrest."

"Feels like I'm her prime suspect. But I didn't kill her, Kari. I swear."

"I know." Her voice choked with emotion. "Meanwhile, Erin's out there somewhere. Probably alone, scared, in pain. You heard her screaming at the séance."

Pangs of guilt filled me. Belladonna Loveless may have been a crazy, evil witch, but why would she reanimate Erin's body? I remained convinced my failed attempt to save Erin with my Faerie magic was responsible.

"If Erin's a zombie, what can we do?" Could I somehow reverse what I'd done?

"She's not a zombie. She's a revenant. There may be a way to fix her and make her human again."

"Well, if I can help in any way..."

"Would you be willing to meet with us?"

"Who's *us*?"

"The Sand Witches."

"Not another séance." The first one was bad enough.

"No, nothing like that. I was thinking lunch at Daniela's."

Daniela's Cocina had been a Wickenburg landmark for decades, known for its authentic Mexican cuisine.

"Sure. Will Roxy be there?"

Kari sighed. "Look, I know you two have a history, but—"

"It's okay. I've forgiven her. I mean, after what I did to Erin, who am I to judge?"

"Then yes, she's coming. I've texted Angel and Thalia too. Meet you there in an hour?"

"I'll be there."

For once, I was the first to arrive. But just as I put a hand on the door handle, I stopped.

A Trump sticker was plastered to the window. Around it were more pro-MAGA stickers.

I was aghast. How could the Latinx owners of this restaurant be pro-Trump? Particularly since he'd sent his ICE stormtroopers to snatch anyone who looked like an immigrant.

All my life, I'd assumed my father was Latino. Even knowing that he was Fae didn't change the fact that I was petite with brown skin and black hair.

People assumed I was Latina. And many probably assumed I was undocumented. Because that was the mentality in towns like this.

I sent a text to Kari.

ME:

Daniela's has Trump stickers in their window. Not sure how welcome we'll be there.

KARI:

Yikes! How about Java Junction? S/B there in 5.

ME:

Meet U there.

JAVA JUNCTION WAS A BRIGHT, open café filled with warm sunlight and the rich, earthy scent of freshly roasted coffee.

A mural of a train crossing the desert at sunrise stretched across one wall.

It was early afternoon, and only a couple of patrons sat nearby, lost in their laptops.

The barista looked about our age, maybe a little younger, in a faded Phoebe Bridgers Punisher tour tee. A thin sunrise-orange braid draped down one side of her head, glowing against her chestnut hair.

I ordered a latte and a sandwich and grabbed a corner table.

CHAPTER 25

Kari, Roxy, and Angel arrived moments later.

"Disappointing about Daniela's," I said.

Angel shrugged. "Not surprising. An Anglo family bought the place out a few years ago but kept the name. Since then, the service and food have gone from amazing to mierda. Another Wickenburg institution gone down the tubes."

"Where's Thalia?" I asked.

Kari shook her head. "Haven't heard from her since last night. I'm a little concerned."

"You think something happened?"

"I'm sure she's fine," Roxy assured us. "Probably preparing for one of her desert survival classes. She often goes radio silent right before a class."

"Does she hate me for some reason?" *Like maybe she knows I'm Fae and doesn't trust me?*

"Of course not," Roxy said. 'Why would you think that?"

"Seems like she's always glaring at me."

"That's just Thalia," Angel replied with a smirk. "Don't take it personally."

"She doesn't hate you," Kari added. "She's just wary around new people. She'll come around."

"I hope so." *Until she finds out I'm Fae.*

"Morgana…" Roxy locked eyes with me. "I hope your being here means you don't still hate *me*."

An overwhelm of emotions clouded my thinking. I fumbled for words. "I… uh… Being a lesbian in this town… It's hard."

Her eyes glistened with tears. "And I only made it worse for you."

"But I know you had it rough being trans. Probably rougher. We both did stupid shit to fit in. I'm willing to let the past go and start fresh. Clean slate."

"Thanks, Morgana." Her voice was barely a whisper, and a smile tugged at her lips. "That means a lot to me. It's important we be there for each other with what's going on."

"Speaking of what's going on…" Angel said. "Seems that loca detective sure has a hard-on for our girl Morgana here. Seems convinced she's the Wickenburg Slasher."

"The what?" I nearly choked on my coffee.

"It's what my editor at the *Sun* dubbed the killer," Kari explained. "Now all the media are calling him, or her, that."

"Despite what Hatathlie thinks, I'm not the Wickenburg Slasher. Not my fault I move back to town right before a serial killer goes on a rampage."

"I've been doing a little digging into the detective," Kari continued. "She worked for the Navajo Nation Police until a few years ago, when she got herself into trouble."

"What'd she do?" Angel asked. "Arrest an innocent witch for murder?"

Kari shook her head. "Not exactly. A Navajo woman named Natalie Tsosie had disappeared. Missing and Murdered Indigenous Persons is an all-too-common issue.

But federal law limits the jurisdiction of Native police for major crimes like murder, kidnapping and rape."

"I've heard." I recalled seeing images of Indigenous women with red handprints across their faces, representing the missing and murdered women and the federal government's lack of response.

"The feds were doing nothing to find Ms. Tsosie. So Detective Hatathlie took matters into her own hands. She tracked down the woman's kidnapper, a white guy named Danny Glenn, who was attending NAU up in Flag. She got Glenn to confess to killing Ms. Tsosie and burying her in a shallow grave near the San Francisco Peaks."

"Good for her," Roxy replied.

"Unfortunately, the Coconino County Sheriff's Office let Glenn go, and prosecutors refused to take up the case, saying Hatathlie hadn't followed protocol. She was eventually suspended from the Navajo Police."

"That's so unfair," I said. "But why's she got a grudge against me and the coven?"

"Witchcraft is viewed differently in her culture. And I'm afraid that might be coloring her perspective."

"And putting my freedom at risk."

"Do you have an attorney?" Roxy asked.

I sighed. "Mom sent one, but I'd already talked to Hatathlie by the time he got there. I don't know what good he could've done. All she has is speculation. Besides, I can't afford an attorney, and neither can my moms."

"We'll help you pay for one, if need be," she assured me. "I have some savings."

"No, I don't want to be a burden to you. This is *my* problem."

"This is all our problem, hermana," Angel said. "We're the Sand Witches. We're familia. We stick together."

"If I can track down the real killer, maybe I can clear my name. I may only be a screenwriter, but I know how to think like a detective."

"The police aren't our only problem," Kari said solemnly. "Someone has turned Erin's remains into a revenant. Not only did it reanimate her body, it trapped her spirit. She's unable to move on. That's why she was screaming during the séance. She's in pain and probably scared. We have to help her."

My anxiety shot up at Kari's words. I still worried that it was my Fae magic that had brought her back from the dead. But what if it wasn't? What if it was this Belladonna Loveless? Or someone like her?

"It must've been the witch Erin trained with before she joined the coven," Roxy suggested. "What was her name?"

"Belladonna Loveless," I replied.

Roxy nodded. "Right. Who else would be capable of reanimating the dead?"

I can think of someone, I thought, squirming in my seat.

"I wonder if she's the same person as Sister Belladonna," Angel wondered, brow furrowed. "She's a psychic who runs a roadside shop off Highway 60 near Morristown."

"You know her?" Roxy asked.

"Stopped in once, a few years ago." Angel grimaced. "Total creep vibes. And you know me. I'm not easily wigged out."

"So how do we break the spell," I asked, "and free Erin's spirit to move on?"

"Cut off its head," Angel said grimly. "Like in *The Walking Dead*."

Kari shook her head. "Won't work. Revenants aren't zombies. The necromancy spell animates the whole body. It... It can keep going, even without a head."

"Yeah, really didn't need that image," Roxy muttered, grimacing.

"Then how do we stop it?" I asked.

"Three possibilities," Kari said. "Option one, reverse the necromancy spell."

"That means knowing exactly which spell was used," Roxy said. "We'd need the grimoire it came from."

Angel made a face. "Meaning tracking down the necromancer and stealing their grimoire? Sounds like a suicide mission. What's behind door number two?"

"Second option—kill the one who cast the spell."

"Trying to kill a powerful witch capable of necromancy also sounds like a suicide mission," I said, assuming it wasn't me.

"Agreed." Roxy nodded vehemently. "Besides, we're not killing anyone. No matter how horrible they are."

"Third option..." Again, Kari's face twisted with emotion. "We use fire. Burn the creature to ash."

"That might be our only real shot," I said. "But if Belladonna Loveless is behind this, she could throw something worse at us. We need help. Someone with serious magical firepower."

"Like whoever summoned that dust storm at the cemetery?" Angel turned to me with a smirk. "Nice work, Morg. Color me impressed."

"Wait—what?" I sputtered. "You think I did that?"

They shrugged. "Summoning a haboob out of nowhere? Not exactly in my wheelhouse. Roxy's the healer. Thalia's all about tracking and animal magic. Kari's got solid elemental chops, but... Kar, you ever pull off anything like that?"

"Way beyond my skill set." Kari met my eyes. "Was it you, Morgana?"

All three stared at me now, their eyes sharp, expectant.

Would they still accept me if I told them the truth—that I was Fae? Sure, most of us were queer, but at least they were human.

Well, maybe not Thalia. The jury was still out on her.

Before I could answer, Kari's phone rang.

"Hello? Thalia! Are you okay? Where?" A pause. "Okay, we're on our way."

Chapter 26

"What's going on?" I asked.

"Thalia's at the O'Briens'. Something's happened there. She wants us to meet her. Follow me."

I tossed my half-eaten sandwich and joined the others in a caravan heading north of town. We pulled up to a sprawling ranch house ringed with manicured shrubs, towering saguaros, and gnarled mesquite trees. Erin's childhood home.

Thalia stood at the foot of the stairs leading to the O'Briens' wraparound porch. She was dressed in a tank top and shorts. No sign of her Land Rover. *Did she walk here?*

I hadn't been here in years—not since Erin's parents banned me for having two moms, who were also witches.

As I stepped out of my car, I spotted paw prints in the sand. At first, I assumed they might be a dog's. But then I recalled lessons learned in a class on wildlife identification at the Hassayampa River Preserve years earlier.

The tracks aren't symmetrical, so not a dog's. Coyote, maybe? But there's no claw marks. Something with retractable claws. Feline. Bobcat? No, too large. Puma.

I knew pumas roamed the area. I'd seen one in our backyard once when I was a kid. They usually avoided people, except when food and water were scarce. But they were ambush predators. You didn't always see them coming. Until it was too late.

A chill raced down my spine. *Had a puma attacked the O'Briens?*

"What happened?" I asked. "Are the O'Briens okay?"

"I tracked the creature here," she replied.

"What creature?" Roxy asked.

"Erin's revenant."

Dread blossomed in my chest. "It came *here*? To Erin's parents' house?"

"From the cemetery, I tracked it to the wash that runs up behind the Wicked Grille."

"Where Jimmie, Linda, and Charlie were killed," Roxy said somberly.

Kari's face was a mask of disbelief and terror. "You don't mean she…"

Thalia nodded. "The creature killed them. I could smell it there. And here." Concern grew in Thalia's eyes.

"Oh my Goddess!" Roxy gasped. "She… it's… here? It went after her family?"

"Are they okay?" I asked.

"I don't know. I haven't gone in. I called as soon as I got here."

Angel looked as terrified as I felt. "It's not still here, is it?"

Thalia shrugged. "Don't know."

"We need to check on them," I said, pushing past old resentments. "Make sure they're okay."

"Her parents are bigoted assholes," Angel added. "You saw how her papi acted at the burial."

"But her sister isn't," Kari said, voice trembling. "We need to make sure they're safe."

We climbed the steps onto the wraparound porch, each creak of the wood tightening the knot in my gut.

The front door stood open. Parallel scratches tinged with reddish-brown streaks marked the door's tan paint. Not good.

I felt a cold prickling at the base of my skull. My nose filled with the combined scents of rotting flesh and something grimy. Dark magic. Had to be.

If I were a detective on *LA Murder Squad*, I'd be drawing my sidearm and calling for backup. But after Hatathlie's interrogation, I knew better than to expect help from the cops.

My heart raced as we stepped into the large entryway. Every instinct screamed at me to run. But if Erin's family were still alive, they may need our help.

"Hello? Sarah? Mr. and Mrs. O'Brien?" I called nervously.

There was no reply. The house was quiet, but a heavy dread hung over the place.

An overturned cherrywood console lay amidst shards of a ceramic vase. Evidence of a fight?

To the left, the cavernous dining room where I'd once shared dinner with Erin's family. To the right, a stuffy living room full of antique chairs no one actually sat in. Ahead, a dim hallway led to the kitchen and bedrooms.

"Maybe we should split up," I suggested. "This place is massive. Erin's family could be anywhere."

Angel shook their head vehemently. "I do not want to face this creature alone. Better to stick together. Safety in numbers and all that."

"It went this way." Thalia said, already striding down the hall. The rest of us followed.

Family photos hung askew on the walls. A hallway lamp lay smashed on the floor. Drops of blood trailed ahead, deeper into the house.

We entered a sprawling, high-end kitchen. Pots and pans dangled above a butcher-block island outfitted with a gas grill. The stench of blood was suffocating.

I slipped on the slick tile and caught myself with the fridge handle. Water, shattered glass, and crushed flowers littered the floor. And then I saw him.

Mr. O'Brien's mangled body sprawled near the shattered pantry door, eyes frozen open, staring blankly at the ceiling. His throat was torn open, and deep gashes lay across his arms and chest. A chef's knife rested just beyond his reach.

"Damn," I whispered.

Thalia knelt and pressed two fingers to his neck. "He's gone."

Bile rose in my throat. Phillip O'Brien had been a bigoted asshole, but he didn't deserve this. Again, I wrestled with the horrible possibility that I, and not Belladonna Loveless, had turned Erin into a homicidal monster.

Roxy and Kari ducked into the pantry.

"Mrs. O'Brien's in here," Roxy called. "She's hurt bad but still alive!"

I poked my head in. Mrs. O'Brien lay curled in a fetal position on the floor, deep lacerations across her back. I wanted to help—to heal her—but what if I made things worse? What if I turned her into another revenant?

Roxy grabbed a kitchen towel and pressed it against the wounds. "Kari, do they have a first aid kit?"

Kari stood frozen, staring at the blood. "I... I don't know. I've only been here a few times. Can you heal her?"

"My magical healing kit's at home. But I can slow the bleeding. We need to call 911."

"Already on it," Angel said, phone pressed to their ear.

A crash echoed from deeper in the house, followed by an inhuman shriek.

My blood turned to ice. "Oh, shit."

"I've got this," Thalia said.

My body trembled with fear, sadness, and guilt. If my magic had reanimated Erin's corpse, I had a responsibility to stop it. "I'm coming with you."

Chapter 27

THALIA and I crept deeper into the house, following the trail of dark magic prickling at the edge of my mind. We passed a guest room then a study straight out of Sherlock Holmes.

With each step, I reached for my magic. But what good was wind or flickering lights against a revenant?

Maybe I could try to summon fire again. All I needed was a little practice, right? No time like the present.

Another bloodcurdling scream ripped through the house, drawing us toward Sarah's bedroom. We stepped inside, and my blood turned to ice.

The grimy, putrid stench of dark magic filled my lungs. Across the room stood Erin, or what was left of her. Her eyes were sunken orbs. Blood streaked her face and the tattered pastel-pink dress she'd been buried in.

Her skeletal fingers clawed at the wall, leaving streaks of blood and gore. No sign of Sarah. I wasn't sure if that was a good thing or not.

"Erin?" I said tentatively.

She turned toward me, tilting her head like a predator. Could she see me through those empty eye sockets?

"Erin, it's me. Morgana. Are you in there?"

Her jaw worked open and shut as if trying to speak. Only a hissing escaped her rotting lips.

Out of the corner of my eye, I saw Thalia kick off her shoes then peel off her shirt and shorts. What the hell? We were facing our undead friend, and she was doing a striptease?

Her body shimmered and blurred in a swirl of mystical energy. The musky scent of a wild predator filled the air. A different kind of magic.

She dropped to all fours as tawny fur erupted across her body and a tail sprouted. Her legs shortened, and her head reshaped. Thalia had become a massive, pissed-off puma.

She's a shifter? That explains the prints outside. But holy shit! I'm trapped between a revenant and a mountain lion.

I backed into the far corner, heart hammering, desperate not to get caught between these two other-worldly predators.

Thalia growled, a low, guttural sound that rumbled deep in her chest as she prowled toward the revenant. Her golden eyes locked on the creature, ears flat, tail lashing. Every muscle in her sleek feline body coiled with threat.

The revenant let out a shrick—a raw, bone-rattling sound of rage and grief. She bared her teeth and launched herself in a blur of bloodstained limbs and snapping jaws.

Thalia sprang. The two collided in midair then slammed to the floor in a snarl of claws, teeth, and ragged limbs. The revenant's nails raked across Thalia's flank, carving deep furrows into her fur.

Thalia roared and bit down hard on Erin's shoulder, yanking her off balance and driving her into the dresser, which cracked on impact.

Erin thrashed wildly, flailing her skeletal limbs with unnatural strength. One blow clipped Thalia's ear, sending a spray of blood across the wall. But Thalia didn't let up. She clamped her jaws around Erin's upper arm and shook.

I stood frozen against the far wall, my breath caught in my throat. The room reeked of blood and sweat and decay. The sounds—the screeching, the guttural growls, the thuds of bodies crashing into furniture—were nearly unbearable.

Erin howled and writhed, snapping at Thalia's throat. Her strength was inhuman but uncoordinated. Thalia was faster. Smarter. She ducked, pivoted, then pounced again, claws slashing across the revenant's midsection. Rotten flesh tore open. A gush of black ichor spilled out, stinking of death and magic.

Still, the revenant kept fighting.

Thalia tried to pin her, but the revenant twisted and bit into her shoulder. Thalia roared, her claws scrabbling for purchase, back legs kicking to shove the creature off. They rolled again, a blur of fur and gore.

I couldn't just stand there and watch Thalia get ripped to shreds. If my Fae magic had brought Erin back, maybe I could pull it out—undo whatever I'd done.

I closed my eyes and reached for Erin with my mind to find the thread of magic inside her and reel it back into me.

But as soon as I did, a wave of nausea slammed through me. I gagged, my mouth tasting like rancid meat. The prickling of dark magic became a thousand needles stabbing through my brain all at once.

Oh Goddess! What have I done? This is bad. Really bad.

I fought to ground myself, to push the toxic magic back out—just as the revenant hurled Thalia into a nightstand with a sharp, painful yowl. Blood poured from dozens of gashes across the puma's body. She struggled to stand as the revenant closed in to finish her off.

No, no, no, you don't!

Furiously, I reached for my Fae magic, willing it to conjure fire. But instead of flames, a spray of Faerie lights shimmered into existence between the two supernatural predators.

Damn it! Why can't I figure this shit out?

The revenant froze, transfixed by the glowing orbs, while Thalia limped backward, keeping her distance.

I couldn't summon fire. My attempt to reverse the necromancy had failed spectacularly. But maybe I could lure the creature away.

I focused on the lights and nudged them into the hallway. To my relief, the revenant followed, completely ignoring Thalia and me.

I lured the revenant down the hallway and out the front door like I was luring a cat with a laser pointer.

Once outside, I steered the Faerie lights toward the mountains and away from town. The creature followed, vanishing over the nearest ridge.

Grief stabbed through me. Erin was reduced to this... thing. But then I remembered Thalia bleeding and broken in Sarah's bedroom.

I sprinted back through the house to find Thalia in human form again, slumped on the floor, gasping. Her body was a canvas of deep cuts. A broken rib poked out of her chest. Blood and ichor were everywhere. Would she turn into a revenant too? Was it like a zombie virus?

"Did... Did you need me to heal you?" Would it even work if I tried? My mind buzzed with a million questions.

She shook her head. "Just. Need. A minute."

Right before my eyes, her wounds knitted closed. The rib disappeared into her chest. The newly healed skin reabsorbed the blood as if by—well, I guess it *was* magic.

"Thank you," she said, her voice strained. "For luring... the creature... away."

"How? What... What are you?"

"Werepuma." Her eyes flicked away, her expression a mix of shame and vulnerability. "I'm guessing you're Fae."

"I'm... I don't..." I stammered, panic flaring in my chest. Then I exhaled and said it out loud. "Yes, I'm Fae. Well, half. On my father's side."

She nodded, pulling on her clothes. "Thought so."

"You don't hate me, do you?" I asked.

She shook her head. "No."

"The others... Do they know? About you, I mean?"

"Your moms do. I think Angel suspects, somehow. But no one else."

My moms knew a lot of secrets, apparently.

"The Sand Witches—they don't know about me, do they?"

"Don't think so."

Sirens wailed outside, growing louder.

With a mechanical hiss, the section of wall Erin had been clawing slid open—revealing a hidden safe room. Sarah O'Brien stepped out, pale and trembling. She was cradling a wound on her arm.

"Sarah!" I rushed to catch her as she started to collapse. "Hold on. Help's coming."

I guided her to the bed, trying to keep pressure on her wounds.

"Is... Is she gone?" Her voice trembled.

"For now."

"Wh-What... what *are* you people?"

Inside the safe room, a panel of security monitors glowed. She'd seen everything. Erin's revenant. Thalia shifting into cat form and back again. And me summoning the Faerie lights.

Before I could answer Sarah's question, Angel poked their head through the doorway. "Cops and EMTs are here. We should bounce."

"Mom! Dad!" Sarah cried and bolted from the room.

I followed—only to come face-to-face with a wall of uniformed officers, weapons drawn.

Chapter 28

All five of us were handcuffed and hauled off to the Wickenburg police station, where they stuck us in a holding cell. Detained by the police twice in one day. My moms were going to freak.

Using my magic to lure away the revenant had left me drained, as if I'd run a 10K in the desert heat. I needed a nap and sustenance. My wrists, now free from the cuffs, were raw and blistered due to my allergy to iron. I wanted to try healing them with my Fae magic but didn't want the others to see.

Roxy noticed the angry welts and gently took my arm. "Oh, Morgana! The revenant do that to you?"

I pulled my arm away and folded it under the other, heat rushing to my cheeks. "It's nothing. The cuffs were just too tight," I muttered, embarrassed.

"Damn!" Angel said. "And I thought mine were tight."

"What happened with... the revenant?" Kari asked Thalia and me.

Thalia glanced at me but this time with a modicum of

respect rather than her usual glare. "Morgana lured it away. She saved my life."

Everyone looked at me. I felt under the microscope.

"How?" Kari asked.

"The truth you must confront," Angel murmured, recognition dawning. "The cards never lie, chica."

"What are they talking about?" Roxy looked confused. "What truth?"

My insides shook. I wasn't sure what scared me more—facing a murderous revenant or coming out of the Faerie closet.

"I'm Fae," I blurted out. "On my bio-dad's side."

I stared at the concrete slab floor and braced for ridicule, wishing I could disappear into a hole.

"For reals, chica?" Angel asked. "That's so cool."

"That's amazing." Roxy slid an arm across my shoulder. "You're not embarrassed, are you?"

"I don't know. Maybe. All this time, I assumed I was Latina. And I'm not. I mean—I'm not even human. Not fully."

"You're still a person," she assured me. "Still worthy of love and compassion."

"And you still saved my ass from the revenant." Thalia's voice was full of admiration and respect, which I wasn't sure I deserved.

"That's why the cuffs burned you," Kari said. "It's your Faerie blood. Iron's toxic to the Fae. If you'd been full-blooded, it could've done serious harm. Possibly killed you."

"Lucky I'm only half." I didn't feel so lucky. I felt exhausted and dysregulated.

"Would you like me to heal the burns?" Roxy's eyes were almost pleading to help.

"Could you?" I recalled Mom saying Roxy specialized in healing magic.

"I can't guarantee results. I don't have my supplies, and I've never worked with anyone who's Fae. But it might help a little."

Her offer seemed genuine. And the burns did sting to the point of distraction.

"Yeah, okay."

She took my arm again. This time, I didn't pull away. Her touch was gentle. She traced a shape above my wrist and began to chant.

Sacred Brigid of well and flame,
Cleanse this wound and ease her pain.
Hands of magic, heart so bright,
Bless this skin with healing light.

Roxy repeated the chant twice more. The pain fading was the first thing I noticed. The blisters shrank and dried, the scorched skin flaking away to reveal healthy pink flesh beneath.

"I... Wow! Thank you."

"Better?" She smiled.

"Much." A rush of heat filled my core. "Though I'm worried about Thalia. The revenant scratched and bit her. Could it turn her into..."

Roxy turned to her. "You're injured?"

"I'm fine." Thalia held out her unscratched arms, her tone steely as ever. "No wounds."

"But I saw..." I stopped myself before I outed her. "I'm sorry. It all happened so fast. My mind's a bit muddled. I was worried you might turn into a revenant too. If it had scratched or bitten you, that is—which clearly it didn't. Sorry."

Kari shook her head. "Scratches or bites won't turn someone. Erin's a revenant, not a zombie. This is necromancy, not a contagion."

Good to know, I thought. "So, y'all don't think I'm a freak? For being Fae, I mean."

Angel gestured toward the group. "Look around, hermana. We all freaks up in here."

"Being Fae is nothing to be ashamed of," Roxy assured me. "Just the opposite. It's amazing. You saved Thalia and Sarah from a monster. You're a hero."

"Well, before you throw me a parade, there's something else I need to confess."

"What?"

I forced myself to meet their expectant gazes. "I reanimated Erin's body."

"What?" all four of them said at once.

"Not on purpose," I rushed to explain. "It's just... when Mom and I found her, she had no pulse. I panicked and used my Fae magic to bring her back. I don't know much about my powers—but I can make things grow. So I thought maybe... maybe I could save her. Like magical CPR. And for a moment, it worked. She started to revive." I swallowed hard, bile rising. "But now she's a revenant. And more people are dead as a result. I tried to take back the healing energy I gave Erin, but it made me sick to my stomach."

"Which further confirms you didn't reanimate her," Kari explained.

I wanted to believe her, but I struggled to let go of the guilt.

"Faeries can do a lot of things with their magic," she continued." Summon the elements. Talk to animals. Disguise their appearance. But I've never heard of any Fae who can reanimate the dead. The revenant was a result of necromancy, not Faerie magic. That's why it made you sick."

"How can you be sure?"

"What kind of Fae was your father?"

"I'm told he was Desert Fae, whatever that means."

"The Desert Fae? Never heard of them. Perhaps they're associated with the Summer Court."

"Summer Court? They're the nice ones, aren't they?" Roxy asked.

"'Nice' is a relative term when it comes to the Fae," Kari explained. "They are the Seelie, ruled by Queen Titania. They can be nice, but even the Seelie can be vicious when offended."

"How's Mrs. O'Brien?" I asked Roxy, trying to change the subject. Talking about my being Fae made me feel self-conscious.

"She lost a lot of blood, but she should pull through," Roxy said. "How's Sarah?"

"Her injuries didn't appear life threatening, but she's been seriously traumatized..." And a witness to both my and Thalia's supernatural abilities. That could be a problem.

"She has a lot of grief to work through," Roxy added.

Don't we all?

"I'm glad you told us about you being Fae," she continued.

"So, what are we supposed to tell the cops?" Angel asked. "That Erin's reanimated corpse is on a killing spree?"

Before anyone could answer, a uniformed cop entered the holding area and unlocked the cell door. "Morgana Quinn, come with me."

CHAPTER 29

THE FEMALE COP led me to the same interview room as before and motioned for me to sit. I would have preferred to curl up in the corner and take a nap. My energy was slowly returning but not as fast as I would like.

She brought me a soda and a candy bar and told me Detective Hatathlie would be in shortly.

Normally, I might have rejected such hospitality from cops who clearly had it in for me. But I was so hungry my belly hurt. Trying to suck in that death magic hadn't helped either.

I considered calling Douglas Tremball to represent me. But the thought of Mom and Mama Joyce forking over thousands, possibly hundreds of thousands, for my legal bills filled me with dread and shame. Bad enough I had to move back in with them. I didn't want to burden them further.

I can get through this on my own.

Hatathlie walked in and eyed me warily. "We don't see much violent crime in town. You know that. You grew up here. This isn't Phoenix or some other metropolitan city. This is Wickenburg. A small town filled with good people."

Bigoted people, more like. But I kept that to myself. No sense digging the hole deeper.

"Until recently, the last murder we had was nearly fifteen years ago. Now we have five inside of a week. Possibly six, if Mrs. O'Brien doesn't pull through. And somehow, you and your friends keep turning up at the crime scenes."

"Coincidence."

"Uh-huh. The only fingerprints we've found at any of the crime scenes are yours and your friends'—in blood. Why is that?"

"Because we're trying to save people. We didn't remove our prints from anything because we haven't committed any crimes. The real killer..." I stopped.

I had initially assumed that whoever killed Erin had also killed the others. But obviously that wasn't the case. The only serial killer was Erin's revenant.

Hatathlie raised an eyebrow. "The real killer what? What were you going to say?"

"The real killer obviously removed their prints. I'm guessing there were no prints on the athame. And none of our prints were at the scene where Charlie and the others were killed, even though we had dinner there earlier that night. None of our prints were in her vehicle, except maybe Kari's, since they were dating."

I think I'd made my point because Hatathlie didn't respond right away.

"How's Saffron Blaise?" she asked eventually.

"What?" Her bizarre change in subject took me a second to realize what she was asking.

"You two are dating, right? How's she doing with you

staying with your mothers here in Wickenburg. She must miss you."

"She's busy shooting the latest season of *LA Murder Squad*. What's that got to do with anything?"

"Lucky you. She's very glamorous."

"I suppose." Where the hell was she going with this?

"Funny thing—I read on *TMZ* that the two of you broke up. What happened?"

My temper surged along with the tingle of magic. I clamped down on it as hard as I could. "I caught her cheating on me. So I left. Happy now, Detective?"

"And moved back home to chase after Erin—your high school sweetheart. Only Erin's dating another woman."

"It's not like that."

"Then tell me how it is."

"I've moved back while I look for a new screenwriting job. I didn't even know she was still in town. In school, she always talked about moving to New York or Paris to be a chef."

"Why were you at her parents' house this afternoon?"

"We were worried about Sarah. She just lost her sister."

"And now her father is dead. Her mother mutilated. And you were there. You certainly had motive this time. They despised you, didn't they? I witnessed the confrontation between you at the cemetery."

"We. Did not kill. Anyone," I hissed.

Sarah had witnessed Thalia and me using our powers. Would she tell the cops that her sister's animated corpse attacked her parents?

"You don't want to take my word for it? Fine," I continued. "Ask Sarah."

"Sarah is in shock. She's not making any sense. Just keeps repeating her sister's name."

Because that's who attacked the house, I thought. "When

she comes out of it, she'll confirm my friends and I showed up *after* her family was attacked." I hoped, anyway.

"Why have so many people been murdered days after you moved back to town?"

Oh Goddess! This question again.

"I don't know."

"Or maybe you *do* know, and you're afraid to say. I'm here to help you, Morgana."

"No, you're here to pin these murders on me and members of my mothers' coven because you're prejudiced against witches."

"That's simply not true." She paused, and I caught what looked like a moment of self-reflection.

"I realize what witchcraft means to my people may differ from what it means to others."

I wasn't sure whether to believe her or not, but I said, "Thank you."

"That said, these murders started when you came back to town. Erin's body was found in front of your mother's bookstore in what can only be described as a ritual murder. So I'm following the evidence, not my prejudices."

"If I knew who the killer was, I'd tell you. But it wasn't me. Or any member of the coven. We're not violent people."

"Nobody is—until they are. People snap sometimes. It happens."

"I didn't snap."

"Just tell me who's responsible. Tell me, and this can all go away."

I debated what to tell her. Would she even believe me if I told her the truth? Or maybe just part of the truth.

"Belladonna Loveless," I blurted out.

"Who's she?"

"A witch Erin studied with before she joined my moms' coven. I believe she's responsible for these murders."

"And why would she go after all these people?"

"She and Erin parted on rough terms a few years back."

"Like the two of you."

"My mom and Loveless were also friends before I was born. But my mom said Loveless became violent, using magic to hurt people. So my mom ended their friendship. Loveless has held a grudge against both my mom and Erin ever since. If anyone would murder Erin in front of my mother's bookshop, it would be Belladonna Loveless."

Hatathlie seemed to consider this. "And where can I find this Belladonna Loveless?"

"I hear she lives in Morristown."

"Wait right here." She left the room.

Could I trust the police to handle things? Probably not. Even if Loveless had killed Erin and the police arrested her, the revenant was still out there, killing people. And then the police would release Loveless, more pissed off than before. It'd be like kicking a hornet's nest.

Detective Hatathlie returned thirty minutes later. She shoved a photograph of a woman toward me. Looked like a driver's license blown up to letter size with the address blurred. She had a weathered face, dead eyes, and long, stringy dark hair streaked with gray. The left side of her face drooped a little.

"This woman's name is Donna Loveless. She runs a psychic-reading business called Sister Belladonna, LLC. Is she who you were talking about?"

"I believe so. You going to arrest her?"

"Nope."

"Why not?"

"I sent a couple of uniforms to her place of business. They had a nice little chat."

"And?"

"A year ago, she suffered a stroke that left her confined

to a wheelchair. Doesn't exactly fit the serial killer profile. So I'm still left wondering, who is murdering the citizens of this town?"

"Ask Sarah. Ask her mom. It won't be me or my friends they'll name. I guarantee that."

She studied me for a moment, no doubt trying to suss out whether I was lying.

"You and your friends are involved somehow. I can feel it. And when I find proof, nothing will keep you out of prison."

I stood to leave. "So I'm not under arrest?"

"Not yet."

CHAPTER 30

I WAITED for the rest of the Sand Witches in the police station lobby. Thalia arrived first and settled into the chair beside me.

"What'd you tell that detective?" she whispered, careful not to be overheard by the desk sergeant.

"I said we stopped by to check on Sarah. Nothing about the revenant."

"You tell her about me?" Her eyes narrowed with a mix of concern and warning.

"About you being a werepuma? Of course not. But who knows what Sarah will say? What'd you tell the detective?"

"Nothing. I know when to keep my mouth shut."

Her tone was sharp, but she wasn't wrong.

"I suggested Belladonna Loveless, Erin's former mentor, is behind the killings."

"And?"

I shrugged. "Hatathlie said she's confined to a wheelchair due to a stroke."

"Being disabled doesn't keep her from controlling the creature and sending it after people."

"No, but Hatathlie doesn't know about the revenant. She's chasing a serial killer, and Loveless doesn't fit the bill."

"Then it's on us to stop it. Somehow."

"Mind if I ask you something personal?"

She eyed me warily. "What?"

"How'd you become a were?"

She let out a low growl of frustration.

"I mean, were you bitten by another werepuma? Or did a—"

"I was born a were. In cat form."

"Oh."

"I spent my first few years in the Wickenburg Mountains. Until a human with a rifle killed my mother," she said with a hiss.

"I'm so sorry. That must have been devastating."

"My littermates and I were old enough to hunt on our own. Until we shifted into human form a month later. We didn't know what was happening. Much less how to shift back. Hunting as a two-legged was impossible. We were slower, less agile. We had no fur to keep warm, no claws or sharp teeth to take down prey. We were dying from malnutrition and dehydration when a hiker found us."

"My Goddess! How horrible."

"My siblings and I were put in separate foster homes. I was placed with a couple in Wittmann. Never learned what happened to the others."

My heart broke for her. I'd never had siblings. At least none that I knew of. But I would have been wrecked to lose either of my moms. "Did your foster parents know you were... different?"

"No. I'd all but forgotten my life before. Until I hit puberty. I shifted back into cat form during the full moon."

"Yikes! As if getting your first period isn't traumatic enough."

"I managed to sneak out before I shifted. My foster parents never knew. But it felt good to be back in cat form. The world felt so much richer. And I could hunt once again."

"Wow, I can't imagine."

"Your mom Selene was the first human I came out to. She helped me understand my nature a little. Over time, I learned to control it. I can shift when I want to—usually."

"Are there other supernatural creatures in the coven?"

"Not that I know of. Thought I was the only one." She met my gaze. "Until now."

"I promise not to out you," I assured her.

Kari joined us a minute later, with Roxy and Angel close behind.

Angel sauntered up to the desk sergeant. "Hey there, big guy—any chance we can get a ride back to our cars?"

The sergeant, a heavyset guy with a porn 'stache, grunted. "This look like a taxi service to you, kid?"

"You people dragged us here. In handcuffs, no less," Angel replied, their temper rising. "The least you could—"

"Angel, leave the man alone." Roxy pulled them away before their mouth got them and us into more trouble.

We stepped outside as Roxy pulled out her phone to request an Uber.

"So... what's the plan now?" I asked.

"I want to check on Sarah and Mrs. O'Brien at the hospital," Roxy said somberly.

I nodded. "Sarah could use some support after all she's been through."

"We need to stop the creature before it kills again," Thalia said.

"How?" I asked. "We have no way to reverse the spell. And no idea where the revenant is."

"I can track it."

Angel scoffed. "Yeah, and then what? Throw a Molotov cocktail at it? The desert's a tinderbox after our non-soon summer. You really want to risk starting a wildfire?"

"We should pay a visit to Belladonna Loveless," I suggested. "If she did reanimate Erin's body, maybe we can force her to reverse it."

"Or just take her out," Thalia added.

"We are *not* murderers," Roxy reminded her.

"No, but the creature she created is. It's killed four people already. Five, if Erin's mom doesn't make it. Taking out an evil necromancer to save innocent lives? How is that not the moral thing to do?"

"She's also got Erin's spirit trapped," Kari said. "As long as the revenant exists, Erin suffers. We have to stop this woman controlling the revenant. And if that means killing her, well, too bad. She hurt the woman I loved. I'm gonna hurt her right back."

"If Loveless is as powerful as they say," Roxy replied, "she may not be so easy to kill. Even if she's in a wheelchair."

"Trust me," Thalia growled. "I can manage it."

Of that, I had no doubt.

"Maybe we can reason with her," Angel suggested. "Convince her to reverse the spell."

Thalia looked skeptical. "How do you propose we do that? Appeal to her *humanity*? You heard what Kari said about her. She's a monster. Monsters deserve to die."

"Let's pick up our vehicles at the O'Briens' and pay this witch a visit," I said. "We'll get a better idea who we're dealing with. And then decide how to stop her."

CHAPTER 31

WHEN WE ARRIVED BACK at the O'Briens', the house was cordoned off with patrol cars and yellow tape. Fortunately, our vehicles were outside the perimeter.

After our Uber drove away, Kari pulled three small cloth sachets out of her purse, each strung on a leather cord.

"I made a few protection charms during the last full moon," Kari said. "Only have three, though."

"I don't need one," Thalia replied. "I have my own protection against dark magic."

Kari handed one to Roxy, another to Angel, then held the last out to me.

"What's in it?" I asked.

"A black tourmaline crystal, a shard of obsidian, and an evil eye bead, plus sage, rosemary, and St. John's wort. Solid protection against hexes and psychic attacks."

Even after I'd discovered I was Fae, encountered Erin's reanimated corpse, and witnessed Thalia shift into a puma and back, my years of skepticism about magic didn't vanish overnight.

Yes, magic was real. But could a pouch of herbs and crystals shield me from a powerful necromancer? Maybe—if I believed in it. But right now, I didn't.

"You keep it. Mama Joyce gave me this." I grabbed the black agate bracelet from my purse and slipped it onto my wrist. "Plus, my Faerie magic should protect me."

I wasn't sure any of that would help, but I'd rather Kari be protected after all she'd been through.

"Let's just get this over with," Thalia said.

Kari slipped the cord over her head. "Okay, then. Let's go meet this witch."

We climbed into our cars and headed south on Highway 60.

Morristown was one of those blink-and-you'll-miss-it communities, best known as the hometown of Grumpy Cat, the frowning feline turned internet meme.

Just past the turnoff for the New River Highway, we pulled into a gravel lot in front of a weathered clapboard house. A sun-bleached sign read Sister Belladonna—Psychic and Medium. Beneath that was written Take Control of Your Future.

"Why'd she set up shop in the middle of nowhere?" I asked. "You'd think she'd get more business in north Phoenix or Scottsdale. Those rich housewives eat that shit up."

"Excuse me?" Angel glared at me. "Divination is not shit, Tinker Bell."

Damn. My cynicism was getting me in trouble. "Sorry. You're right. Not shit."

A yellowed plastic Open sign hung in the window of the weathered front door. When I gripped the doorknob, my hand tingled at the touch. It must have been made of steel.

I ignored the allergic reaction, turned the knob, and

stepped inside. The prickling sensation of dark magical energy shot through me, making my skin crawl. But the grimy stench of rotting flesh I'd come to associate with necromancy was noticeably absent. Perhaps that only meant that the revenant wasn't here.

A wrought iron chandelier hung from the ceiling, its bloodred bulbs bathing the entryway in a hellish glow. Shelves lined three walls, packed with candles, potions, crystals, and other metaphysical tchotchkes for sale.

In the corner, a raven sat perched on a saguaro skeleton. Panic gripped me. Had Loveless kidnapped—no, bird-napped—Mom's familiar, Lenore? When it didn't move, I realized it was dead. Stuffed. Had this wicked bitch *killed* Lenore?

But the dead bird lacked Lenore's distinctive white tail feather. Not her, thank Goddess! Unless the white feather fell out somehow.

A woman about our age sat behind a desk with a laptop and a Big Gulp cup. Not Belladonna, I guessed. Her daughter, maybe? Or new apprentice? Or just a receptionist?

Her pale thin face contrasted with her scarlet lips and inky-black hair. She sat unraveling a knitting project, brows furrowed, as if she'd dropped a stitch a few rows back.

A plum-colored velvet curtain behind her desk separated the lobby from the rest of the converted house. Murmuring voices drifted through the fabric. Maybe Loveless was in the middle of a reading.

Roxy shut the door behind us with a creak and a thud.

"Can I help you?" The woman's voice dripped with boredom. She didn't bother to look up from her knitting disaster.

"We're here to see Belladonna Loveless." I planted myself in front of the desk, trying to look intimidating.

Hard to accomplish when you're five two. But I could glare with the best of them.

"Got an appointment?" Still, not even a glance at me or the others, who now flanked me.

"We're not here for a reading," Angel said. "We're here about the necromancy spell that bitch cast on our friend."

That got her attention. She looked up, face unreadable. "She's busy with a client. You'll have to make an appointment and come back another time."

"We need to see her now," Thalia growled, looming over the desk.

The woman's uninterested look shifted into a menacing glare. "You people need to leave."

"Not till we talk to Belladonna," I said, trying to sound as intimidating as Thalia.

She dropped her knitting and muttered something under her breath. Her hands twisted into odd shapes.

Holy shit, she was casting! I was so not letting that happen.

I clapped my hands over hers, locking them into a tight ball. A surge of magical energy radiated from her fists and rippled through me. My Faerie magic exploded like a bucket of gasoline thrown on a campfire. Wind and rain gusted around the small room like a mini-hurricane.

"We need to see her now!" I shouted over the gale.

Alarm spread across her face. She struggled to free her hands, but I tightened my grip, determined not to let her fire off whatever spell she planned to use against us.

"What the hell's going on?" a gravelly female voice said.

A woman with leathery skin and long, scraggly hair pushed aside the velvet curtain and stepped into the lobby. The tempest I'd conjured evaporated instantly.

Belladonna Loveless, no doubt. She'd been pretty once—cute nose, dazzling eyes, heart-shaped face. The acrid stench of stale cigarette smoke clung to her. Tiny creases around her lips told me she was a lifetime chain-smoker. Also, no wheelchair and no droop on the side of her face to suggest she'd had a stroke. That was interesting.

An aura of powerful magic buzzed around her, equal parts seductive and terrifying. When she turned her gaze on me, it felt like being caught in the glare of a spotlight. Naked. Exposed. Vulnerable.

A sneer slithered across her face. "Well, well, what have we here?"

"My name is—"

"I know who you are, Morgana Quinn."

I swallowed hard. Maybe she'd seen me at the Emmys. Though she didn't strike me as someone who watched much television, much less award shows.

Before I could ask, she continued. "I remember when your mother got herself knocked up at Beltane. 'Oh no, Donna! I'm pregnant. What do I do?' Stupid cow."

"How dare you!"

"Of course, I offered her a remedy to get rid of it—to get rid of *you*. But she got all paranoid, afraid I might poison her. As if. I even offered to drive her to the clinic. But no, she refused that too. Got it in her little head that aborting you would bring down the wrath of the Fae. She was so full of shit. What Faerie would want to fuck her?"

My hands balled into fists. I wanted to punch this woman's lights out. But I held off, in case she could reverse the necromancy spell.

Instead, I let my magic wreak more havoc in the lobby. Soaking her merchandise, toppling candles and spell jars, blowing out light bulbs.

Who's full of shit now, bitch?

Then all at once, I shut it down and stared up at her, anger coming off me in waves. The only sound was the slow *drip-drip-drip* of water from the shelves, the chandelier, and that poor old stuffed raven.

She swept her gaze across the wreckage. "Well, look at you. I suppose Selene fucked a Faerie after all."

"What did you do to Erin O'Brien?" I demanded.

"Erin O'Brien?" Her laugh—dare I say, cackle—was condescending and cruel. "That ungrateful little twat?"

"How dare you—"

"Save it, you half-breed pixie. I tried to teach that girl magic. *Real* magic—not that pathetic Wicca nonsense dreamt up by that raging bigot Gardner. No, I taught her spells with teeth to deal with the holier-than-thou bullies in school."

Erin had always seemed so resilient. Had she been struggling more than she let on? So much so that she turned to Loveless for help?

"Then that little witchling got all squeamish. Worried I was teaching her dark magic. Hah! If you can't punish people who hurt you, what good is it? But Little Miss Goody Two-shoes ran away, stealing several of my potions and a couple of grimoires in the process. But I guess she got what was coming to her, didn't she?"

"What'd you do to her?" I snapped.

"Nothing. Last I heard, she ran off to New York to play kitchen witch."

"You're lying," Thalia hissed. "You killed her and turned her into a monster."

Loveless wheeled on her. "Hello, kitty! Come for a saucer of milk?"

"We came for answers!"

"Answers? And what, pray tell, is your question?"

"Ms. Loveless," Roxy said, in a forced-calm tone. "Someone murdered Erin then reanimated her corpse.

You're the only one we know of with that particular set of skills."

Loveless let loose with another unsettling laugh. "Having zombie trouble, are we, darling?"

"Revenant," Kari corrected.

Loveless narrowed her gaze at her. "I know what they're called, little girl. I create them. Even taught Erin how to do it. The spell itself isn't that hard. But the girl lacked discipline. Damned things kept going rogue on her."

My breath caught. Erin had used the spell?

"You need to reverse it," Angel insisted. "She... it... has killed people. And will kill more if you don't stop it."

"Oh, the sad little witchling freaks need my help. How precious." Loveless sneered at me. "What's wrong? Mommy can't teach you proper magic?"

"You created that thing," Thalia growled. "You need to uncreate it."

"I didn't murder Erin. Nor did I reanimate her ginger-headed corpse. Though I'll admit I'm curious who did."

"You're lying," Thalia snarled.

"Careful, little cougar!" Belladonna hissed. "Or I'll make a coat out of you."

"We're just trying to stop the carnage in Wickenburg," Roxy explained. "Even if you didn't cast the spell, we need your help to reverse it."

"Wickenburg could use a little thinning out. Nothing there but a bunch of hoity-toity, self-righteous rednecks. Sure, I can reverse the spell. But I won't."

"Innocent people are dying," I insisted. "You've got to do something."

"No, pixie girl, I don't. You and your sorry band of misfits are on your own."

I locked eyes with her, my blood boiling. What I wouldn't give to probe that dark mind of hers. Figure out a way to reverse the spell. But who knew what other horrors I might find there?

"Come on," I said at last. "Let's get out of here. She won't help us."

We turned to leave.

"Not so fast!" Belladonna grabbed my arm with surprising strength for an older woman. "You soaked my lobby with your damned Faerie magic."

I pulled my arm away, her nails leaving scratches on my skin. "It's Arizona. It'll dry."

I stormed out.

Chapter 32

The sun was low in the western sky, gilding the scrub desert in honeyed light.

Beads of blood welled up where Loveless had scratched me. I pressed a hand to the wound and tried to use my Fae magic to heal it. When I peeled my hand away, the scratches were still there, oozing blood and itching.

"Dammit!" I hissed as we regrouped in the parking lot.

"What's wrong?" Roxy asked.

I showed her my arm. "Bitch scratched me."

Just as Roxy had done to my handcuff burns, she traced a shape above my wounds and whispered a chant. This time, her magic stung like alcohol. Tiny bubbles of liquid sizzled along the scratches.

"Ouch," I said, resisting the urge to pull my arm away.

"Hold still. Almost done."

The bubbling stopped. The wound dried and scabbed, and the pain faded.

"Better?" she asked.

"Uh, yeah. Why did your healing magic sting this time?"

"It wasn't my magic causing the pain. When she scratched you, she left lingering traces of her own magic in the wounds. Nothing serious, I think. Should heal completely in a few hours."

"Thank you. Again." I realized I was feeling butterflies in my stomach from her touch. What was that about?

"I'm going to the hospital to check on Sarah and Mrs. O'Brien," Roxy said. "Anyone want to come with me?"

"I'm in," I blurted out before I could stop myself.

Kari and Angel chimed in with quiet nods.

"Thalia?" Roxy asked. "You coming, or should I drop you at your place?"

"Don't know Sarah. And her mom? Couldn't care less if she lives or dies. But sure, I'll tag along."

I shared Thalia's indifference toward Sarah's mother after the horrible things Erin's parents had called my moms and me over the years. Devil worshippers. Perverts. Groomers.

Still, I felt sorry for Sarah and her mom. Losing two family members in one week? Brutal. Even if her father was a dick.

"I have a question," Angel said, eyeing Thalia. "What was with all the cat references, chica? Belladonna called you a cougar and kitty, asked if you wanted milk. Why would she do that?"

Thalia remained stone-faced. "How the hell should I know? She's a crazy old witch."

Angel didn't look convinced. But before they could press the issue, my phone rang.

"Hey, Mom, what's up?" I asked.

"Mama Joyce and I were wondering if you're coming home for dinner."

"We're actually headed to the hospital."

"Oh my Goddess, sweetie, were you hurt?"

"No, Erin's family was attacked."

"What? Are they okay?"

"Sarah has a laceration on her arm. Her father was killed. Her mom's in rough shape. Not sure if she'll make it."

"Was it the Wickenburg Slasher?"

"There's no slasher, Mom. It was the revenant. It's real. We saw it."

"Oh, dear Gaia!" Mom exclaimed. "Who'd create such a thing? Who's even capable of that kind of magic?"

"We confronted your old pal Belladonna Loveless."

"You confronted her? Morgana, honey, you need to stay far away from that woman. Goddess knows what she could—"

"It wasn't her, Mom. At least, I don't think so."

"Did she know you're my daughter?"

"Yes. But it's okay. We got out of there without any problems." Aside from me turning her lobby into a water park and her scratching my arm as payback.

"I wish you'd stayed away from her. Nothing to do about it now, I suppose. You want us to meet you at the hospital?"

"If you want."

"Sounds like Sarah could use some support. We'll meet you there."

"Oh, and Mom? I told them I'm half Fae. Roxy and the others."

"Oh? Wow! Big step. How did it go?"

I sighed. "Better than I expected."

"We should have a coming-out party. I'll bake Faerie cakes. Invite the whole coven."

Mom looked for any excuse to throw a party. As if the eight annual Sabbats and the dozen or so full-moon rituals weren't enough.

"Thanks, but I'll pass. I'd rather keep things close to the vest for now."

"Fair enough. Mum's the word. I'll meet you at the hospital."

I ended the call and turned to my fellow Sand Witches. Corny as it was, I was warming to the nickname. Better than the Scooby Gang. "Let's roll and see how Sarah's doing."

On the drive back to Wickenburg, I kept circling around the same question. Who was the necromancer? Belladonna Loveless topped the suspect list. She was certainly capable, if my sense of her dark magic was any indicator.

Still, my gut said it wasn't her. She looked genuinely surprised to learn about the revenant. Disgustingly gleeful but surprised. And curious.

Plus, her little shop of horrors—though crackling with dark energy—lacked the smell I'd picked up at Erin's grave and from the revenant itself. That felt significant.

Just as I pulled into the hospital parking lot, Mom sent me a text: *Sarah's in room 147. Meet us there.*

WE FOUND Mom waiting outside the room.

"How's Sarah?" I asked.

"Shaken up. Mama Joyce is in with her now."

Roxy asked, "How's her mom?"

"Still in critical condition down in the ICU. Not sure if she'll pull through or not."

"Can we see Sarah?" I asked.

"I think she'd like that."

The room was dim, lit only by the fuzzy twilight filtering past the drawn shade.

Sarah lay reclined on the bed, her face blotchy and

streaked with tears. A bandage encircled her wounded arm. Mama Joyce sat beside her, holding her hand. They looked up when we entered.

"Hey," I said softly.

"Hey," Sarah echoed, her voice barely above a whisper.

Mama Joyce stood to give me a quick side hug. "Glad y'all are here. Sarah's got something to share with you."

Sarah opened her mouth to speak, but emotion overtook her. She broke down, sobbing.

"It's okay," Roxy said gently. "We're all here for you. Whatever you need to tell us can wait until you're feeling better."

"No," Sarah managed. "It can't."

We gave her a moment to pull herself together.

Finally, she said, "It was me."

I was confused. "What do you mean? What was you?"

"I... I tried to bring Erin back."

"Wait, what? You're a witch?" Kari asked.

"No, I... When my folks and me stopped by to pick up a dress to bury her in, I found a book in her closet. Figured it was an old diary. I wanted something meaningful that belonged to her. Something besides an old photo." She looked up at Kari. "I'm sorry."

Kari offered a weak smile. "It's okay. What's this book got to do with bringing Erin back?"

I got a bad feeling in my stomach. "This book... What'd it look like?"

"Red leather. It was a spellbook, I think."

"Erin's grimoire is blue," Kari replied. "Still sitting on our bookshelf, last I checked. What kind of spells were in the one you found?"

"Most seemed kinda boring—talking to animals, locating lost objects, that sort of thing. But then..." Again, Sarah choked up. "I found a spell to raise the dead."

"And you cast it?" Thalia snapped. "Why the hell would you do something so stupid? You don't know the first thing about magic."

I shot Thalia a glare. "Ease up!"

"I just wanted her back. I missed her so much. So I tried to cast the spell. It said to make a doll, so I did and took it to her grave and recited the words in the spellbook. At first, I didn't think it worked. But then..."

A look of horror spread across her face. "I heard a large *crack* deep in the ground and then a scuffling noise. Like something digging. That's when I saw it. Hands reaching out of the grave. And a scream—a scream like I've never heard before and never want to hear again. That's when I ran."

"Except it didn't really bring her back, did it?" Angel said coldly. "You created a monster."

"People are dead because of you," Thalia added.

"Hey, you two! Lay off," I shot back. "She didn't know what she was doing. She was just grieving for her sister. No need to pile on."

"Morgana's right," Roxy added. "She needs our support, not our judgment."

Thalia crossed her arms. "We need to stop this thing before someone else dies."

"Did the grimoire say anything about reversing the spell?" I asked.

Sarah gave a helpless shrug. "I... I don't know. If that's not Erin, what is it?"

"A revenant," Kari said.

"Like a zombie," Angel added.

"Why did it attack us?"

Kari appeared to consider the question. "If the spellcaster doesn't control it, I'm guessing it acts on instinct."

"How?" I asked. "What instinct?"

"It may have some residual memories," Kari explained. "After all, Erin's spirit is still connected to it."

"So it goes to places it's familiar with, like the restaurant and her parents' house," I said as I worked things out in my head, unsure what pronouns to use to describe this thing that once was Erin. "And attacks those who treated her badly in life."

It would explain her going after Jimmie and Linda as well as her parents. But what about Charlie? And Sarah? Were they just collateral damage?

"Why would Erin have a spell like that in her book?" Sarah asked. "I thought you witches didn't use those kinds of spells."

"We don't," Mama Joyce assured her. "Our coven forbids magic like that. Any witch caught using such spells would be cast out of the coven."

"Then how'd it end up in Erin's spellbook?"

Mom sighed. "Before Erin joined our coven, she trained under another witch. Someone cruel. Manipulative. That grimoire must be from that time. We should destroy it."

"Not until we deal with the revenant," Thalia said. "We may need the grimoire to undo the spell."

"Where's the grimoire now?" I asked.

"In my dresser," Sarah said, sniffling. "Top drawer. Under my bras."

Mama Joyce turned a stern eye on the rest of us. "Y'all listen up. Leave that grimoire alone. Ya hear? Don't go messing with dark magic."

"We gotta find a way to reverse the spell, Mama. The Fall Festival's tomorrow night. If the revenant shows up there..." I didn't finish the thought. I didn't need to.

"I'm a horrible person," Sarah whimpered.

"No, you're not," Mama Joyce said, giving her hand a

gentle squeeze. "You're just a young woman, grieving a terrible loss."

"You saw a chance to bring your sister back," Roxy said softly. "It may have been a mistake, but it was motivated by love."

"But I just made everything worse. Now Dad's dead. Mom might die too. And it's all my fault."

I wanted to tell her everything would be okay—but that would've been a lie.

"I know what it's like to hurt someone and not be able to take it back," I said. "Sometimes the only thing you can do is forgive yourself."

Roxy slipped an arm around my shoulders. "She's right, kiddo. Just gotta acknowledge it, let yourself grieve, and give yourself grace. We'll find a way to stop this thing before it hurts anyone else."

"Can we borrow your house key to retrieve your sister's grimoire?" I asked.

Sarah shook her head, dabbing at her eyes. "My purse is still at home. No keys."

"Don't worry. We'll figure out a way in," I reassured her.

Mama Joyce stood and looked each of us in the eye. "I still say this is a bad idea. You mess with dark magic, you could make it worse."

"Worse? How much worse can it get? That creature is killing people. It's a chance we'll have to take."

Mom pulled me into a hug. "Stay safe, baby girl." Then to the others: "Y'all watch each other's backs."

"We will," I said.

Chapter 33

Instead of taking separate cars, we all crammed into Roxy's Trailblazer. I snagged the front seat while Thalia, Angel, and Kari squeezed into the back.

I probably should've let Thalia take shotgun—the girl had legs for days—but the more time I spent with Roxy, the more drawn to her I felt.

Was it friendship? A silly rebound crush? Something deeper? I didn't know. With everything that had gone down lately, my emotions were a tangled mess.

When we pulled up to the O'Briens' house, a Wickenburg patrol car sat out front. Yellow crime scene tape stretched across the front porch.

"Well, crap," I muttered as the patrol car turned on its flashing blue lights. "Now what?"

"It's been hours," Angel muttered. "How long does it take these clowns to bag evidence?"

"Everyone, just play it cool," Roxy replied.

A uniformed officer stepped out of the patrol car— early thirties, narrow jaw, and a no-nonsense expression.

"You folks need to turn around. This is an active crime scene."

"Doesn't look so active," Angel said with a smirk.

"We understand, Officer... Brennan," Roxy said, reading his name tag. "We're friends of Sarah O'Brien. She's in the hospital. Asked us to grab a few things from the house."

"What things?"

"Her purse, phone charger, pajamas."

"Sorry, no can do. The department's still processing the scene. Until they finish, it's off-limits. Try again tomorrow afternoon."

"Listen, asshole, Sarah lives here," Thalia shouted from the back. "She has a right to her stuff."

Officer Brennan shined his flashlight into the back seat. "We gonna have a problem, ma'am?"

"No, Officer," Roxy assured him. "We're leaving."

"Y'all have a good night," he replied, stepping back.

Thalia let out a low growl as Roxy backed the Trailblazer out of the driveway and headed toward the main road.

"I could've taken him," Thalia muttered.

"We don't need more trouble with the police, Thalia," Roxy warned. "Not tonight."

Angel barked a laugh. "Them cops will have a *lot* more trouble if we don't stop that thing."

"Pull over," Thalia said. "I have a plan."

Roxy stopped in front of a nearby ranch house. A small corral stretched beside it, and a horse trailer sat parked in the gravel driveway.

Roxy turned to Thalia. "Okay, let's hear it."

"I sneak in the back and grab the grimoire."

I wondered if she meant as a human or a puma.

"How?" I asked. "There's a ten-foot retaining wall

around the back. How are you going to get down that without twisting an ankle?"

"Ten feet's nothing, if you know how to land."

"The back door's probably locked," Kari said. "How will you get in?"

"Bust it open if I have to."

"And alert Officer Hardbody in the process," Angel said dryly. "Great plan."

"You got a better plan, goth girl?" Thalia shot back.

"I'm not a girl," Angel snapped. "I'm nonbinary."

"If it comes to it, I'll take him out."

"No," Roxy said. "We're not killing innocents."

"Innocent," Thalia snorted. "All cops are bastards, remember?"

"I can unlock the door," I offered.

"With your Faerie powers?" Angel asked, intrigued.

"Actually, no. Just a spell my moms taught me. Getting past the cop's the real issue."

Kari turned to me. "Maybe not. The Fae are experts at going unnoticed. They can vanish right in front of you. It's called Faerie glamour."

"You're saying I can become invisible?" If only I'd had that trick back in school. Could've avoided a lot of trauma.

"Not exactly invisible," Kari said. "More like unnoticeable. Sort of a magical camouflage. You fade into the background."

"How do I do that? Aside from Faerie lights and a little wind and rain, I haven't a clue what I'm doing."

Kari thought for a moment. "Go behind that horse trailer. Close your eyes, reach out with your mind, and imagine that you're one with the night. Listen to all the sounds. The chirping of the crickets, the staccato drone of the nighthawk, the rustle of the wind through the scrub. Imagine they are a part of you. Then when you're ready, step out from behind the trailer and walk around to Roxy's door."

"That's it? Just listen to the crickets?"

"No, don't just listen—connect. Become one with the natural world."

"And that will make me invisible?" It didn't make sense to me.

"Unnoticeable."

"How do you know this?" I pressed her.

She shrugged. "I read a lot of old arcane texts."

"I guess it can't hurt to try." Wouldn't be the first time I looked ridiculous. Definitely wouldn't be the last.

"You've got this!" Roxy said, squeezing my hand.

"Show us what you got, Tinker Bell." Angel grinned. "We believe in you."

"Goddess! Stop calling me that!"

Thalia gave my shoulder a solid pat. "Magic's in your blood, girl. Use it."

I climbed out of the truck and into the dark. "Hope I don't step on a rattlesnake or get stung by a scorpion." I was always more of an indoor kinda gal.

"Too cold for rattlesnakes," Kari said.

Good to know.

My shoes crunched on the gravel as I circled behind the horse trailer, which reeked of manure. I didn't see how this was going to work, but what the hell?

I stood out of sight, closed my eyes, and listened.

Insects buzzed. Birds chirped. I felt—more than heard —the rush of wings overhead, accompanied by sharp, high-pitched squeaks. Probably a bat. *Yeesh!*

I'd never realized how alive the desert was at night. Aside from bats, scorpions, and coyotes, I figured every-thing would be asleep.

I reached out with my consciousness, trying to connect

to the creatures around me. To my surprise, I could feel their energies—dozens, no, hundreds of animals. Maybe thousands.

Birds nesting in trees. A raccoon rustling through the brush. Coyotes with pups emerging from a den. An owl gliding overhead. A mule deer buck nosing along a game trail. A jackrabbit nibbling prickly pears. Javelinas, snorting softly, their babies squeaking beside them. Crickets chirping for a mate.

Then I reached farther and sensed creatures not discussed on any Arizona wildlife websites. One looked like a cottontail... until I noticed the antlers. A jackalope? I thought those were a joke.

A flurry of small winged creatures zipped around a pumpkin patch behind the house. Not bats. More like hummingbirds—except they weren't. Their energy felt different. Wild. Fae.

Pixies! Just like the ones I'd seen at my moms' place and the one I'd encountered at the Hassayampa River Preserve.

I stretched farther and felt a presence—humanoid, maybe female—hovering near a tall saguaro, basking in starlight. Some sort of nymph, maybe?

My energy flowed into the desert's rhythm, merging with it like crisscrossing waves. Wind whispered through creosote and brittlebush, carrying me with it.

I stepped out from behind the reeking trailer, focused on staying connected to the flurry of activity around me, and crept toward Roxy's SUV.

"You see her?" Angel whispered.

I could feel all of them now—each pulse of energy.

"Not yet," Thalia muttered. "Must still be behind the trailer."

"When you're ready," Kari called gently, "come on out."

I was already in the headlights—but none of them noticed.

"Well?" I said, when I reached Roxy's open window.

Her eyes went wide with shock, and she clutched her chest. "Morgana! Goddess! Nearly gave me a heart attack."

I couldn't help but laugh. "You seriously couldn't see me? I walked straight past the headlights."

"Nada," Angel said. "Gotta admit, I'm impressed, hermana."

"Go get that grimoire," Roxy said. "You've got this."

I still wasn't sure they weren't just humoring me. But either way, we needed that grimoire. Now or never.

"Here goes nothing."

I stepped back from the window and let myself sink into the night again, letting the nighthawk's steady drone pull me under.

"Holy shit! Where'd she go?" Kari asked.

"That is *wild*," Angel breathed.

I slipped away from the Trailblazer, heading toward the O'Briens' house. I kept my focus locked on the desert around me. One stray thought, and I feared the glamour would drop.

The patrol car came into view. I forced myself not to focus on the cop inside—just the desert. The trees. The creatures. The wind. The hum of the O'Briens' backyard pool pump.

Minutes later, I rounded the corner and reached the back door. I took a slow breath. The night still buzzed around me. I could feel everything.

Was I still cloaked? I didn't know. Didn't matter. I just needed to grab the grimoire and get the hell out.

Chapter 34

At the back door, I gripped the knob and reached out with my magic. "Lorem ipsum dolor sit amet. Lorem ipsum dolor sit amet," I whispered. After a third repetition, I tossed in an "Abre la puerta" for good measure.

I felt the tumblers align. The deadbolt released with a soft clack. I turned the knob and eased the door open.

A thrill pulsed through me as I stepped inside—part witch, part burglar. Technically, I had Sarah's permission. Mrs. O'Brien, though? She'd probably call it breaking and entering.

The stench of decay and the prickle of dark magic still lingered in the air. My pulse quickened—had the revenant returned? No. I'd driven it off. And there was no one left to attack. Except me.

I hesitated at the light switch. The cop was out front, watching for trespassers. If he did a patrol around the house, I didn't want to tip him off. I could also try summoning Faerie lights again, but that would only drain me if I used it too long. I was already feeling it from using my glamour. I flicked on my phone's flashlight instead.

I crept through the game room with its massive flatscreen, a PlayStation, and a wall of DVDs. Down the hallway, I turned into Sarah's bedroom, bathed in the soft sapphire glow of a nightlight.

The grimy, putrid stench of necromancy melded with the musk of shifter magic and the metallic smell of dried blood. Thalia and the revenant locked in a savage brawl replayed in my head with me all but helpless to stop them.

I shoved the memories aside and moved to Sarah's dresser.

The top drawer was filled with neatly folded underwear on the left, socks in the middle, and bras on the right. Reaching under her bras made me feel less like a cat burglar and more like a creepy stalker, invading Sarah's privacy. Still, I had to do what I had to do.

My fingers wrapped around a small, thick, leather-bound book.

My blood ran cold the instant I touched it. The extreme wrongness of this grimoire radiated from its very cover. I recoiled on instinct. Its energy tasted metallic, like sucking on nickels, and felt like scorpions skittering across my skin. I didn't want to be anywhere near it.

But this grimoire was our only way to destroy the creature and keep it from hurting anyone else. I had to take it with me.

With a steadying breath, I wrapped the book in one of Sarah's T-shirts from the drawer below. I spotted a dark leather purse atop the nearby nightstand. With my free hand, I slipped the strap over my shoulder and crept out of the room.

I should've bolted with my cursed prize. Instead, I stepped across the hall into Erin's old bedroom.

The greasy, putrid reek of necromancy was oddly

stronger in here. Beneath it lingered Erin's old perfume—sweet with a hint of sophistication.

Goddess, I missed her. Missed everything that could have been between us. Even if it had just been a lifelong friendship. I'd been such an idiot to push her away.

A sound of movement caught my attention, followed by a low hiss. Panic exploded inside me. I fumbled for the switch, and the room blazed with light.

"Oh shit, shit, shit!"

Under the desk in the far corner, the revenant lay curled into a ball. It shrieked and shielded its face from the sudden brightness.

My heart thudded in my chest.

Why the hell's it back here? How'd it get in?

Then I saw the shattered window.

Dammit! I just had to come in here.

The revenant focused on me, hissing low and guttural. Its head tilted like a predator studying its prey, deciding whether to kill me.

It still looked sort of like Erin. Aside from the sunken eyes, decaying flesh, and tattered, blood-smeared dress. But the growling creature before me was not the girl I knew. The energy coming off it was not human—not entirely. More like a nightmarish entity that wanted to destroy anything alive.

It rose and stepped toward me. Every instinct screamed *run*—but my feet refused to move. Like I'd fallen into a childhood nightmare made real.

I held up the grimoire instinctively to ward off a pending attack. The revenant recoiled with a shriek, like a vampire flinching from a cross.

That was... unexpected. Did the creature fear Erin's old grimoire?

I wanted to bolt. But could I leave this thing here? What

would it do when the cops returned to investigate? Or when Sarah and her mother were released from the hospital?

Then again, if it stayed here, at least we'd know where it was when we figured out how to break the spell and put Erin to rest once again.

I backed away, holding the grimoire high like a shield. The creature hissed again and slithered back underneath Erin's old desk.

The moment it disappeared from view, I bolted out the back door without bothering to lock it. What would be the point? The damn creature had its own entrance now.

I'd just rounded the side of the house when a voice barked, "Hey, you! Stop!"

Shit! I'd been so distracted—and terrified—by the revenant that I'd forgotten to raise my glamour. Last thing I needed was for that cop to confiscate the grimoire.

I ducked behind a shrub and hurriedly tried to summon my glamour. But my heart was hammering in my chest. My brain was spinning like a windmill in a hurricane. I couldn't focus.

His boots crunched on the sand, growing closer with each step.

My thoughts raced. *Gotta get outta here, gotta get outta here.*

The air stirred, and suddenly the wind whipped in furious gusts. I focused on it, intensifying it, spinning it like a dust devil, and sending it straight at the cop.

"What the hell?" he shouted, wind battering his voice.

I drew a deep breath and reached out with my senses, tuning in to the nighthawk's warbling drone to connect me to the night.

Up the hill, a coyote let out a volley of yips and high-pitched howls, soon joined by a dozen others. A family of skunks tottered along the road. A ringtail skittered up a tree, heart pounding ten times faster than mine, perhaps hoping not to become a late-night snack for the 'yotes.

"Come out, come out, wherever you are." The cop walked past me, swinging his flashlight to and fro, oblivious to my presence. He turned and stared right at me.

Shit, shit, shit! He sees me. He sees me. Wait... does he see me?

He turned away and trudged back to his cruiser, muttering under his breath, "Damned creepy-ass guard duty."

I reached Roxy's Trailblazer and slumped into the front seat, exhausted from using my magic.

The others jumped when the door closed.

"Morgana!" Roxy yelped. "You scared the crap out of me —*again.*"

"Sorry. Faerie glamour." *When I remember to use it.*

"Did you get the grimoire?" Kari asked.

I nodded. "Got it. And Sarah's purse. Figured she'd need it. Oh, and the revenant's back."

"She was in there?" Kari's voice cracked with grief.

I met her sorrowful gaze. "Yes."

"Where is it?" Roxy asked. "It didn't attack you, did it?"

"Erin's old room. Curled up under her desk. And it's afraid of the grimoire. Cowered when I held it up."

"No wonder," Angel muttered. "That grimoire's throwing off some seriously nasty vibes. Feels like snakes slithering through my brain."

"I feel it too," Thalia said grimly. "That's one evil book. Every instinct tells me to burn it."

"Not yet," Kari insisted. "We need to break the spell so Erin's spirit can move on."

I stared at the book, nestled in the shirt. The magic radiating off it felt so toxic. "How do we do this? I'm scared to even touch it."

"We should wait until daylight," Angel said. "Easier to contain dark magic."

"We don't have that luxury," Thalia warned. "That creature could hurt someone else."

Roxy eyed the book warily. "I'm with Angel. We should hold off until daybreak. Baneful magic this powerful is better dealt with in daylight. And we should stick together. Strength in numbers. You're all welcome to crash at my place."

"I'm in," I said. *More time with Roxy? Yes, please!*

"Sounds good," Kari agreed.

"Ooh, slumber party!" Angel chortled. "We can stay up all night, paint each other's nails, talk trash about boys. Or girls."

"Or nonbinary people," I added, though I had no intention of staying awake all night. I wasn't sure I'd remain awake on the ride home.

"I plan to sleep, thank you very much," Roxy said with a smile. "Better to deal with necromancy. But you do you, boo. What about you, Thalia? You in?"

Thalia appeared to consider it. "If we must wait, then fine. Better we stay together. We'll mount a stronger front should trouble arise."

CHAPTER 35

I CALLED Mom on the drive back to the hospital to pick up our vehicles. It was just past nine, and visiting hours were over, so I figured she and Mama Joyce had already headed home.

"You okay?" she asked, the worry evident in her voice.

"I'm good. How are Sarah and Mrs. O'Brien?"

"Sarah was sleeping when we left. The nurses said Mrs. O'Brien's out of immediate danger, but they're keeping her in ICU. Lucky you and the others showed up when you did."

"Is Lenore back?" I should've asked earlier at the hospital, but we'd been too focused on Sarah.

"No. I tried scrying but couldn't get a bead on her. I'm worried something's happened. Mama Joyce suggested astral projection, but it's been years since I tried."

I remembered the stuffed raven at Sister Belladonna's but didn't mention it. Probably wasn't Lenore. No use worrying Mom unnecessarily.

"She'll turn up," I assured her. "Maybe she met a cute male raven."

"Maybe." Mama chuckled. "You find Erin's old grimoire?"

"I did. Also picked up Sarah's purse. I'll drop it off tomorrow." I sighed. "This grimoire... It's got some seriously spooky energy. I'm afraid to touch it barehanded."

"You should bring it here. The coven elders are better equipped to handle this type of magic and unravel the necromancy spell."

She was probably right. But I wasn't sure if the Sand Witches would surrender it at this point. And honestly, I owed it to Erin to free her from the grip of this spell.

"We got it under control, Mom. We're crashing at Roxy's. We'll dig through it tomorrow. Locate the spell Sarah used and reverse it."

"Who's 'we'?"

"The Sand Witches. Roxy, Angel, Kari, and Thalia. And me."

"Forming your own coven now, are we?"

I couldn't tell if she was joking.

"No, Mom. But we've got this. If anything goes sideways, I'll call."

She paused. "Okay, sweetheart. Just... be careful. This type of magic is extremely toxic. And seductive. It's not something to play around with."

"I know. We'll be fine. See you tomorrow."

"You still helping me at the Wiccanburg booth at the festival tomorrow?"

"Sure. After we've stopped the revenant."

"Okay. Get some rest, sweetie! We love you."

"Love you too. Good night."

We caravanned through El Burro Loco's drive-thru on the way to Roxy's place. The googly-eyed cartoon donkey on the sign brought back a wave of nostalgia and childhood memories of Friday night dinners with my moms.

Roxy's home was elegant, modern, and alive with welcoming energy. The living room walls were lined with framed prints that read things like Believe in Yourself and One Day at a Time, alongside photographs of a coral reef, California's redwoods, and Sedona's red rock formations. I wondered if Roxy had taken them herself or if she bought them somewhere.

Over the next hour, we ate, swapped embarrassing stories, and tried to laugh. But the laughter felt strained. I wondered if the grimoire's negative energy was sucking all of the joy out of the place.

The food energized me. I no longer felt so drained. And I kept catching myself staring at Roxy. Butterflies of happiness fluttered through me whenever I looked at her. Was it a silly crush? Couldn't be love. We'd only just met, and I was on the rebound.

I'd had my period a couple weeks ago, so my oxytocin levels were probably spiking, coupled with my ADHD wreaking havoc with my other neurotransmitters. And I didn't have my meds with me. Dammit! Oh well. I'd pick them up in the morning. I should start carrying some with me.

Still, every time I glanced at her, those butterflies swarmed inside me, filling me with warm feelings.

Roxy was only a few years older than me, but she seemed so much more mature. Maybe because, unlike me, she had a successful career. Lucky her.

"I'd been doing tarot readings for six months when this college girl comes in," Angel said between bites of burrito. "She told me that she and her boyfriend just got engaged but wanted to make sure he's *the one*."

"No such thing as *the one*," Roxy said.

"And anyone who needs tarot cards to tell them

whether their partner is a good match is already screwed," Thalia added.

Harsh, I thought.

"Nevertheless, I set out a compatibility spread," Angel continued, a little frost in their tone now. "But the cards I was pulling... Ten of Swords, the Tower, Death, the Devil, Five of Cups. All the most ominous cards in the deck. And it kept going. Eight of Swords, the Hanged Man. I'm, like, damn! Who is this woman? Her energy was all sunshine and daisies. But the cards I was pulling? So freakin' dark."

"Sounds a little familiar," I muttered under my breath, recalling the reading they'd done for me. "What'd you tell her? That everything would be fine in the end?"

Angel narrowed their eyes. "I didn't lie, if that's what you're implying. Just told her some challenges were headed her way. Advised her not to make any major decisions. Maybe hold off on her nuptials. But she brushed it off. Said her fiancé was a total catch."

"And?" I asked.

Their face darkened. "A week later, she was on the news. They found her chopped-up body in a Phoenix canal. Police charged her fiancé with first-degree murder."

A shiver raced down my spine, and before I could filter myself, I snapped, "Guess no five-star review from her on Yelp."

Angel stared at me. "Wow. Really?"

I winced. "Sorry. I don't know why I said that. I didn't mean it like—"

"Cards never lie." Angel shook their head. "People just don't want to hear the truth."

"I don't know about that. Your reading for me said big opportunities were headed my way. So where are they?" I fired back, the heat in my voice catching me by surprise.

"Once you face up to a truth you've been avoiding."

"I have! I'm Fae. I accept it. So when do I level up, smart-ass? I've been applying for new screenwriting jobs but so far, nada. What the hell else am I supposed to—"

"I don't know, Morgana. The cards don't lie, but neither do they give an exact timetable for when things happen. Maybe you being Fae is only part of the thing you must face and accept."

"Or maybe you're just full of shit!"

"Okay, everyone take a breath," Roxy interrupted, though even her voice was frayed around the edges. "Let's not turn this into a screaming match. Sometimes, Morgana, you just have to trust the process."

"Goddess! You sound like my moms." I tossed my half-finished burrito back onto my plate, feeling my appetite fade. No more butterflies now.

"Your mothers are two of the wisest people I know," she said coolly.

I sighed and pushed away my food. "Yeah. Sure. Whatever."

Roxy wasn't wrong. My moms were wise. But lately, my life felt like it was circling the drain. I'd lost my girlfriend, my job, and my Santa Monica condo. Now I was at risk of losing my freedom, possibly my life. And no advice from them or Angel or anyone else seemed to be helping.

I stared at the grimoire, still wrapped in Sarah's shirt and sitting in the center of the table.

"What the hell are we going to do with that thing overnight? It feels..." I searched for the word. "Toxic."

"It's just a book," Kari said. "It's not going to cast spells on its own."

"Morgana's right," Thalia said. "There's something wrong with that thing. I can feel it filling the room with bad energy. It's infecting us—making us act like assholes. A salt circle could help."

We all looked at one another, the tension in the room palpable. Was it just the awful things we'd been through today? Or was the grimoire's energy fueling our conflict with each other?

Roxy nodded slowly. "Be right back."

She returned with a large wooden cutting board and a canister of iodized salt. "Don't want the salt to damage the dining room table. The cutting board, no big deal."

She laid the cutting board on the table, and I placed the grimoire on top. Roxy then encircled it with a line of salt.

"I don't feel any different," I said. "Maybe we are all just assholes."

"Hold on a sec." Angel reached into their messenger bag and drew out a wand made from unpolished wood, one end wrapped in leather.

"Always carry a wand with you?" I asked, half joking.

"Don't you? Made it from a saguaro rib." They focused on the salt. "By the power of Santa Muerte, La Virgen, and the five sacred elements, I charge this circle to protect us from the grimoire's energy. So mote it be."

"So mote it be," the rest of us muttered.

Instantly, it was like someone had shut off an invisible alarm buzzing inside my skull. The static faded. My shoulders dropped. I finally exhaled.

"Much better," Thalia said. "Nice work, Angel!"

I glanced around the table. "Sorry for... acting like an asshole."

There was a beat of silence—then everyone burst out laughing.

Around ten o'clock, Roxy stretched and said, "Don't know about y'all, but I'm wiped. As far as sleeping arrangements, I don't mind sharing my king-sized bed with someone."

My hand shot up. "I'm game." Heat rushed to my face. "I mean, if that's cool."

Roxy smiled. "More than cool. For the rest of you, I have a queen-sized bed in the guest room. And the living room couch is a pull-out. No drinking, smoking, or use of mind-altering substances in the house. Beyond that, knock yourself out."

I followed Roxy back to her room. The walls were sunshine yellow—warm and bright, even in the dim glow of the overhead light.

I suddenly felt awkward, wrestling with a jumble of emotions, most notably my growing attraction to her. I felt like a lost puppy.

We're just friends, I reminded myself. *She's not into me. At least not in that way. And why the hell am I having sexy thoughts about her? I just broke up with Saffron.*

"You sure it's all right? Me sleeping with you. I mean, sharing your bed?"

Oh Goddess, could I be any more awkward?

"You planning to attack me in the night?"

My face burned with embarrassment. "What? No! Of course not. I just... I don't know."

She laughed. "You should see your face. I'm teasing you. Of course it's all right. We're both adults." Then softer, "You're not weirded out about me being trans, are you?"

"What? No. Not at all. I'm just—my brain's still playing catch-up. Everything's been so much lately. I'm in a weird headspace."

"You're not the only one. Feels like the world's turned upside down."

"Yeah. Part of me wonders if I should've stayed in LA."

"And miss out on all the fun?" She pulled a set of pajamas from her dresser. "I'd offer you a spare set, but considering our size difference, you'd probably drown in them."

"I can sleep in my T-shirt and underwear, if that's okay."

"Perfectly okay."

She changed in the bathroom and came back wearing teddy bear pajamas. An actual teddy bear sat propped on her pillow.

"Her name's Kimberly Anne," she said, after catching me noticing the bear. "I bought her after I got out of rehab. I was dating another user at the time—Nicole. She refused to get clean, so I ended things."

"Must have been hard." We slipped under the sheets, and she wrapped an arm around the bear.

"It was. And the bed felt so empty at night without her. My sponsor suggested getting a teddy bear. Felt silly at first —grown woman, stuffed animal—but it helped. She's been with me ever since. Crazy, right?"

"Not crazy at all. I think it's sweet." *I think you're sweet*, I wanted to say but didn't.

"Thanks. Well, good night."

CHAPTER 36

I LAY NEXT TO SAFFRON, her brown eyes glittering in the morning light, her normally perfect hair deliciously tousled—which somehow made her even sexier.

"I've missed you," she whispered.

"I know. I missed you too." I leaned in to kiss her.

Her lips were soft and full, exactly how I remembered.

Long, elegant fingers cupped my cheek then slid down my body, teasing my breasts, grazing my nipples until I gasped. I returned the favor, coaxing moans and shudders of pleasure from her.

It felt like we hadn't touched in eons—like our need had been steeping in silence, finally boiling over into raw, aching want. Her hand slid between my thighs, found my clit, and began to circle it.

"Oh, Goddess," I moaned.

"You can just call me Saffron," she teased, slipping one finger inside me then another, sending a burst of pleasure rocketing through my body.

"Morgana?" a voice called.

"Don't stop," I begged. "Please don't stop—"

"Morgana, I think you're dreaming." That voice. Not Saffron's.

My eyes flew open.

Roxy lay beside me, propped up on one elbow, a wry smile playing at the corners of her mouth. "Good morning."

Oh Goddess, had I been talking in my sleep? Or worse—had I...? Nope. Not going there. Not even thinking about that.

"I, uh... Good morning," I croaked, voice thick with mortification.

"Good dream?"

My face flamed with heat. How embarrassing! I pulled the pillow over my head and groaned. Maybe I could just disappear into the mattress. Or a black hole.

"Please tell me I didn't do or say anything... inappropriate," I sputtered.

"You invoked the Goddess a few times, rather urgently," she said, clearly amused. "But nothing I'd call inappropriate."

"Just kill me now!"

She laughed softly. "No need to be embarrassed, Morgana. We're sexual beings. Erotic dreams are perfectly natural."

"Yeah, well, maybe under normal circumstances. But with everything that's been going on..."

"Just because we're battling the undead doesn't mean we stop being human. Dan Savage once said, 'During the darkest days of the AIDS crisis, we buried our friends in the morning, we protested in the afternoon, and we danced all night. The dance kept us in the fight because it was the dance we were fighting for.'"

"Meaning?"

"Meaning it's okay to dance. And dream. And have sex."

"Or dream about having sex," I muttered, setting aside the pillow, struggling to meet her sweet smile.

"Exactly. Because this is what we're fighting for. Joy, pleasure, life! We have to keep dancing."

Goddess, she was smart. And insightful. *And please, Morgana, for the love of Gaia, stop thinking about how kissable she looks right now.*

"Food for thought."

"Speaking of food, I should throw something together for breakfast. Also, would you care for a latte? I have my own espresso machine that puts Starbucks to shame."

"That'd be wonderful. Thank you. Mind if I use your bathroom? I gotta pee something fierce."

"Help yourself."

After a quick pee and a splash of water to the face, I pulled on yesterday's clothes and headed into the dining room.

The others were already there, sipping lattes and eating bowls of fruit, cereal, and yogurt. Someone had moved the cutting board with the grimoire into another room—probably so we didn't lose our appetites.

Roxy handed me a latte topped with a heart-shaped design in the foam. Was she flirting? Or just being nice? *Goddess, lesbians are impossible to read sometimes.*

After breakfast, we cleared the dishes, and Roxy brought the grimoire back. Even though she set it down gently, I still felt a heavy thump—like a pressure wave rippling through the room. Even through the salt ring, its energy thrummed, steady and malignant, like some generator of evil.

"Has anyone tried opening it?" I asked.

"Not yet," Kari replied, eyeing it warily.

"I vote Morgana does it," Angel said, nodding at me. "You're the one who brought it here."

"Fine," I muttered. "But I barely know anything about spell work beyond basic circle-casting and a little herb magic."

"You grew up with two witchy moms," they replied. "Surely, you picked up something."

"We'll look through it together," Roxy offered. "Everyone here brings something to the table. Just... keep your emotions in check, okay? We don't need a repeat of last night's meltdown."

My pulse quickened. "Here goes nothing."

The moment my fingers broke the salt circle, the buzzing returned—low and insistent in the back of my skull. A hum of malevolence. Anger. Jealousy. Cruelty. The sensation sharpened the instant I lifted the book and set it in front of me.

The leather cover was bloodred, stamped with the word Grimoire and ringed with glyphs I didn't recognize. I probably didn't want to. Whatever they meant, it couldn't be good. For all I knew, opening it might trigger a magical booby trap.

The spine cracked as I lifted the cover. A faint whiff of bitter incense drifted from the paper. Erin's elegant handwriting filled the pages—her signature style ever since she took that calligraphy class.

Slowly, I flipped through the book. Erin had taken copious notes on casting circles, cleansing magical tools and spaces, the how-tos of creating a poppet, and the uses of sundry herbs and crystals.

About twenty pages in, her first spells appeared. One to make flowers bloom on command. Another to talk to animals. A scrying charm. A lie-detection spell. Even one to disguise the caster's appearance.

Then the spells turned darker. One to kill plants.

Another to invade someone's dreams. One to bind a minor supernatural being and force obedience through pain.

The ingredients shifted, too—moon water and herbs gave way to blood, hair, and bits of flesh. Some from the caster. Most from animals or other people.

Halfway through, I found the spell Sarah must've used. Erin's handwriting—once graceful—had devolved into a jagged scrawl. The spell described how to reanimate the recently dead, yanking the spirit back from the afterlife and chaining it to its old body.

A chill ran through me. It was horrifying to think Erin had tried this more than once—unsuccessfully, according to Belladonna Loveless. And now Sarah had cast it to raise Erin from the dead.

"This is it." I pointed at the page. "This must be the one Sarah cast."

Angel leaned in, eyes narrowed. "How'd she even pull it off? She's not a witch."

"Magic is essentially energy plus intention," Kari explained. "If the spell is written well enough, it can be followed by just about anyone. Like a recipe."

I read through the spell. "It uses a poppet embedded with a body part of the dead person such as hair, skin, or a fingernail. The caster recites the incantation written here three times then activates the spell with the caster's own blood on the head of the poppet."

"What's the incantation?" Angel asked.

"'Dark Moth—'"

"Stop! Don't read that aloud!" Thalia snapped.

"It's okay," Kari assured her. "It can't work without the blood and the poppet. What does it say?"

"'Dark Mother Hecate, I call upon your powers. Assist me in this midnight hour.'"

The buzzing in my skull spiked. Was Kari wrong? Could the words alone trigger something?

Against my better judgment, I continued. "'Recall the spirit of... insert name here... from the other side, and chain it to where it did once reside. Raise this body from the dead. Thus I command with my blood so red.'"

The buzzing became a sharp stab of pain. I gasped. The world around me fell away as life-and-death energies swarmed me like furious hornets. Someone was calling my name from a thousand miles away. I clung to the sound, fighting through the pain. I knew that voice.

It was... it was...

Erin.

Crying. Pleading. Begging to be freed.

<h1 style="text-align:center">CHAPTER 37</h1>

———

In a blink, I was back in Roxy's dining room. The grimoire was gone from my hands. Panic surged through me as I scanned the room, frantic to reclaim it.

Kari held the book, murmuring some kind of spell over it.

How dare she take it away from me! Thieving bitch!

"No! Give it back!" I demanded. "It's mine."

Kari backed away, still chanting.

Roxy stepped between us, locking eyes with me. "Morgana. Focus. Look at me."

For a second, her voice pierced the frenzy in my head. Then the need returned—raw and ravenous. I had to have that book. I'd tear it from Kari's hands if I had to.

I lunged for it, but Roxy and Thalia held me back. "Give it to me! Keep your damn spells off it, you stupid bitch!"

"Morgana, stop," Roxy said firmly. "That thing is poison. You don't want it."

I raised a hand to slap her, but Thalia caught my wrist in an iron grip.

"I need it! Give it to me! Now!"

I didn't even register Roxy's face closing in—until our lips met in a fierce, passionate kiss.

Instantly, the frantic hunger for the grimoire dissolved, replaced by a different kind of longing. The storm inside me cleared—like clouds parting after a summer monsoon.

What the hell just happened? Why had I lost control like that?

"Roxy?" I breathed. "Did I... Did you just..."

"Kiss you? Yes. How are you feeling?"

I almost laughed. How could I put my turmoil of dysregulated emotions into words? Embarrassed? Ashamed? Terrified? Oh, and the desperate need for her to kiss me again. And again. And again.

"I, uh... I'm... okay. I guess."

"Deep breaths," Roxy said. "You're safe. You're with us. You're with the Sand Witches."

I obeyed, breathing in slow, shaky gulps. The pull of the grimoire faded. Kari gently laid it back on the table.

"What just happened?" I asked, my thoughts still scattered. "Kari said reading the chant wouldn't do anything."

"It didn't activate the spell. How could it? There was no body to reanimate."

"But it still did something. I felt it." Then the memory hit. "Oh, Goddess—I tried to hit you!"

Roxy gave me a soft smile. "That wasn't you. That was the book."

"The grimoire pulled you into its grip," Kari explained. "That's the nature of malevolent magic. It's very seductive. But I've cast a spell to seal it off."

"Like the One Ring in Tolkien," Angel said. "You went full Gollum."

I nodded slowly. "Felt like I'd been transported between worlds. I heard Erin crying and pleading for help. At least, I think it was her. Hard to be sure. The grimoire created this painful buzzing in my head. But when Kari took it away... Goddess, it felt my heart had been ripped out of my chest. I would've done anything to get it back."

"I got that way when I was jonesing for a fix," Roxy said.

"Like I said last night," Thalia growled, "we should just burn it."

"Not until we unmake the revenant," Angel replied. "That's our mission, right? To keep more people from dying?"

"Maybe burning the grimoire will break the spell and destroy the creature. And if it doesn't, I'll tear that creature to pieces myself."

"It nearly killed you," I said, recalling the blood pouring from her tawny hide when she was in puma form. "You could have bled to death if you hadn't..."

The others turned to me, waiting.

Roxy tilted her head. "Wait... Thalia got hurt? When?"

Shit. I nearly outed her. "Sorry. I... I'm not making sense."

"Morgana, what are you not saying?" Angel pressed.

"She's trying not to say I'm a werepuma," Thalia said flatly, her tone edged with resignation. "But I am."

All eyes swung to her. My cheeks burned. I wanted to crawl under the table.

"At the O'Briens', I shifted to fight the creature. But it was faster and stronger than I anticipated. If I hadn't shifted back, I might've bled out."

"You're a... a werepuma?" Kari asked, wide-eyed.

"I am."

"I knew it!" Angel exclaimed.

I felt bad. "I'm so, so sorry for outing you."

Goddess! Could I be more pathetic? First, I nearly slapped the girl I'm crushing on, and now I'm outing my friends?

"It's fine," Thalia said. "Truth was gonna come out sooner or later."

The grimoire and our situation with the revenant were all but forgotten as the others peppered her with questions.

How'd she become a were? Did it hurt to shift? Who else knew? Did she belong to a pack? How'd she avoid shifting during full-moon rituals?

"Is that why Belladonna Loveless kept making cat references? She knew you were a shifter?"

"Enough questions," Thalia said, her tone sharp. "We need to break the spell and end this thing."

"There wasn't anything in the grimoire about reversing the spell," I admitted. "I should've searched Sarah's room for the poppet when I had the chance."

Then it hit me—Sarah's purse. What if she had it with her?

I rummaged through the zippered compartments, pulling out a wallet, a pack of tissues, and lipsticks. Then my fingers brushed something dry, ribbed, and papery. A small corn husk doll.

When I pulled it out, the buzzing pain returned, low and sharp behind my eyes. The doll had been crafted by folding corn husks and using string to form the head and the waist, fanning out at the bottom like a skirt. A tightly rolled husk had been inserted through the middle to form arms. On its head, a rust-brown smear that could only be Sarah's blood.

"This is it—the poppet Sarah made. It's thrumming with energy like it's powering the revenant."

"A corn doll?" Thalia asked. "Would that work?"

"Why not? It's all about intention," Kari replied. "The spell didn't specify what the poppet had to be made of. Corn husks are available at any grocery store."

"Now I'm craving tamales," Angel muttered, smirking.

"Okay, so how do we break the spell?" Roxy asked.

Kari studied the corn doll. "The grimoire doesn't say. Either Loveless never taught the reversal or Erin didn't write it down. But with a lot of poppet magic, taking it apart is enough to undo the working."

"Let's try it." I tugged at the string around the doll's head, but it wouldn't loosen. "Anyone got scissors or a knife?"

Thalia pulled out a pocketknife, flicking the black blade open with the press of a button. "Will this do?"

I blinked at the switchblade. Well, that was Thalia. Cats had retractable claws.

"Thanks." I sliced through the string, unfolding the husks layer by layer. Nestled inside was black candle wax melted onto strands of coarse red hair. Erin's, no doubt.

I laid the husks, hair, and wax on the cutting board. The dark energy faded to a faint pulse.

"I don't think the spell is broken. We should burn it," I said, looking up at the others. "Along with the spell page from the grimoire."

"Screw that," Thalia said. "Burn the whole damned thing."

Roxy nodded. "I'll get a fire started."

I carried the board into the living room behind her. Roxy set an artificial log on the grate and lit the gas flame. The fire crackled to life—cozy, under any other circumstance. But this task felt a lot more sinister.

"Whenever you're ready," Roxy said.

I dropped the grimoire and the poppet remains into the flames. The fire flared green and black, and acrid smoke billowed up the chimney. Finally!

Chapter 38

I RELEASED a breath when the flames returned to their usual yellow-orange. "I think that did it. If Kari's right, the revenant is..." I stopped short of saying "dead." That wasn't the right word.

"Gone," Roxy finished for me. "Should be just Erin's remains now. Her spirit is now free."

That was a relief. It broke my heart to lose Erin so soon after I moved back to Wickenburg. Even more so to think she was suffering because of her sister's attempt to bring her back from the dead.

"Maybe it's gone. Maybe it's not," Thalia said. "We need to go to the house and confirm the creature is destroyed."

"And if Erin's body is there—unanimated—we should call someone to retrieve it, so it, or rather, she can be reburied," I said, a wave of sorrow mixed with relief tightening my chest.

"I know someone at Houston's Funeral Home," Roxy said. "They handled her burial."

"I wonder if that cute cop's still guarding the house," Angel said, a mischievous glint in their eyes.

"I hope not," I muttered. "I'm so over cops right now."

"What can I say? I love me a man in uniform." They sighed dreamily. "Although being locked in the back of a cruiser isn't exactly the handcuffing role-play I have in mind."

We headed back toward the O'Brien house in Roxy's SUV. As we drew near, a column of black smoke spiraled into the sky.

Dread coiled in my gut. "You don't think..."

Sirens wailed behind us, and Roxy pulled onto the sandy shoulder to let a fire truck roar past.

"I got a bad feeling about this," Angel murmured, their voice tight with worry.

Roxy eased back onto the road, following the firetruck. "Guess we'll find out."

As I feared, the O'Briens' house was ablaze. Wickenburg PD patrol cars had sealed off the driveway.

"Did burning the corn doll and the grimoire cause this?" I asked. *Had I just added to the O'Briens' tragedies?*

"I don't see how." Roxy parked on the shoulder and put a reassuring hand on my arm.

"Maybe breaking the spell lit the revenant up too," Angel said. "As above, so below."

"Hopefully, now Erin's spirit is free to move on." Kari squinted at the officer by the tape. "Wait, I know her. Maybe I can find out what happened."

We climbed out of the Trailblazer and approached the patrol officer standing inside the yellow police tape.

As we drew near, the officer raised a hand. "Sorry, folks, this area's off-limits."

"Hey, Brenda. We were wondering what happened," Kari said.

"Kari? What're you doing here?"

Kari sighed before answering. "This is Erin's parents' house. We wanted to know what started the fire."

Conflict crossed the officer's face. "Can't give you any intel right now—not even off the record. We won't know the cause until the fire inspector does his thing. I can tell you a neighbor reported smoke coming from a bedroom window at the southeast corner of the house."

Southeast corner. Erin's bedroom. Had to be.

"Any bodies?" I asked. Had they found Erin? I didn't want to imagine what her remains looked like. Probably charred beyond recognition.

"Not that I heard. Call me this afternoon, Kari. I might have something then. Off the record, of course. And, hey... sorry about Erin. I hope we catch the Slasher soon."

"Thanks, Bren." Kari turned back to us, the sorrow evident in her eyes. "Let's go."

As we walked back to Roxy's SUV, I said, "Erin's bedroom is in the southeast corner of the house—same place the fire started. The revenant must have ignited when we burned the grimoire and poppet. It's gone."

"And Erin's spirit is free," Kari said, wiping a tear from her cheek. "Thank the Goddess."

We pulled one another into a group hug then piled into the Trailblazer.

The ride back was quiet. I hoped the fire hadn't done too much damage. One family shouldn't have to suffer this much in a single week. My heart ached for Sarah and her mom.

Back at Roxy's, Angel said, "I need to change and set up my tarot booth at the Fall Festival—it starts in a couple hours. Will I see y'all there?"

"I'll be there," Kari replied. "I'm reporting on the festival for both the *Wickenburg Sun* and *Phoenix Living*."

Thalia shook her head. "I have a desert survival class to

prep for, but I'll be reachable for the rest of the day in case the revenant isn't destroyed after all."

And then there were two. I wanted to stay and spend the day with Roxy. But I had other obligations.

"I promised Mom I'd help man the Wiccanburg Books booth. Are you coming?" I asked. "I'll treat you to a corn dog and some deep-fried pickles. Or whatever you're into."

Wow, I sound like a nervous kid asking someone to a school dance. Goddess, I'm such a dweeb.

Her eyes sparkled. "Corn dogs and deep-fried pickles, huh? You sure know how to show a girl a good time."

"Not that I'm asking you out on a date. I mean, I just... I don't know... wanted to thank you for letting me sleep with you. I mean, not sleep *with* you—not in *that* way. I meant, in your bed. Oh Goddess, I don't know what I'm saying."

She laughed, and I practically melted on the spot.

"Unfortunately, I have a shift at work I'm already late for."

Disappointment punched me in the gut. Probably just letting me down easy.

"But I'll swing by this evening. We can have our date then."

Serotonin, oxytocin, and dopamine lit up my ADHD brain like fireworks.

"You mean it? You actually want to go on a date with me? Even though I'm technically on the rebound? Ugh, sorry. Probably shouldn't bring up my ex."

"You didn't, technically. And I'd love to go on a date with you. I don't care if you're on the rebound. There are no rules. And we're not making any long-term commitments. We're just two women getting to know each other."

Her warm hands wrapped around mine. That simple touch sent all the romantic butterflies fluttering inside me. When was the last time Saffron made me feel that way?

Dating her had been a manic roller coaster. One minute she was treating me like royalty, the next like a cheap whore. Always extremes with her.

But Roxy wasn't like that. And she wasn't like the guy she'd been in school. She was tender and caring. When she looked at me, I felt she saw through to my soul. That should have terrified me. But oddly, it didn't. She didn't even care that I was Fae.

"Two women getting to know each other, huh?" I repeated. "I like that. I'll see you tonight then."

Without warning, she leaned in and kissed me. Not a full-on make-out session but more than a peck on the lips. It was enough to make me feel like I was floating.

Chapter 39

Before heading to the Fall Festival, I stopped by the hospital to return Sarah's purse—and break the news about the fire. A woman her parents' age sat with her.

"Hi, I'm Morgana Quinn," I said to the woman.

"Gloria O'Brien, Sarah's aunt."

"Pleasure to meet you." I turned to Sarah. "How are you feeling?"

"Better. Physically, at least. The doctor says I'll be discharged this afternoon. I'll stay with my aunt until Mom can go home." Her voice was flat and numb. Understandable, given everything she'd been through.

"How's your mom doing?"

"She'll be here for a few more days."

"I brought your purse." I set it on her bedside table. Unsure what to say with her aunt there. But I figured Sarah had told her what had happened. "We reversed the spell. The creature that attacked you and your family—it's gone."

Tears streamed down her face.

"It's not your fault," I reassured her. "Honestly, I might've done the same."

"No, it's not her fault." Gloria O'Brien looked me dead in the eye. "It's yours. All of you witches."

"What?" I felt dumbstruck. Totally did not see that coming.

"If you and your moms hadn't lured Erin into your coven, she'd still be alive. So would my brother. This is all your fault."

"Hold up! My moms had nothing to do with that grimoire Sarah found. That came from Belladonna Loveless, another witch Erin studied with before she joined the coven."

"I don't care. You're all evil in my book." Clearly, Gloria and her brother shared the same bigoted attitudes toward witches. I tuned her out and focused on Sarah.

"You took your sister's grimoire. And you cast the spell to reanimate her body. We're simply the ones who cleaned up your mess."

"My mess? That's my sister you're talking about."

"That creature may have used her body, but it wasn't Erin anymore. We freed her spirit to move on."

"Move on to what? Hell?"

"To whatever's next. Personally, I don't believe in hell. But if anyone deserves to go there, it's people like your father who make life a living hell for Erin and people like us. People who are queer. And Pagan. If you want to blame anyone, blame him."

I regretted the words the moment they left my mouth. She'd lost everything, and here I was piling on.

She started bawling. Her aunt comforted her then turned back to me. "Get out."

"Look, I'm sorry. I just wanted you to know we reversed the spell." I hesitated. "Also, your house caught fire. I think the creature caused it."

Technically true. Probably.

"You burned down my house?" Sarah wailed.

"What? No! It was the revenant. I swear. And I won't tell the police or fire department you reanimated Erin's body."

"Just leave. You people ruined my life."

I didn't know what else to say. So I walked out and drove downtown to help Mom and Mama Joyce set up for the festival.

"Don't take it personally, hon," Mom said as I arranged books on the display racks.

The tables had been arranged in a U shape under a canopy tent. A "Shoplifters Will Be Hexed" sign hung on the back wall. Next door, Angel was already giving a reading to a client.

Mama Joyce set out candles in a rainbow of colors, each with its own purpose. "Grief makes people lash out. Sarah's looking for a scapegoat to avoid her own feelings of guilt."

"I thought she was okay with Erin being a witch," I said. "Unlike her parents."

"Her aunt is there, filling her grief-stricken mind with more hate."

"Give her time, honey," Mom said. "She'll come around."

"Has Lenore returned?" I asked.

Mom opened a box of deity statues. "No. But, I can still sense our connection. Feels like she's traveled somewhere. If she'd died, I would have felt the breaking of our bond."

"I'm sure she'll turn up."

I filled them both in on the reversing of the necromancy spell.

"You think burning the corn doll and grimoire made the revenant catch fire too?" I asked.

"I wouldn't think so," Mom said. "But who knows how that spell was constructed?"

"I think you did right, destroying that grimoire," Mama

Joyce said. "No good can come from anything that woman taught Erin. She was a bitter, nasty woman who used magic as a way to hurt and manipulate people. Best steer clear of her from now on."

"I intend to."

When the festival opened, more people than expected wandered through our booth, flipping through books and eyeing the merch. Mama Joyce called it the *Practical Magic* effect.

Most of the year, they were God's frozen chosen—condemning anything their preachers labeled evil—witches, immigrants, queer people, unhoused people.

But this time of year, a sense of magic was in the air, and curiosity drew them in like moths to a flame.

Many attendees wore costumes—especially the kids. Probably a test run for Halloween, just a few nights away.

More than a few asked what we knew about the Wickenburg Slasher, often in whispered voices. I told them I didn't know anything other than what was in the papers. I didn't get the impression they believed me, but I didn't really care.

As the day dragged on, I kept checking my phone for a message from Roxy. So far, nothing.

Around four thirty, Dave and Melinda Talbot showed up while I was ringing up a customer. They stood just beyond the canopy, staring daggers at me.

"Murderous bitches," Melinda hissed at us. "You got a lot of nerve showing up here."

"Thanks for your business," I told the customer, handing her the book on magical herbs she'd purchased along with a receipt.

After she left, I turned to Dave and Melinda. "What do you want?"

"We want you dead," she snapped. "You and your witch cult murdered Jimmie and Linda."

"Actions have consequences, lesbo," Dave sneered. "You people are gonna pay—one way or another."

"We're not the Wickenburg Slasher. We haven't hurt anyone."

"You made my hair fall out in school!" she shot back. "Now you're back from Hollyweird, and suddenly, people start dying left and right. Coincidence? I think not!"

"Your hair fell out because you messed with my stuff. Actions have consequences."

Dave charged me, fists raised and murder blazing in his eyes.

I raised a defensive hand and unleashed a gust of wind that knocked them both on their asses. Guess I was finally getting the hang of my Faerie magic.

"What the hell?" Dave shouted as he got to his feet.

"Get your holier-than-thou asses out of here—unless you want to see what else I can do."

Not that I could do much more than summon wind, rain, and Faerie lights. But they didn't know that.

"Watch your back, bitch!" Melinda spat, brushing herself off as they stormed away.

People were staring at me. *Shit!*

"Be careful throwing around Faerie magic in public," Mama Joyce murmured when they were gone.

"What was I supposed to do? Let them beat me up?"

"Just... be careful. We don't need to give the cops any more ammunition to use against us."

She was right. But I didn't know how else to respond.

Needing a dopamine hit, I checked my phone again. My heart soared when I saw a text from Roxy: *Just walked thru the gate. C U soon. Thalia's on her way.*

"Good news?" Mama Joyce asked.

"Roxy's here."

"Ohh..." she said, eyes twinkling. "Someone got a date?"

I blushed. "Maybe."

A shriek tore through the air from the direction of the festival entrance. At first, I figured it was someone on a carnival ride—until another scream followed. Then another. A whole chorus of panic filled the air. My blood turned to ice.

"Roxy."

Chapter 40

Gunshots punctuated the rising screams.

I sprinted toward the festival entrance, weaving like a salmon upstream through a flood of panicked people fleeing the chaos. A sharp prickling ignited at the base of my skull. Dark magic.

An inhuman screech filled the air as the last of the crowd vanished behind me. Dozens of bodies lay twisted and bleeding on the ground. In the center of the carnage stood a humanoid figure, its body scorched black, skin peeled back in places to reveal raw red muscle.

The revenant. It hadn't been destroyed after all.

At its feet, Roxy writhed in agony, her clothes torn and slick with blood.

"Leave her alone!" I bellowed at the creature.

A massive tan shape rocketed from the shadows and slammed into the revenant with bone-jarring force.

Thalia! In puma form. It had to be.

They collided like wrecking balls and rolled across the ground in a blur of claws and teeth. The revenant shrieked, flailing with jagged fingers while Thalia raked its sides and bit hard into its shoulder. Her deep growls were raw with fury and pain.

The revenant retaliated, latching onto her flank with blackened claws, tearing a bloody gouge into her flesh.

I wanted to run to Roxy but couldn't get close enough without risking being caught in the melee. Desperate to do something, I called forth my magic to summon Faerie lights, hoping to draw off the revenant.

But panic muddled my focus. Roxy was still screaming. Blood soaked the ground beneath her.

A few lights flickered to life then sputtered out.

"Shit," I muttered.

A police officer appeared at my side, his gun drawn and eyes wide. "What the hell is that thing? How did it get in here?"

I wasn't sure if he was talking about Thalia's puma or the revenant. And I was too focused on trying to intervene to care.

Thalia and the revenant broke apart, circling each other, both crouched low and panting. Thalia's lips curled back in a snarl. The revenant hissed, its burned chest heaving, head twitching erratically.

Gritting my teeth, I drew on the storm inside me, channeling my fear and rage into magic. More lights sparked to life—ten, twenty, a hundred—and swirled in a glowing cloud above the revenant's head, pulsing brighter and brighter.

The revenant looked up, entranced for a split second. That was all Thalia needed.

She pounced, slammed the revenant to the ground, and locked her powerful jaws onto its neck. The creature shrieked, thrashing wildly, but Thalia held on. Bones crunched beneath her jaws as she shook it like a rag doll.

A gunshot split the air.

Thalia screamed, stumbling back. Blood streamed down her hind leg from a fresh bullet wound. She released the revenant and fled, limping into the parking lot.

The revenant staggered to its feet, ignoring the Faerie lights. Its head lolled grotesquely to one side. With a sickening *pop*, the head snapped back into place and locked its gaze on the cop and me.

The creature lunged at the officer with superhuman speed. More gunshots followed but did nothing to stop the revenant from slashing with lethal claws. In seconds, the officer was down, blood pouring from a gash in his neck.

When it turned toward me, I hurled a storm at the creature—howling wind, cold rain, a full blast of raw elemental force. The revenant tumbled backward, limbs flailing, but landed on all fours and came charging.

"No, you don't!" I yelled.

I reached deeper. Baseball-sized hailstones pummeled the revenant, battering it relentlessly. It shrieked, staggered, then bolted lightning fast back toward the parking lot.

I pursued it, hurling wind and ice with everything I had until I lost it among the pickup trucks and SUVs.

When I was sure it wasn't coming back, I scanned the lot. "Thalia? Can you hear me? Are you okay?"

No response. Was she alive? Hiding? Had she shifted, healed, and run off?

Dizzy with fatigue, I stumbled back to the festival, calling Thalia's name. But she was nowhere in sight. I was on the verge of collapse by the ticket stand when I remembered Roxy.

"No," I whispered. "Can't. Stop."

Operating on fumes, I pushed myself until I collapsed onto my knees beside Roxy's motionless body. Deep cuts crisscrossed her arms and torso. In the hazy dusk, her face looked bone white.

Kari appeared and knelt opposite me, tears streaming down her cheeks. "Hang in there, Rox. We're gonna get you help."

"Stay... with us," I cried.

I pressed my hand against her wounds to slow the bleeding. She screamed in pain—but that meant she was still alive.

"Help! Somebody!" I croaked, my voice drowned by the other screams around us.

Kari gripped my shoulder, her eyes locked on mine. "Save her, Morgana. Use your Faerie magic."

"Not. Sure. I can. So. Tired." I swayed, the world spinning like one of the carnival rides.

"You have to try," she pleaded. "Please, Morgana. Save her!"

Bizarrely, a scene from *The NeverEnding Story* bubbled up in my mind—the Childlike Empress begging Bastian to save her world.

I hadn't saved Erin—I'd been too late. But maybe, just maybe, I could save Roxy.

An idea occurred to me. It was a long shot, but my own magical energy was depleted. I closed my eyes and reached beyond my magic to another world.

"Titania, Queen of the Summer Court, please help me. As the daughter of Rhaedoryal, your loyal subject..." I didn't even know if Titania really existed or, if she did, that my father was a part of her court. "I call upon the magic of your kingdom—er, queendom—realm to heal my friend, Roxy."

In my mind's eye, I stood in a glowing moonlit oasis. Bioluminescent plants and flowers shimmered all around me—like something out of *Avatar*.

Was this the realm of Faerie? Or just my exhausted imagination?

I drew on the oasis's energy, envisioning tendrils of healing light flowing through me and into Roxy. Magic stirred—along with something vast and divine.

Roxy's cries quieted, and for a terrifying moment, I feared she was slipping away. But then her breathing evened out—strong and steady.

"Keep going," Kari urged. "It's working."

More and more life flowed through me from that mystical oasis into Roxy.

Out of nowhere, memories flashed through my mind—waking up next to Roxy, kissing her outside her house, her teasing me about corn dogs and fried pickles.

"Pickles," I murmured.

The vision continued. The sparkle in Roxy's eyes, the warmth of her smile, the way she smelled like lavender and rain.

Then a different memory surfaced—Roxy in high school, mocking me, calling me a lesbo and a perv. The vision shattered. Everything went black.

⁊

"MORGANA? HEY! PLEASE, WAKE UP."

My eyelids felt too heavy to open. "Just ten more minutes, Mama."

"Morgana, it's Kari."

"What? Where am I?"

It all came rushing back. Fall Festival. Revenant. Puma. Thalia. Hailstorm. Roxy. Shit! Roxy.

I forced my eyes open, my lids feeling like lead weights. Kari hovered over me, her face tight with worry. Dusk had given way to night, and the festival lights cast harsh shadows across her cheeks.

She slipped an arm behind my back and helped me sit up. "You okay?"

I drew a shaky breath and let it out slowly. "Aside from feeling limp as a rag doll."

Roxy's eyes were open and locked with mine. Her face seemed to have more color, though it was hard to tell in the glare of the festival lights.

"You're... alive," I rasped.

"Hey," she murmured.

"Was afraid... we lost you."

"Me too. But you... saved me. I felt it. Healing magic. Different... from mine, but... thank you."

I wiped tears from my eyes and leaned down to kiss her. Not sure why. It just felt right. I didn't even care that Kari was beside us, watching.

To my relief, Roxy kissed me back.

Paramedics arrived and loaded Roxy and the others into ambulances. Kari helped me to my feet.

"We should follow them," I said, watching the flashing lights disappear into the night.

She eyed me warily. "You okay to drive?"

Was I? I could barely keep my eyes open. "Not sure."

"Come on," she said. "You're riding with me."

On the drive over, I noticed two missed calls from Mom and a text from Mama Joyce.

MAMA JOYCE:

You OK? Where are you?

ME:

OK. Roxy hurt. Headed 2 hospital.

MAMA JOYCE:

We're packing up the booth. Will meet you there.

The emergency department was a madhouse. Dozens of festival casualties packed the waiting area, in addition to others with medical emergencies.

"We're here for Roxy Monroe," I told the woman at the check-in desk, once Kari and I reached the counter. "She came in by ambulance."

The woman's hair stuck out in every direction, and her expression screamed, *Get me out of here.*

She handed us visitor stickers. "Room twelve. Through the double doors, turn right. Seventh room on the left."

"Thanks."

Roxy lay in the hospital bed, the worst of her wounds already bandaged, a blood pressure cuff on her left arm and a pulse-ox sensor on her right index finger.

"How're you feeling?" I asked.

"Like I tried to give a pill to a lion—and lost." She managed a tired smile. "But I'm alive. Thanks to you."

My thoughts leapt to Thalia. Was *she* still alive? Had she shifted back and healed?

"Thalia was there—in puma form," I said. "She had the revenant by the back of the neck. Until some idiot cop shot her."

"Oh Goddess!" Kari's eyes went wide. "Is she okay?"

"I don't know. I looked for her after I chased off the revenant, but..."

"The revenant..." Roxy whispered. "Looked like a burn victim. Blackened flesh."

Kari shook her head. "I don't understand. Burning the doll and the grimoire should've destroyed it. I mean, it clearly caught fire."

"Powerful spell," Roxy murmured.

"I'm just glad you're okay," I said. "I'm sorry you got hurt."

"Lucky I have a Faerie watching over me." Her smile brightened.

"I swear, if you call me your Faerie godmother..."

Roxy laughed then winced. "No. But I owe you my life."

The last thing I wanted was anyone feeling indebted to me. I was no hero. "Buy me a corn dog and a deep-fried pickle, and we're square. Ugh, Goddess, I'm starving."

"Me too." Kari shifted awkwardly. "You two talk. I'll find a vending machine."

Once we were alone, Roxy met my gaze, her eyes twinkling. "Guess we missed our date."

"You really want to date me?"

"Yes, if you're willing. No pressure."

"You don't mind that I'm Fae?"

"Nope." She snorted. "You mind that I'm trans?"

"Of course not."

"You forgive me? For what I did in school?"

I remembered how that flash of memory had short-circuited my healing. Time to let it go for good.

"Forgiven and forgotten. We both did dumb stuff back then."

We kissed again—slowly and carefully. I didn't want to hurt her while she was on the mend.

When I pulled back, I asked, "How are we going to stop the revenant?"

"Mood killer."

"Sorry, but... people are still dying."

"We'll figure it out."

A frazzled nurse bustled into the room. "Good news, Ms. Monroe. You're being discharged."

"Already?" I said, incredulous. "She nearly died."

"She's stable, and we're short on beds. I'll bring your release papers shortly."

My phone rang. Mom calling.

"How's Roxy? I heard several people were killed."

"She'll be all right. Kari and I are with her at the hospital. They're releasing her now."

"Thank Goddess."

"But I'm worried about Thalia. A cop shot her while she was in puma form. Haven't seen her since."

"Oh Goddess! I hope she managed to shift in time to heal."

So Mom did know about her. What other secrets were she and Mama Joyce keeping?

"It was the revenant, wasn't it?" Mom asked. "Erin's reanimated corpse?"

"Yes. We thought we'd destroyed it, but..."

"I warned you, messing with necromancy... It's not for beginners. This is advanced-level stuff."

"And yet somehow a non-witch like Sarah was able to do it."

"And you see what's happened. People are dead because of it."

"No need to say, 'I told you so,' Mom. I get it."

"But we may have a way to stop the revenant for good."

"How?"

"Meet us at home when you can. We'll explain there. We're unloading everything at the bookshop now. The festival's been canceled."

"Yeah, okay."

Kari returned ten minutes later with a wry grin. "I half expected to walk in on you two going at it like rabbits."

CHAPTER 41

"ARE YOU OKAY TO DRIVE?" I asked Roxy as we helped her toward the exit.

The same question Kari had asked me earlier. Fortunately, a couple of vending-machine granola bars and a bottle of Gatorade had revived me enough to gain a little executive function.

"I'm sore, but I'll manage."

"I can drop you both at the fairgrounds to grab your vehicles," Kari offered.

"Thanks," I replied. "My mom thinks she knows how to stop the revenant for good. Are y'all in?"

Kari nodded. "Whatever it takes."

Roxy gave a weak shrug. "Don't know how helpful I'll be, but I'm in."

The fairground's parking lot was ablaze with red-and-blue flashing lights. Fortunately, we were allowed to retrieve our vehicles and make our way to my mothers' house.

To my surprise and my mom's relief, Lenore was back and perched on her wooden stand in the kitchen. Mom,

Mama Joyce, and Angel were sitting around the table, drinking rooibos chai tea, its earthy scent calming my frayed nerves.

"I heard from Thalia on the drive over," Kari said. "She managed to shift and heal in the parking lot. She's resting at home and will join us in the morning if we need her."

I breathed a deep sigh of relief before bringing everyone up to speed on what I'd witnessed at the festival—from the revenant's rampage to Thalia's attack and the hailstorm I'd summoned to drive the thing off.

"And then she used her Fae magic to heal me," Roxy added. "Saved my life."

"My daughter, the hero," Mama Joyce said, beaming.

"You raised her right," Roxy said.

I blushed. "Glad my freaky powers were good for something. But how do we stop this thing? We burned the poppet and the grimoire, but that thing's still going, even if it looks like a half-cremated corpse."

"Before the festival attack, Officer Brenda Gomez, my contact at Wickenburg PD, texted me," Kari said. "A trail of sooty footprints was found leading from the rear of the house to the backyard pool."

"Sooty footprints?" I thought about it. "The revenant. It caught fire, ran out of the house, and jumped into the pool?"

"How can a mindless revenant know to do that?" Angel asked.

"I don't know," Kari said. "Perhaps it has some sort of primal survival instinct."

"Okay, but how do we destroy it once and for all?" I asked.

Lenore made a series of clicking sounds, croaked three times, then said, "Quoth the raven. Lenore is a good bird. Good bird. Boop. Boop. Nevermore."

Mom nodded, as if what the bird had said was anything but random mimicry.

"We may have a solution. Or, rather, Lenore does." Mom sighed heavily. "She sensed we were in danger and sought out someone she thought could help."

"Who?" I asked.

"Grandmother Raven."

Kari gasped. "Wait! *The* Grandmother Raven? I thought she was an Indigenous myth, like Coyote, Elder Brother, or Kokopelli."

I raised an eyebrow. "You've heard of her?"

"She's a primordial being who can shape-shift into a raven. She's associated with creation, the balance of life and death, and ancient wisdom. Some scholars have compared her to the Navajo's Changing Woman or the Hopi's Spider Grandmother."

"According to Lenore, she's not a myth but a real-life immortal being," Mom explained. "Her home lies in a mountain cave somewhere."

The raven. In the mountain. That's what that infuriating pixie had said that day by the lake at Hassayampa River Preserve. Now the pieces were starting to fall into place.

"I think she's right. I ran into a pixie at the Hassayampa River Preserve a few days ago."

All faces turned to me, with expressions of surprise.

"You saw a pixie?" Angel asked. "Like Tinker Bell?"

I nodded. "She mentioned a raven in a mountain being the one that can help us."

"Why didn't you say anything about this before, honey?" Mom asked.

"Because the damned pixie was speaking in riddles. I didn't understand half of what she was saying. Until now.

But she also warned that Grandmother Raven was as likely to eat us as to help us."

Kari nodded. "It's said she doesn't part with knowledge easily. There may be a price to pay for her help."

I sighed. "Always comes down to money, doesn't it? How much would she want?"

Mama Joyce shook her head. "Doubt she's interested in money, peanut."

"What then? My firstborn child? My voice? A year of servitude?"

"Maybe," Kari answered. "Or she may ask for your true name or a memory."

"Doesn't sound so bad."

Mama Joyce gave me a pointed look. "Trust me, sugar. Those are no small things."

"Giving her your true name could give her power over you," Angel said. "She could make you her slave. Permanently. Which could be kinda fun if that's your kink."

"Or the memory she takes could be of Mom or someone else you love." Mama Joyce glanced at Roxy. "You'd remember everything else but not them."

A chill crept through me. "Would she really do that? Is she that evil?"

Lenore croaked twice, followed by a rattling purr. "Hi. Lenore's a good girl. Boop. Boop. Nevermore. Mwah!"

I looked to Mom. "Translation?"

"She insists Grandmother Raven isn't evil. She doesn't want human slaves." Another three croaks. "But she *is* an ancient being and may require you to fulfill a task to prove you're worthy of her help."

Something about the way she said that sounded ominous. "A task? Like what? How do I prove I'm worthy?"

"Possibly something that goes against your principles," Roxy suggested.

"Something *not* your kink," Angel added, grimacing.

"Or something impossible," Mama Joyce said. "Remember the Baba Yaga stories?"

When I was little, Mama Joyce read me stories from Clarissa Pinkola Estés's *Women Who Run with the Wolves*. Her favorite was the story of Baba Yaga, Vasilisa, and the doll.

Abandoned by her father and abused by her stepmother, Vasilisa seeks help in the woods with a doll blessed by her late mother.

There, Vasilisa finds Baba Yaga's house standing on chicken legs. The witch gives Vasilisa three impossible tasks, which she completes with the doll's help.

Impressed but wary, Baba Yaga asks how she accomplished the tasks. Vasilisa says her mother's blessing helped her.

An enraged Baba Yaga kicks Vasilisa out but not before giving her a skull with flames for eyes. Vasilisa brings it home, where it incinerates her wicked stepmother, and she's reunited with her father.

It always struck me as a weird little story. But then, most faerie tales were.

Mom shrugged. "Honestly, I'd rather we find another way to destroy the creature and restore Erin's remains. But I don't know how."

"And tomorrow night is Samhain," Mama Joyce added. "A revenant has a foot in both worlds, the living and the dead. It may be harder to destroy it when the veil between worlds is at its thinnest."

I turned to Kari. "You said there were only three ways to unmake the revenant. One, reverse the spell using the grimoire. But there was no reversal in the book. And we burned it besides. The second option was to destroy the corpse with fire. We tried that, but it's still killing people. Which leaves only one option…"

"Kill the spellcaster," Kari muttered.

"Which we will not do," Roxy snapped. "Sarah was reckless but doesn't deserve to die."

"Agreed. Not an option," I replied. "So, if this Grandmother Raven can stop this creature, then that's our solution. And if I have to strike a deal with the devil—or Baba Yaga—or whatever she is—I'm willing."

Mom's jaw tightened. "No. You've done enough. You fought the revenant and saved Roxy. You're already a hero. No need to risk yourself anymore."

"Look, I know I'm not some *chosen* one." As a writer, I always hated that trope. "But if not me, then who?"

"I'm going with you," Roxy said. "Before I got clean, I was a master manipulator. A lot of us addicts are. Anything to get our next fix. Maybe I can use those skills to help Morgana negotiate a deal."

"I'll go with her too," Kari added. "Perhaps my knowledge can help."

"I'm in," Angel said nervously. "Even if it's just to check this chica out. I mean, how often do you get to meet an ancient raven shifter?"

"How do we find her?" I asked. "Where exactly is this mountain? It could be anywhere."

Lenore answered with a series of caws and croaks. Mom translated.

"The mountain is a rocky outcropping east of Apache Junction."

I found this less than helpful. But Kari seemed to have an aha moment.

"Rocky Outcropping! Of course! Tseh'-Hos-Keet! That's what the Apache called the Superstitions."

"Lenore can lead you to Grandmother Raven's cave. But

you'll need to wait until morning. The terrain is rugged in daylight. Impossible at night."

I was impatient to get started, but Mom was right. I wasn't exactly outdoorsy. It'd been years since I'd hiked any mountains. And the thought of crawling through a cave freaked me out a little. Well, more than a little. Finding Grandmother Raven's lair wasn't going to be like the guided tours at Kartchner Caverns.

Better to wait. Maybe Thalia could join us, since she taught desert survival training. If she was up for it.

"We'll head out at daybreak," I said then turned to Roxy. "You want to stay the night?"

She smiled at me, and I melted.

"Sorry, but I didn't bring a change of clothes," she said.

My heart sank. "Oh. Yeah. I understand."

"But I can swing by my place, pick up what I need, and come back."

Joy flooded through me like the sunshine after a thunderstorm. "I'd like that."

Mom cocked her head, the way Lenore sometimes did. Weird. That bird was rubbing off on her. "So, are you two an item?" she asked with a teasing smile.

Heat rushed to my face. "I, uh…"

"We've developed a fondness for each other," Roxy said, coming to my rescue. "We're taking it a step at a time."

"Cue the U-Haul," Angel quipped.

Kari swatted their shoulder. "Behave."

"You're all welcome to stay over," Mama Joyce said. "And tomorrow, with a little luck, we can break this necromancy spell for good."

CHAPTER 42

I TEXTED THALIA BEFORE BED.

ME:

How R U feeling?

THALIA:

Sore but recovering.

ME:

Lenore's back w/ news. Ancient wereraven
may help destroy revenant.

THALIA:

G-ma Raven?

ME:

U know her?

THALIA:

Heard stories. Scary powerful.

ME:

She lives in a cave in the Superstitions.

THALIA:

I know the area. Will bring map & gear. Can be @ ur place at 8am.

ME:

C U then

Lying beside Roxy in my queen-sized bed, I felt the urge to kiss her senseless and explore her body.

But she needed rest to continue healing. And I needed to recharge. Especially with our upcoming excursion to the Superstitions.

So we settled for some gentle kisses before drifting off to sleep.

Morning came too soon, heavy with dread. I wanted more than anything to destroy the revenant and set Erin's spirit free. But the thought of negotiating with an ancient shape-shifter to prove I was worthy scared the hell out of me.

What would she demand for her help?

Roxy stirred beside me, opening first one eye then the other. "Morning."

"Good morning. How do you feel?"

"Better." She kissed me gently on the lips.

I kissed her back, passion blossoming in my core. Our hands began exploring each other's bodies, only to be interrupted by a knock on the door.

"Who is it?" I grumbled, feeling frustrated.

Roxy giggled beside me.

"Breakfast's ready," Mom called through the door.

I checked the clock and groaned. It was already seven thirty. Normally, I was up by five.

"Guess we should get moving," Roxy said.

"Suppose so. Time to save the world."

In the kitchen, Kari and Mom had cooked a feast—scrambled eggs, hot oatmeal, fresh fruit, Greek yogurt, and peanut butter toast. Roxy commandeered Mama Joyce's espresso machine and whipped up elaborate lattes for the coffee drinkers among us.

By the time Thalia arrived, we'd cleared the table. She unfolded a large topographic map of the Superstition Mountains.

"Where exactly are we headed?" she asked.

Lenore cawed and croaked then hopped onto the table and pecked at a spot on the map.

Mom translated. "She says that's where the cave is."

Thalia studied the spot where Lenore's beak had dented the paper. "Massacre Falls. I know the area. There's a lava tube high up on the mountain. Could be Grandmother Raven's lair."

"Massacre Falls?" Angel asked, visibly uneasy. "Well, that's not ominous. What'd she do? Wipe out a village or something?"

"The massacre happened in the mid-1800s," Kari explained. "Miners working for the Peralta family were digging for gold on sacred Apache land. The Apaches repeatedly told them to leave, but the miners refused. So the Apaches slaughtered them."

"Note to self," they replied. "Don't go mining on sacred Indian land."

I studied the map. The maze of squiggles showed the general lay of the land, but I had trouble gauging how rugged the terrain was. "How hard is it to reach this lava tube?"

"The hike to the falls isn't difficult. Everyone will need hiking boots. No sneakers. And we'll need to carry water. I don't know about the climb up to the cave. I brought along some climbing gear, but I hope we won't need it. We've got enough to worry about without newbie climbers risking a fall."

"Looks like it'll take a while to get there," Mama Joyce said. "It's on the far side of the valley, past Apache Junction."

"Couple hours' drive to the trailhead," Thalia replied. "Then about two hours on foot to the falls. But after that? No clue how long it'll take to find Grandmother Raven. If we want to be back before dark, we should leave now."

Roxy, Kari, and Angel dashed home to change clothes and grab hiking gear. I threw on a tank top, jeans, and a pair of boots I hadn't worn in four years. Fortunately, they still fit. I wrapped a bandana over my head to keep off the sun.

In the back of my closet, I found an old hydration pack with pockets for snacks, sunscreen, and a first aid kit. I filled it with water and took a sip. Tasted like old plastic. I was probably ingesting BPAs or phthalates or Goddess knew what carcinogens. Oh well. It was just a day hike... to track down an ancient being... who would probably kill us anyway.

When everyone returned, geared up for a rugged hike, I noticed Mama Joyce was dressed in scrubs.

"You're not coming with us?" I said.

"Wish I could, peanut. But I have patients to see." She kissed me on the forehead, a worried expression on her face. "Keep each other safe. Okay?"

"We will."

Mom and I piled into Roxy's Trailblazer, with me riding shotgun. Kari and Angel rode with Thalia in her Land Rover.

We headed southeast on Highway 60. At Morristown, we turned onto New River Highway to I-17 south then followed the Loop 101 around metro Phoenix. Eventually, we picked up the Loop 202 east to the Superstitions.

At noon, we arrived at the small gravel parking lot for the Massacre Grounds Loop Trailhead. A handful of hikers milled around parked cars, either gearing up for a hike or cooling down from one.

Jagged pinnacles rose sharply above the flat scrub desert to the east. Though the summer heat had overstayed its welcome this October, the air was cool and breezy. I took it as a good omen.

"Lot of people on the trail today," I said, grateful to stretch my legs after two hours in the car. "Must be the cooler weather."

"Most folks just stick to the loop trail," Thalia said. "Hardly anyone takes the side trail up to the falls unless it's rained recently."

"Why's that?" I asked.

"The falls only flow after a heavy rain."

"Bummer," Angel said.

Thalia opened a green canvas bag she'd brought and handed each of us a brightly colored helmet with a light mounted on the front. "You'll need these once we enter the cave. For now, just strap them to your belts."

"You hike here a lot?" Roxy asked.

"Now and then." Thalia paused for a moment before continuing. "I read a news article from ten years ago. A four-year-old girl was found wandering naked in an Apache Junction neighborhood. No one knew who she was or where she came from. I thought she might be... a were-puma like me."

"Were you able to contact her? Is she a werepuma?"

"Her records were sealed. Never found her. Guess I'll never know."

"There's gotta be more like you out here," Angel said. "Could be a whole pack of werepumas."

Thalia shook her head. "We don't travel in packs like wolves do. Pumas tend to be solitary once we've reached maturity. I've encountered a few pumas on my hikes over the years. But none were weres."

Mom gave her a sideways hug. "Well, I'm glad you're part of our witchy pack."

"Perhaps Grandmother Raven knows more about your kind," Roxy suggested.

"Maybe."

The Massacre Grounds Loop Trail meandered through low, gently rolling hills. Thalia led the way, with Mom beside her. Roxy and I followed close behind. Kari and Angel brought up the rear.

Saguaro, prickly pear, and cholla dotted the landscape, alongside ocotillo, brittlebush, and countless plants I couldn't name. Rabbits and lizards darted between rocks. Hawks and vultures gyred overhead, riding the thermals.

I'd never been the outdoorsy type, preferring to stay indoors and write. But I was in decent shape. And I was learning to appreciate the desert's rugged beauty. My Fae side stirred, sensing more than my eyes could see.

I extended my consciousness and tapped into the energy flowing all around me.

Life here was a struggle due to the harsh climate, made worse by drought and urban sprawl. Still, the plants and animals found a way.

I felt the cycles of life, death, and rebirth. Everything around me was an expression of the universe made aware of itself.

How had I never noticed this before?

And then I remembered I had as a child. Before Mama

Joyce bound my Faerie nature with that talisman. Now, the binding was gone. And I was open to it all once again.

Just as I was savoring this new experience, my boot caught on a rock. I stumbled, pitching myself face-first toward a teddy bear cholla and coming to an abrupt stop with my nose a few inches from its golden barbed spines.

Roxy pulled me back upright, having grabbed the back of my shirt just in time.

I stood there dazed, my pulse racing at the near disaster.

"That would've been painful," she said. "You all right?"

I took a deep breath, steadying myself. "I... uh, yeah, I'm okay. Thanks to you. Guess that makes us even."

She laughed. "Not even close. You saved my life. But watch your step out here. Not a place to be daydreaming."

"I was opening up my Fae senses. I can feel the life around us. Every shrub, every lizard, every bird, every insect. It's kind of a trip. I didn't, like, go invisible, did I?"

She laughed. "Nope. But if you're not careful, you could end up as a Faerie pincushion."

"Good point," I said with a smirk.

As we hiked on, we passed through a fence, and the slope grew steeper, the terrain rockier, and the vegetation denser. My breathing became labored. Maybe I wasn't in as good a shape as I'd thought.

Chapter 43

Thirty grueling minutes later, the trail ended at the base of a thirty-foot rock face. Palo verde, cats claw, myrtle, and mesquite ringed a shallow pool of water. Blackened sections of the cliff hinted at where the waterfall intermittently ran.

"The falls are spectacular after a good rain," Thalia explained.

"Maybe we'll come back another time after a storm," Mom said.

Angel, panting harder than I was, wheezed, "When we're not... bargaining away... our lives... with ancient beings... to kill the undead."

Yeah, that kinda killed the whole beauty-of-nature vibe.

"Where to now?" Roxy asked.

I extended my senses again. A herd of mule deer grazed a hundred yards to our right. To our left, a mother bobcat and three kittens huddled in their den. A pack of javelinas rooted through the scrub behind us, while a Gila monster sunned itself on a nearby rock.

When I pushed further, a jolt of magical energy

slammed into my skull, nearly knocking me on my ass. The intensity bordered on painful. Like grabbing a high-voltage cable barehanded.

I doubled over, clutching the sides of my head.

"Morgana? You okay?" Roxy asked. "Slow, deep breaths."

Her hand on my back steadied me. I drew in a long breath, filling my lungs, trying to relax my senses.

"I'm... all right. I connected to a powerful source of magical energy. It felt... primordial. As old as the mountains themselves. And yet, I'm weirdly drawn to it."

"Where is it?"

"Up there." I pointed toward the slope on our right.

The climb was steep but looked doable, with perhaps the need for handholds farther up. I could make out a large alcove in the rock about fifty feet above us. Could that be the entrance to Grandmother Raven's cave?

"Looks like a hell of a climb," Mom said. "I'm not sure this old body's up for it."

"I can stay with her," Kari offered.

Mom shook her head. "No, you go with them. I'll be fine. There's some shade. The weather's nice. And I've plenty of water and an energy bar. I'll just relax and enjoy the scenery."

"¡Ay, mami!" Angel eyed the cliff warily. "That's really steep. You sure there's no other way? Maybe we could lure her out."

"You don't have to go if you're not up for it," Roxy assured them.

"And miss out on a seeing a raven-shifter abuelita? Not a chance. Assuming I don't die of a heart attack on the way."

Mom took my hand. "Be careful, lovebug. That goes for all of you. Think before making any bargains. Grandmother Raven may not be evil, but she's not human either."

Neither am I.

"We'll be okay," I assured her. Whether I believed it was another matter.

Mom reached into her pocket and pulled out a rutilated quartz crystal wrapped in silver wire and hung on a matching chain. "Take this."

"What's it do?" The golden threads inside the crystal glittered in the afternoon sunlight.

"The rutilated quartz will help you tap deeper into your Fae nature. In short, it's a power-up for your magic. Mama Joyce and I also blessed it with a protection spell."

"Thank you, Mom." I hung the chain around my neck and hugged her tight. "I won't disappoint you, I swear."

"You never disappoint me, sweetie."

"Looks like you're taking the lead," Thalia said. "Show us the way. I'll bring up the rear to keep an eye on Angel."

I extended my senses just enough to lock onto the primordial magic like a beacon. Leading the group felt strange, especially without a defined trail. I hoped I didn't guide us off a cliff. Or worse.

Soon, we encountered petroglyphs etched into a massive boulder—tan markings standing out against the darker stone. I recognized deer, snakes, cacti, and human figures amidst abstract shapes. One looked like a rainbow, maybe. Above it, a bird with strange lines radiating from it. Grandmother Raven, perhaps?

The slope steepened until we were crawling on all fours. Not steep enough that we needed Thalia to break out the climbing gear. But one bad step could send me tumbling—and possibly take the others with me.

I was not in shape for this kind of workout. Judging by Thalia's constant encouragement, Angel was struggling too.

Just as my legs were starting to shake, I reached the alcove, roughly ten feet across. The rocky floor was rippled—cooled lava, I guessed. The mouth of a cave yawned at the back, disappearing into darkness.

I sat gasping while my pulse throbbed in my temples. Ancient magic thrummed in the air around me. What the hell was I getting us into?

Angel wheezed, their face flushed dark red. They lifted their water bottle and drained the last of it between ragged breaths.

"Need more?" I offered mine, which was still half full.

They nodded, and I passed it over. They took a few gulps then handed it back.

"Thanks."

"No problem."

Roxy laced her fingers through mine. "How're you holding up?"

"My hands feel raw. Like I've been scrubbing them with sandpaper."

"Wrecked my manicure, that's for sure." She eyed the cave's entrance. "I'm guessing Grandmother Raven lives in there?"

"Something does. I can feel it."

After a moment, Thalia stood and eyed the cave warily. "If everyone's ready, let's go. Helmets on, headlamps lit, and eyes open for anything."

Angel hesitated. "Anyone else suddenly claustrophobic?"

"If it's like other lava tubes I've explored," Thalia replied, "there should be plenty of headroom. I don't expect we'll be crawling through any wormholes."

"Wormholes?" Angel looked like they'd accidentally swallowed a worm.

"But watch your step," Thalia continued. "Could be loose rubble from the ceiling."

"You mean the cave might collapse?" I asked.

"Unlikely. But chunks do fall sometimes." She knocked on her helmet. "Thus, the head protection."

"Any other dangers we need to worry about, Catwoman?" Angel asked. "Mountain trolls? Orcs? Gelatinous cubes?"

"We're tracking down a prehistoric wereraven. Best to be prepared for anything."

I strapped on my helmet and switched on the lamp. "Follow me."

Chapter 44

The lava tube reminded me of an LA subway tunnel—minus the buskers and drunks. It smelled less like piss and vomit and more like scorched stone, ancient forests, and dry bones. The magic thrumming through the rock made my head pound.

Time seemed to slip away as we trudged deeper into the tunnel. Only the crunch of our boots and the occasional drip of water broke the silence.

How far in does this thing go?

"Tell me something," Angel said, breaking the silence. "If Grandmother Raven's so powerful, why does she live in a disgusting hole like this?"

"Maybe she likes the isolation," I said. "I mean, have you met people? Most of them suck."

"What keeps hikers from coming in here, I wonder?" Roxy asked.

"Maybe she eats them," Angel said with a nervous laugh.

My headlamp caught something glittering on the walls. Thin veins of gold snaked through white rock. "Whoa."

Everyone stopped and stared at the gleaming threads around us.

"Wow! It's so pretty." Roxy traced a vein with her finger.

"I wonder if this was Jacob Waltz's mine," Kari said.

The name didn't ring a bell. "Who?"

"The so-called 'lost Dutchman' whose mine was never found. Technically, he was German, not Dutch. Some say he rescued a survivor of the Peralta Massacre. This could be the legendary Lost Dutchman Mine."

"We're rich!" Angel exclaimed, opening a pocketknife.

"No!" Thalia warned. "This cave belongs to Grandmother Raven. Steal from her, may as well dig your own grave. Leave it."

"Come on! She'll never know." Angel dug the knife blade into the rock surrounding the thick vein.

The magical energy in the cave shifted sharply. No longer just ancient and powerful but threatening.

"Angel, stop!" I warned. "Something's happening."

Angel's headlamp flickered wildly then blinked out. "Dammit! Thalia, this light's defective." They smacked the side of their helmet to get it working again. It stayed dark.

Everyone else's headlamps flickered and died, plunging us into total darkness. Not even the faintest glimmer of light like you saw in movies.

"Hang on," Thalia said. "I've got a flashlight."

A sharp beam cut through the black—then flickered and died like the rest.

"What the hell's going on?" Angel cried, their voice edging toward panic. "I'm sorry! I won't steal any gold! I swear!"

The magical buzzing in my skull swelled into a migraine, making it nearly impossible to focus. I took three deep breaths and wrapped my hand around the amulet that Mom and Mama Joyce had made. The buzzing quieted, pushed out by my mothers' magic. I felt reconnected to my own Fae energy.

A single Faerie light flickered into existence, exceedingly bright in the deep dark. Then another. And another, until the chamber glowed with their pulsing radiance.

"That's amazing," Roxy breathed, followed by oohs and aahs from the others.

"Pixie Girl to the rescue," Angel said, half laughing. "Praise the Goddess for Faerie magic."

"Well done," Thalia said. High praise, coming from her.

We continued deeper into the tube until a wall of rubble blocked our way. A ceiling collapse, most likely.

"What now?" Kari asked. "Is there a way around?"

I reached out with my consciousness, tuning in to the ancient magic that had to be Grandmother Raven. This deep into the mountain, the energy surrounded us, making it harder to pinpoint.

"We're close," I said.

I focused on the Faerie lights, wondering if maybe...

They swirled and undulated like a murmuration of starlings. Searching, searching, searching...

A cluster vanished into a gap in the rubble, while the rest hovered and circled the opening—beckoning us in.

"There." I pointed at the gap.

It was tight—maybe two feet wide and barely tall enough to crawl through.

"A wormhole," Thalia murmured.

I recalled all those movies set in caves, in which some idiotic character said, "Well, it has to come out somewhere." Often about an underground river.

I didn't have to be an outdoor survivalist like Thalia to know that was bullshit. Underground rivers vanished into bedrock cracks or lakes filled with blind fish and no outlet.

And this wormhole? Who knew where it led, if anywhere?

"No, no, no, no!" Angel backed away. "I am *not* crawling through that. We have no idea how far it goes. It could narrow or dead-end. Emphasis on *dead*."

"Please don't tell me we came all this way for nothing," Kari muttered.

Roxy sighed. "Maybe there's another way to stop the revenant."

"How?" Angel asked. "Throw a Molotov cocktail at it?"

But I wasn't ready to give up. I reached out again. This time, the Faerie lights didn't just glow—they spoke to my mind, giving me the dimensions of the wormhole. And more importantly, what waited beyond.

Dread gripped my chest. My magic had reached the source of this other magic. Grandmother Raven. It had to be. So unbelievably primordial and feral.

"The wormhole's about fifteen feet long," I said. "Doesn't narrow. Opens into a wide chamber. And there... That's the source of the magic I've been following. It's Grandmother Raven. She's there. And she's waiting."

"You're sure?" Kari asked.

"I feel it too," Thalia said. "It's ancient."

"How can you tell?" Angel asked.

Thalia shrugged. "I just do. The way a forest can feel old."

Roxy studied the wormhole while Faerie lights danced and swirled around the entrance. "Well, either we go through or turn back."

"I'm going in. Whatever happens, happens," I said.

I climbed over the rubble toward the wormhole, hauling myself up hand over hand. Footsteps scraped behind me, though I didn't know whose. With each step and handhold, I expected the whole place to come down on me.

What would Mom do if we didn't come back? Would Search and Rescue attempt to save us in so remote a spot? Would their electric lights still work?

The mouth of the wormhole seemed even narrower, now that I was looking into it—like a fifteen-foot-long coffin. My pulse raced, and my dysregulated brain buzzed with countless worst-case scenarios.

"Just breathe," I whispered, echoing the words Mom and Mama Joyce had drilled into me.

"You'll have to take off your pack," Thalia instructed. "Push it ahead of you, then pull your body along after it."

"You've got this," Roxy called from behind. "Also... great ass."

I laughed, grateful for her attempt to cut the tension.

"Perv," I shot back with a grin.

"And proud of it."

I took a final sip from my hydration pack, slipped it off my shoulders, and shoved it into the hole as far as I could.

With a heave, I wriggled into the narrow tunnel, pushed the pack farther ahead of me, then dragged my body forward on my forearms. No room to use my legs. Push, pull. Push, pull. Over and over.

Faerie lights swirled around me, illuminating the wormhole. Far ahead, a faint glow shimmered from the chamber beyond. What waited for us there? What if something decided to come this way? A swarm of bats? Or Grandmother Raven herself?

Just focus on the task at hand, nitwit. Push, pull. Push, pull. Rinse and repeat.

"There's light up ahead," I called over my shoulder.

A slow, rhythmic pounding echoed around me—like a heartbeat, syncing with the magical thrum inside my skull.

"What's that noise?" Angel called from a ways behind me.

"Sounds like drums," Kari said, somewhat closer.

"Great," Angel grumbled. "Cue the part where the cavern fills with bloodthirsty orcs."

"You want to turn around, be my guest," I snapped back.

"Can't. Thalia's behind me. If I try to back out, she'll probably shift and bite off my foot."

"Damn right I will."

"Easy, Angel," Roxy assured them. "Just keep moving."

Suddenly, I was almost there. Five feet. Three. My fingers found the edge—then nothing but open air. The rhythmic pounding sounded less like drums now and more like the beating of... wings? Hundreds of them. Perhaps thousands.

Relief surged through me at the thought of getting out... followed by dread at whatever awaited us.

I eased my head out of the tunnel—and froze. The steady beat of wings ceased abruptly.

The wormhole opened into a cathedral-sized chamber with a ceiling that yawned overhead. A heavy musk of feathers mingled with the smell of scorched rock, dry bones, and fetid swamp water. I also caught the metallic tang of old blood.

A natural skylight pierced the roof of the chamber, casting a shaft of golden sunlight onto the stone floor. Dust motes and downy feathers drifted through the beam in slow spirals, lending the space an eerie, suspended stillness. My Faerie lights danced around me, almost protectively.

I hauled myself out of the hole, trying not to faceplant onto the uneven floor. I landed hard, graceless, and scrambled to my feet to take in my surroundings.

Around the edges of the chamber, shadow reigned,

deep and impenetrable. I sensed movement just beyond sight. The occasional deep-throated croak of a raven echoed, its call carrying an intelligence that made the hairs on my arms stand on end.

A massive stone slab table stood beneath the skylight at the far end. Black feathers, animal skulls, and strange trinkets made of silver and bone lay scattered across it.

Without a sound, a hunched female figure emerged from the darkness. Grandmother Raven. Her form wavered between shapes—human and raven—the light shimmering off the folds of her dark robes like the sheen of feathers.

She had a beak-like nose and very little chin. Her eyes were embers of eerie red light that seemed as if they saw my very soul. She regarded me with a mix of amusement and threat.

CHAPTER 45

THE MOMENT STRETCHED while the others got to their feet next to me. The lair seemed to breathe around us, alive with the caws of countless ravens and the hush of unseen wings flapping.

"Well, don't you look tasty!" Grandmother Raven croaked in a raspy voice that chilled my blood. "Five little witchlings come for dinner."

"Mierda," Angel muttered under their breath.

Not for the first time, I wondered if this was less of a Hail Mary and more of a suicide mission.

"I won't let you hurt us!" I summoned a gust of wind, filling the air with feathers and dust.

She cackled and waved a taloned hand. "As if you could stop me if I wanted to. Which I don't—yet."

My Faerie wind died instantly. *Shit!*

"A child of the Fae, though not pureblood."

"So what?" I shot back. "We're here to stop—"

"I know why you're here, Faeling," Grandmother Raven muttered with a mirthless laugh. "Your raven told me. You created an abomination. Playing with powers you can't begin to comprehend. But now your spell's gone awry. Humans are dying. So you've come to beg my help."

"We didn't cast the spell. The girl who did isn't even a witch. We burned the poppet and the grimoire she used, but the revenant's still killing people. So yes, we need your help."

She flew at me, obsidian robes flaring like wings, until we were nose to beak. Her eyes blazed like fiery coals. My skull throbbed under the pressure of her magic. Panic clouded my mind, making it hard to focus or even breathe.

"A child of the Desert Fae doesn't know how to unmake a revenant? Queen Verdanya would be ashamed if she knew."

"Queen who?"

The ravens around us began squawking in what could best be described as laughter. At my expense, no doubt.

"Quiet!" she instructed the birds. "Queen Verdanya, estranged daughter of Queen Titania. How is it you are ignorant of such things?"

"I... I only just learned I was Fae. Or half Fae, as the case may be."

She snorted derisively. "Pathetic. Humans and their secrets."

"Please! We need your help. People are dying."

"Humans die every day. Why's it my concern? You steal lands that don't belong to you, slaughter animals for sport, poison the air and water. Why should I help you? Better I let your dark creation kill every last one of you. Let you go the way of the mastodons and dire wolves that once roamed this land."

"You represent balance," Kari said from beside me.

"And what would you know of balance?" Grandmother Raven hissed.

Angel stepped to my other side. "Our coven protects the

environment. We teach stewardship and responsibility, as well as peace, love, and compassion."

"Do you now?" The ancient wereraven turned her fiery gaze toward Angel, who looked like they were ready to pass out.

For an instant, huge dark wings stretched out from her ancient body, resolving back into a cloak a heartbeat later. "Did you not seek to steal the gold from the very walls of my home, like so many before?"

"Sorry," Angel squeaked, staring at the floor.

Thalia took a step toward her and growled, low and rumbling. "No one's taking your gold, old raven. Now back off!"

Grandmother Raven whipped her head sharply toward Thalia then cocked it sideways like a bird. "What have we here? A mountain cat skulking into my lair? Hunting for birds, are we, puma?"

"You don't scare me."

She flew at Thalia and wrapped taloned fingers around her throat. "You're not the only predator here with killing claws, kitty cat."

"We're willing to strike a bargain," I said through gritted teeth.

She released Thalia and turned back to me. "A bargain. Of course. Typical Fae. Everything's transactional with you."

"Or you could help us for free," Roxy suggested. "Out of kindness. Make the world a better place?"

"This world was better before the pale skins arrived. It will be better once they're gone." She paused, locking eyes with me. "But I will help you, Faeling—so pitifully ignorant as you are of your magic and your people."

I dared to breathe a sigh of relief. "Thank you."

"In return, you will do me a favor."

Shit.

"What favor?" I asked warily.

"The Fae stole something from me. An artifact of sorts. You will go to Faerie and retrieve it."

"What sort of artifact was it?"

"Does it matter? You have a creature to destroy. That's your priority, is it not?"

"The details do matter," Roxy said firmly. "Tell us what was stolen and where it is. Otherwise, no deal."

Grandmother Raven glared at Roxy. "Who are you to dictate terms to me, witchling?"

Roxy put an arm over my shoulder. "Morgana's my girlfriend."

Wait, did she just say girlfriend? *We haven't even had an official date. Not that I'm complaining.*

Roxy continued. "I won't let her be manipulated into a bad bargain. Not by you or anyone else."

The old raven twirled a finger, conjuring wisps of pungent smoke. The stench was familiar. Something I remembered from a visit to a cleared-out flophouse with an LAPD detective. Black tar heroin.

"I know the deals you like. Remember how it made you feel? What wouldn't you give for just one more hit?" She drew out the words teasingly.

Roxy's eyes glazed over, their lids half closed. "Oooh..."

What the hell? Freakin' bitch was using Roxy's addiction against her? *Not gonna happen!*

I gripped the rutilated quartz crystal Mom had given me and again summoned wind. More furious this time. Enough to shove Grandma here back a few steps and disrupt her hold on Roxy.

"Stop it now!" I growled at her, less from fear and more to threaten.

The narcotic haze dissipated, and Roxy's eyes cleared.

"What's it to be, Faeling? Do we have an accord? I help you unmake the abomination. You return what was stolen by your people. Or does your misbegotten creation kill every last two-legged in this land? Personally, I prefer the latter."

I stepped back and whispered to the others. "Thoughts?"

"I'd prefer we knew more details," Kari replied. "Like what was stolen."

"You don't even know how to get into Faerieland," Angel pointed out. "Or which court might have what she says was stolen."

"But we must stop the revenant," I insisted. "This may be our last shot."

"Not if it means risking your life for some trinket," Roxy said. I was glad to see her back to her usual self.

Grandmother Raven's eyes blazed. "What was stolen was no mere trinket, witchling! It was a powerful artifact. And without it, this land will burn along with all of its inhabitants."

"Why not get it yourself, if you're so powerful?" Thalia asked defiantly.

"Shall I show you how powerful I am, little cat?"

I felt her magic fill the room, dark and feral. The air filled with dozens—maybe hundreds—of ravens who dove perilously close to our heads with outstretched claws and razor-sharp beaks.

Thalia swallowed hard and lowered her gaze. "No, Grandmother Raven."

The ravens once again settled in the shadows. Cawing and croaking their threats of violence.

The ancient wereraven turned back to me. "It was the Desert Fae who took it. Only one of your kind can retrieve it."

"I'm only half Fae. And I've never been to the world of Faerie. I wouldn't know how to get there."

"Figure it out, child! Do you want my help or not?"

"Yes."

"Then after the creature is destroyed, you will return here by the next full moon. I will tell you what was stolen, and you will travel to Faerie and retrieve it. Do we have a bargain?" She extended a hand, talons gleaming in the flickering Faerie lights.

I glanced at Roxy, looking for guidance.

She shrugged, her expression tight. "Your call, babe."

The term of endearment surprised me, but I liked it. It boosted my courage a little.

I locked eyes with Grandmother Raven. The thought of accepting this quest terrified me.

But people had been dying since I returned to Arizona. Maybe not because of me. But perhaps I could stop the carnage. With her help.

"We have a bargain." I shook her hand, feeling like I'd made a deal with the devil.

As I pulled away, one of her claws sliced open my palm, drawing blood.

"What the hell?" My hand burned like I'd touched a hot stove. I gasped and pushed down hard against the pain.

"Blood seals the deal. No backing out, Faerie child."

I hurriedly wrapped my bandana around the wound. "Fine! Now tell me how to unmake the revenant."

In the shadows, the ravens stirred once again—fluttering, shrieking, and cawing in outrage.

"Silence!" Grandmother Raven waved an arm. The birds ceased their racket. To me, she said, "It must end where it began."

"What the hell's that mean?" Angel snapped. "We came for answers, not riddles."

"She means Erin's grave," Kari said. "That's where Sarah cast the spell."

"Ah, the clever one. Yes, at the grave."

A raven landed on the stone table, picked something up in its claws, and deposited it in the old woman's hand.

"Take this fetish." She handed me a foot-long cholla skeleton. A corroded double-A battery had been lashed with twine to the woody lattice.

Seriously? This was supposed to help me bring down the revenant? Damned ravens and their trinkets!

"This? It's a bunch of junk."

She cocked her head. "Is it? Then give it back."

I hesitated. Was this a test? A trick? "Okay, not junk. But how do I destroy the creature with it?"

"With fire, of course."

"We tried that," Thalia said. "It didn't work."

"Because she jumped into a pool," Roxy reminded me. "No water at the cemetery."

"But how do we set it on fire again?" Angel asked. "Douse it with lighter fluid and toss a match? Give it the old Dean Winchester treatment!"

"Ordinary fire won't break the spell," Grandmother Raven croaked. "But Faerie fire will."

Naturally. The one element I can't control.

"I've tried summoning fire. I can't do it. Wind and rain? Fine. Even hail. But fire? All I get is Faerie lights." The ones I'd conjured danced around the chamber, as if to emphasize my point.

"I gave you the fetish. Must I feed you every last detail? Figure it out, Faerie child. I'm not here to hold your hand." She fixed her blazing eyes on me. "I have honored my part of the bargain. By the next full moon, you will return here to fulfill yours. Refuse, and you will perish. Quite painfully."

Her gaze dropped to my neck. With a hiss, she snarled, "What's that wretched thing at your throat?"

Instinctively, I gripped the rutilated quartz. "An amulet of protection. A gift from my mothers."

"A mother's blessing?" She hacked and spat. "I want none of that here. Get out! All of you! Or my children and I shall dine on witchling this night."

In the blink of an eye, she transformed into a gigantic raven, massive wings unfurling as she took to the air. Three times she circled overhead before vanishing up through the skylight, followed by a steady stream of ravens.

CHAPTER 46

I SHOVED the fetish into my pack, ignoring the sting in my palm where Grandmother Raven's claw had sliced it open. "Let's get the hell out of here."

"Wait," Angel said. "What other goodies are on that altar?"

"Leave it," Thalia warned. "Unless you want her and her minions to rip you apart."

Angel heaved a theatrical sigh and rolled their eyes. "Fine."

I led the way back through the wormhole, Faerie lights bobbing ahead as the only illumination. Even with the boost from my mothers' amulet, keeping them lit this long was draining me. But without them, we'd be lost in the dark.

Once we squirmed through the narrow gap, we bolted down the lava tube and burst into daylight.

"Oh my Goddess!" Angel wheezed as we collapsed in the alcove outside the cave. "Never been so happy to see the sun. And coming from a goth, that's saying a lot."

My mind flooded with dysregulated emotions. Fear.

Anger. Despair. Shame. Hope. I wanted to curl up on my bed and disappear for a year. Unfortunately, that was not an option.

"We just made a bargain. With a primordial being," was all I managed to say.

"Correction, Tinker Bell." Angel shook their head. "*You* made a bargain with a primordial being. I didn't agree to squat. She scared the hell out of me. I may have to sleep with the lights on for a week."

"Guess it *was* just me, huh?"

Even if I reversed the necromancy spell, destroyed the creature, and laid Erin's body to rest, I alone was oath-bound to steal a magical artifact from the Fae. Total suicide mission. And if I failed or refused? Goddess knew what she'd do to me.

"But," Angel added with a grin, "we Sand Witches stick together."

I glanced at them, their face still flush from sprinting out of the cave. "Truly?"

"You kidding? A heist in Faerie? Hella road trip."

Thalia gave a curt nod. "We're a team. Even if Sand Witches is a stupid name."

"Absolutely," Kari said, her voice calm but resolute. "We're with you, Morgana."

Roxy put a hand on my arm. "We got your back, babe."

"Did you mean what you said earlier? About me being your girlfriend?"

"I did—if you're cool with that."

"It's a little sudden." Warmth bloomed in my chest. "But I'm totally cool with it."

"You were seriously badass in there," she said.

"I was?" I blinked at her.

"When she..." Regret filled Roxy's eyes. "When she used

my addiction against me, you pushed back. Against someone like her, that's totally badass."

"I wasn't going to let her hurt you. I don't care who or what she is. Besides, you stood up for me. So we're even."

We sat in silence for a long moment.

"How's your hand?" Roxy asked.

I unwrapped the bandana, which was smeared with dried blood. "Looks like the bleeding stopped, but it still burns like hell."

"Want me to try healing it?" she offered.

"Can't hurt, I suppose."

She began tracing a sigil over the wound but yelped in mid-chant. She jerked her hand away as if she'd touched a hot stove. "Yow!"

"What's wrong?" I asked, alarm trilling in my voice.

"That's not just a cut, Morgana. It's a mark. Her mark."

"Blood seals the deal," I murmured, echoing Grandmother Raven's words.

"Her way of making sure you can't back out," Kari said.

My pulse spiked as a thousand worst-case scenarios swarmed through my brain at once.

"What was I thinking, striking a deal with her? Will that fetish even do anything? It's just junk."

"Maybe it's not," Roxy said. "You think you can summon Faerie fire?"

"No clue. How do we draw the revenant back to Erin's grave?"

"I think I can help with that.," Angel said. "We'll each need to bring something that had personal value to Erin. A photo or memento. A gift she might have given. I'll handle the rest."

"Not like we've got a ton of options," Thalia muttered.

"We should head back to Wickenburg," I said. "End this thing once and for all."

Climbing down from the alcove was tricky. Footholds were harder to find when looking down. But eventually we reached the bottom.

The moment Mom spotted us, she raced over and hugged me tight. "Oh, honey. I've been worried sick. Are you all right?"

"We're fine." Shorthand for "I don't want to talk about it."

"Did she give you a way to destroy the creature?"

"I think so. We'll see."

"What did she demand in return for her help?" The concern in her voice was palpable.

"I agreed to retrieve a magical artifact the Fae stole from her."

Her face drained of color. "Morgana, no! Do not mess with the Fae. You'll only get yourself deeper in trouble."

"Don't have much choice, Mom." Goddess knew, I wished I did. "We need to go. The longer we wait, the more people the revenant could hurt."

The hike back to the trailhead was long and quiet. Nothing but the crunch of our boots and the occasional birdsong announcing the end of the day. The setting sun cast long shadows across the trail as dusk approached.

My ADHD brain kept looping through everything that happened in Grandmother Raven's lair. Had I swapped one nightmare for a whole new set of horrors?

How would we even get *into* Faerie? And what the hell would we find there? Some bizarre mashup of Alice's Wonderland and Harry Dresden's Nevernever? A world ruled by sadistic queens and crawling nightmarish monsters? Mortals had vanished into that realm for years. Sometimes decades.

Still, part of me was curious. The Fae were technically my kin. Maybe I could find my father. What would he think of me? Would he help me master my magic? Or scorn me for being a half-breed?

"You okay?" Mom asked when we reached the parking lot.

"I'm fine." An obvious lie.

What was I supposed to say? That I was terrified? That I should've listened to her and Mama Joyce and never struck a bargain with Grandmother Raven?

Mom placed her hand on mine. "We believe in you, sweetie."

"You got this, babe," Roxy assured me.

"I just hope I can summon fire. Otherwise..."

"We all get sliced into steak tartare," Angel deadpanned.

"You've faced that thing twice already," Kari said. "Both times you drove it off."

"Total dumb luck. The Faerie lights were an accident. And the hail... I was just so pissed it hurt Roxy..."

"It wasn't luck," Mom said. "It's your intuition. You've got a gift, sweetie. You're a natural. You'll figure it out."

"If I'm so gifted, why'd I beg an ancient bird woman for help and get myself into a worse mess?"

"Because you're still learning," Roxy said. "Nobody's born knowing how to wield magic. Keep trusting your Faerie instincts. You'll figure it out."

On the drove home, Mama Joyce texted me saying Sarah's mother had been released from the hospital. Sarah was still blaming us for what happened to Erin.

Two vehicles sat parked in our driveway when we arrived home around seven. One was a Wickenburg PD police cruiser. The other was unfamiliar, though I had a feeling I knew who was inside.

CHAPTER 47

I SIGHED. "Seriously? Again? How many times do we have to say it—we're not the killers."

"Just play it cool, babe," Roxy said. "Let's hear them out, see what they want."

I passed her my hydration pack. "Hold onto this for me. The fetish is in one of the side pockets."

"Will do," she said. "Good luck."

"Promise you'll visit me in prison," I said, only half joking.

"I'll bake you a cake with a hacksaw blade hidden inside it."

I gave her a quick kiss. "Thanks."

The moment I stepped out of Roxy's SUV, two uniformed cops emerged from the police cruiser.

"Trick or treat?" I said.

I couldn't help it. It *was* Halloween, after all.

Detective Hatathlie stepped out of the other vehicle. "Morgana Quinn, you're coming with me." Anger rolled off her in waves.

"This is harassment, Detective," Mom snapped, stepping between us. "My daughter has nothing to do with these murders."

"Don't lecture me, Ms. Quinn." Hatathlie held my gaze, her dark eyes glinting in the glow of the headlights. "Four more people died last night—two of them police officers. More than a dozen others are in critical condition."

"I know," I said. "I was there. I stopped it."

"Did you? Seems you've been there for every one of these attacks. This was a quiet little town until you returned. So either you're involved or you know who is. Officer Riggs, place her in custody."

Mom turned to me, her voice cool. "I'll call the lawyer. Don't say a word until he gets there."

I threw my arms around her. "I love you, Mom. I'll be okay."

Officer Riggs cuffed me and read me my rights then shoved me into the back of the cruiser—right in front of Roxy and the others. What if she didn't want to be with me after this?

Sure, she knew I was innocent. But that didn't stop my ADHD from flooding my mind with shame. The burn of the steel against my flesh didn't help either.

Riggs drove me to the station with full lights and sirens going, dumped me back in the same interrogation room, and—thank the Goddess—uncuffed me. The steel had burned fresh welts into my wrists. I tried to soothe them with magic, but nothing happened.

Ten minutes later, Detective Hatathlie swept in, a stack of case files and a laptop tucked under one arm, and set them down on the table between us.

She glanced at the bloody bandana on my hand then the raw welts circling my wrists. "Do you require medical attention?"

"No." Doctors probably couldn't remove Grandmother Raven's mark. And the welts? They'd fade eventually.

"You've been read your rights?" Her tone was clipped and harsh. No fake sympathy. No offers to "help me out of a jam."

"Yes."

"Knowing that, are you willing to answer my questions?"

I hesitated. Didn't want to spend the rest of my life in prison—or worse, face the death penalty—for something I didn't do.

But I didn't want my moms going broke over legal fees. And the sooner we ended this necromancy nightmare, the sooner the town would be safe again. I just wanted it over.

"I'll tell you what I know."

"Then explain this." She opened the laptop, tapped a few keys, and turned it to face me.

A shaky video played, most likely recorded on someone's phone at the Fall Festival. It showed the scorched revenant attacking someone. When other people tried to intervene, it attacked them as well, mowing them down like a landscaper with a chainsaw.

She stopped the video and closed the laptop.

"What *the hell* is happening in my town? And don't even think about playing dumb—you're neck-deep in this."

"You wouldn't believe me if I told you."

"Try me. I'm open-minded." She absolutely wasn't. "Who is that?"

I struggled with what to say. This was a person who already had a grudge against witches. Telling her the truth would only reinforce those beliefs.

"It's a revenant."

"A reve-what?"

"A reanimated corpse."

"You mean like a zombie? You're telling me a zombie is slaughtering the citizens of my town? Morgana, I don't have time for faerie tales."

I snorted. *Faerie tales.* "I told you that you wouldn't believe me. But I'm telling you the truth."

"The Wickenburg Slasher is not a zombie. But you know who the killer is. And if you don't tell me the truth, I'll arrest you, your moms, and your friends—anyone associated with that witchy cult of yours. I'll search your homes, your businesses—I will not stop until one or all of you are rotting in prison for these crimes. Am I making myself clear, Morgana?"

Fury surged through me. "Leave my moms and friends out of this!"

The overhead light stuttered, flared, then burst with a loud *pop*. Darkness swallowed the room, save for a faint glow under the door. Above us, Faerie lights shimmered to life, flickering like fireflies.

Well, shit! Guess my magic's out of the broom closet now.

Hatathlie gawked at the lights, eyes wide with wonder. "What the...? You... you're doing this?" She reached up to touch them then jerked her hand back. "It tingles."

"It's magic," I said. "It does that."

Weariness washed over me. The Faerie lights winked out, leaving us in darkness.

"Aw, where'd they go?" she murmured, voice full of wonder and a hint of regret.

She cracked the door to let in some light.

I considered making a run for it, but I knew it wouldn't fix anything. If I wanted to clear my name, I had to level with her.

"Magic is real, Detective. And most of the time, it's harmless."

"But not all the time."

"No. Necromancy's not harmless. And no, I didn't do it."

"Necromancy?"

"Someone reanimated Erin O'Brien's corpse. That's why her body is missing from her grave."

"Reanimated? Like in *Frankenstein*?"

"Not exactly. Someone cast a spell to bring her back."

"So, which one of you witches cast the spell? Because we know you were there the night her body went missing."

"No one in my moms' coven would do such a thing. They've got strict rules against that kind of magic."

"Then who was it?"

I didn't want to throw Sarah under the bus, even though she had turned on us. She'd been through enough. But I couldn't lie convincingly either. *Damned Faerie blood.*

"The O'Briens found Erin's old grimoire at her apartment while picking out a dress for her funeral."

"A grimoire? Is that like a spell book?"

"Yes. It had a necromancy spell that Erin learned from Belladonna Loveless."

"The lady in the wheelchair?" Hatathlie looked skeptical. "The O'Briens despise witchcraft—especially Erin's dad."

"He was distraught over her death," I added. "Any father would be. He would've done almost anything to bring her back." Technically true. Even if he hadn't actually done it.

"You're saying Phillip O'Brien, a devout Catholic, cast this spell? Convenient that you pin it on him, seeing as how he's dead and unable to defend himself."

I simply shrugged.

"Necromancy sounds like advanced magic. Did you and your friends help him?"

"We had nothing to do with it. He hates us. We only learned about the revenant after we went to the cemetery late that night. After the spell was cast, Erin's corpse clawed its way out of the grave. Later, we tracked it to the O'Briens'. But we were too late."

"And why were you tracking this thing?"

"To destroy it before it could hurt anyone."

"I take it you were unsuccessful—seeing as how it killed a whole bunch more people at the Fall Festival." She glared at me.

"Yes, so far we've been unsuccessful. But I think we can destroy it now," I said. "If you let us."

"Why would Erin attack her own family?"

"I don't know why. Perhaps because of how they treated her. Same as with Jimmie and Linda Collins."

"And Charles Ralston?"

"I don't know. I don't have all the answers. My friends and I were just trying to help."

Hatathlie shook her head, clearly weighing how much of this she actually believed. "You realize how insane this all sounds?"

"That's why I didn't tell you before. I knew you wouldn't believe me. But it's the truth."

She went quiet, clearly waiting for me to say something incriminating. I wasn't playing.

"If Erin's zombie-revenant thing is the Wickenburg Slasher, which one of you killed Erin?"

Another tsunami of emotion rolled through me. Anger. Grief. Shame. And once again the Faerie lights flickered to life above us.

"It wasn't us, Detective," I yelled at her, letting it all out, tears of fury rolling down my cheeks. "We all loved Erin. And despite what you think, I didn't resent her being with Kari Sullivan. I'm glad Erin and Kari were together."

I took a deep breath, not so much to ground but just to push everything out.

"I treated Erin badly when I broke up with her in school and was hoping for the chance to make up for it. I am racked with guilt over how I humiliated her. She was a good person. She didn't deserve what happened to her. And if I knew who killed her, I would tell you in a heartbeat, no matter who it was. Because despite what you might think about me and my moms and their coven, we care about people. Our being Pagan doesn't make us evil. It's not the witches you should be afraid of. It's the people who burn us. As for who killed Erin, you tell me. You're the detective."

"We didn't find any fingerprints at the scene except yours. Still waiting on DNA."

"What DNA?"

Her fierce expression softened. "Erin O'Brien had human skin under her fingernails. We're hoping the DNA will give us a match. But the Phoenix Crime Lab's backed up."

Hatathlie stared for a moment at the twinkling Faerie lights and eventually met my gaze.

"So, how do we stop this revenant-zombie-thing?" she finally asked.

"Fire."

"Fire? This town is a tinderbox. The wildfire risk is very high with the lack of rainfall."

"Not ordinary fire. Faerie fire. Don't worry. I can summon rain if we need to put it out. At the festival, I drove off the creature by summoning hail."

"You did that?"

"Yes," I said proudly.

"Several vehicles sustained hail damage that night. The owners might want to have a talk with you."

"I was trying to save lives," I growled through gritted teeth.

"And you can summon fire as well?"

I sighed. "I'm not sure. Grandmother Raven thinks I can." I immediately regretted saying her name.

"Grandmother Raven? She a member of your coven?"

"No. She's a wereraven who lives in the Superstition Mountains."

She barked out a dark laugh of disbelief. "A wereraven? As in a person who can turn into a bird?"

"You think I'm making this up?"

Detective Hatathlie folded her arms and shook her head. "Honestly, I don't know what to think. Magic, monsters... I'd have laughed it off yesterday. But now..."

"You asked for the truth. I gave it to you."

"Do you really think you can stop this revenant from killing again?"

"Yes." I hoped.

"Then you better get to it. The town council's ready to fire my ass for not catching the Wickenburg Slasher."

DOUGLAS TREMBALL, Mom's attorney, showed up just as I was leaving. He was dressed as a Hollywood version of Dracula—slicked-back hair, white face paint, ceramic fang extensions, cape. The whole vampy enchilada.

"Seriously? A bloodsucking lawyer?" I asked. "A little on the nose, don't ya think?"

"I was on my way to a party when your mom called," he said flatly. "You spoke to the police without me? Again?"

Dude, at least ask in a cheesy Bela Lugosi accent.

"Yes," I replied defiantly.

"Not smart. Cops take serial homicide seriously. Especially when some of the victims are their own. You could've landed yourself in prison. Permanently."

I rubbed the welts on my wrists. "It's fine. They let me go. No charges."

He snorted and shook his head dismissively. "Need a ride?"

"Thanks, but I'll grab an Uber. Cheaper."

He smirked. "I'm headed in that direction anyway. No charge."

I sighed. Halloween night—probably be an hour or more wait for an Uber.

"Fine. But try to drink my blood, and I'll go all Buffy on your ass." *Gotta set boundaries.*

On the way home, I texted Mom and the other Sand Witches and let them know I wasn't facing any charges. We agreed to meet at the cemetery at nine.

Only Mom and Mama Joyce were at home when I arrived. The house smelled amazing—pot roast? Meat loaf? Whatever it was, my stomach growled. When had I last eaten? I couldn't remember.

"What were you thinking?" Mom snapped once she found out I hadn't waited for Tremball.

She was livid—a rare sight. She and Mama Joyce sat me down at the kitchen table like they had when they caught me smoking one of Mom's joints at sixteen.

"Morgana, sweetheart," Mama Joyce said, her voice calm and steady. "I know you're trying to save us money, but your freedom's far more important."

"It's fine. I told the detective everything—the revenant, Grandmother Raven, what we're doing to stop the killing."

"You what?" Mom exclaimed. "She doesn't understand about these things, sweetie. To her, all witchcraft is evil."

"I think she's starting to see we're trying to help. I... I showed her my Faerie magic."

"You *showed* her?"

"Just the Faerie lights," I replied, guilt creeping into my voice.

"She knows you're Fae?" Mama Joyce asked, voice sharp with alarm.

"No, just that I can do magic. She let me go. No charges."

"You should've waited for Mr. Tremball, baby girl."

Mama Joyce rested a hand on my arm. "But I'm glad things turned out okay. Are you hungry?"

I was starving—but we had bigger problems. "We need to get to the cemetery. End this before the revenant kills someone else."

"You need your strength," Mom said firmly. "That trip to Grandmother Raven's and getting grilled by that detective took a toll. I can see it in your face. You look like death warmed over."

"I made my grandmother's stew," Mama Joyce said. "I'll fix you a bowl."

After inhaling a bowl of stew—despite Mom's cautions to slow down—I went to my room to search for something to lure the revenant. A memento that meant something to Erin.

I drew a blank.

Aside from our brief encounter at the bookshop, it had been years since the two of us spent time together. Every token of our friendship had been lost or tossed out long ago —mostly out of guilt. We'd both moved on. Or tried to.

I dug through my desk drawers. Maybe that old keychain from Castles N' Coasters—the one from her thirteenth birthday—was still around. Nope.

I scrolled through my laptop and phone. No photos of her. Not even a selfie of the two of us.

I ransacked my closet, hoping for an old T-shirt or something I'd left behind when I moved to LA. Still nada.

I sat on my bed, feeling despondent. Erin had been my best friend for most of my life—and I had nothing to remember her by. Nothing to use in the spell. Just guilt. Goddess, I was a terrible person.

Just as I was about to ask my mothers if they had anything, I spotted the framed photo from our tubing trip down the Salt River on my desk. She'd lost her designer shades but didn't care because we were having too much fun.

I picked up the photo, closed my eyes, and let the memories pour in. Countless movies. Late-night sleepovers when she told her parents she was at Megan Hopkins's house—because they didn't approve of her crashing with my witchy lesbian moms. That one summer monsoon that drenched us while we were hiking the Vulture Mountains.

I remembered the first time we tried sushi. She loved it. I hated it—especially when I mistook wasabi for guac and shoved the entire blob into my mouth. I was convinced my whole head was going to explode. She laughed so hard she could barely breathe.

The memory pulled a smile from me. For the first time in years, I felt truly connected to her spirit. I could sense her pain—her desperate struggle to break free from the creature and move on. Would the photo be enough to draw the revenant in? To set her spirit free? I had to believe it would.

I stepped into the bathroom and splashed cold water on my face. Grandmother Raven's mark still burned a little. But I had bigger problems to deal with.

"You ready?" I asked my reflection.

The woman staring back at me looked exhausted. Broken. Sad.

I should throw on some makeup, I thought. *Roxy would like it.* But honestly, I didn't have the energy.

"As ready as I'll ever be," my reflection murmured back to me.

"I've invited the rest of the coven to the cemetery," Mama Joyce said as we prepared to leave. "It is Samhain, after all. And we've postponed our ritual because of this."

"Why invite them to this?" I had hoped it would just be the Sand Witches. The five of us had forged a special bond.

Most of the rest of the coven were strangers to me. "It could put them in danger."

"The more magical energy the better," Mom said. "We can cast a protective circle around you."

"I don't know. This is so last-minute. Who knows how long it'll take them to show up? We've already delayed too much."

"We'll cut them into the circle as they arrive."

I wanted to argue. Would the revenant show up with so many witches? It was turning into a chaotic event. I just wanted to get this over with.

"Do what you think's best," I said with a sigh, resigned to whatever was going to happen.

We arrived at the cemetery fifteen minutes later. Roxy, Thalia, and Kari were already in the parking lot. Angel pulled in a moment later.

I hugged Roxy, letting her warmth ground me. "Hey," I said.

"Hey. How you holding up?"

I shrugged. "I'm... not really sure. I just want it to be over."

"Same."

Thalia handed me my hydration pack. "Fetish is still in the side pockct."

I retrieved it then dropped the pack in Mama Joyce's car. "Thanks for keeping it safe."

I stared at the corroded batteries lashed to the cholla skeleton. How was I supposed to summon fire with this? Grandmother Raven had told me to use the tools I had. But the only tool I had was this. I could sense no magic coming off it now that we were away from her lair. Maybe it really was just a piece of junk. And if that were the case, we were screwed.

But I kept my thoughts to myself.

"I did some scrying before I came. The revenant's close." Angel handed me a scrap of paper. "And I wrote this incantation to summon the creature once we've placed all the personal items on Erin's grave."

"And then the fun begins," Thalia muttered, venom lacing her voice. "We end this—for good."

"The rest of the coven's on the way," Mom said.

"I saw the text," Kari said. "The more energy the better."

"Shaping up to be quite a party." Angel grinned. "I should've brought booze. What's a revenant banishing without spirits?"

Using flashlights and phones to light our way, we wound through the grave sites until we reached Erin's. It looked pristine again as it had before Sarah cast the necromancy spell.

"Please tell me we don't have to dig up her casket," Angel said, worry etched across their face.

"I don't think so," I said. "Grandmother Raven didn't mention it."

"Thank the Goddess."

We gathered around the grave. I placed the photo from the Salt River trip on the sandy ground. Beside it, Roxy laid a greeting card I assumed Erin had given her. Thalia set down a small Bast statue. Angel, a scrying stone on a silver chain.

Kari placed a ring box on the ground and opened it to reveal her diamond-and-sapphire engagement ring. A wave of sadness filled my heart for what could have been a beautiful marriage.

Mama Joyce set down a candle in the shape of a tree trunk decorated with skulls. Beside it, Mom placed a paperback on kitchen witchery.

Though I didn't know the story behind each item, I

could feel the emotional energy pulsing from them all. "I guess we should cast the circle."

We took our places. Mama Joyce pulled out her wand and walked clockwise around us, laying down a barrier of protective magical energy. "I cast this circle as a space between worlds. May it protect us from those who wish us harm during this working of the Craft."

The circle thrummed to life. Through my Faerie sight, I saw a silvery wall of magic, solid as stone. Nothing spiritual or ethereal could cross it. But the revenant wasn't just a spirit—it had a body. Could it still break through? I didn't know.

"Call the quarters," Mama Joyce said. "Kari, will you start?"

One by one, we invoked the guardians of the East, the South, the West, and the North, calling upon the energies of air, fire, water, and earth, respectively. Angel invoked Spirit, Mama Joyce called upon the Goddess, and Mom, the God.

A surge of magical energy swirled around us. I sensed unseen presences gathering at the circle's edge. It was now or never. Time to summon the monster.

Chapter 49

I PULLED the paper on which Angel had scrawled the incantation from my pocket. Their handwriting took me a second to decipher.

"BLOOD AND BONE, death's hold denied.
   Corrupted magic, a spirit tied.
   By Faerie fire and Raven's will,
   Return to the grave, again be still."

I DIDN'T KNOW if Angel intended for me to repeat the chant. But the coven loved doing things in threes, so I repeated it twice more.

With every line, a pulse of energy rippled out from our circle—growing stronger and more urgent with each repetition.

After the third round, Kari asked, "Is it working? How long do we wait?"

"I don't know," I said. "Angel, you sure this incantation will work?"

"Trust me, sweetheart. The incantation's fine. It might just take some time. It's not like she can just magically transport here."

"Just hang in there," Roxy added. "I'm sure it'll show up soon."

"Maybe I should keep chanting."

So I did.

As time passed, more coven members arrived. We cut each one into the widening circle, and with every addition, the energy surged. The chant gained weight, power, momentum.

A bloodcurdling screech ripped through the night. I stopped chanting in mid-word.

"Is that it?" Angel asked, fear thick in their voice.

The back of my mind prickled with the presence of dark magic drawing near. I reached out with my senses and felt the creature closing in.

"It's coming." I pointed down the hill in the direction of the approaching threat.

Coven members swung their flashlights in the direction I indicated, followed by gasps of fear and stifled shrieks of horror.

The revenant emerged like a predator stalking its prey, hissing and growling as it advanced. The prickling in my mind sharpened to the point of distraction.

"Steady now," Mama Joyce said. "It can't cross the circle."

"You sure about that?" I squeaked. Images of the carnage from the festival flashed brightly in my memory.

Thalia let out a low rumbling growl. I hoped she wouldn't shift. It would only complicate matters.

Swallowing my fear, I stepped to the edge of the circle closest to the revenant.

It stopped only a foot away, just on the other side of the shimmering barrier. Mama was right. It couldn't cross. Thank the Goddess!

"Time to do your Faerie thing," Thalia said.

I held Grandmother Raven's fetish in both hands and pointed it at the revenant. I hoped like hell this worked.

I reached deep into my Faerie magic. "Fire," I whispered.

Nothing happed. *Shit!*

"Fire!" I called. Maybe the elements were a little hard of hearing.

The revenant only screeched louder and seemed to inch closer.

I tried channeling my Faerie energy through the tube of the cholla skeleton. Maybe that was how it was supposed to work. "Fire!" I screamed with all my energy.

Again, there was no fire.

I closed my eyes, wrapped my hand around the rutilated quartz crystal Mom had given me, and reached deep for my Faerie magic, desperate to destroy this creature that had hurt so many people. Wickenburg might be a town full of more bigots than I'd like, but it was my home. And I was going to defend it.

But no matter how far I reached, there was no fire. Just not in my wheelhouse. Not even with Grandmother Raven's useless fetish.

"Come on, Morgana! Kill that thing!" Angel shouted next to me.

I remembered the festival—the air thick with terror and the metallic stench of blood. The roar of emotions ripping through me as Roxy lay dying on the ground. Erin's lifeless body in front of the bookshop. Her look of betrayal when I turned her down for junior prom.

A surge of energy swelled inside me—and the sky rumbled in response. Wind whipped my hair. The scent of rain thickened in the air.

The revenant hissed and clawed frantically at the barrier as if to tear out my throat. I met its hollow, rage-filled eyes.

The sharp scent of stale cigarette smoke hit me. The blood in my veins turned to ice. The wind fell still.

"That's quite a power you've got there, Faerie girl," said a raspy voice from the darkness.

Belladonna Loveless emerged into the glow of the flashlights, her presence thrumming with menace.

"What are you doing here, Belladonna?" Mom asked angrily.

"Well, well, Selene. Been a minute, hasn't it, darling? Got yourself a new girl, I see. And a half-breed daughter."

"You need to leave."

"What's wrong? Afraid of a little hex from your ex?"

Belladonna Loveless was Mom's ex? Yikes! And I thought dating Saffron Blaise was a disaster.

"You dated her?" Mama Joyce asked, just as stunned as I felt.

"It was a long time ago," Mom murmured, embarrassment obvious in her voice. She turned to Loveless. "What do you want? This is a private ritual."

"You summoned my creature, so I followed to see what was going on. Glad I did. Would've hated to miss the party. And on Samhain, no less. Beats handing out candy to ungrateful brats in store-bought costumes."

"*Your* creature?" I asked. "Sarah O'Brien cast the necromancy spell."

"That foolish girl!" Loveless cackled. "Dumb bitch had

no idea what she was doing. Just like her sister—no discipline, no control."

"You have no right to talk about Erin that way!" I spat back.

"She was my apprentice. I'll speak of her as I choose. As for you, Morgana Rhiannon Quinn," she sneered, "you thought you were clever, wrecking my shop. Drenching my lobby like a monsoon had rolled through. But turnabout's fair play, child."

She held up a small spell jar. I had no clue what was inside, but it couldn't be good.

I remembered her scratching my wrist. She had my blood—and she knew my full name. *Shit, shit, shit!*

She lifted the spell jar and muttered a single word, "Trennan."

It felt as if a blade had cut me in half. Not physically. But my Faerie magic... It was... gone! My knees buckled. "What... what's happening?"

"I felt it when you broke that pathetic dimwit's spell. Burned the grimoire and the poppet, did you? But you couldn't finish the job, could you? Stupid girl. Now I control the creature—and you."

Loveless raised a gnarled wand. "Come to me. Now."

An invisible force wrapped around my heart, yanking me toward the edge of the circle. "No!" I screamed.

I slammed into the magical barrier, every muscle straining to hold my ground.

Mom's voice rose strong. "By east, by south, by west, by north. Through the spirit that connects us, the Goddess who protects us, and the God who strengthens us—assist us now in the working of the Craft. Siblings, repeat after me."

Voices rose around me in unison, repeating the chant. The coven.

Loveless's grip faltered, but I still struggled to resist her hold.

I dug deep into my Fae self, fighting to remember the name of the queen Grandmother Raven had mentioned. Veronica? No, that wasn't it. Vidalia? Nope, that was an onion. Verdanya! That was it.

"Queen Verdanya, hear me now. Come to my aid," I whispered, struggling to ignore the chaos around me. "I call upon the Fae magic within and without. I call upon the creatures, mortal and immortal. I call wind. I call rain. I call hail."

Wind howled and whipped around us, rising to a deafening roar. Rain struck my face—first scattered drops then a pounding downpour. The shrill voices of coyotes cried out. Wings whooshed overhead.

My hand tightened on Grandmother Raven's fetish. Nothing but junk. A cactus skeleton and corroded batteries.

My ADHD brain latched onto the word. Batteries. Batteries.

Holy shit! Batteries!

A flash of lightning lit up the clouds above, followed by a rumble of thunder.

Use the tools that you have, she had told me. Not the damned fetish. Wind. Rain. Hail. Lightning! Countless wildfires had started with a lightning strike.

I changed the chant. "I call wind. I call rain. I call lightning. I call wind. I call rain. I call lightning."

With every repetition, the magic surged around me, growing stronger.

I opened my eyes—nose-to-nose with the revenant, separated only by the shimmering circle. It hissed, shrieked, and clawed, desperate to reach me or the keepsakes we'd laid on the grave. Perhaps both.

Loveless loomed nearby, muttering in a language I didn't recognize. Her hand curled as she reached for me.

A blur of black wings shot toward her, and claws slashed her face. Lenore!

Go, you brilliant bird!

She dove again and again, drawing blood with each strike.

I turned back to the shrieking corpse before me, reached deep into my core, and again called lightning.

"Erin," I whispered. "If you can hear me, I'm so sorry—for everything I did to you in high school. I was wrong to hurt you, to humiliate you. You were the bravest person I knew. You stood up to bullies, even your own family. And I... I was a coward. Always hiding, even with two loving, supportive moms."

I didn't know if Erin could hear me, but I had to say it.

"And I'm sorry... truly sorry... for what I'm about to do." Tears blurred my vision and slid down my cheeks.

A blinding flash and a thunderous crack exploded in front of me, throwing me backward.

࿓

FOR A MOMENT, all I could see was the searing afterimage burned onto my retinas. My ears rang with the echo of thunder. I was dizzy, nauseated. The acrid stench of ozone and scorched flesh flooded my nose.

Then—darkness. Silence. I sat up, dazed and alone.

Moonlight filtered through trees. Nearby, a stream burbled softly in the dark.

Where the hell am I? How did I get here?

As my vision adjusted, I saw a familiar silhouette approaching—and caught a floral scent I hadn't smelled since...

"Erin?" I asked warily. My heart beat a rapid staccato. Was it really her? Or the revenant?

"Hey, girl." Her voice was playful. She sat beside me, slipped an arm around my shoulders, and hugged me. "Missed you."

My throat choked with emotion. "I... I missed you too. Where... where are we?"

"Not entirely sure. A space between worlds. It was terrifying at first. But now, it's kind of peaceful."

"Huh," was all I could think to say.

"Thank you," she said, her eyes catching the moonlight like tiny stars.

"For what?" I asked, caught off guard.

"For freeing me. Being bound to that... that thing... It was agony. I saw all the horrible things it did—helpless to stop it."

"Did it hurt? The lightning, I mean."

She paused, considering. "Only for an instant. Then came a wave of relief. I'm free now."

Guilt pressed on me. Tears welled in my eyes. "I'm so sorry I hurt you in school. I was a coward and an idiot. I ruined everything."

"You were scared. Those bullies made life hell for both of us."

"But you stood up to them. I just hid."

"You were bullied a lot longer than I was. For having lesbian moms who were also witches. That couldn't have been easy. In any case, I don't hold grudges. Not anymore. I'm beyond all that now."

"Who killed you?"

She shrugged. "I don't remember. And honestly, it doesn't matter anymore."

Rage flared through me like wildfire. "I'm going to find out. And I'll make them pay."

"Do what feels right. Like I said—I've let it all go."

Another figure appeared, female, radiant, powerful. My breath caught, and my whole body tingled.

"Ready, Erin?" Her voice chimed like silver bells.

"Are... are you..." I stuttered.

She smiled, and joy, peace, and calm flooded through me—beyond anything I'd ever known. Like tubing the Salt River on a perfect spring day... or biting into a mango at the peak of ripeness... or maybe, yeah, like an orgasm that just kept going on and on and on.

"I have many names, child. But yes, I am she."

"Erin, please don't go. Goddess, can't you please bring her back to life? Not like a revenant but as her old self?"

"It's her time to move on, Faerie child," she explained. "And time for you to let go."

"What's next?" Erin asked.

The Goddess smiled. "And ruin the surprise? Don't worry—you've got incredible adventures waiting."

Erin and I stood and hugged each other tight.

"I love you," she whispered, her breath warm against my ear.

"I... I love you too. I don't want to lose you again. Not ever."

But before I finished speaking, Erin and the Goddess were gone.

A cloud slid over the moon, leaving me in absolute darkness.

"MORGANA! CAN YOU HEAR ME, SWEETIE?" a nearby voice whispered urgently.

My teeth chattered. My whole body shook from cold,

wet, and exhaustion. At least the rain had stopped, and the wind had calmed to a gentle, if chilly, breeze.

Someone squeezed my hand. Another voice—full of fear and worry—whispered, "Open your eyes, babe. Please."

My mind grasped at the name of the voice's owner. Roxy.

Roxy!

I forced my eyes open. I could just make out the outline of her face, inches from mine. I wanted to kiss her but felt too weak and shaky.

Her gentle hands cupped my cheek. "Morgana, thank Goddess. You scared us for a second."

"I... I'm... alive."

"Yes. Yes, you are," Roxy said with a relieved chuckle.

She helped me to sit up, and vertigo spun the world until my brain settled.

"Where... where's the revenant?"

"Destroyed. You did it. Your lightning strike broke the spell."

"Just a crispy corpse now," Angel said. "Sorry, Kari."

"No, it's all good. It can't hurt anyone now. And Erin's remains can be reinterred."

"And Erin's spirit has moved on," I said, a little sadly.

No one asked how I knew, for which I was grateful.

Mama Joyce and Roxy helped me to my feet. I wobbled, still dizzy and completely drained.

The circle was open, the barrier gone. Erin's remains lay scattered in a depression roughly ten feet wide, scorch marks charred into the sand around it. The lightning strike didn't just unmake the revenant—it obliterated it. I was both relieved and a little sickened.

Ten feet away, Loveless lay sprawled on the dirt, blood

oozing from deep slashes on her arms and face. Had the revenant turned on her somehow?

"What happened to her?"

"Thalia… Well, she shifted into a puma and pounced on Belladonna," Mom said. "I called her off before she could finish the job. Then I used a binding spell—one Belladonna taught me, back when we were still… friends. How's that for irony?"

"She won't hurt anyone else," Roxy said. "At least not with magic."

The Sand Witches and the rest of the coven gathered around Erin's remains.

"May you find peace," I whispered to Erin, wherever she was. "Blessed be."

"Blessed be," the rest of the coven intoned quietly.

We wrapped Kari in a tight group hug, only breaking apart when a voice shouted, "Everyone, put your hands in the air."

Ugh. Not again.

CHAPTER 50

DETECTIVE HATATHLIE STOOD twenty feet away, weapon raised, flanked by what looked like the entire Wickenburg police force. Every officer had a flashlight trained on us—and presumably a pistol too.

I pointed at Erin's smoking remains. "That's the Wickenburg Slasher. Or what's left of it." I then gestured toward Belladonna Loveless. "And she was responsible for controlling it."

A rumble of uneasy laughter, laced with muttered expletives, rose from the cops.

Hatathlie holstered her pistol and said to the other officers, "Wait here." Then she stepped closer to me and whispered, "What are you telling me, Ms. Quinn?"

"I destroyed the revenant, just like I told you I would. And Belladonna Loveless sent the revenant on a killing spree. If you're going to arrest anyone for the murders, she's the one you want."

Hatathlie glanced at Belladonna's unconscious form then back to me. "She controlled the creature? How?"

"Necromancy. Like I told you."

"You have any evidence?"

I scrambled for something—anything—but came up empty. I couldn't think of any concrete proof. I had no idea how she'd taken control of the revenant.

"No," I admitted.

"All I see is a group of people trespassing in a cemetery after hours with a mutilated corpse. And the person you're accusing of being a serial killer is a disabled, unconscious woman suffering similar wounds to the other Slasher victims."

"She's not disabled," I said. "She walked up here on her own two feet."

Mom and Mama Joyce approached Hatathlie and me.

"She's telling the truth, Detective," Mom said. "Belladonna and I knew each other from way back. We learned witchcraft together—until she started using it to hurt people. So I parted ways with her. Years later, Erin O'Brien became her apprentice. That's how Erin learned the spell that was eventually used to reanimate her body."

"By her father?" Hatathlie asked.

"Yes," Mom said—lying rather convincingly. "Only he lacked the proper training to control it. The revenant turned on him."

"And then Ms. Loveless took over and used it to kill the others," Mama Joyce added.

Hatathlie looked back at Loveless. "Is she... dead?"

"Just sleeping," Mom said with a smile. "She'll wake soon, though."

Hatathlie's gaze shifted to Erin's remains. "So that's the... the creature? The one that did the actual killing?"

"It is," Mom said.

"What's left of it," I said, solemnly. "The spell's broken. No more murders."

"Looks like it got hit with a grenade," Hatathlie said.

"Lightning, actually," I said with more than a little pride.

Belladonna stirred and let out a low groan.

Hatathlie rubbed her temple and muttered, "What the hell am I supposed to do with this? You're telling me Loveless used magic to control a corpse and kill a dozen people—including two of my officers? I can't exactly charge her for illegal use of magic, much less homicide."

"It's the truth," Mama Joyce insisted.

Hatathlie sighed. "And if we don't arrest her?"

I shuddered at the thought. Loveless had used a single drop of my blood to nearly sever me from my Faerie magic—and that was just because I trashed her psychic-shop lobby.

Now she'd be really pissed at us. We'd destroyed the revenant. Thalia and Lenore had assaulted her. And Mom... A small, satisfied smile tugged at my lips. Mom had bound her magic. Loveless shouldn't be a threat to anyone now.

"You really want to take that chance?" I asked. "She used that creature to murder two of your fellow officers and several other citizens. Goddess only knows what she'll do next. And obviously she lied to your officers about being disabled. I'd say it warrants a closer look into her involvement in the Wickenburg Slasher cases."

Hatathlie started at Loveless, who was beginning to stir.

"Officer Riggs," Hatathlie called. "Take Ms. Loveless into custody."

"For what?" Riggs asked, clearly baffled. I recognized him from my own arrest.

"Grave robbery, mutilation of a corpse, and suspicion of murder."

"But Detective, she looks more like the victim than the perpetrator. The woman uses a wheelchair."

"Do you see a wheelchair, Officer Riggs? She lied. Tell

dispatch to send an RA unit to provide medical care, but she's under arrest. Got it?"

Officer Riggs still looked disbelieving, but he nodded and said, "Yes, ma'am."

Hatathlie stepped in close and whispered, "I'm staking my career on this. If I find out you lied to me, I'll bring down the full weight of the law. And if these killings start up again—so help me..."

"They won't," I replied. "Loveless was controlling the revenant. And as you can see, it's been destroyed."

"Fine." She stepped back then raised her voice. "I'm ordering all of you to disperse. If you don't, you'll be charged with trespassing. Am I clear?"

"Yes," we all said in unison.

I considered leaving the Salt River photo on Erin's grave but decided to keep it: a reminder of the friendship we once shared. The other Sand Witches quietly collected their mementos as well.

Back at the parking lot, I pulled Roxy into a hug and kissed her.

"You were amazing," she whispered.

"I couldn't have done it without all of you. Loveless nearly had me with that spell."

"That's the power of the coven. We're family."

"Attention, everyone!" Mom called. "I think we've had our Samhain ritual for the year."

The coven members laughed darkly.

"As is tradition, we are still having the party at our place. Music, food, chosen family, and of course, midnight margaritas. So for those who are joining us, welcome. For anyone else, have a happy and safe Samhain."

"You coming?" I asked Roxy, my chest tight with hope.

"Unfortunately, I have to work in the morning."

My heart sank. "Damn."

She kissed me. "But how about an official date tomorrow night?"

"Sounds perfect." I kissed her deeply, suddenly feeling invigorated despite the night's events.

"Morgana! Let's go!" Mom insisted.

"Bye," I said, stealing one last kiss. "Happy Samhain!"

I woke at eleven the next morning, still drained from pushing my Faerie magic to the limit—and a few midnight margaritas.

Three voicemails waited on my phone. The first was from Roxy.

"Hey, girl. Just checking in while I have a break between sessions. Hope you're doing well. What do you think about dinner and a movie tonight? There's a dine-in Harkins Theatre in north Phoenix. Food's really good. Not sure what's playing, but we can figure it out. Give me a call between noon and one if you're up. Catch ya later, girlfriend."

Warmth flooded my body—like butterflies and sunshine all at once. I had a girlfriend. Someone grounded and kind who accepted me, Fae and all. A damn good reason to stick around Wickenburg.

The second voicemail was from Detective Hatathlie.

"Ms. Quinn, I wanted to inform you that Ms. Loveless's prints matched those found at the scene of an unsolved homicide in Peoria a few years ago. We also uncovered evidence of financial fraud."

I laughed out loud. "Thank the Goddess."

"Also, we got the DNA report back the Phoenix Crime Lab on the Erin O'Brien case. The skin under her fingernails belonged to David Talbot. We also found Erin's blood in the back of his SUV. A search of his phone turned up text conversations between Mr. Talbot, James Collins, and Charles Ralston. It appears they conspired to kill Erin in order to take over her restaurant. We have arrested Talbot, though it's likely he'll make bail. We'd like to charge him with the other Slasher murders, but since we have no evidence..."

Holy shit! Charlie conspired with Dave and Jimmie to kill Erin? Why?

Then I remembered Kari saying the two had butted heads over the Wicked Grille menu and that he'd had problems with other chefs he'd worked with. After the burial, he was talking about taking over as owner, already introducing classic French dishes to Erin's upscale Western menu. Maybe he was one of those guys who couldn't stand playing second fiddle to a woman.

"Also, I want to apologize for accusing you and your coven of the Slasher murders. You have changed my mind about your coven. For now. But don't give me a reason to change it back."

I tapped Play on the third message.

"Hi, Morgana, this is Elyse Calder with the Sterling Talent Agency. I've reviewed your work following your Emmy win for *LA Murder Squad*. I'd like to talk about possible representation. Joanne Rosenberg's putting together a series you'd be perfect for as head writer. If interested, call me back and let's talk."

I nearly dropped my phone. My screenwriting career wasn't dead after all. And Joanne Rosenberg? Holy shit! She'd been the showrunner for the recent *Lisbeth Salander* series on Netflix, and before that, she produced one of the *Dexter* spinoff series.

Would I have to move back to LA? The progressive attitudes and milder weather were tempting. But California housing prices were insane. Plus earthquakes. Landslides. And Governor Gavin Newsom had become a transphobe, talking shit about our community to the likes of Charlie Kirk.

Besides, what would that mean for Roxy and me? Maybe I could figure out a way to stay here in Arizona.

❦

I RETURNED Elyse Calder's call.

"First off, I have to say how impressed I was with the writing on episodes of *LA Murder Squad* where you were lead writer. You had me crying one minute, laughing the next. You're truly gifted."

Heat rushed to my cheeks. My instinct was to deflect, but Mama Joyce had taught me to just say thank you.

"I... uh, thanks."

"Secondly, Runaway Girl Studios just greenlit a crime thriller series about a female motorcycle club. Sort of a feminist queer *Sons of Anarchy*. You'd be perfect as head writer. If you're interested in representation, I'd love to pitch you to Joanne Rosenberg, the showrunner. What do you think?"

I wanted to say yes, but I had one question. "Would I have to move back to LA?"

"Not necessarily. You'll probably need to fly in once in a while, but Runaway Girl Studios does work with writers who work remotely."

"Then yes." A surge of excitement pulsed through me— so intense the lights flickered and the phone crackled. I drew a deep breath, reining in my magic.

"Great. I'll send over the contract. Let me know if you have any questions. As soon as I get the signed copy, I'll reach out to Ms. Rosenberg."

Mom and Mama Joyce were as excited as I was.

"I told you, darling girl. Setbacks are inevitable but only as permanent as you let them be," Mama Joyce explained. "You've got what it takes to make a name for yourself in this business."

"It's not a done deal," I said. "It's just representation—no guarantee Joanne Rosenberg will want to work with me."

"And if she doesn't, your agent will find something else that's a better fit," Mom assured me. "Meanwhile, you can live here and save up money, avoiding another crisis like you had with what's-her-name."

"Saffron."

"See, I already forgot."

"I've actually been thinking of getting my own place. In Arizona, not LA."

"I'm glad to hear it," Mama Joyce said. "I missed seeing you on a regular basis. Plus, you and Roxy seem to have a little somethin'-somethin' going on."

I blushed. "Yeah, we do." I then summoned the courage to reveal something that had been bothering me. "I think Grandmother Raven cheated me."

Concern wrinkled Mama Joyce's brow. "How so, peanut?"

"When I tried to use the fetish she gave me to summon Faerie fire, it didn't work. I don't even feel any magical energy coming off it at all. She tricked me into agreeing to help her get back whatever the Fae stole from her."

"Are you wanting to back out of the deal?" Mom asked. "Because while I'd rather you not risk your life to retrieve this magical MacGuffin, backing out of a deal with Grandmother Raven might not be a wise idea."

"Did she say it would summon Faerie fire?" Mama Joyce asked.

"I... I can't remember exactly. I thought so. She said I would need it."

"And did you?"

"I summoned lightning to destroy the revenant. But I did that all on my own." I remembered that intense moment from the night before. "Although looking at those old, corroded batteries is what gave me the idea."

"So the fetish did help."

"I suppose. In a roundabout way. But why didn't she just tell me to do that?"

Mom shrugged. "She's an ancient wereraven. Who knows why they do what they do?"

I called Roxy during her break. We agreed to meet at her place and drive down to the Harkins Lake Pleasant CinéGrill in North Phoenix for dinner and a showing of Guillermo del Toro's *Frankenstein*.

I spent the afternoon helping Mom at the bookshop, though I still had to defer to other employees for a few customer questions. Which crystals attracted success? What herbs repelled negative energy? Did we have a public restroom? Okay, that one I knew the answer to.

Between tarot readings, Angel came out to chat.

"Did you hear?" they asked. "The cops released a statement saying the Wickenburg Slasher is a none other than Dave Talbot."

"Hatathlie called me," I said solemnly. "His DNA was found under Erin's fingernails. He and Jimmie conspired with Charlie Ralston to take over the Wicked Grille. And they're charging Belladonna Loveless for an old homicide in Peoria—plus a laundry list of financial crimes."

Angel snorted. "Why am I not surprised? Karma's a bitch."

"Yeah."

Around five, I hugged Mom goodbye.

"Don't be out too late," she warned.

"Mom, I'm not fifteen anymore."

"I know. But you know I'll worry."

"I might even spend the night."

"Well, if you do, call or text and let me know."

"I will. Promise."

Roxy opened the door in a stunning red silk dress. Her hair was pinned up, and her makeup—flawless yet subtle —highlighted her natural beauty. Her perfume held notes of lilac, lavender, and wild blackberry.

I glanced down at my faded *LA Murder Squad* tee and worn jeans. I wasn't wearing any makeup. Leave it to me to screw up a first date. I should've put on something nicer.

"I... uh, didn't realize... I guess I should've dressed up, huh? Sorry I'm such a dork. Please don't be mad."

I remembered all the times Saffron got pissed when I didn't meet her exacting standards—especially the night of the Emmys.

But Roxy just smiled and pulled me into a hug.

Goddess, she smelled incredible.

"Why would I be mad? We're going to a movie, not a dinner party. You're dressed just fine. Honestly, I might've gone overboard—I was trying to impress you."

"You don't need to impress me. I'd like you even if you weren't wearing a thing."

A sly grin tugged at her lips. "That can be arranged. But later."

My brain spiraled with a flurry of hormone-fueled thoughts.

Goddess, she's so pretty. So smart. So kind. When's the last time I felt this way about someone? Even Saffron... No! Stop thinking about her. You're with Roxy. What's she like in bed? What does she like? Will she like me? Would she prefer someone taller? Or, I don't know, human? Will she get sick of me like Saffron did?

"Morgan?" Concern flickered in Roxy's eyes.

My mind snapped back to the present. "Oh, sorry—ADHD brain squirrels. What did you say?"

Instead of answering, she leaned in and kissed me. My body lit up with magic, arousal, and need. My mind went quiet. I let myself enjoy the moment. For once.

About the Author

Dharma Kelleher writes thrillers and urban fantasy novels where queer women kick ass and bad guys get got.

Her works include the Jinx Ballou Bounty Hunter thriller series, the Shea Stevens Outlaw Biker thriller series, the Avery Byrne Goth Vigilante thriller series, and the new Witches of Wiccanburg urban fantasy series.

Her action-packed stories are filled with exciting twists, grit, and heart. Sometimes a little magic and romance.

They explore powerful themes of queer representation, found family, overcoming trauma, and social and criminal justice.

Dharma lives in the Sonoran Desert with her wife and a black cat named Mouse. Learn more about Dharma and her work at https://dharmakelleher.com.

ACKNOWLEDGMENTS

Thanks to Lynn McNamee, Brittany Meyer-Strom, and Virge Buck at Red Adept Editing for helping transform a typo-riddled manuscript into a polished novel.

Special thanks to members of the Spirit of the Sacred Journey who have become my witchy family and a source of strength in these difficult times. Blessed be, lovies!

Thanks also to Chelle and Laylla, hosts of the *Back on the Broomstick* podcast, for sharing your wisdom and knowledge of witchcraft and paganism. Thank you for helping me keep it witchy!

Thanks to Carol Beth Anderson, Jay Myers, Rich Miller, and the many members of the ACX/Audiobook Narrators Facebook group for your expertise and encouragement helping me to create the audiobook version of Desert Magic.

Thanks to Mark E. Pry, author of *A Town on the Hassayampa: A History of Wickenburg*; Anna Moore Shaw, author of *Pima Indian Legends*; and Tony Hillerman, author of the Joe Leaphorn/Jim Chee book series, for teaching me more about the history and stories of this amazing land we live in.

Thanks to Jim Butcher, Yasmine Galenorn, Malinda Lo, and Julie Kagawa for all of your wonderful faerie stories. You have literally inspired me.

Thanks to the staff of the Hassayampa River Preserve for helping to maintain a beautiful and literal oasis in the desert and educating the public on the beauty and wonder of this magical place.

And thanks most of all to my beloved wife, Eileen. Without your encouragement, none of this would ever have happened. You are the person I dreamed of being with ever since I was a kid. You are literally my dream girl. And I'm so grateful to have spent the past 27 years with you. Thank you for picking me.

www.ingramcontent.com/pod-product-compliance
Lightning Source LLC
Chambersburg PA
CBHW051434190726
48289CB00001B/186